THE KING'S COIN

AMBITION IS THE ONLY FAITH

PAULA CONSTANT

For Chloe and Taylor
Who kindly indulge my delusion of being a parent figure in their lives

LIST OF PRIMARY CHARACTERS

For the most part character names have been anglicised. There are some exceptions, notably Count Ilyan of Septem. Rightly his name should be rendered as Julian. However, as there was already a Julian of Toledo, I kept the Spanish pronunciation for ease of reference.

A note regarding fictionalisation of characters

All kings are verified by church records of the time. Unless stated below as fictional, all those mentioned as 'count' or 'duke' are equally attested, usually as signatories to the well documented Councils of Toledo. That said, I have in many cases created the family relationships between characters, based upon my understanding of geographical, political, and genealogical associations. My characterisations are not meant to be definitive but are rather my own perceptions. The Visigoths of Spain series is a work of my own imagination, interweaving fictional characters and events with what is known from primary sources of the time.

Lælia of Illiberis
Fictional
The township of Illiberis is attested in numerous church records

(please see 'Place Names' following this page), as is a Count of that place. Evidence of horse worship in the area is plentiful, and horses from the region are mentioned from Roman times, both in Spain and on foreign shores. Lælia herself is a fictional character.

Count Paulus of Illiberis
Actual
Count Paulus is attested as one of King Reccesuinth's *seniores*, or senior advisers, in the Councils of Toledo records, but not associated with a particular place. His association with Illiberis is fictional as are his personal relationships.

Acantha of Illiberis (Baeticus)
Fictional
The name 'Baeticus' is found on early Roman graves in the Illiberis area, denoting the local chiefs/power holders found when Romans first arrived in the region. Acantha is a generic Gothic name. The tradition of female inheritance was both Gothic law and associated with tribes indigenous to the area.

Yosef ben Radhan
Fictional
The Rhadanite merchants are famous, though largely associated with southern France. The Jews of Garnata are well attested, however, and a man named Yosef from Garnata became well known in Moorish Spain. Yosef is a fictional amalgamation of those elements.

Arun ben Radhan
Fictional
Arun is entirely fictional.

Theudemir of Aurariola
Actual
Count Theudemir is well attested in numerous documents as the Count of Aurariola, later Orihuela, on Spain's west coast. I have created a fictional backstory for him, as there remain no truly reli-

able records of his lineage. His relationship to rebel king Geila is my creation.

Alaric
Fictional
I created Alaric to represent the military expertise of the time.

Athanagild
Fictional
Athanagild was created to represent the Church culture of the time.

Count Suinthila of Aurariola
Fictional
Since Geila's descendents are unknown, I made him the patriarch of Theudemir's family, and Suinthila's father (Geila's brother was the great king Suintila). The circle of nobility was small and highly interconnected during the period, meaning most noble families were familiar with one another if not directly linked by blood or marriage.

Geila (Iudila)
Actual
Geila (Iudila) is described as 'one of the greatest generals' of Visigothic Spain. His brother, King Suintila, was also described as great military strategist, who during his reign oversaw the unification of Spain and expulsion of Greek Imperial forces. Coins minted in Illiberis and Emerita named Geila as king in opposition to Sisenand, suggesting his support was found in the south of Spain.

Duke Theodofred of Corduba
Actual
Theodofred was a son of King Chindasuinth, and Duke of Corduba during the reign of Egica. He is widely attested in documents of the period as the husband of Riccilo and father of Roderic.

Riccilo

Actual

Attested as wife of Theodofred and mother of Roderic. Her relationship to Illiberis is fictional.

King Erwig

Actual

Attested as son of Ardabast (a Greek), husband of Liuvgoto, and father of Cixilo.

Liuvgoto

Actual

A formidable figure, Liuvgoto is well attested as the daughter of King Sisebut; wife of King Erwig; and mother of Cixilo. Her relationships to Sunifred and Suinthila are fictional, however her very interesting backstory allows fertile ground for speculation.

Cixilo

Actual

Liuvgoto and Erwig's daughter, wife of King Egica, and mother of Wittiza.

King Egica

Actual

Well attested as the son of Ariberga (son of King Tulga), husband of Cixilo, and father of Wittiza, Egica is also strongly regarded as fathering the illegitimate Oppa.

Oppa

Actual

One of the most shadowy figures of the era, Oppa is nonetheless well attested in varying roles throughout history, including as a Bishop of Hispalis. His parentage was murky, though it is generally accepted he was a royal son.

Wittiza

Actual

Wittiza was Egica and Cixilo's legitimate son and co-ruled with his father for several years.

Giscila
Actual character, gender unknown
Giscila is often considered as having been female, however in Gothic nomenclature the name is a masculine one, and evidence is nebulous at best. I have heavily fictionalised this character so whilst a 'Giscila' certainly existed as Egica's offspring, the rest is my invention.

Ariberga
Actual
Ariberga is attested as Tulga's son and Egica's father. His treason is my invention based upon the disappearance of Tulga's infant sons following Tulga's forced tonsuring by Chindasuinth and the brutal coup surrounding his fall from power.

Wamba
Actual
Archbishop Julian of Toletum wrote 'The Book of Wamba' on this king's rule, one of the few intact documents of the time.

Dahiya (or Diya, Dihiya, Kahina, Al Kahinat)
Actual
Dahiya (or Diya, Dihiya) was an Amazigh leader, or amgar, in the Sahara attested by multiple sources.

Bagay and Khanchla
Names attested, characters fictional
Dahiya's sons are spoken of in legends of the time, but their existence cannot be verified. Their lives are my creation based on my research.

Count Ilyan
Actual

(Anglicised, 'Julian') was an actual Governor, or Count (known as both) of Septem.

Mohammed bin Marwan

Actual

Mohammed bin Marwan was the brother of Caliph Abd al Malik bin Marwan, and a great military general in the armies of the Caliphate.

Neboulos

Actual

Head of the Slavic contingent of the Imperial army at Sebastopolis.

Leontios

Actual

Leader of Imperial army at Sebastopolis, Byzantine Emperor AD 695-698

Archbishop Julian of Toletum

Actual

Attested in church records.

Bishop Felix of Hispalis

Actual

Attested in church records.

Bishop Sisebut

Actual

Sisebut's role in the church and in Sunifred's rebellion is attested, however his proclivities are my creation - based on decisions made in the 16th council of Toledo.

Bishops Idalio, Maximo, and Mumulo

Actual

All attested in church records.

Laurentius Severianus
Name attested, character fictional

A scholar by the name of Laurentius is mentioned as possessing 'one of the best libraries in Toletum' in writing of the period. A Count Severianus appears repeatedly as a signatory to the Councils of Toledo. I have associated Laurentius with this name, as it is a Roman one, and the name itself with the lineage of Isidore of Seville, as this house was well known as one of Roman aristocracy and scholarship. The connection is of my making and used as an example of the old Roman ruling class that still held (symbolic) power two centuries after Gothic conquest.

Shukra
Fictional

Entirely fictional but based on Zoroastrian warriors attested in Imperial forces of the time who escaped the Arab conquest of Persia or were simply conscripted. In Shukra's lifetime there was widespread destruction and burning of Zoroastrian fire temples under the Arabic conquest.

Apsimar
Actual

Apsimar is known to history as the Greek Emperor Tiberius III.

Sunifred
Actual

Sunifred is attested in coins minted in his name and records of the time as a rebel King during Egica's rule. I have made him a son of Ricimer, which would make him Liuvgoto's cousin, and give him the perceived right to make a bid for the throne. Given the small circle of nobility and his lofty position, he must have been related or connected in some way to the ruling families of the time.

Frogellus
Actual

Attested in church documents during the rebellion against Egica.

Egilona
Actual
Egilona is an extraordinary character who plays a larger role in later books in this series. She is attested in multiple records. However her origin story as Theo's sister is one of my creation.

Rekiberga
Fictional
Alaric's betrothed is a fictional creation. I named her for King Chindasuinth's wife.

VISIGOTHIC KINGS, AD 586 - 687

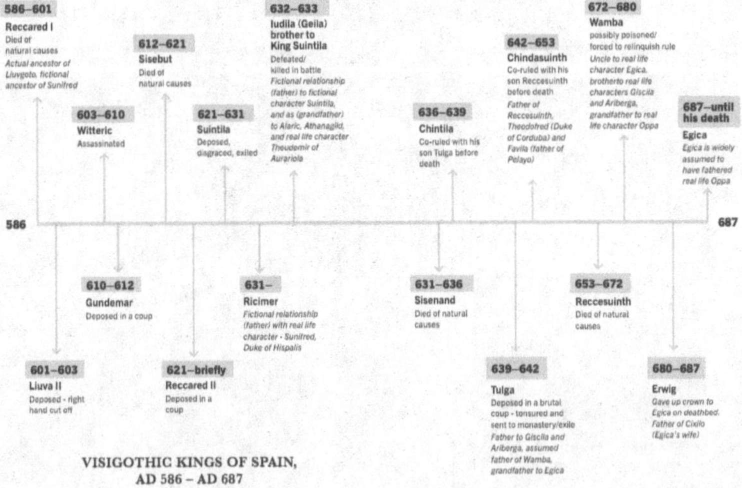

VISIGOTHIC KINGS OF SPAIN, AD 586 – AD 687

VISIGOTHIC SPANIA, AD 690

LÆLIA AND THEO FAMILY TREES

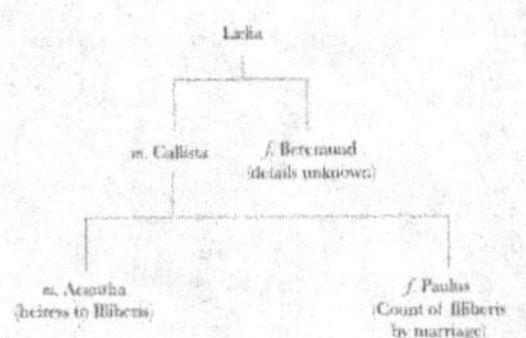

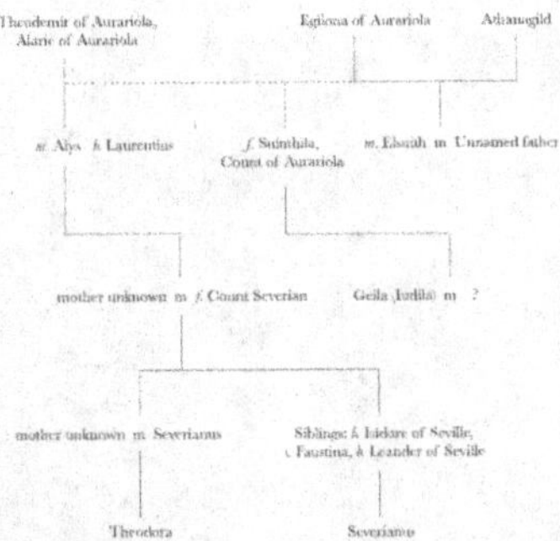

YOSEF'S JOURNEY

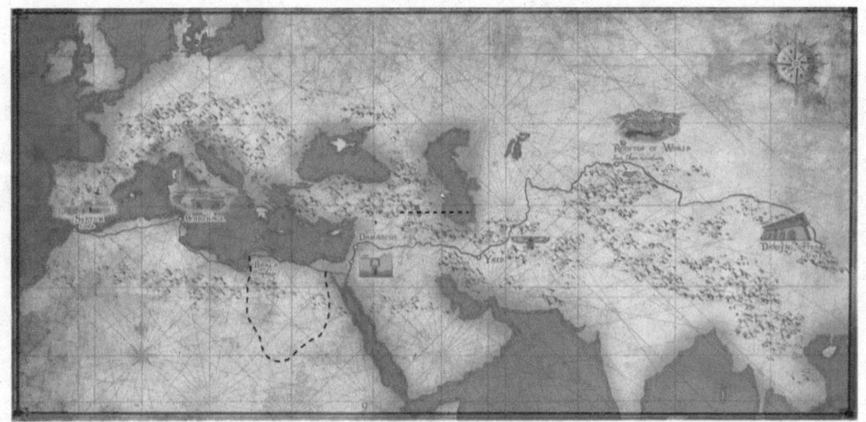

PROLOGUE
LAURENTIUS

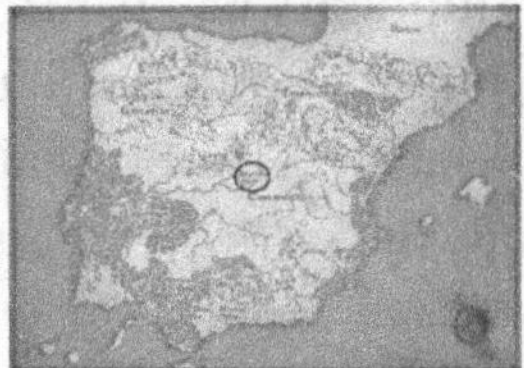

AD 687, eight months before the coronation of King Egica
Toletum, Spania
Toledo, Spain

His father's library smelled of parchment, cedar, and cinnamon. The familiar scent struck Laurentius Severianus in a way nothing else had since news of his father's death had reached him in Constantinople. He clutched the door frame, breathing deeply to steady himself, glad there was none but the spring breeze to witness his homecoming.

The servants had made ready the villa for his arrival, but at his request none had entered the library. Long accustomed to the arrival of cedar chests from distant shores, they knew better than to handle the contents. The family of Severianus held one of the most esteemed libraries in all Spania. Now the son of the house had returned with new treasures to grace its shelves, but the one man who would have revered them was gone, and the chests that had been meant for him lay unopened on the stone floor.

Laurentius traced the chestnut shelves and the books they

contained. The air seemed to quiver with his father's presence. He felt the old patrician in every dust mote and leather casing. A large, purple-covered copy of the Gothic monk Ulfila's translation of the Bible lay in pride of place on a stand by the desk. It was open at Romans.

"For if the first fruit be holy, the branch is also holy; and if the root be holy, so are the branches: *þandei ufarskafts weiha, jah daigs, jah jabai waurts weiha, jah astos*," he read aloud.

The Gothic words sounded soft on his tongue. He tried them again, letting the round, purring sounds trill through his throat.

Every language is a treasure. He heard his father's voice as clearly as if Severianus stood before him. *Its gifts remain hidden until your tongue can unlock them. Spania is a Gothic country now. Our laws are made by Goths, our customs dictated by theirs. Learn their tongue, or you will never understand either their treasures or their fault lines.*

"I learned it well," whispered Laurentius aloud. "Gothic at your knee, Greek at sea, just as you taught. And so much more, Father, that only you would have understood. But you are no longer here."

It was this that hurt the most: that all he had learned, all he had striven to understand and acquire in the long years wielding both sword and pen in the furthest and strangest of lands, could not be shared with the one person who would value the endeavour. With whom would he now share his ideas, his vision of Spania's future, the almost unbearable weight of the knowledge he carried about the enemies they might soon face?

Pressing his forehead against the iron lattice of the window covering, Laurentius gripped the shutters so hard they cut into his hands, his chest tight with emotion. Laurentius Severianus was twenty-six years old. He had not stood in this house since he was half that age and preparing to sail for Constantinople. The study was just as it had remained in his mind, its scent present in the rare letters that had reached him over the years, treasured rolls of vellum so dear he had held them to his face at night and breathed in the presence of his father, feeling his strength and wisdom contained in the wry humour of words written in his own hand.

He was almost unaware that he was striking the lattice repeatedly with his forehead until a noise at the door disturbed him.

Laurentius swung about with lightning swiftness, sword drawn and at the ready.

"Athanagild." Laurentius smiled ruefully. "I have been too long amongst men and steel. I jump at shadows, I am afraid."

The young man hovered hesitantly at the door. Although yet to be formally admitted as an acolyte, he wore plain homespun robes that hung loose on his slender frame, the dark colour throwing his pale skin and auburn hair into sharp relief.

"Bishop Sisebut sent me to enquire about a codex. I can return at another time —"

"No." Laurentius gestured him in. "And you are my nephew, not a visitor. You must make use of my library whenever you wish."

"Your nephew by marriage." An odd shadow passed over the young man's face. "Not by blood."

Laurentius inclined his head. "That is true," he said, smiling. "But you are no less welcome."

A hectic flush had risen on Athanagild's neck. "Do you find your home much changed on your return?" The question mirrored Laurentius's recent introspection with uncanny precision, but when he looked at his nephew, Athanagild was looking away, clearly unsure of himself. Laurentius, long accustomed to commanding men and recognising introversion disguised as reserve, sat down and poured them both wine. Athanagild perched uncertainly on the *lectus* opposite, holding the wine cup self-consciously.

"The house is unchanged." Laurentius smiled at him. "But it was my father's house, and without him inside its walls, it no longer seems like my home."

"And you are no longer the person you were when you left it." Athanagild looked directly at him when he spoke. The sun falling through the lattice caught his face as he did, turning the hazel eyes to rich topaz and his hair to flame above the pale skin. The effect was startling, but it was the expression in his eyes that jolted Laurentius, as if Athanagild saw straight through the years of blood and war and command to the boy Laurentius had been when he bid his father farewell in this same room.

"Yes," said Laurentius slowly, hearing an uncharacteristic roughness in his voice. "I am not the person I was when I left."

Athanagild nodded as if the answer was no more or less than he had expected. For a time, neither of them spoke. The atmosphere felt rich with leather and parchment. Laurentius turned the wine cup in his hand, a strange feeling stealing through his body.

"It is peace," said Athanagild, then coloured at Laurentius's quizzical expression. "The feeling I have in this room," he explained. "It's peaceful here. I imagine it must be a luxury after so many years at war." He smiled, a sudden blaze of joy that was gone as swiftly as it came, fading back to wary stillness. Laurentius had an unsettling desire to draw forth that unguarded joy again.

"And you?" Feeling the need to readjust the balance of the conversation to a place in which he was more familiar, Laurentius gave Athanagild what he hoped was a cool smile, detached but still interested. "Do you find the surrounds of the monastery peaceful?"

"There is much that I might learn there." In the moment before he turned away, something flashed in Athanagild's face that was so savage Laurentius thought perhaps it was a trick of the light. Before Laurentius could ask anything further, Athanagild went on, "Is Constantinople truly as magnificent as the stories we hear?"

"Oh, more so." On a topic so well suited to capturing the imaginations of young men, Laurentius was able to speak without any risk of the uncomfortable intimacy he had felt moments earlier. Athanagild listened eagerly, asking questions that at times were so unexpected that Laurentius found himself openly laughing. It was only as the shadows grew long and Athanagild stood to take his leave that Laurentius realised they had not touched again on his life at the monastery.

"How do you find the instruction of Bishop Sisebut thus far?" Laurentius said as they walked through the silent villa. "I understand you are to study under his direction. It is a great honour."

"He favours me." There was a certain edge to Athanagild's voice. "Not least because of my family's connection to yours. Sisebut is an ambitious man. He realised early that I could prove of benefit in his rise in the Church." Laurentius did not miss the hard gleam in his eyes as he spoke.

"Ambition is not a sin," he said lightly, watching the boy's face as he did so.

"No, ambition is not." Athanagild paused at the door, his expression carefully blank. He looked at Laurentius with that same disquieting directness. "I would like to return here," he said. "To your library." He coloured, the same hectic flush, and Laurentius found himself again moved by the glimpse of vulnerability.

"You must come whenever you wish." He gripped Athanagild's arm, surprised at the whipcord strength beneath the cloth. "Your father, I think, trained you with sword," he said, smiling to cover his sudden disquiet.

"Not like you." Athanagild met his eyes. "I wish I could have seen you fight." He spoke with a quiet intensity that hit Laurentius like a gut blow. "I can imagine you there. Amidst the smoke and flame on the water, fighting for your life." The awareness in his eyes sent a trickle of heat down Laurentius's spine. He dropped the arm as if it were a hot coal.

"I can assure you," Laurentius said lightly, "it was nothing so impressive."

Athanagild's mouth lifted in a brief, hard smile that seemed much older than his years. "I doubt that," he said softly. He held Laurentius's eyes just long enough to turn the trickle of heat to a raging blaze, then walked away, leaving Laurentius staring after him until the gloaming faded to night.

AD 687, SEVERAL MONTHS LATER
HISPALIS, SPANIA

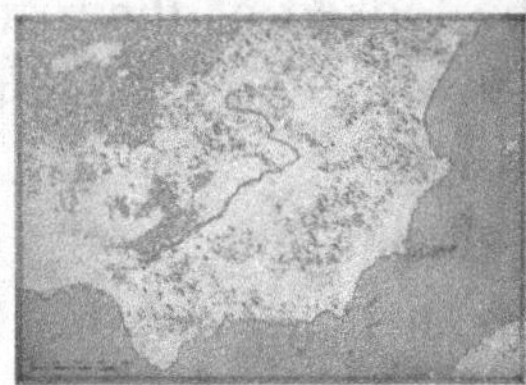

Seville, Spain

The room was thick with the scent of wine, meat, and men.

Autumn had cooled the nights in Toletum before Laurentius rode south with the royal entourage, but here on the flat plains by the River Bætis, the air was sultry. The dank smell of mud drifted through the open windows of the *œca* and from the atrium beyond. King Erwig, Laurentius had learned, did not travel well in the heat. He wore an unnatural pallor, and his hands shook when he drank.

Laurentius bore one of Spania's most honourable names, dating back to the old Roman aristocracy. Now, however, observing the drunken spectacle in the once great domus of Sunifred, Duke of Hispalis, he felt himself a stranger in his own land.

Sunifred sat to the right of King Erwig at a long table set on the dais. The duke was a man of expansive gestures and an even more expansive waistline. His voice had grown as much as his girth during the interminably long feast, and now it carried clearly across the clatter of dishes, punctuated by wild gestures of his wine cup, the contents of which decorated both the red mass of his beard and the table in front of him.

"Your mother was a niece of Chindasuinth," he was saying now, for at least the tenth time that night, Laurentius noted resignedly. Clapping the king's shoulder with one great paw, Sunifred waved the wine cup dangerously close to Erwig's face. "Your father may have been a godforsaken Greek, but you have some of Chindasuinth's blood in you. That is why we supported your claim. But, by God, we have seen little in the way of thanks!"

He raised his cup and the men of his *thiufa* roared in approval, returning his salute with their own raised cups. It was a good thing, Laurentius thought as he looked at them, that weapons were not permitted in the king's presence. The night had an undertone of savagery that he didn't care for.

Erwig seemed almost comically small beside the vast bulk of Sunifred. He was not a tall man, and his hair, cut square in the Greek fashion, framed a thin, anxious face. Beside his towering Gothic cousins, long haired and bearded, boasting elaborate jewelled torques and brooches, his own royal purple faded into insignificance.

"Whilst you squabble over land in Toletum, we in the south fill your treasury with our oil and grain and maintain our own thiufae to hold your borders against the barbarians from Africa. And what help do we get?"

Sunifred's hand on Erwig's shoulder pushed the king to one side with such force that the smaller man almost toppled from the lectus. Guards moved toward him, but he gestured them away, recovering himself to jeers from the men on the floor.

Laurentius released a breath he hadn't realised he was holding. In another time, not so long distant, Sunifred's action would have meant war. Looking at the thunderous expressions on the faces of the Toletum court, Laurentius was not entirely certain that it would not still.

Back in Toletum, the aristocracy had long since adopted Gothic-style halls, with the king seated on a chair at the head table. In the capital and to the north, the distinction between Roman and Goth had long faded to no more than a memory. But here in the south, it had been barely a generation since the last imperial forces had been expelled. The old customs remained, as did the greatest of the old villas. It was plain that the Toletum nobility found reclining on lecti an insult to their dignity. Whilst the Hispano Romans of Hispalis lounged comfortably, picking at their plates with their hands, the northerners sat stiffly upright, swaying without the support of the high-backed chairs to which they were accustomed, unable to find solid purchase amongst cushions on the low-backed lecti. Laurentius, whilst of the Toletum party, sat amongst his Hispalis peers, glad to be removed from the theatre playing out on the dais. Since his return to Spania, he had been almost constantly travelling in the king's retinue. A decade and more abroad in the imperial naval force, the *Karabisianoi*, had lessened his tolerance for men who talked of war whilst sending others to do the fighting. He was grateful for a night where he was at least nominally removed from their immediate vicinity.

The southern Goths lacked the easy elegance of the Hispalis Roman nobles but were both untroubled by the distinction and more at ease than their Toletum counterparts. Sunifred rested one foot on the lectus, his elbow propped on it as he faced the king. He was not quite as drunk as he chose to appear, Laurentius thought; the blue eyes watching Erwig were shrewd and calculating. Sunifred could trace his descent from the legendary King Liuvguild and was long accustomed to the power his name and blood conferred upon him. The condescension of the old Roman nobility concerned him as little as it had his famous forbears. Unlike Erwig and the self-conscious Toletum court, he revelled in his Gothic heritage, wearing its garish trappings of gold armbands and jewels woven into his long hair with casual arrogance.

"My men have fought off ten raids at sea this summer alone," he was saying now. "When will we see the Chrismon-and-peacock standard amongst our ranks? We have no coastal forces. When does your *Comes Exercitus* plan to answer our pleas for help?"

The taller man to Erwig's left stirred, and cold eyes met Sunifred's. Following his wedding to Cixilo, King Erwig's daughter, it was Count Egica who held the title of Comes Exercitus, Count of the Army. It was he who signed the orders that commanded the provincial armed forces: the thiufae, and their leaders, the *thiufadi*.

"You speak much of these raids," said Egica coolly. "Yet by all accounts the Arab army was vanquished in Africa five years ago, their forces scattered into the desert sands. These vessels that – you claim – threaten our shores can be no more than opportunists looking for plunder. And pirates, surely, your great warriors can easily expel."

Sunifred's eyes narrowed. He licked his lips, stained purple from the wine. Egica held his gaze, and the chatter in the room died away.

Laurentius found he was again holding his breath.

"Do you name me liar, Egica sunau Ariberga?" Sunifred's Gothic accent thickened his speech. "In my own *gards*?"

One broad hand dropped to his side, instinctively feeling for the *spatha* that was not there. Egica's dark eyes did not miss the gesture.

"I am merely saying that whilst our forces fight a very real foe in the mountains to the north, protecting Mater Spania from neighbours who covet her riches, the south hoards wealth that belongs by right to the Crown. Your coastline squabbles deny us men who could help us protect our northern border as we must."

Sunifred slammed his cup on the table, and Erwig jumped nervously as the big red head leaned around him to address Egica directly. "Do not think that I, nor any other in this room, are ignorant as to your ambitions, Fráuja." Sunifred spat the honorific with contempt. His voice was low, but the menace in it carried clearly throughout the œca. "We know you come amongst us as the next King of Spania – and be warned, Fráuja, that we are all watching the manner in which you conduct yourself. Neither your marriage nor your bloodline assures your succession. We elect our kings. They do not inherit. There are others amongst us who hold equal right to the throne – and require no marriage to substantiate it."

The two men stared at each other, fierce blue eyes meeting hooded black. Erwig shrank between them, his thin figure swallowed by the larger presence of those on either side. Looking at Egica's hand, white knuckled as he clenched his eating knife, Laurentius felt a rivulet of cold sweat trail down his spine.

"*Fráujan minus.*" The voice that broke the tense standoff belonged to Julian, archbishop of Toletum. He had moved forward from the rear of the room and stood now behind Erwig's lectus, one pale hand resting on the king's shoulder. The large ruby of his office glinted on the third finger, and candlelight lit the gold thread worked into his white robes. "Our Lord watches us all." His stern eye and tone of authority stilled the room. "It is by His grace that Flavius Erwig wears the crown, and only in His house should such discussions take place."

The noble seated beside Laurentius gave a low, ironic chuckle. "Erwig rules by the grace of Archbishop Julian, who did him the good favour of poisoning his predecessor," he muttered.

His wasn't the only murmured aside. A hum of comment passed through the œca like a wave, and the tension was broken. Erwig flushed but took the opportunity to turn and talk to Julian, who leaned forward to listen.

Sunifred settled back on his cushions, raising his cup to Egica in mock salute. Egica himself did not move.

He is still and dangerous as a serpent waiting to strike, Laurentius thought, watching him. Whether Egica's venom was directed at Julian or Sunifred was hard to say; the dark eyes flickered between both. Laurentius, taking a large gulp of wine to still the rapid thudding of his heart, shivered at the hatred in their depths. The whispers surrounding the death of King Wamba, Egica's uncle and Erwig's predecessor, were persistent. They had become more so since Egica had married the new king's daughter and risen so high at court.

Egica, Laurentius was aware, did not share his father-in-law's passivity. Laurentius had watched him closely during the long weeks they had ridden together and developed a wary respect for a man he sensed was both ambitious and venal.

The men of Sunifred's thiufa burst into raucous song. It referenced the old pagan gods, Tyr and Berkana, and Julian's face tightened with annoyance.

"It takes little to scratch away the veneer of sophistication, no?" murmured Laurentius's neighbour. "They are barbarians themselves, these Goths. Two centuries have done little more than put a shine on the unfinished product."

"They achieved what our forefathers could not," replied Laurentius coldly. He had little time for the supercilious chattering of the old Roman nobility. "They unified Spania beneath one ruler, and they created a code of law to protect it."

"By blood and the sword," sneered another.

"By blood and the sword was the Empire created," replied Laurentius.

"Well, if one studies Livy —" began a third.

"Excuse me," said Laurentius abruptly.

Ignoring the shocked expressions of his elegant companions, he stood and strode through the open corridor to the atrium, where he stopped and inhaled the cool air gratefully. He should have been more gracious, he knew, but he had never found the haughty snobbery of the old families anything but grating, even if he was honest enough to admit that he privately shared some of their outrage at Gothic crudity. As if to prove their words, an old fountain, long dry, crumbled in the centre of the atrium. Looking at it, Laurentius felt a familiar flash of irritation. He glanced around, noting the uneven surfaces where lumpy plaster covered the beautiful mosaics beneath. A clumsy tapestry on one wall depicted the Christogram, the only image permitted by the laws of the Hispanic Catholic Church, which outlawed all iconography. He allowed himself the luxury of imagining the old artistry beneath and wondered, as he often did, what treasures were lost forever beneath the crude piety of the Goths.

"Art is God's spirit working through man."

Laurentius turned to find Julian standing beside him. The archbishop smiled, the large gold pectoral cross about his neck seeming almost too heavy for the thin body beneath. He looked tired, Laurentius thought, wearied from long days in the saddle. Julian was a man meant for scholarly pursuits, not the rigours of travel. In his mid-forties, he looked much older.

Laurentius touched the wall where glimpses of old colour still showed through. "I know they depict terrible sin," he said. "But it seems – if you will forgive me, Your Grace – an insult to God that they are no longer visible."

"If God had intended them still to be seen, they would be." Julian smiled gently. "In time, God will find His artists amongst our own."

They were interrupted by the quiet arrival of Felix, bishop of Hispalis and a student of Julian's. Laurentius liked Felix; the man had a subdued integrity that did not quite conceal the strength beneath. *He is no fawning acolyte,* thought Laurentius, as Felix turned to him now.

"Not only will God find those to wield a brush. He will also find leaders who will rule in the light of God instead of by the edge of the sword," he said softly, dark eyes afire with the strength of his convictions.

Laurentius returned Felix's smile. He could not help but like both men of God, although there was reason enough to do otherwise. "I admire your faith," he said. "I fear my own falters at times."

"You are an educated man." Julian gestured around them. "And this was the world of your father's father. Such things test our faith."

"Knowledge tests our faith?" Laurentius looked between the two men curiously.

"Of course it does," said Felix calmly. "It raises questions only God can answer. That is why it is best left to those in the bosom of Our Holy Father. Learning must always be tempered with spiritual understanding."

Julian cast a wry glance at Laurentius. "And this is why I have ever encouraged first your father, and now you, to join our ranks, my friend. You would be a most welcome addition." He gave a low laugh. "At the least, I could then enjoy our conversations without fearing for your immortal soul."

Laurentius did not meet his eyes, though he laughed in return. "I suspect you simply wish to gain access to my library," he said lightly.

"Ah, yes." Julian accepted his deflection with grace. "I would be lying if I denied it."

"I do hope you will continue to speak with me despite my refusal to take orders."

"It would be my sincere loss if I did not." Julian stepped back. "I am tired, my lord Laurentius, and we have long miles to ride tomorrow."

Laurentius inclined his head. "I shall anticipate your company with pleasure, Your Grace." He nodded at both men, remaining in the atrium as the archbishop made his slow progress into the night, given strength by Felix's arm.

Turning to leave, Laurentius found himself confronted by a young soldier of the king's guard. Clad in a short tunic and breastplate armour, the soldier's bronze skin gleamed over hard muscle.

"I am sent to escort you back to your chambers, Fráuja." His tone was quite proper, but the warm brown eyes and sensual half smile made an offer of quite a different kind. Laurentius had already sampled the delights offered beneath the brief tunic – had been sampling them nightly, since Toletum, in fact. But now he shook his head once in dismissal.

"I have no need of an escort tonight," he said coolly. His own eyes, grey and clear, met those of the young soldier, who was pouting. "The dangers from this point in the journey," Laurentius added, "lie not on darkened streets, but in the ears and eyes upon them." He stared at the boy until he was certain his meaning had been taken. "I will alert your commander if I require an escort beyond tonight."

"As you wish, Fráuja." Nervous watchfulness had replaced the sulkiness; the boy had more to lose even than Laurentius himself should he be discovered.

Walking through the night to his family's domus in Hispalis, Laurentius pushed the boy from his mind with an effort, reflecting instead on Julian's offer. His family, he knew, had expected him to take the cloth. His house had already produced the famed Isidore of Hispalis, and his great aunt, Faustina, had founded over a hundred monasteries throughout Spania. The family's libraries, at Laurentius's estate in Toletum and here in Hispalis, were consulted by scholars the world over. His own entry into the clergy would come with political power and assured ascension through the ranks.

His sexual nature constituted a mortal sin. Laurentius knew it, had spent many dark nights contemplating the vagaries of a God who would make man as He had made him, condemned to live in eternal purgatory even before death. But he was honest enough to know that taking the cloth and devoting himself to God would not stop him pursuing the pleasures of the flesh.

Laurentius was an intelligent and educated man. He was also an honest one. His was a passionate nature. The fire ran beneath his skin, hidden far beneath the cool exterior of aristocratic birth but undeniably a force to be reckoned with. His lithe form was whipcord strong, and he was as happy behind a sword as a book. He did not find release only in the taking of what he desired sexually; Laurentius knew the thrill of battle blood-rush and relished it as much as the cut and thrust of politics.

It was not that he did not desire the power that came with Julian's offer, he thought, as he pushed open the side door of his family home. The *posticum* was dark and silent, the servants gone to bed, and he passed into the peace of the atrium unseen. But whilst he knew it to be a mortal sin, Laurentius had no intention of spending the rest of his days in the hypocrisy of indulgence followed by repentance. He was not ashamed of who and what he was, and the integrity of his character precluded him from pretending other- wise. He would live his purgatory in quiet privacy, the price he paid for choices made; but he would not pretend to himself, nor to the God he loved, that he truly repented. Laurentius had searched the depths of his own soul and concluded that the God of Our Lord Jesus Christ, who had made Himself manifest in Word to man after so many centuries of relative silence, would have small tolerance for a man who knew His truth in his heart but pretended on the surface to be ignorant.

But in the company of Archbishop Julian, and the increasing hold the prelate had over the throne of Spania, it paid to be cautious indeed.

And Laurentius was, first and foremost, a very cautious man.

For a moment he remembered a pair of wide hazel eyes set in a pale face. He felt again the odd shock he had felt upon meeting Athanagild, who was stepbrother to his nephews Theo and Alaric. "I am not your nephew," Athanagild had said, colour staining his face as he met Laurentius's gaze with quiet dignity.

For the hundredth time Laurentius replayed the meeting. He had lived too many years with his nature not to recognise the signs in another. *Yet what kind of man,* he thought, as he had every time he contemplated the matter, *would take advantage of a youth barely old enough to know his own mind — especially one who has taken orders in the Church?*

Raised to a code of honour far deeper than any laid down by Church or law, Laurentius knew in his heart that to give in to such desire could only ever be moral transgression.

He made for his bedchamber, heartsick and lonely, regretting that he had turned away the young soldier, whose presence these past weeks had at least served to temporarily drive away the ever-present memory of that pale, angular face and the haunted expression in the wide hazel eyes. He thought for a moment of Shukra, his oldest friend, who was even now in Aurariola with Athanagild's brothers. Shukra was perhaps the only man to know Laurentius's secret and find no fault in it. He heard the little Persian man's voice, his comments so many years ago when first he had surprised Laurentius with one of his male companions: *Do you think Ahura Mazda cares with whom you take your pleasure, aziz-am? What matter is it where you are finding love, so long as it is love you find? Pah! Are you thinking your God has nothing better to do than concern Himself with whom you choose to lie?*

Then Shukra's light-hearted voice and laughing eyes disappeared, replaced once more by the deep, solemn hazel of Athanagild's. Laurentius leaned his head against the cool stone of his bedchamber, one clenched fist hitting the stone beside his face.

"I will not give in to this," he muttered. "I will conquer myself. I will."

ATHANAGILD

AD 688, ONE YEAR LATER, AFTER ERWIG'S DEATH AND
EGICA'S CORONATION

Toletum, Spania
Toledo, Spain

The hour was late, and the monastery silent, when Athanagild heard the stealthy creak of the wicket beyond its walls.

Slipping silently from his pallet, he crept through the sleeping figures of his fellow students, out through the communal hall, to the low entrance to the chapel. It had been a long time since he had truly slept; he preferred to be awake if Sisebut came to his bed. That way, at least he could ensure they removed to Sisebut's own chambers rather than forcing the others in the dormitory to witness his humiliation.

It was late even for Sisebut. By now the priest was generally wine soaked and maudlin, a state Athanagild had come to appreciate since at least it meant he would be spared his attentions.

Sisebut was not drunk tonight, however. He was seated in the chapel, head bowed as if for prayer, and the man who entered from the rear of the chapel was clad in the robes of a monk, his face covered. Moments later another monk joined them, and then, finally, another. There should have been nothing remarkable about their presence in the chapel. But there was something in the way

17

they walked and held themselves that made Athanagild alert; that, and the odd hour and place they had chosen for their prayer. Monks tended to remain within the confines of their monastery. They were, in Athanagild's experience, hardly inclined to seek city chapels in the early hours of the morning. Then one of the men put his hood back, and the others did the same. Athanagild shrank back into the shadows, his heart thudding with tension.

The men in the chapel were not monks. They were bishops: Maximo of Emerita, Idalio of Barcelona, and Mumulo of Corduba.

Athanagild crept closer. Barefoot, clad only in his homespun robes, he moved silently across the stone floor, concealing himself behind a carved pillar only feet from where the men sat. After greeting, all pulled their cowls back over their faces. They sat in two pews, all facing the altar in an attitude of prayer. Had any entered the chapel, there would have been nothing to witness other than four monks, all praying.

"Egica has grown bold since becoming king," said Maximo grimly, without preamble. "Does he not recall that the Church put his predecessor on the throne – and can just as easily remove Egica from it?"

"Whilst Julian lives," said Idalio, "Egica will remain on the throne. The archbishop is too concerned by his squabbles with Rome to countenance any upheaval at home."

"But Julian will not live forever." Mumulo's dry tones dismissed the others. "And when he is gone, we will take care of this king, just as Julian did his predecessor."

An uncomfortable silence met this statement. Athanagild held his breath. He had only ever heard rumours, whispers, of the actions that had resulted in Wamba's death and Erwig's taking the throne. To hear it so blatantly stated was shocking.

"Whether he lives or not, Egica is not Erwig." Athanagild could sense the barely restrained excitement in Sisebut's voice. "If we wish to truly take control of Spania, more drastic measures must be taken. If we allow Egica to sit on the throne for long, he will find a way to undermine the Church – and in doing so, undo the great gains we have made."

"I will not see murder done twice," Maximo interjected. Athanagild felt his blood turn to ice. Barely breathing, he strained to listen.

"We do not know King Wamba was poisoned –"

"Yes, we do." Maximo cut off Idalio's words brutally. "We all of us turned a blind eye to Julian's plot with Queen Liuvgoto, and with good reason. We needed her husband on the throne. Erwig was pliant. Wamba would have seen us all die in his battles and taken the spoils of what was left. Conscripting men of the Church to fight, like any common man, in the Crown's wars? It was unconscionable. But that was then, and a different time. We cannot be seen to interfere now."

"Then what?" Mumulo's voice was thick with distaste. "I, also, will not be party to murder."

"Rebellion is brewing in the south." Sisebut leaned in and the others drew close to listen. Athanagild held his breath. "Sunifred has sent word, and I have met with him. He has both the men and cause to take Toletum – but he cannot hold the capital without our support."

"You are speaking of treason," said Idalio, shocked.

"Not I." Sisebut smiled unpleasantly. "Sunifred. What can the Church do, once Toletum is taken? We are forbidden to take up arms ourselves. What choice do we have, after the city falls, than to anoint the king that God has favoured in battle?"

Mumulo sucked in his breath. "And after this anointing? What then? Do you have any idea what kind of man Sunifred is? Because I do, Brother – and believe me when I say that his is not the rule that Spania needs."

"Of course it is not," said Sisebut, the excitement in his voice clear now. "But Sunifred's rule is exactly what we – the Church – *do* need. Egica is dangerous. He is smart, cunning, and calculating. He understands the power of the Church and is determined to cauterise it. Sunifred, on the other hand, is an eager fool with a sword and a love of power. He is a fighting man, with nothing but contempt for the rule of God. He believes, as all pagans do, that God is there simply to serve his own interests; that with the right offerings, he can bribe not only God himself, but those who represent him on earth. It does not occur to him that the Church may have knowledge and foresight that he himself does not. The arrogance of the man precludes any such understanding."

"And how are we advantaged by such a man sitting on the throne?" asked Maximo, interested despite himself.

"Because Sunifred will fail spectacularly," said Sisebut. "He may win Toletum at the point of his sword. But what of it? Do any of you believe Sunifred has the diplomacy – or even the will – to rule?"

Mumulo gave a dry laugh. "The man cannot see beyond the next prize in his sight," he said. "And the only way he knows how to rule a chamber is by shouting at it and insisting upon his right to do so."

"Exactly." Sisebut looked at each face with satisfaction. "Sunifred will not last a year on the throne before Spania erupts into outright disarray, the nobles begging for someone – anyone – to restore order. And who is able to do that?"

"Those who hold the *Lex Visigothorum*," said Idalio, his voice slow with comprehension. "Since Braulio of Saragossa edited the Visigothic code of law in the time of Reccesuinth, the Church is the ultimate authority – even over the king."

Sisebut's eyes gleamed. "My brothers," he said, "the Church has been passive enough. God's very will in Spania is threatened by Egica's rule, and by the ambitions of all those he represents. Will we stand idly by and watch as Spania falls from the light of Christ into the darkness of sin – and possibly even heresy?" The pale blue eyes glittered with excitement. "Julian ages. His time is nearly done – and when it is, we must act, and act quickly. If I am able to bring Sunifred's plots to fruition, do I have your word you will support my accession to the primacy of Toletum?"

"If you can do what you say," said Mumulo, "then we – and the Church itself – will owe you a debt that can never be repaid."

"I can do it," said Sisebut, his voice high with excitement. "It is already happening." He held out his hand, and one by one, they each kissed the ruby ring on its third finger.

Unseen by any of them, Athanagild shrank from the chapel. He had stopped shaking. His skin felt icy cold, as numb as his heart. *They are plotting to undo the very fabric of Spania,* he thought. Around and around in his head the words travelled, making no more sense the more he thought of them. *Who can I tell?*

Archbishop Julian's face crossed his mind, only to be instantly dismissed. Even if Julian believed him, what could the archbishop do against a plot Athanagild could never prove, that was to be implemented on his own death? One by one, he considered those he knew and loved. He thought of his stepbrother Theo, somewhere far away on foreign seas, fighting with the Karabisianoi, and of Theo's betrothed, Lælia, whom Athanagild already thought of as a sister. Of his other stepbrother Alaric, already riding to support Sunifred's cause, blind to the trap he would be caught in. Then Laurentius's cool grey eyes passed before his face, and Athanagild shuddered with mingled longing and shame.

He allowed himself the rare luxury of recalling the day he had come across Laurentius in the library at his villa in Toletum. In the moments before Laurentius had realised he was there, Athanagild had seen the stark loneliness on the older man's face, a terrible despair that had made his heart twist in sympathy. A scar ran down the back of Laurentius's neck, a livid red welt that was usually hidden from view by his robes. When he had grasped Athanagild's arm, he had felt the rough callouses on the other man's palm, a hardness that came from oar and steel and battle. Somewhere amidst the scars and the books, Athanagild thought, lay a complex soul who seemed in his own way to be as alone as Athanagild himself. He longed to reach out to him, to offer comfort and receive it in turn; but such desire sent him spiralling into shame and self-doubt. The thought of Laurentius's rejection was as terrifying as it was inevitable.

I cannot go to him, he thought fiercely. *He carries enough of a burden already. And if he knew what I had become, he would despise me.*

Kneeling by his pallet, he bowed his head. *Holy God,* he prayed silently, *who should I tell? What should I say – and to whom? How can I prevent corrupt men from committing terrible acts in Your name? From twisting the ministry of Your Word to suit their own human ambition?* For a moment, he heard the echo of Shukra's voice, long ago: *I think there is much you see, aziz-am, which others do not.*

Yes, Athanagild thought, and the realisation opened a door in his mind hitherto unconsidered. *Sisebut thinks me his plaything. The others barely know my name.* His prayers stopped, replaced by a tense stillness. He felt both slightly sick and oddly excited. *I have chosen the Church,* he thought. *If I am to truly be a man of God, then I must learn to do His work in His house. I will serve those I know work for Spania, and trust to God that He has placed me here for His own purposes and that He will not inflict upon me any suffering I cannot bear.* He felt his body straighten with his resolve, hope stealing through his veins. *I may be Sisebut's plaything,* he thought, *but suffer I will, if it means I can prevent what I know is against God.*

From the corridor beyond, he heard the soft slap of footfall, the clumsy shuffle that meant Sisebut had drunk more than his fill. The plump figure filled the doorway, and Athanagild rose, moving silently to the bishop's side.

"Athanagild," slurred Sisebut, stroking his face with one hand, the other sliding along his thigh.

"Father," Athanagild murmured, manoeuvring Sisebut out of earshot of the sleeping acolytes, toward his chambers. "I was praying you would come."

1

THREE YEARS LATER
LETTER FROM ATHANAGILD TO SHUKRA

March, AD 690

Shukra —

Archbishop Julian is dead.

I doubt many saw the farce of his funeral for what it was. At King Egica's command, Julian's body was carried through the city. People lined the streets, aromatic herbs and flowers were cast upon the ground. Julian lay with hands crossed. In one of them was a cruet of holy oil; the Book of the Gospels rested on his chest. The corpse lay on a byre and women wept as it passed, holding their babies up to see the body, hoping they would be touched by the great archbishop's grace. Egica, of course, followed behind it on foot, his head bare and bowed in respect, and the people seemed convinced he truly mourned Julian — the same man Egica hated as much as any man can loathe another.

I walked behind the king, beside the bishop Sisebut, the man who will now succeed Julian. The man to whom I am clerk and closest companion. A man I know to be corrupt at his core. One who will destroy Spania and all that has taken centuries to build. A man more dangerous than even Egica himself, though I had not thought such a thing possible.

Sisebut trusts me, for reasons that would offend you, God, and all men.

23

Should Laurentius discover what manner of man I am, he could not accept the only worth I may offer, which is the information that Sisebut's trust allows me access to. You, who do not follow our God nor bow to our customs, are better able to understand the value of information. I am grateful you accept my offerings and pass what I may send you to Laurentius without disclosing the source of your information. I can send these letters amidst Church documents and ensure they reach you with the seal untouched. None so far suspect we meet — as you suggested, none question a priest who visits a pleasure house by the river. It is, sadly, far more common than men might wish to believe.

Perhaps it is only you to whom I may speak openly, now that my brothers are lost to me and Lælia is gone. Of Theo, we have no word other than the coin he sent Lælia as a reminder of their promise to each other. He is far away, fighting on foreign shores, where only my prayers may be of aid to him.

Lælia herself is gone to Septem, to Ilyan's court. She knows it was Giscila who killed her mother, and now she sails to the very shores where his dromons lie. I cannot believe she does not mean to search him out. Lælia is as wild and fierce as she is determined. Her presence in Africa is meant to be secret, but the Church has eyes everywhere. Strange that men do not see the man who wears a cross and browncloth. We are the most invisible of creatures, and yet it is to us that all men — even kings — must bow. It is a dangerous privilege.

Of Alaric, I have heard little. I fear that in following Sunifred he seeks to replace our father, who cannot support this rebellion, believing as he does that it is destined to fail. Even if Alaric, too, believes that, his love for Rekiberga, Sunifred's daughter, means he cannot shun the father. He and I must both work with forces we know to be corrupt. He at least has the fleet, your company, and Laurentius to console him.

I envy him that.

It sometimes feels that all have a destiny, a purpose, whilst I, who am privy to the most destructive plots man in his hubris might devise, must rot in brown homespun amidst prayers and old parchment, unable to so much as carry a sword in defence of my family or country.

For God, family, and Mater Spania,

—Athanagild

2

LÆLIA
MAY, AD 690

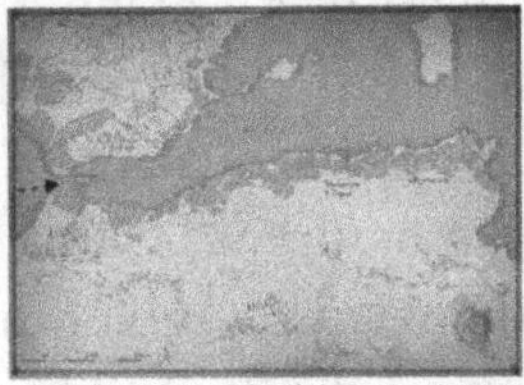

Septem, Mauretania
Ceuta, Morocco

"Ilyan."

The tall woman strode brusquely through the great wooden doors of the palace in Septem, looking neither left nor right as she approached the dais. "Your men said it was urgent. I must hope they did not lie, for the Arabs land to the east, and fighting season approaches."

Lælia, sitting in an alcove to one side of the dais, stared at the woman in amazement as Ilyan stood, reaching out his hands in welcome. "Dahiya. You honour me."

Making an impatient sound, the woman seemed about to sit when she caught sight of Lælia. The almond-shaped eyes narrowed, their colour deepening to liquid amber. "You do not customarily bring your whores to our council, Ilyan."

Ilyan opened his mouth to reply, but it was Lælia who spoke. "My grandfather, Count Paulus of Illiberis, says all men see what they expect to see when they look at a woman. I had not, however, thought a woman herself would do the same – particularly one who commands many thiufae of men."

"The Count of Illiberis." Dahiya did not offer an apology, but she looked at Lælia now with curiosity rather than hostility. "Yes, I see the resemblance. I met your grandmother once. Did she tell you?"

Lælia nodded. "She did."

"I take it this is the reason for your summons." Dahiya's eyes swivelled back to Ilyan, who was watching the exchange with the detachment of the consummate diplomat. Lælia, who had been in Septem and Ilyan's palace for a quarter of the moon, had yet to decide what the man's true nature was. Tall, thin, and restless, Ilyan seemed as mercurial as the winds that blew across his rocky port, his wild shock of hair seeming a direct representation of the thousand thoughts he juggled in his mind every day. He strode now across the room, turned, and strode back, whipping his robes behind him as he did so.

"It *was* the reason," said Ilyan, his stress upon the second word indicating other events had taken precedence. "Until I discovered a certain friend of ours has re-entered my waters."

Dahiya frowned. "Do not give me your riddles, Ilyan. You have more friends than I do enemies. What is it now?"

"Giscila."

The name fell across the room like a shadow. Lælia felt the old tightness squeeze her throat in the place where her words had once been stilled by her mother's dying whispers. It was by Giscila's hand her mother had died. Giscila, uncle to Egica, the present King of Spania, though long exiled from his home for his crimes. Giscila, of whose existence and pivotal role in her life Lælia had only recently learned.

Dahiya's eyes flickered to her once again. *She must know,* thought Lælia. *Of our history, and what he did.* She met the older woman's gaze unflinchingly. *I know the stories of the revenge you took on the man who killed your father,* Lælia thought. *Look at me and know that I, too, am capable of such rage, granddaughter of a Spanish count though I may be.* A quarter moon in Ilyan's court had taught her the fear and awe with which men regarded Dahiya, Queen of the Jerawa, the fighter who so terrified her Arabic enemies that they called her Al Kahinat, the Sorceress. Lælia felt both compelled by Dahiya's legend and painfully unequal to it. Lælia might have faced enemies across the battlefield of the Toletum court, but at the same age, Dahiya had already gathered an army and led it to victory in battle.

"And what business do I have with Giscila?" Despite Dahiya's disdainful tone, Lælia, who had lived too long in silence not to see what was unsaid, felt the tension and interest behind the words.

"It is not Giscila alone who sails close to my port. He comes to meet another, one who does not dare land on my shores but who travels even now to meet his kinsman. A man even closer to the Crown of Spania – Oppa, King Egica's bastard son."

The name sucked the tightness from Lælia's throat, replacing it with a cold, hard fury. "You did not tell me this," she said in a low voice, staring at Ilyan.

"I did not know it myself until this morning." Ilyan shrugged and waited whilst a slave poured Dahiya wine, putting a plate of olives, dates, and nuts before her, another with bread and oil. Cross legged, her spine perfectly straight, Dahiya swallowed the wine, ignored the food, and stared at Lælia.

"You know the king's bastard," she said.

"I do." There was so much more Lælia wanted to say: that it had been Oppa who forced Yosef, her childhood friend, into exile; who had pursued Theo, the man to whom she was betrothed, far across the seas; who had tried to force Lælia to marry him. Despite her skill in masking her emotions, some of what she felt must have shown on her face. Dahiya's mouth twisted in a strange smile.

"Yes," she said, watching Lælia closely. "I see that you do."

"If Oppa is meeting with Giscila," Lælia said, "it can be for no good purpose."

"I am inclined to agree with you." Ilyan paced the room again, turned, and strode back. "The last time the two entered my waters together, an entire fleet of the Karabisianoi's new recruits were attacked, most of them lost."

"Most," said Lælia sharply. "Not all."

Ilyan gave her a small smile. "Not all. Your Theudemir of Aurariola, I believe, made a rather miraculous escape." Lælia's heart thudded and caught, then began beating again, more rapidly than before.

"Only you, Ilyan," said Dahiya dryly, "would call being discovered in a slave market in Carthage a 'miraculous escape'."

"I would most certainly call it that. The boy could have died in chains."

"Chains?" Lælia's voice felt rough in her throat. "Theo was enslaved?" A glance passed between Dahiya and Ilyan that made her throat tighten. "What?" She looked between them. "What is it you aren't saying? Is Theo…?" She swallowed, unsure what she wanted to say. "Was he hurt?"

"He was enslaved, child." Dahiya's tone was brusque. "One does not survive enslavement unharmed. But he is whole. He fights now in the Karabisianoi, the imperial fleet, beneath one of the Greeks' greatest commanders – Apsimar. He is fortunate."

"Fortunate indeed," agreed Ilyan, a small smile playing around his mouth. Dahiya looked studiously out of the window, oblivious to Lælia's shock.

"You've seen him." When Lælia found her voice, it sounded as if it belonged to a stranger. "Theo. You've actually seen him."

"Barely six months past." This time when Dahiya met her eyes, there was an understanding in them. "I fought beside Apsimar at the Battle of Barca. Your Theudemir was there." She nodded, remembering. "He fought well," she said simply.

Ilyan raised his eyebrows at Lælia. "Praise indeed," he said. Questions churned inside Lælia, all the things she had wondered in the long years since Theo had been taken from her, when everyone – everyone except her – had feared him dead. Now that she had a chance to ask them, she didn't know where to begin.

"We can speak of this later." Ilyan caught his robes behind his back in a tighter twist. "Now, however, we must discuss what is to be done with you." He nodded at Lælia.

"Me?" She looked between them. "What do you mean?"

"You cannot sail back to Spania," said Ilyan bluntly. "All of Septem knows you are in my palace. By now, Giscila does too. We do not know why Oppa is here. Little more than a year has has passed since you humiliated him in his father's Toletum court by refusing to marry him. That wound is unlikely to have healed. It is very probable he comes in search of you – and his family does not have a good history when it comes to yours."

Seeing Dahiya shoot Ilyan a warning glance, Lælia interrupted: "I know Giscila killed my mother. Acantha, my grandmother, told me the story." *After I discovered it for myself,* she thought, but did not say. Her resentment at being lied to for so long had yet to entirely fade.

"Then you can see why I would prefer not to have you on open water," Ilyan continued. "Capturing you would achieve a great many of Oppa's goals. He would have a bargaining tool with which to discover the real destination of your Jewish friend, Yosef, and why your betrothed, Theo, was prepared to die to protect it. No matter even if I could rescue you. By the time I did, you would be reeved, ravaged, and married, with Illiberis in the hands of Oppa's father – a fate I am certain we agree is an unacceptable risk."

Lælia nodded silently. She could not argue with anything he said, even if his words raised questions she was forced, for now, to swallow.

"In Spania, too, you are vulnerable." Ilyan frowned. "If all you have told me is true, rebellion is growing on your shores. Illiberis is the most powerful latifundium in the south. That makes you a target – one reason, I imagine, why your grandfather took the rather unusual step of sending you to me in the guise of a tribeswoman from the horse herders."

"You bring horses from Illiberis?" Dahiya seemed far more interested in this than anything else said thus far.

"Almost a hundred," said Lælia, her pride in her family's famous bloodline undimmed despite the serious nature of their discussion. "I trained many of them myself."

"Almost a hundred?" Dahiya's eyes gleamed with unmistakable longing.

"Then that is decided," said Ilyan briskly, striding across the room again. "You will ride with Dahiya into the sands, Lælia, and show her your horseflesh. Like this, you will be safe, and I can send word when I know more of what Oppa does here."

Dahiya and Lælia stared at him with equal surprise.

"I can't leave," said Lælia. "I came for news of Theo, and Yosef. I must take it back to my grandfather. Rebellion in Spania grows. Illiberis needs me —"

"Yosef rode with Dahiya." Ilyan cut her off. "And it was Dahiya who last saw Theo. She is better suited than I to answer your questions and undoubtedly will take more pleasure in doing so."

"I have already played nursemaid to one Spaniard for you, Ilyan." Dahiya's eyes flashed. "The last time it resulted in my sending my own two sons to accompany Yosef into enemy territory. I have no more sons to give, Ilyan – and even less patience."

"I don't require a nursemaid." Lælia was indignant. She turned to Dahiya. "And nor do I need your help. If I decide to enter enemy territory, I will do it at night, and none will see me."

At the anger in her voice, a low growl rose from behind the lectus. Dahiya looked around warily, her hand going to her knife. The long, sleek body of a lynx prowled into sight, head lowered and tail swinging slowly behind her. Lælia made a silent gesture and the cat dropped to its belly, staring at Dahiya with wary topaz eyes. "Her name is Jadis," said Lælia defensively. "I raised her from a kitten." At Dahiya's raised eyebrows, Ilyan tilted his head and lifted one shoulder, his wry smile answer enough.

"So." Dahiya shook her head in grudging acceptance. "I take another of your Spaniards into my sands, Ilyan. At least this one brings gifts my men will understand. And what then? Do I swathe her in the *tasuwart* of our women and leave her in the *adwwar* whilst they make henna patterns on her feet?"

"I don't —" began Lælia, her eyes flashing furiously, but Dahiya held up one hand, her gesture so imperious, and so terribly reminiscent of Acantha's command, that Lælia subsided despite herself.

"What you think does not, at this moment, concern me." Dahiya pinned Ilyan with a stern eye. "Well, Ilyan?"

"Ride to your mountains, and then for Carthage. I will send word by sea to the port there." He nodded at Lælia. "I will also send envoys to Spania to tell your grandfather what occurs and to discover what business Oppa has here. If I learn anything before you arrive, I will send riders to find you and bring you back." The look he gave Lælia was not unsympathetic. "I understand this is not what you had planned. But I do believe it to be the safest course."

Lælia had lived too long under her grandparents' grim command not to recognise it when she saw it in another. In truth, even had she been given the choice, she knew she would have followed Dahiya, and not only for news of Theo and Yosef, though the thought of speaking of them to one with recent news was as seductive as a kiss.

Lælia would have followed Dahiya because in her company she sensed an adventure that as the heir to Illiberis, the granddaughter of a count, and the desired wife of greedy men, she would never have the chance to live.

Dahiya met her eyes, her mouth twisting in that same wry smile. "You think it will be an adventure," she said, reading Lælia's mind with uncanny accuracy. "But you have never lived in the sands. Drink your wine, child, and eat your meat – for tomorrow there will be neither."

3

YOSEF

AD 689

Tripolitania, Libya
Ténéré, Libya

E ven at the beginning of the hot season, the incessant desert wind had a malevolent will of its own. Yosef could barely see Bagay's camel in front of him. He peered through slitted eyes at the sun, red and angry behind the swirling sands. Swathed within the folds of his turban, hot wind roaring in his ears, he felt detached from everything he had known, lost in a yellow world of sand and heat. The only reality lay in the swaying gait of his camel and the dim shadow of the figures before him. They had been riding hard through the big sand seas for days now, and the camels were tired.

"We cannot delay here," Khanchla had said tersely when the dunes first came into sight. "We must be through the dune sea before the moon makes a half cycle, or we and the camels both will be dead. Nothing lives here."

Yosef had crossed dune seas before, when they rode with Dahiya's army, but none like this. After three days he had ceased to have any sense of direction. At night he could pick out the constellations, the glittering carpet above him like an intricate tapestry, clearer than he had ever seen. But during the day, when the wind roared and the dunes climbed up and down in an endless, treacherous pattern, he was lost. There was no wood for a fire on which to cook. They had eaten the last of their bread by the fifth day. By the seventh the last of the dried goat's meat was gone. Now they had only nuts and dates. Yosef found he wanted little else. His appetite was fading, just as his camel was grown thin and tired. He felt scoured down by the wind and sand, as if the very flesh were fading from his bones. Often he wondered if they would ever make it out of the tall walls of sand.

"We will be through the dunes by tomorrow."

He had grown so accustomed to the silence that Yosef was startled when Khanchla spoke. The stars shone so brightly they cast a shadow on his friend's face and found a reflection in the dark eyes watching Yosef. "How do you know?" Yosef's voice rasped.

Khanchla nodded toward the east. "The sand has changed," he said. "Can you not see it?"

They spoke in Tamashek. Yosef found the smooth clicks and whirrs of the dialect soothing and oddly simple to understand, particularly here in the dune sea. He wondered, in the strange recesses of his mind that opened here, amidst the nothingness, if languages belonged to different geographical areas just as animals and plants did. Perhaps he would forget Tamashek when he was no longer amongst the sands that were its home. He picked up a handful of grains and let the sand filter back to earth, admiring the smooth pattern it made. "It feels the same to me," he said.

"No." Khanchla picked up another handful. "It is heavier here. And there is a little more heat in it. Slightly bigger pieces. Tomorrow we will find water."

"You have ridden through here before," said Yosef.

Bagay and Khanchla looked at him, odd smiles on their faces. "No," said Bagay. "We haven't."

Yosef stared at the two brothers. "You mean we rode into this without knowing if we would make it to the other side?"

"Others have crossed it before us. And I made the journey once."

"When?"

Khanchla grinned, a sudden flash of white teeth that lifted Yosef's spirits more than even the promise of water. "As a baby, riding in a basket on the side of a camel."

Yosef shook his head. "We could have died."

The smile faded from Khanchla's face. "People die every day," he said, softly. "But how many of them die amongst the great dunes? If a man must die, then let it be here."

Yosef felt the sweetness of the date in his mouth. Above him, the cold stars glittered so brightly it was as if he could feel them on his face.

"I am glad we did not die," he said quietly.

Khanchla grinned again. "I also," he said.

"Can you teach me what you know?" Yosef looked between his friends.

Bagay shrugged. "You learn with every footstep," he said.

"The next dune sea," said Khanchla, "you will lead us."

BEFORE THE NEXT DUNE SEA, though, they reached the trading centre of Agadès and faced the great wasteland of rock and plain through which Hausa merchants drove a long, swaying salt caravan, over a hundred camels strong, to the oasis at Bilma.

"We are late in the season and must go now or wait until after the summer. It is too dangerous for us to wait," said Khanchla. They were eating a warm stew of millet and goat's meat. After the long, hard silence of the dunes, Yosef thought nothing had ever tasted so rich. He savoured every bite.

"If we arrived at a coastal port from the west, we would immediately be identified as Dahiya's people, the same 'barbarians' who have beaten back the Arab forces and cost them many lives. We would be taken for slaves, or worse. Amongst the Hausa we will become invisible, part of a tribe none notice. Men see what they expect to. When we arrive at the coast, men will no longer see what we are but what they expect us to be."

"Which is worse?" Yosef asked, grinning.

Khanchla did not smile. "You are a Jew," he said. "And you travel in secret, with no family or goods, accompanied by tribesmen rebelling against both the Greek occupiers and the Arab invaders. Beyond Africa, where none know or care for our troubles, we are merely travelling merchants, just like the Hausa with their salt goods. But to those with an interest in Africa's affairs, we are more easily killed than questioned. We have taken a long route, it is true. But if it makes us invisible, as our mother intended, it is a route worth taking."

Bagay looked curiously at Yosef. "What is it you carry that is so valuable you must be invisible?"

Yosef coloured and looked down at the plate from which they ate with their hands. "I cannot explain it," he said quietly.

Khanchla gave his brother a quelling stare. "And you were told not to ask," he said. He looked at Yosef. "It is none of our concern what business you have," he said gently. "We follow our mother's orders – and Dahiya told us to take you as far as Damascus, further if we must." He smiled ruefully. "And that is still a long way, brothers. A very, very long way."

The salt caravan travelled at a different pace than they were used to. At first it seemed slow and meandering, the deep-voiced Hausa allowing their camels to stop often to graze. The frequent pauses chafed at Yosef.

"We graze whilst we can," said one of the men, his eyes roaming the horizon restlessly. "When there is no more grass, we must move quickly." He was right. One day the grass dwindled into nothing, and the pace picked up.

The Hausa drove their camels at speed for nearly a full turn of the moon. Yosef and the brothers dismounted and ran with the others alongside the caravan, feet pounding the earth. Within days, Yosef's thin sandals had worn away and dropped off. Then he ran barefoot with the others. It was agony at first. His feet bled and blistered, and he winced at every stone underfoot, often falling far behind the caravan, limping into camp to the jeers of the others, long after dinner had been eaten. But after ten days he learned to place his feet carefully and to ignore the sharp edges that cut the soles. By the end of the Ténéré he ran as fast and silently as the salt carriers, his feet tough and leathery.

The heat grew to become an overwhelming hell. The hotter it became, the faster they moved, running through the cooler hours of night to ensure they did not become stranded in the great wastes, the flat ground allowing them to move at the hard pace.

The running became hypnotic, the great expanse clearing his mind, allowing thoughts to enter it that Yosef had carefully suppressed until now.

What is it you carry that is so valuable? Bagay's words ran through his head, over and over.

Occasionally Yosef touched the scrolls sewn into the hem of the white desert robes he wore, his cloak bundled on the camel. *Always, you will carry these on your body.* He heard Shukra's voice in his mind. *They are more valuable than anything. More valuable than your life. If your life is in danger, they must be destroyed – or carried to one of your own blood, by one you can trust.* But months later, after losing his father and his home, after watching men die as they battled for their homeland, and now, traversing the great sands, Yosef dared to ask himself the question his younger self had never thought to, bound as he was by ties of blood and duty.

What, he thought, was the true point in this journey?

The letters were written in tongues he did not understand to people he had no idea how to find. In the madness and grief of losing his father, he had known nothing but the orders of Laurentius and Shukra, the smuggling of goods to the Jews of Septem. Those goods, though rich indeed, were nothing out of the ordinary – oil, wine, grain, cloth. Their sale in Septem, and the taxes paid to Ilyan to ensure his protection and silence, had bought him the means to travel the vast distance to Serica – and to purchase what must be bought there.

His family's trade was cloth. Material had surrounded Yosef his whole life: linen and cotton, dyed wools, and embroidered silk from afar. Once, the lands between Garnata and Illiberis, upon which flax grew in such abundance, had been owned by his father's family, and many of the people of Garnata were employed by the house of Radhan. But now, and for many years, such manufacturing had been forbidden to Spania's Jews. Garnata had become dependent on the Illiberis latifundium, the Count of Illiberis now owning those same lands and masking the skills and expertise of the Garnata merchants under his own title. It was for the secrets of cloth that Yosef had been told this journey was necessary, to forge new relationships, partnerships of mutual benefit that would stand his house in good stead for years to come.

Here, amidst the Hausa merchants of the Ténéré, he was surrounded by a veritable wealth of goods from the salt pillars they carried as their main trade to other, lesser but not unimportant, goods: ivory and gold, frankincense, and ink and parchment, both of which, to his surprise, had been much in demand here in the midst of the sands. Yosef had done his duty and negotiated terms of trade, drawing up yet another letter of agreement signed by both parties. The letter defined the terms on which goods would pass through the hands of the Hausa and what portion they would take as their share. It gave Yosef a sense of satisfaction to know that the terms he negotiated would be taken as law by those involved in the passage of goods for some years to come, all being well.

But even this did not help with the feeling that his journey had no true purpose. The negotiation of trade terms seemed to him something that could have been done by a third party. It was the reason behind the scrolls that held the purpose to his leaving his homeland: the discovery of the means and method of making silk. Thus far, Yosef had no idea, still, what that secret was. It had begun to feel, of late, that he was simply moving through time and space for the sake of moving – that both he and his journey had no real purpose at all.

The land of Serica, where he was meant to discover those answers, felt distant, mythical even. He remembered his father speaking of Serica and the family he must find there. But long before he would reach Serica, he must pass through the lands of the Arabs. He must make allies of them, these same Arabs against whom his friends wielded steel, who even now threatened the lands and lives of those he had come to love. The same Arabs who threatened his own shores, even if Spania did not realise it.

Yosef ran, feeling lost and confused, asking himself the question he had dodged since leaving Septem: when he reached the palace of the caliph, what, exactly, would he do?

It had been his destination for so long – the first port of call, so to speak, on the way to the land his father called Serica. He had but the vaguest notion of Serica and its whereabouts. He knew it was the place from which silk came. He was aware that in recent years, as the Christian persecution of Jews had increased across the lands of the Greeks and Romans, trade in the products of Serica had become difficult. On the surface of it, this journey was a mission to create a new trade route.

But here he was. Alone in the Ténéré amidst a caravan of camels carrying salt, on his way to yet another oasis, thinking only of how to best place his feet amongst the stones. Serica was as far away as it had ever been and Yosef, so far as he could tell, had yet done nothing at all to advance his cause. He had done nothing but follow the lead of other men and be guided where he was told to go. He understood nothing of how he was to achieve this goal others seemed to believe he could. He thought of the trust placed in him by his father, by Laurentius, by Shukra; he thought of the help of Ilyan and the great Dahiya, whom he respected more than anyone he had ever met; he thought of Theo, the raw, livid scars on his friend's face, the way he had nearly died so that Yosef himself might finish this journey.

And he felt nothing but terrified and inadequate. As he ran through the Ténéré wastes, Yosef realised, with a terrible clarity, that he had no idea what exactly he was meant to do.

Even worse, whatever the task was, Yosef felt certain he was the last person qualified to complete it.

At night beneath the vast, glittering sky, the hot desert wind restless on his skin, his mind touched on the memory of Sarah, the girl he had last seen bleeding and crying after being raped at the hands of one of Oppa's men. She hovered at the edge of his dreams, a soft presence he both longed to touch and turned from in shame. In his dreams it seemed she was cocooned from him, swathed in a protective cloak that seemed to hide something of great importance that he, Yosef, was not part of. He felt a sense of both wonder and sadness. Often when he woke it was to find tears on his cheeks and a bittersweet ache in his heart. He knew it unlikely he would ever see Sarah again. Even if she was by some miracle still unmarried when he returned, she would never wish to lay eyes again on the man who had witnessed the horrors done her and been powerless to save her. Still, the dreams became his secret solace, the place he disappeared to and emerged from renewed. In the absence of Sarah's presence, the fantasy of it – for Yosef knew his dreams could be no more than that, no matter what he knew in them – was a secret comfort from which he derived more solace than anything else.

Yosef ben Arun Radhan ran beside his camels toward the lands of his ancestors, toward Bethlehem, his dreams his only comfort on a journey he no longer believed in. The only thing Yosef knew for certain was that he was unworthy, unknowing, and, above all, doomed to fail all those who had invested their hopes in him, just as he had once failed the girl he loved.

4

OPPA

JULY, AD 690

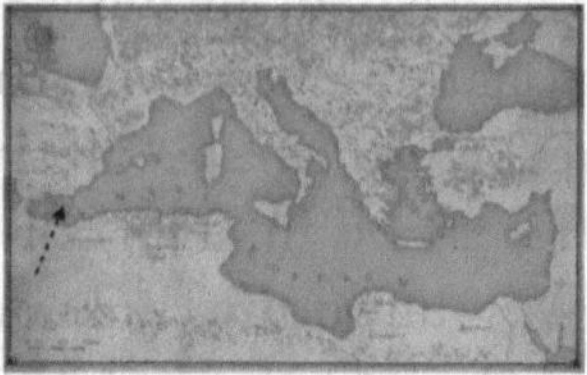

Mare Ibericum
Mediterranean Sea near Spania

"My father intercepted your letter to me." Oppa fingered the thick coils of his whip as he stared coldly at Giscila. Behind him the sea was slick and glassy, the rugged coastline of Spania hovering above the sea haze like a mirage. "Fortunately for you, his discovery of your news had a positive outcome."

"Then you will follow the fleet, as I suggested?" Giscila spat over the side of the dromon. His scarred face was narrow and pinched with the long years of exile, his once-hard body stooped. Oppa looked at him disdainfully. His own form was lean and supple, his robes, as always, impeccably pressed, the dark, pointed features smoothly shaven. The stolid figure of Nicalo, son of Vitulo and Oppa's ever-present shadow, stood silently behind him, far enough that he was out of earshot, close enough if he were needed. Oppa did not trust Nicalo, but he kept him close. Nicalo knew too much to be left alone in Spania.

"We will follow the fleet. Not because you suggested it, but because my father, the king, has ordered me to do so." His emphasis on the word "king" was unmistakable.

Giscila's face darkened. He opened his mouth as if he would speak. Oppa's fingers caressed the coils of the whip again. Giscila closed his mouth sullenly.

"Yes," said Oppa softly. "The coin that funds our ventures may have come from my father's coffers, but he has entrusted it to me, in the knowledge that when I return, it will be with a fortune far greater than his original investment. Do not confuse to whom you answer, Uncle. My father might be king in Spania. But upon these waters, it is I who give the orders."

He nodded over Giscila's shoulder to where the rocky point of Septem jutted into the sea. "I cannot return to Ilyan's port. The man is no friend to our family. We will head for Carthage. You wrote in your letter that it was there you saw Theudemir of Aurariola and had news of the Jew he helps."

"The fleet has long since left Carthage. It is far east of here now, if you wish to pursue it."

"*If* I wish?" Oppa frowned. "Have I not told you that is what I plan?"

Giscila inclined his head. "You have. But perhaps you are not aware of what – or who – currently enjoys Ilyan's hospitality in Septem."

Oppa's eyes narrowed. "Go on."

"A shipment of Illiberis horse landed there several weeks past. Disguised amongst the tribesmen accompanying them was Lælia." When Oppa did not react, Giscila went on: "The Count of Illiberis's granddaughter. The one betrothed to Theudemir of Aurariola –"

"I know who she is."

The savagery in Oppa's voice silenced the older man. Water lapped flatly at the dromon. The sun beat down, still fierce with the last of summer's heat. Insects hung over the still surface in a dull cloud, men slapping them away and scratching irritably at the small red bites they made.

Oppa ignored them. He was thinking. Why would Paulus send

his granddaughter to Ilyan? Oppa's tidy mind dismissed the question almost immediately. That was a mystery he must unravel. The greater mystery, and of far greater interest to Oppa, was the fact that his father had not known of it.

Turning away from Giscila, Oppa stared out across the metallic surface to the distant smudge of Septem on the horizon. Unseen by his uncle, he gripped the edge of the dromon so hard his knuckles turned white. The memory of Lælia's voice in the Toletum court taunted him: *You will find, I believe, that it is customary to not only wait the full twelvemonth before declaring a man dead but to also have witnesses who will verify his death ... And aside from you, Fráuja Oppa, are there any here who can claim to be witness to the death of Theudemir of Aurariola?*

He willed the memory from his mind as he had done every day since he had stood in court before all the Toletum nobility and suffered the open humiliation of being ruled against by his father's own archbishop.

An archbishop who now rots in hell, he thought savagely, but the thought gave him no satisfaction. Nothing, Oppa knew, would truly satisfy him until he had Lælia of Illiberis on her knees before him, and the bastard from Aurariola watching as he took her.

He hardened at the mental image. His mind began to clear.

He returned to his original thought, uncaring of his uncle waiting behind him for a response. *If my father had known of this, I would also know.* This much Oppa was certain of. He had travelled in the company of his father's men until here. He had stocked his dromons in eastern ports where messengers arrived regularly from court. If Lælia had arrived in Septem weeks ago, his father should have known – and he didn't.

Not for the first time in recent weeks, Oppa pondered what else his father might not know. *The Arabs are godless savages,* Egica had bluntly stated, *as are the barbarians of Africa. They will never launch an attack on Mater Spania – they know they could never prevail.* Oppa had recollected those words almost as frequently as he had relived his humiliation at court. Accustomed to automatically granting Egica ultimate superiority in all matters, it had never before occurred to Oppa that he himself might have knowledge his father did not. In the matter of the Arabic threat, however, Oppa had realised he had the greater understanding. Now it seemed that, once more, he was in possession of knowledge his father was not. The question was: how to use it?

"Does Theudemir of Aurariola know his little bride is come to Africa?"

He asked the question without turning around. Oppa did not wish Giscila to see the savagery he knew was still raw on his face.

"It is impossible," said Giscila flatly. "I learned of it myself only yesterday, and I took the liberty of killing the priest who brought the news. He came directly to me, believing I would pay the highest price for his information, something I have made certain men in every port understand. I am certain no other knows what he did." He smiled unpleasantly. "Had he lied, he would have told me. By the time I was finished, his tongue was the only part of his body that still worked."

Oppa nodded absently, his mind still working. "It may be," he said slowly, "that there is more to this alliance between Illiberis and the Jews of Garnata than we understand. If Ilyan hosts Lælia, it is not merely horseflesh he is interested in. Ilyan harbours Jewish merchants, most of them Spanish exiles."

Should an Arabic army succeed in crossing Africa, Oppa thought, it was also Ilyan who stood to lose the most. He did not, however, voice this thought. An idea was dawning on the edges of his consciousness. An idea, Oppa realised, that had been growing for some time, certainly since the meeting with his father, and possibly even before that.

What if… instead of forcing her submission, I won it? Oppa thought, once again allowing himself to imagine Lælia on her knees before him. The thought was as novel and enticing as an intoxicating wine. *What if instead of killing Theudemir of Aurariola and the Jew Yosef, I allied with them?* He shivered, the idea so startling it gave him a visceral thrill. He thought of the Arabic horde he had seen last year. *They are coming,* he thought. *Of that I am certain.* What if there was a bigger game at play? One his father had not yet begun to grasp but that he, Oppa, was perfectly positioned to play?

Getting his emotions under control, he turned back to Giscila. "Are you aware," he said, careful to maintain a neutral tone, "that my father intends to name his son, Wittiza, as his co-ruler?" Giscila looked confused by the change in subject. "It is true." Oppa nodded. "Though Wittiza is barely ten years old, already my father tells his court that he will associate his rule with his son."

"Such dynasties do not work, as your father should well know." Giscila frowned. "Sunifred and the southern lords will not stand for it."

"No." Oppa's tone was careless. "I daresay they will not. Sunifred's rebellion gathers momentum. War, it seems, is inevitable, as my father well knows and plans for."

"Then why speak of this now?"

Oppa looked at him meditatively. "What roles do you think my father plans for you and me in this new Spania he envisages?" Giscila stared at him but didn't answer. "Ah." Oppa smiled silkily. "You begin to see my point, Uncle. After we uncover the reason for the alliance between Illiberis, the Jews of Garnata, and Ilyan of Septem – then reveal it to my father in Spania – what do you think happens to us?" He took a gold coin from his robes and held it up so it gleamed in the sun. "Gold, perhaps? My father is generous with his coin when he is pleased, it is true." He flipped the coin to Giscila, who caught it neatly, though his eyes had not left Oppa's face. "Lands?" He shrugged. "Perhaps – though in Spania, I wear the robes of a priest, a role my father is eager I should continue to play, for he does not like the power the Church wields over his reign, so he places me amongst his enemies that I may serve his interests in the Church he intends to build. Bishops occupy abbeys. They rule monasteries. They do not hold titles and lands, even if they do hold power and coin." He nodded at Giscila. "As for exiles," he said softly, "even under a sympathetic king, have you ever known a murderer and exile to return to Spania and receive lands and a title?"

Giscila, seeming to emerge from a stunned stupor, spat into the sea once more. His eyes had not left Oppa's face whilst his nephew spoke. Now they had turned an ugly shade of black, hard and angry as the metallic surface of the sea. "I believe I begin to understand you, nephew. And perhaps I might offer some insight of my own in return."

Oppa nodded. "Speak."

"Theudemir of Aurariola knows you come for him. He knows, too, of the whereabouts of the Jew, Yosef ben Radhan – but whatever alliance they once shared, it is now gone. Theudemir of Aurariola fights now for himself alone. He has offered to expose the Jew to me." He spat to one side. "In exchange for leading you to him."

It was Oppa's turn to stare at his uncle. "Did you intend to tell me this," he said finally, "or do Aurariola's bidding?"

"Perhaps the latter." Giscila smiled unpleasantly. "But that was before I heard you speak like a smart man, Oppa, bastard son of my kingly relative. Now you begin to see the reality of our position."

Oppa raised his eyebrows. "You impress me, Uncle."

"Then perhaps you will hear my suggestion." Oppa inclined his head. "The Illiberis heiress is too valuable a piece to roam unmarked."

"Agreed."

"One of us, then, should make it their mission to capture her. When it comes to negotiations with Theudemir of Aurariola, she could be useful."

"Perhaps," said Oppa slowly. "Or perhaps, in this instance, we may capture more flies with honey." He was careful to keep his expression bland. "I think it would be preferable to monitor her movements and contrive a meeting with her."

Giscila raised his eyebrows incredulously. "And do what? Smile and introduce myself as her parents' killer, enslaver of her betrothed, and uncle of the man who recently tried to force her into marriage?"

"Yes." Oppa gave him a half smile. "That is, a man who wishes to make amends. A man who seeks forgiveness, a pathway to redemption."

"Why would she wish to offer me one?"

"She does not need to offer it. Only to know your desire for it exists." Oppa looked out over the sea. "Tell her that if the time should come when Illiberis needs hands to defend it – from my father's forces, for example – you are a resource upon which she might call for aid. You might also mention you have met with her betrothed, made of him an ally of sorts."

Giscila stared at him. "Are you sea addled, nephew? Do you think after I make such an offer that we will drink wine together and embrace?"

"I think she will dream of thrusting a knife through your belly." Oppa smiled coldly. "But she loves Illiberis and that whoreson from Aurariola more than she does even revenge, I think. If she considers you of possible benefit in safeguarding either, you open an infinitely easier road to Illiberis than if we take her by force."

"Whilst I am paving this road," Giscila said, "am I to assume you will follow the fleet?"

"Given that is what my father has ordered me to do – and what you have agreed with Aurariola – I believe that the wisest course."

Giscila looked at him narrowly. "And what is to prevent you from making a deal of your own with him?"

"Nothing." Oppa met his uncle's eyes evenly. "But I hold my father's gold, and I have no intention of handing it to you. Nor do I intend to give my father any reason to distrust me."

"What guarantee do you then give me?"

"Only this." Oppa stepped forward and spoke in a low tone only his uncle could hear. "When the Arab forces come for Spania – and we both know they will, Uncle – I will need those at my side I can trust. And if we cannot trust family" – his smile was as cold and venal as Giscila's had been unpleasant – "who can we trust?"

After a brief pause, Giscila took Oppa's proffered arm, gripping it at the elbow. "Where shall I await your return?"

Oppa nodded. "I will send word to Carthage." He nodded to Nicalo's silent figure. "Come, Nicalo." He turned and stepped across the narrow gap of sea that separated his dromon from his uncle's. Oppa's mind was whirling.

If Theo had indeed turned on his friends – which Oppa doubted very much – then his allegiance could be valuable indeed. If he had not, then an opportunity existed for him, Oppa, to become part of whatever plans had been made to forge an alliance between Illiberis and Garnata. Those plans, Oppa knew, pertained to Spania's future. A future Theudemir understood by now in the same way Oppa did. A future that encompassed the threats Oppa's father did not see – and planned for them.

A vision arose in Oppa's mind, a gleaming, shining image that would once have been unthinkable.

He, riding at Theudemir's side, ahead of a force great enough to defend their homeland from the Arabic army. Theudemir, kneeling before him, laying his sword at Oppa's feet. *"I give you my allegiance, and my sword…"*

Lælia, her face filled with the glowing admiration Oppa had once seen as she gazed at Theudemir, but now, gazing instead up at him: *"I was wrong about you all this time… it is you I love, Oppa."*

And Oppa, the bastard son of a ruthless king, born in a brothel and raised in the shadows, felt the one thing he had carefully schooled himself never to feel, the one thing that he had learned from the cradle gave a man weakness and his enemies a weapon. Oppa felt hope.

5

THEO

SEPTEMBER, AD 690

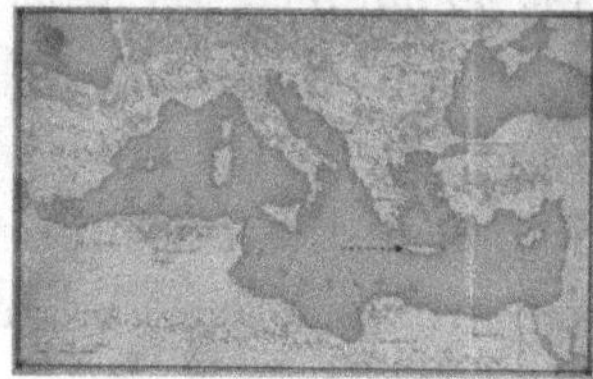

Gortyn
Crete

Theo himself frequently forgot about the brutal facial scars left by Oppa's whip, but every new port gave him occasion to recall them. He stepped out of the dromon on shaking legs, trying to ignore the gasps of horror and covert glances of the dockworkers.

Gortyn was a bustling port, a small but vital resupply point between the shores of Africa and the metropolis of Constantinople. The passage here had been lean on supplies and hard on the body. Apsimar's fleet, it seemed, had been urgently recalled by Emperor Justinian II. Theo was learning that when his *droungarios* desired a particular outcome, he spared no man to achieve it. When the wind had not blown, as happened often during late summer days on the flat water, every man took shifts on the oar. Regardless of rank, they rowed. Hard.

"Well!" Silas clapped him on the shoulder, looking about with satisfaction. "Even the mighty Apsimar must pause whilst the dromons are resupplied – and for once, it is not us who must carry the barrels." The whites of his eyes gleamed against the pitch-black, scarred face as he pulled Theo away in the act of reaching to take one of the supply crates from a passing dockworker.

"Then what must we do?" Theo watched the crates pass, feeling oddly at a loss.

"We must get drunk." It was Leofric, his other companion, who answered. "And find whores. It seems we will finally get the coin we are owed." The Slav grinned widely and gestured to where the other *skutatoi* of their rank queued before a harried-looking man with parchment and pen. Beside him was a somewhat more brutal-looking man of tremendous bulk and dull face. He had a bare torso and stood in front of an iron chest, arms folded. As each man stepped forward, the scribe checked the stigma on his hand, then glanced at the man's *kentarchos* for confirmation before reaching around the broad figure of the guard, into the chest, and withdrawing gleaming coin, which he counted into the man's hand.

"The best part of being raised to *skutatoi* in the emperor's service," grinned Silas, putting a hand on Theo's other shoulder, "is that we risk our necks now more often than our backs. And are paid for it before the others, also. Come, *wenkai*." They collected their coin and walked away from the port into the rapidly falling dusk. The night was mild, and figs grew ripe on low-hanging branches as they passed through thick stone walls into the small city on the hill.

The night smelled dusty and exciting, and Theo looked around in interest, ignoring the shocked glances and whispered asides of the locals. They made an odd party, he knew.

Silas stood a good head and shoulders above the tallest of men, and his permanent smile had the unsettling impact of appearing much like most men's killing look, made all the more chilling by his bald scalp and tribal scars. Leofric was thickset and hard, hairy as one of the bears he described from the dark forests of his home, and, at six feet, just as powerful. He moved with a silent menace that carried at all times the vague threat of violence, and the scars crossing his body made it clear he had both endured and inflicted his fair share.

Theo suspected that he, too, presented a fearful sight, given the way other men shrank from him. The months training at sea had hardened his body into that of a man, and he stood taller than Leofric now. He did not often look upon his own face, but he could see the ridges of skin on his arms where Oppa's lash had caught him, and he knew, by feel, those on his face to be the same. They felt as if the skin had been melted and pushed into a new form, then frozen – hard, unnatural ripples both smooth and brutal to the touch.

Long hair and beards were forbidden for soldiers of their rank, so he lacked even their fragile protection. When he had asked Silas quietly if the scarring was very obvious, the big black man had raised his eyebrows and grinned crazily, tilting his head from side to side. The reaction hadn't been reassuring.

Nevertheless, Theo strode through the city, feeling the comforting weight of iron at his side and caring little for the stares they attracted. He was a *skutatos* in the emperor's service – and, more importantly, he carried Lælia within. He touched the amulet at his neck, and Leofric caught the gesture.

"This may be one time when is best you forget your child bride," he said, grinning. "A man should not think of wife when with whores. It will spoil what we are about to enjoy."

"What you are about to enjoy, perhaps," corrected Theo mildly. "I am merely here for the wine."

"*Wenkai.*" Silas paused outside the low entrance to a tavern and faced him, taking his shoulders in two large hands and gripping him tightly. "Believe me when I say there are some things all men need when they fight in the emperor's service. Wine is one. Women are another. No man can wield a sword if he does not take it from the baldric once in a while, no?"

Chuckling, Leofric clapped him on the back and pushed open the door. The tavern was clean and well swept, with low wooden stools set by whitewashed walls. As they entered, a young girl spotted them and came immediately to their side, smiling in greeting. Despite glancing briefly at Silas and Leofric, her eyes, which Theo saw sparkled the same brilliant blue as the sea they had just crossed, remained locked admiringly on his own form.

She was scarcely older than Lælia would be now, he thought;

then, noting the rich swell of breast and the barest hint of a nipple straining the thin cloth of her gown, he coloured and turned away. His mind, unwilling to relinquish the mental pathway, continued on to envisage Lælia dressed thus. Theo was suddenly hit with such a bolt of longing it literally took his breath away.

"Ah," murmured Silas at his side. "And already you are finding yourself convinced, I think."

"My name is Elpis," said the girl, in Greek. She smiled shyly. Placing three cups on the table, she bent across him to pour wine from a terracotta jug. Glancing at Theo, she looked likely to speak when a tiny scrap of a girl scurried beneath her legs and peeped out at them through a long fringe of white-blonde hair. "Pelagia!" Elpis whirled, red faced, and knelt to speak to the child. "What are you doing in here?"

"There's a man," said the small girl, eyes examining the men at the table with frank scrutiny. "At the docks."

"What are you talking about?" Frowning, Elpis turned to the men. "Please excuse my sister," she murmured, blushing prettily. "She is just a child."

But Theo had leaned forward, elbows on knees, and was returning the girl's stare with a smile. "Would you care to share some of my bread, Lady Pelagia?" he asked gravely. The little girl looked up at him with wary eyes. "I have been at sea for a long time," said Theo, still smiling. "I am afraid it means that when I come ashore, my legs are a little unsteady and my appetite is gone."

"Lots of men from the boats get sick when they come ashore." The girl reached up and, quite unafraid, touched the stiff scar tissue on his cheek. "Your face looks funny," she said.

"Pelagia!" Frowning, Elpis tried to bustle her sister away.

"Don't worry," said Theo, putting out his hand to the young girl. She reminded him so much of Egilona, the young sister he had left behind, that he felt his heart twist. "Yes," he said, smiling at her. "I imagine it does."

Elpis pulled Pelagia close to her. "My sister is just a child," she said protectively, her face clouding over. Theo recoiled as if he had been struck.

"Of course," he said, frowning. "I have a sister the same age. Her name is Egilona."

"Oh." Elpis looked relieved. "I'm sorry. It's just that some men —"

"We are not such men." Silas spoke gently, covering Theo's shock and Leofric's grunt of disgust. Pelagia tugged at her sister's gown, which, Theo noticed, was grubby and torn at the side. He felt his heart twist with pity; what must her life be like, in a tavern by a port, with men like him searching for a moment's pleasure? Filled with an uncomfortable sensation of self-disgust, his colour deepened, and he turned away to his wine cup.

"The man at the docks," said Pelagia, more urgently now, glancing between Theo and her sister. "He gave me coin —"

"Pelagia!" Giving her sister a fierce look of warning, Elpis nodded tightly at their group before hurrying the little girl away. Theo saw her bend down to talk to her urgently by the wall.

"Well," said Leofric, looking about the room. "We might have found your entertainment for the night, *magare*, but I am seeking something a little more rounded." He made a gesture with his hands at chest height. Silas chuckled, shaking his head.

"What about that one?" He nodded across the room, where a dusky girl with lush rolls of flesh laughed at a comment from one of the customers. Her laughter had a rich, suggestive tone, and Leofric's eyes lit up.

"Now that," he said, draining his cup, "is almost worth a year on an oar. Make sure you do not sail without me." Jingling the coin in his tunic and whistling through his teeth, he rose and sauntered over to the girl. As they watched, he put an arm about her shoulders, whispering something in her ear that made the girl laugh aloud and look at him suggestively through lowered lashes.

"Well," said Silas in his low, rich voice, white teeth flashing at Theo. "We had best make our choices before the rest of the fleet discover this place and take all the beautiful girls."

Theo smiled. "You do what you must," he said, holding his hand up to order more wine. "I will wait for you here."

"Are you afraid, *wenkai*?" Silas asked quietly. He leaned forward. "Perhaps it is better — at first — to take a woman, not a girl," he said.

"They are less trouble – and more fun." He grinned, but his voice was kind.

Theo flushed. "I am not afraid." He glanced at Elpis, who had finished talking to her sister and was looking in their direction again. "She… I feel sorry for her." He looked back at Silas, who was frowning as his eyes moved between Theo and Elpis.

"She is a whore, *wenkai*."

"I know." Theo watched a group of men come in, already clearly the worse for wine and shouting for more, making lewd comments at the girls within. The tavern was filling up; the girls were disappearing. "But when I look at her," he said quietly, "all I see is Lælia. All I can imagine is someone like me, paying her for –" He broke off, shaking his head. "I can't, Silas," he said, with a finality in his tone that made the other man sit back and regard him with dark eyes.

"This Lælia of yours," Silas said thoughtfully. "What is it that makes you so certain she will not have found another? There is a good chance she must think you dead, after all."

Theo frowned. "I have sent word that I am not."

Silas shrugged. "Word that may or may not reach Spania – and may or may not be believed if it does."

"It doesn't matter." Theo shook his head. "She will know I am not dead. Just as I know she will not find another."

"*Wenkai*." Silas's voice was kind, but he looked at Theo with something akin to pity. "Even if you are right and your Lælia waits faithfully for your return, how will she ever know that you took your pleasure with a woman you will never see again, in a tavern far away? Would you deny yourself every pleasure simply to hold to the rules of your priests in brown robes?"

"It is not for their rules." Theo struggled for the words. "I just know how I would feel if I thought that she… that someone else…" He closed his eyes briefly, an image crossing them of Oppa, holding a knife to Lælia's throat. His hand tightened about the wine cup so hard his knuckles turned white. "If I begin to betray what I left behind," he said quietly, "where does it end, Silas? Which step is it that takes me over a cliff from which I cannot return?"

Silas turned his wine cup on the table. "What I know," he said slowly, "is that if the path you walk is too narrow, the risk of falling from it is far greater. Perhaps you might wish to choose places where you can widen the way you walk and thus find yourself on more stable ground." One great hand briefly gripped Theo's shoulder. "But I warn you – no man can sit in a room like this all night turning away the girls without causing insult." He tilted his head to one side and looked about the tavern. "And, I am not sorry to say, I do not intend to keep you company." As a wide-hipped beauty with skin almost as dark as his own made her way across the room, Silas drained his cup and grinned at Theo. "Enjoy the memories of your girl bride," he said, standing. "I hope she appreciates it – for I certainly don't understand it." Standing, his head nearly reached the low beams of the ceiling, and the dark girl's eyes widened and her face split in pleasure as he reached her.

Theo watched them go, annoyed and relieved at once. He settled back into the corner with the wine jug, for now at least content to sit and watch the night unfold before him.

"It is a pleasure few men understand – that of observing others undetected."

Theo started, then he leaped to his feet when he recognised the looming figure as Apsimar. The commander wore a dull cloak that hid the gold of his rank and an old felt hat in place of his helmet; he was quite disguised.

"Sit." Apsimar waved him down. "A man does not make the effort to dress so badly only to find himself saluted." Theo grinned despite himself. He imagined it was not easy for a man such as Apsimar to go undetected. "You are observant." It was not a question. "It is a trait I noticed back in Africa, during training. A trait I value." Unsure how to respond to such a compliment, Theo drank his wine and said nothing.

"Your uncle Laurentius fought under me for many years." Apsimar's voice was low enough to go unheard amidst the activity of the night. "With time, I realised he did more in my service than merely fight. But he never allowed his private business to interfere with the business of war, and I never asked what his business was."

Apsimar poured himself more wine and took a long swallow, his eyes roaming the forum meditatively. "I will not continue with the fleet when it sails," he said.

Theo could not hide his shock. "I had hoped to continue under your leadership," he said.

"And I hoped to continue leading. But I serve at the emperor's pleasure, and Justinian II" – Apsimar's mouth curled – "has other things, I believe, in mind. In Sebastopolis, where your dromons are bound, you will find yourself under the leadership of a man called Leontios." His eyes continued examining the crowd, and Theo realised Apsimar was not there for pleasure. Nor was he drinking deeply of his wine. He was there for a reason.

"Why are you telling me this?" Theo asked.

"Several reasons." Apsimar spoke without looking at him. "You are a good soldier. More than good. You could rise far in the Karabisianoi. If you do, I can ensure your rise does not stop there. I return now to Constantinople, but you remain here. Sooner than any of you think, you will be at war again. There will be opportunities for your advancement. I am prepared to pass on a recommendation to Leontios that he consider you for higher command. We do not agree on much, Leontios and I" – a wry smile twisted his mouth – "but in matters of war, he will listen, at least a little."

"Thank you." Theo did not know what else to say.

"You have not heard my other reasons." Apsimar leaned slightly closer across the table. "Sebastopolis, your destination, is a dangerous place. You speak many languages and have a gift for learning more. You also have the advantage of being Spanish, which means you do not have allegiance to any of the forces you will find there. Like Laurentius, it is possible for you to be both diplomat and warrior." His eyes cut directly to Theo, piercing blue in the gloom. "Amidst those roles, you might also find time to pursue the interests that brought you here. As with Laurentius, I do not need to know of them. But I say this to you, Aurariola: think hard on what it is you truly aspire to be, now and on the voyage to Sebastopolis. Perhaps you have allegiances, as Laurentius did, that preclude you from remaining in the emperor's service and giving your life to imperial affairs. Perhaps, too, you have other things that draw you home." His eyes fell to the amulet about Theo's neck, which hung still on the plaited cord made of horsehair he and Lælia had woven together. "Do not think I do not understand the pull of such things," Apsimar said. "I do. Better than you could imagine."

Theo remembered the tall woman, Dahiya, who had led her Riders into battle and with whom Yosef had been riding. Theo knew, as did the entire fleet, that Apsimar was her lover. From what he had seen between them, he suspected they shared a depth of emotion not dissimilar to that between him and Lælia.

"For now," Apsimar went on, "these are choices that do not matter. You will fight. You will see things in Sebastopolis that other men do not, and you will draw your own conclusions. What you choose to do with them is your choice." He looked directly at Theo. "When you leave here, a woman will sail with you whom I believe you know. She is known to most as a whore keeper, though I suspect you might know her by another name."

"Athanais?" Theo stared at him. "She sails with us?"

Apsimar raised his eyebrows and smiled. "You are surprised. Do you think all a commander's information comes from official sources? Men are most unguarded when their loins are bare. Athanais is a valuable resource, one I will continue to rely upon. I tell you this" – he leaned forward – "because Leontios may not always prove willing to listen. Athanais, however, will. What she hears will reach me. There may be times in the coming months where the balance of loyalty and right are very difficult to discern. It would relieve me to know I have a set of eyes on the ground in Sebastopolis upon which I might rely."

"You want me to spy for you," Theo said flatly.

"You might call it that." Apsimar did not shy away from the accusation. "But is it spying when we work for the same force and goal?"

"It is if I do it without Leontios's knowledge."

"It seems very simple to you."

"It is." Theo regarded his commander with folded arms and a grim face.

"Then I will ask you this." Apsimar seemed not at all bothered by Theo's anger. "If you knew the bastard son of your Spanish king – the same man who, I understand, gave you those scars – was ally to Leontios, would you feel so certain of your commander's integrity?"

Theo stared at him. When he finally spoke, his voice sounded hoarse to his own ears. "Oppa?"

"I have it on good authority that, even now, his dromons are drawn up on these same shores. Laden with Illiberis horse and a gift of coin from the Spanish king." Apsimar's mouth twisted wryly. "Such gifts do not pass ports without men speaking of them. Word of gold crosses the seas faster than any dromon could, passed from one mouth to another."

"Oppa is evil." Theo's hand tightened on the wine cup. "If he sails for the fleet, it is to find me, and for no other reason."

"Perhaps." The smile had fled Apsimar's face. "But it is my experience that such men, bearing such gifts, have ambitions beyond doing the bidding of their masters. Leontios is not the type of man to turn away such gifts, nor the alliances that accompany them. Leontios, too, is ambitious. He is also Emperor Justinian II's creature." He leaned across the table. "And Justinian II is a greedy fool."

"Those are dangerous words."

Apsimar eyed Theo grimly. "Not nearly so dangerous as Justinian II's contempt for an enemy he does not understand and Leontios's willingness to indulge it. I fear pressure might be placed on Leontios to take foolish actions. The Spanish king's bastard offers a convenient resource that Leontios might use to aid him in carrying out those actions." He searched Theo's face. "Now, perhaps," he said in a low voice, "you understand why I wish to be kept apprised of developments in Sebastopolis."

"I will not do anything to betray the fleet." Theo's own eyes were hard. "Or to put my men in danger."

"I would not wish you to." Apsimar sat back. "I ask this of you," he said quietly, "because you are precisely the man who would *not* do either of those things." His mouth twisted. "You are that rarest of things, Aurariola," he said. "A man of honour. Sadly, you are about to find yourself fighting beneath a man who has none, for a cause nobody clearly understands."

Theo frowned. "What manner of war is that?"

Apsimar stood, drawing on his cloak so it hid his face.

"The same one we always fight," he said, turning to go. "A war for coin we will never touch, won for men who never bleed."

The following morning, Theo was polishing his armour when his companions returned.

"You are quiet for a man who did not drink his own weight in wine last night," Silas grunted, attempting a smile despite his own obvious suffering.

"What is it that happen to the girl you talk with, hm?" Leofric looked at him beadily through red-rimmed eyes, his accent thick, as it always was after he drank. "You don't reeve this one, Theo? And if not, then why? Do you have cock, man, or willow stick?"

Theo grinned and had opened his mouth to answer when he was interrupted by a cool voice from beside them. "It is fortunate that Theo has such friends to ensure my ladies do not feel neglected." The men swung around in astonishment, for the voice that had addressed them was a feminine one.

"Athanais." Theo took her hand with genuine pleasure. In such squalid surroundings, the Persian woman's beauty seemed even more pronounced, her mellow ivory skin and rich eyes turning every head on the dock.

"This is no place for woman," said Leofric, with admirable dignity. He frowned fiercely from beneath dark, lowered brows. His forbidding countenance failed to move his opponent, who simply watched him with a look of faint amusement tugging the corners of her mouth.

"Indeed, Master Leofric, I am agreeing with your assessment. The ladies who are sharing your beds last night are telling me you and your friend are generous gentlemen who, I am hoping, will forgive my intrusion."

Leofric frowned at her in confusion. "The ladies what shared our... but you, I think, was not one of these ladies – and how are you here? You were in Barca..." His voice trailed off.

Theo bit back his laughter and saw Athanais do the same. "How may I help you, my lady?" he asked politely. "I had thought you gone to Spania until Apsimar told me differently."

"Spania?" Leofric regarded them in confusion. "Apsimar?"

"Stop talking," said Silas wearily, pulling him away.

"But —"

"Stop. Talking." Rolling his eyes at Theo, Silas drew a still protesting Leofric away to a diplomatic distance.

"I am pleased to see your friends remain vigilant as ever." Athanais smiled. "I sent a messenger to Spania in my stead." She touched his face briefly. "Do not fear. Your coin, and your promise, were delivered."

"Lælia?" Theo searched her face eagerly, but Athanais shook her head, not unsympathetically.

"I know only that she got the message."

Theo looked away, trying to master his disappointment. "I am sorry," said Athanais softly. "I know what she means to you."

"You have a tavern here," said Theo, changing the subject. He could hear the harsh note in his voice but could do little to change it.

"Girls. Not a tavern. I was waiting for Apsimar," said Athanais, giving him a small smile. "Now we sail with the fleet, for Anatolia and the port of Sebastopolis." Her smile faded, and she lowered her voice. "Did Apsimar tell you there are those sailing in our company who constitute a danger to you, Theo?"

"I know of whom you speak," said Theo. "Apsimar told me he would come but that he is not here yet."

"Good," said Athanais, appearing to relax. "Until Sebastopolis, then, you will be safe. Perhaps." She looked keenly at Theo. "But you must be vigilant, you are understanding me?"

Theo nodded. "I know." He looked at her curiously. "But why would you come to warn me of this, my lady? And how do you know what Oppa is to me?"

Even from a distance, Silas spun around at that, hand at his dagger, his face murderous. "Oppa? That bastard is here?" He looked about as if he expected the dark figure to emerge on deck. "Where is he?" he growled. "I will kill him."

"And I," said Leofric, his eyes glinting as he stared at Theo.

"Apsimar told me Oppa has made an alliance with the fleet," said Theo quietly. "With Leontios."

Athanais brushed aside their sudden rush of questions and fury with an impatient hand. "Last night," she said, "you gave bread to a young girl."

Theo nodded. "I remember. Pelagia. Her sister works for you."

"Just so." Athanais nodded. "Pelagia was paid coin these last days by that same man. He paid her so well she may have even considered accepting his invitation – had she not realised what he was."

"His invitation?" Theo's eyes narrowed.

"To sail, with the other children." Athanais spat the last word in contempt. "The children he ordered Pelagia to gather up. Children from the streets, who have no home and no family. Children too young, yet, to be accepted into a tavern – or a whorehouse."

The colour drained from Theo's face, and he remembered Oppa, standing behind Lælia, fondling the strands of his whip, an expression of unguarded lust ugly on his face. "He trades in them," he breathed, his fists clenching at his sides.

"Just so," Athanais nodded. "Oppa, it seems, knows well the value of flesh."

"Yes." Theo's mouth tightened. "It is said he was born in a whorehouse." His fist spasmed at his side. Athanais nodded.

"We must be careful," she said simply. Turning, she made to leave.

"My lady." Athanais stopped and looked at him, eyebrows raised in enquiry. "Pelagia – and her sister." Colour flooded his face, but Theo went on. "Elpis. Can you take them with you?"

Athanais's eyes narrowed. "Might I ask why?"

Theo swallowed. "I would not like to see them… taken advantage of. I am happy to pay their passage."

Seeing him reach for his coin, Athanais waved him away. "Why would you do this, Theo?" She looked at him curiously. "Do you desire the girl?"

Theo looked away from her, unsure how to answer. He didn't know what drove him, only that he could not bear to imagine them left here, in a port tavern, at the mercy of men such as Oppa. Athanais must have discerned something of his thoughts, for a resigned expression passed over her face. Her tone was nevertheless slightly grim when she answered. "If they are still here, they may sail with me to Sebastopolis where you yourselves are bound. But I have a warning for you, Theo, and I trust it is one you will take as from a friend: your heart is already given. Take Elpis if you wish, but take her with coin, not with promises of something you are not free to give. There is no harm in taking a woman for comfort. But lying to one is cruel." Her dark eyes resting on his face were gentle. "You cannot save everything that is broken, Theo. Sometimes the harder path is also the kindest."

"It seems everyone, of late, has an opinion on which path I should take." He heard the hard note in his voice, but Athanais seemed unconcerned.

"That is because we all wish you to choose one that you might survive," she said gently, "without losing either yourself or those you love." She touched him on the arm and was gone.

"What," said Leofric, staring after her in astonishment, "in the name of Tyr, was she talking about?"

6

LETTER FROM ATHANAGILD TO SHUKRA

SEPTEMBER, AD 690

Toletum, Spania
Toledo, Spain

Shukra –

Egica has acted swiftly in the wake of Julian's death, holding a council in the province of Tarraconensis, far distant from the scrutiny of the capital, in which it was decreed that the two queens should be cloistered "for their own safety". Sisebut and I were tasked with conducting Egica's own lady wife, Cixilo, and her mother, the old queen Liuvgoto, to an abbey some distance from Toletum. All know, of course, that it is simply another step in Egica's ambition to separate Liuvgoto from those who would ally themselves to her cause, such as her own cousin, Sunifred, Duke of Hispalis. The old queen is both wily and proud. Egica is rightly wary of her. Liuvgoto has survived worse than Egica, and she will not quietly rest behind God's walls. Her daughter, Cixilo, is made of weaker stuff, and she is now even further cowed, since she was separated not only from her allies but from her son, Wittiza, who remains in Egica's care.

My father, along with Duke Theodefred of Corduba, tries still to speak for peace in the king's council. We all know, however, that his is a lost cause. Egica has done all he can to provoke Sunifred and the southern lords to war. He wants to flush his enemies into the open so all may see them tried for treason. I cannot imagine how painful it must be for my brother to stand so close to a cause he must surely know to be flawed. If, as you say, Sunifred prepares to march on Toletum, Alaric will have no choice but to march at his side. It will break our father's already frail heart. I wish I could mend the rift between them, just as I wish there were news of Theo. I know no more of him — nor of Oppa, from whom nothing has been heard from the moment he sailed.

The silence, I believe, is ominous.

I am not, I confess, surprised that Lælia is not returned. If she discovers Giscila's whereabouts, I doubt she will return until one of her arrows has ended his life. I have learned never to underestimate her.

I thank you for bringing news of Alaric. It does not surprise me to learn that he is in dark humour. He loves Rekiberga as few men love their women. That Sunifred now delays their wedding is a cruel twist indeed, and it is undoubtedly contrived to ensure Alaric remains at his side, bringing our father's forces in Emerita to his cause. It is an impossible bind for Alaric. My only consolation is that he trains in the new fleet Laurentius builds there, under your combined guidance.

I must also remind you of the promise you gave not to disclose the source of your information to Laurentius. I could not bear his ill opinion of me.

I pray for you, though I know it is not to my God you look.

—Athanagild

7

LAURENTIUS

SEPTEMBER, AD 690

Hispalis, Spania
Seville, Spain

"Are all of you Goths so slow like this? Or is it just the air in Spania?"

The only parts of Shukra that moved were his arms, parrying blows from two young swordsmen from his stance on the bowsprit. He spoke in his customary unhurried lilt, grinning as he did so. "I am being very glad I am not now on open sea, fighting an enemy, for the flames of war-fire would be stinging my – oh, dear, *aziz-am*. Is the water very cold?" Shukra's white teeth flashed in a smile as he peered over the edge of the dromon to where Alaric and another youth gasped for air, their heavy armour cumbersome as they tried to clamber out of the river.

It was before dawn proper and the light was fine grey, shadowy and deceptive. After Toletum's chill winds, Laurentius found himself grateful for both the mild air of the lingering Hispalis summer and the comfortable familiarity of Shukra's company and military routine.

The youths pulled themselves from the river to the good-natured ribbing of their fellows. Alaric, Laurentius noticed, was not smiling, but rather glaring at Shukra's back, his face dark and sullen. Laurentius sighed. He had trained a hundred and more young men. There was nothing new to him in Alaric's anger. But never before had Laurentius felt responsible for being the cause of it.

He clenched his fists unconsciously by his side. Theo was lost somewhere beyond Spania's shores. Athanagild was silent and distant, as unreachable behind the monastery walls as if he were in a foreign land. And Alaric was wounded and angry, estranged from his own father and longing for a woman he had thought won only to then lose her in a trap deep enough to destroy the strongest man. Laurentius was a soldier, and yet he had never felt more helpless. Guilt was his constant companion, chafing his conscience raw every time he witnessed Alaric's hurt and anger.

"You know," murmured Shukra as he leaped to the dock, landing lightly as a cat, "it is a pity your coin did not stretch to lamellar armour. They will be dead in an instant beneath that absurd iron plate they wear."

"They will likely be dead on a Spanish field long before they face the sea." Laurentius was unable to disguise his bitterness. "We are fortunate they train at all. I am astonished Egica has not ordered us to cease."

"Egica worries only for his crown," said Shukra. "And Toletum cannot be attacked from the sea." Laurentius would have responded, but Alaric's voice, tight with frustration and pent-up rage, interrupted them.

"Now you will face me with a sword, as true men do."

The hubbub on the docks subsided. All eyes swivelled to where Alaric stood, dripping, on the stone landing by the river. Behind him the half-built dromons lay like forgotten skeletons in the water. He was glaring at Shukra.

"Alaric," began Laurentius, frowning, but he never got to the next word. In a sudden swirl of black cloak, Shukra was behind Alaric, his knife at the young man's throat. "How is it that you are thinking 'true men' fight?" Another quick movement and Alaric was on his knees, arms painfully bound behind his back. "Are you thinking men stop to agree upon the rules before battle?" Shukra leaped over Alaric and, with one slash, cut him free again, tossing him the knife he had managed to take without any of them noticing. "You will show me these rules, *aziz-am*. You will be showing me how a Goth from Spania conducts himself in these games you think are war."

Alaric's eyes glittered with the tight anger that had simmered ever since he had been forced to choose Sunifred's rebellion over his father's opposition. Laurentius sighed, crossing his arms and stepping back. Shukra's lessons were no doubt preferable to an actual sword fight with Sunifred. That fact did not lessen their brutality. Alaric drew his longsword and faced Shukra in a fighting stance.

"It is not yet dawn," said Shukra softly. "We have come out of the sea mist to a foreign shore. You are stepping onto it for the first time, and you are not knowing, *aziz-am*, what you will be finding there. Are you drawing your big sword already?"

Alaric thrust at him and Shukra moved easily away, appearing behind him. Alaric whirled to face him, clutching his longsword in both hands. "We could meet an enemy as soon as we step onto land," said Alaric. "Yes, I have my sword."

"A big army of men are making sound," said Shukra. "And not only sound. Even if they are hidden, even if they are masters of concealment, men are smelling like men; an army is smelling like an army. If you are closing your eyes, *aziz-am*, are you smelling an army?"

Laurentius closed his own eyes and inhaled, smiling as he remembered the first time he and Shukra had taken this same lesson, remembering the scents of cinnamon and mint and frankincense that he always associated with Constantinople, recalling the faint cry of donkeys in the distance and the stench of city and people – and then the contrast, many months later, when together they had faced the stench of metal and sweat and fear.

He opened them abruptly at the sound of Alaric's sword clattering on stone.

"Now you are dead already," said Shukra silkily, grinning as he circled Alaric. "Because one man with silence and a knife who rules himself is faster and deadlier than an army with longswords who obey the rules of others. No battle is won because the men fighting it had big swords and played by rules." He twisted and flowed around Alaric until he held the knife at his throat once more. "Battles are won in the mind first," he whispered, drawing the other youths close to hear him. "In Eran, we are teaching this one thing: good thoughts, good words, good deeds. Are you knowing why we are teaching this?" They shook their heads. Shukra released Alaric, sending him spinning clumsily across the ground. Alaric stood up, scowling.

"Because," said Shukra, coming forward to meet Alaric again, throwing the younger man his knife and sword, "everything is coming from your thoughts. Victory, defeat. All of it is happening first in your mind." He moved swiftly past Alaric again as the younger man lunged toward him. "You are seeing first, Alaric is thinking he will pierce my side." Shukra spoke lightly, parrying another thrust. "But he is thinking this so loudly, it is blowing through the air like a storm at sea, so I am feeling his thought before his hand has moved. And now – see – he is thinking to strike my other side, and this time even his eyes are speaking aloud."

Laurentius could not help but smile at Alaric's frustration, the increasingly wild thrusts. No matter how many times he had watched Shukra work, still it was poetry to him. The others watched in wide-eyed amazement as Shukra ducked and weaved, speaking in an unhurried, conversational tone as Alaric thrust and panted with increasing frustration.

"You – don't – stand – still," said Alaric through gritted teeth, as he missed again. Shukra leaped and whirled through the air, an impossibly lithe acrobatic movement that defied logic and expectation, and Alaric was once more helpless on the ground, face down and weaponless.

"And now your words join your thoughts," said Shukra, his voice cutting through the dawn just as light began to grow. "You are thinking I am cheating, and so you are waiting for me to somehow play by your rules. And then you are saying aloud that I am not standing still. And now your body and your mind are believing two things: first, that I am playing a game you do not understand and second, that I am not standing still long enough for you to kill me. And because you are believing these two things, your body and mind are already dead, for they have decided the battle is impossible. And so here you are finding yourself, *aziz-am*. On the ground, helpless."

He looked around the group of observers, dark eyes watchful. Releasing Alaric, he pushed him to his feet and threw him his weapons again.

"He is still wet," pointed out one of the young men watching, ignoring Alaric's dark look, "and clad in heavy armour. He cannot move as fast as you like this."

"Wet! Wet is your thoughts!" Shukra pushed him hard enough that the lad nearly toppled into the river. "First we change your thoughts – then we see if you can fight or not. Wet, not wet. This is not my problem. Now we train."

Laurentius watched as the boys began their drills again, his eye taking in those who had promise and those who would spend their time repairing barrels rather than wielding a sword. For all Alaric's rage, he was a fighter, and a good one. Laurentius knew that Alaric baited Shukra not least because he needed an opponent against whom he could safely throw his full might. Now that he had exercised his rage, Alaric moved between the young men, murmuring a word of encouragement here, correcting a stance there. Subjecting himself to daily humiliation at Shukra's hands did nothing to harm his standing amongst them. If anything, Laurentius noted approvingly, Alaric's anger matched their own, and his willingness to accept repeated lessons inspired their own dedication. Alaric was a different man to his brothers, a blunter instrument in some ways. *But men will follow him*, thought Laurentius. *They know he will never shy from a fight.*

An unexpected vision of Athanagild's face flitted across his mind. He, too, would be immersed in training of his own at this moment in the monastery in Toletum. The stark contrast between the two worlds struck Laurentius as much as the visual difference between the brothers. As he watched Alaric's powerful form fight back against his opponent, a memory crossed his mind of Athanagild's hectic colour, the wide hazel eyes, like a deer startled by a forest pool. He felt again the odd twist in his heart he had felt when they settled on him, the desire to draw the thin form close and protect him against a world that seemed too harsh for one so delicate.

I am not your nephew.

Laurentius frowned into the distance, the sound of swords fading away, thinking again of the strange look on the boy's face. Could he have guessed? Could he be disgusted?

No.

Laurentius shook his head in frustration, wanting to clear any such thought from his mind, unwilling even to think of his own, hidden, inner life at the same time as Athanagild.

Must it always come back to that? he thought tiredly. *Must everything I ever do, think, or see be perceived through this one aspect of myself that I cannot change? Will I never be free to meet others simply as I am and who they are? Or will I ever be wondering if they see the truth — and if they do, if they will condemn me?*

Shukra's voice pierced his reverie, and he focused on the sword-play in front of him, welcoming the mental discipline of training as he always had.

He watched Alaric, nodding in satisfaction to see him adjust his own technique to Shukra's training, accepting the corrections with good grace and the kind of bluff good humour that put the others at ease. When finally Alaric succeeded in disarming his opponent, Shukra bestowed a rare smile. "Still you are pointless as a blunt knife," he said, shrugging, "but at least now you are not dead today. Go and wash the river scum from your clothes. We are done until after breakfast."

Alaric, his anger temporarily forgotten, joined the bantering of the others as they left the docks.

"He is angry," said Laurentius as he stood by Shukra, watching them go. "But I am glad he trains here rather than spending all his day at Sunifred's side, hoping the man will change his mind about the daughter. Better he expends his anger on training than in that bastard's service."

"Anger is good," said Shukra lightly. "Anger is life. Anger is hope." His eyes rested on Laurentius thoughtfully. "I am thinking there are worse things than anger."

Laurentius turned away from the dark gaze, busying himself with a tangle of ropes.

"Hm." Shukra watched him shrewdly. "You cannot run from what you feel, *joon-am*. I have taught you this, no? But here in Spania you seem to forget your lessons, and you have much in your mind always. Not so much time for the heart, here, in this land."

Laurentius laughed humourlessly. "There is never time for the heart, Shukra. Not for me. And especially not in Spania."

"And yet the heart is all there is."

Stepping forward, Shukra gently lifted the coils of rope and deftly folded them. He turned and faced Laurentius, and there was such compassion in his eyes that Laurentius had to look away.

"Thoughts are not only for battle, *joon-am*. They are our life, also. What you feel here" – he put a hand on Laurentius's heart – "is deciding what you are thinking here." He tapped his own head. "When Alaric is swinging his sword without direction, do you think it is only his head deciding to swing it? Of course not. It is his heart, the feelings of anger and frustration in his heart, which are talking to his head and his hand. 'Good thoughts' are not being only in your mind, *joon-am*. They are your heart also."

"I thought your training was done for the day?" Laurentius's tone was sharp.

Shukra's mouth twitched; Laurentius bit his lip, turning away.

"Guilt is as dangerous as anger," said Shukra softly to his back. "It is a river in which a man will drown if he does not find a way to swim across it."

"I have made my choices," said Laurentius harshly. "And I must live with their consequences."

"Must you always find something with which to punish yourself?" said Shukra. "And what will you do, I am wondering, when happiness comes searching for you instead of pain?"

Laurentius began walking away without answering.

"What you are feeling will find what it searches," Shukra called after him. "Just as steel finds war so does guilt find punishment, loneliness exile. You are bringing to you what you run from, my friend."

"And what would you have me do?" Turning, Laurentius faced him, speaking in a low, fierce tone. "What would you have me feel?"

Shukra stepped close to him. He was no longer smiling, his eyes dark and full of compassion.

"I would have you feel joy," he said quietly. "I would have you feel joy in who you are instead of searching for shame around every corner. And I would have you find joy in another."

Laurentius felt the slow beating of his heart, the horrible desert of loneliness an ache in his throat. He was very aware of Shukra's searching gaze. His friend's eyes narrowed. "What is it, that weighs upon you? What is it you will not say? Speak, *aziz-am*."

"You will despise me." The words rasped from his chest.

Shukra snorted. "I am Persian, *aziz-am*."

The ghost of a smile crossed Laurentius's face. "Even your Ahura Mazda, I fear, will not forgive me this."

Shukra merely tilted his head, waiting.

"Athanagild." Laurentius could not look at his old friend. "He… that is, I think… or suspect…" He swallowed, his customary eloquence deserting him completely. Shukra, for once, did not attempt to finish his words. "I believe Athanagild and I are… similar." Laurentius finally looked up, defiance and shame warring within him, to find Shukra watching him with eyes that were curiously opaque.

"And Athanagild," said Shukra quietly. "Have you spoken of this with him?"

"Of course not," Laurentius snapped.

"Why not?"

"Why not?" Laurentius stared at him. "To what end? What possible purpose would be served by asking the boy such a thing? One who has devoted himself to God, no less?"

"Perhaps," said Shukra, watching him carefully, "to reassure him that he is not alone, *aziz-am*."

"I could not."

"Or is it that you will not?" Shukra's eyes narrowed. "You said I would despise you. Why would I despise you for suspecting

Athanagild shares your nature, *aziz-am*? Or is there something else you do not say to me?"

Laurentius's mouth tightened, but he did not answer.

"It is not only that you suspect he shares your nature." Shukra spoke slowly. His eyes seared Laurentius's face like sun burning through mist. "You hope he does."

Laurentius met his eyes then, unable to speak. Shukra sucked in his breath. For a terrible moment, Laurentius thought his friend would turn away from him, and already he felt the shame and sadness of the loss. Then Shukra strode forward, his hands gripping Laurentius's shoulders.

"The danger you would be in," he muttered harshly, and for a moment the Persian lilt was all but gone from his words. "Both of you, should you be discovered." Then, as he looked into Laurentius's eyes, his grave expression softened, his mouth curving in a sad smile. "But you must talk with him, *aziz-am*. If you are right, you cannot allow the boy to carry this burden alone. And if he returns your feelings..." His hands tightened on Laurentius's shoulders. "You will no longer be alone," he said softly.

Laurentius shook his head in despair. "I cannot, Shukra," he said hoarsely. "You know I cannot. Even if he did feel that way, you and I both know it is wrong. And you said it yourself. The danger I would put him in." He met his friend's eyes. "He has already lost his brother because of me," he said. "How can I bring him more pain still?"

"Perhaps," said Shukra quietly, "you should allow Athanagild to make that choice for himself. And as for the danger – well." He shrugged, a flash of his old humour lighting his eyes. "I have never known you to run from a little danger, *aziz-am*."

"Not for myself, perhaps. But I cannot endanger him, Shukra. I will not."

Shukra opened his mouth to argue, then, seeing the hard resolve on Laurentius's face, closed it again.

"Enough." Laurentius's voice was hard as stone. "I will not, Shukra, and that is an end to it." Seeing the resignation on his friend's face, Laurentius nodded, feeling his customary bland mask slip back into place. "We will not speak of this again," he said coolly, waiting long enough to see Shukra's reluctant nod.

Then he turned and walked away.

I can't, he whispered to himself as he walked. Hazel eyes crept across his mind, full of loneliness and uncertainty.

I just can't.

8

ALARIC

SEPTEMBER, AD 690

Hispalis, Spania
Seville, Spain

Alaric had changed his clothes after the morning's training when he came to Sunifred's œca. He found the Duke of Hispalis pacing across the marble floor. His face was already flushed with wine despite the early hour. In response to Alaric's greeting he growled and waved a letter in the air. "Even now, after your father knows full well it is Egica's bastard son who attacked your brother at sea, Suinthila refuses to ally with me!"

Alaric stood quietly beneath his tirade. Beside him, Teudolfo, one of his father's men who had been at Alaric's side since he left Aurariola four years ago, cast his eyes skyward behind Sunifred's back. Alaric stifled a grin. Teudolfo's stolid good humour was one of the few things upon which he could rely in Hispalis's volatile atmosphere.

"For all his faults," murmured Teudolfo, "your father shows uncommon good sense, *magula*."

"Don't call me boy," Alaric murmured back, but there was no

sting in his tone. Teudolfo was his lone ally in Sunifred's volatile court, and the two had become close friends.

"Hm?" Sunifred turned hard blue eyes on them both. "What is that you say?"

"It is nothing, Fráuja," Alaric said, turning a carefully bland expression to the duke. "We wondered what else my father writes." He tried to keep the longing from his tone. Since Alaric had walked from the Toletum court at Sunifred's side late last year, publicly choosing the duke's rebellion over his father's diplomacy, he had exchanged no direct word with him. Suinthila had been ill for some years now and rarely left Aurariola. Last year's news that Theudemir, Alaric's younger brother, had in fact survived the attack at sea and was alive somewhere on foreign soil seemed to have lifted Suinthila's spirits somewhat. At least, that was what Alaric understood from Athanagild's letters. He hoped it was true.

"Suinthila reminds me of the betrothal contract between you and my daughter." Sunifred's eyes on Alaric were shrewd.

"Ah." Alaric tried not to let his excitement show. Sunifred gave a grunt of laughter.

"Now that he knows Theudemir lives, his alliance with Illiberis is safe, thanks to that damned hellcat granddaughter of Paulus's. But don't think I don't remember Suinthila broke with me last year and was set to marry you to the Illiberis wench when he thought Theudemir was dead. Now he comes scurrying back, reminding me of a contract he would have broken in a trice. Man has no stones, no loyalty."

Alaric clenched his fists. Teudolfo's reassuring hand was steady on his back. "Don't rise," murmured the other man. "You know it is just his way."

"Ha!" Sunifred had not missed Alaric's tension. "Like it or not, boy, you chose me when you walked from that council. And if you want my daughter in your bed, you had better mind that loyalty."

Alaric tensed at the crudity, forcing himself not to react. *He means no harm*, he told himself. Sunifred was a man of war, of action. He goaded everyone thus. It did not pay to rise, as Teudolfo said. And besides, for all Sunifred's crudity, the man was strong in a way Alaric understood. Unlike his own father, Sunifred did not waste time on diplomacy. He saw what was needed, then acted. Alaric missed his father. But he knew that if he were to stand in the basilica today faced with the same choice, still he would choose Sunifred, and war. The time for peace, he thought with a surge of strength, was gone. No matter what the outcome of Sunifred's rebellion, Alaric would never again be rendered passive by the secrecy and lies of his father's choosing.

"Suinthila will not so much as cede the men he commands at Emerita Augustus to my cause!" Sunifred's face was dark with anger.

"Emerita Augustus is the seat of the king's military headquarters." Alaric spoke steadily. "Many of the men who train there are taken from my father's lands in the area, it is true. But though he has commanded the training of the military for many years, the men in Emerita are sworn to the king, whoever that may be. Egica sits beneath the votive crown in Toletum. The men of Emerita are sworn to him."

"And what if I defeat Egica, am crowned king? Would they not then answer to me?"

Alaric bowed his head. "They would, Fráuja."

"Then why not declare themselves for me now?" Sunifred moved in front of Alaric, his eyes flashing. "Why don't you command them in your father's stead?"

Alaric stared at him, taken aback. "I could not do that. It would be treason, against everything my father has taught."

"Well, it isn't your father who holds the key to my daughter's bedchamber, now, is it?" said Sunifred softly. "Rekiberga!" he commanded, without taking his eyes from Alaric's. "Come in here, girl! I know you are listening at the door."

The heavy wooden door opened. Alaric caught his breath as Rekiberga entered the œca.

Thick auburn hair, held by a silver band, hung to her waist. She wore a tunic of sheer emerald green over fine cotton, and it moved and glistened in the airy light of the hall like a sea creature on land. Her skin was the palest porcelain, with a faint scatter of freckles across the nose, and she had her father's brilliant blue eyes.

"Fráuja Alaric." She greeted him simply, with open hands and a warm smile. Alaric felt as if his own hands were strangers to his body. He watched them rise to take hers, felt the shock as cool, slender fingers slid into them. Surely, he thought, she would recoil at his touch.

But she did not, and from a great distance Alaric heard himself return her greeting. "My lady Rekiberga. It has been too long since we met." *Almost a year*, he thought, but did not say. Sunifred, he knew, exploited men's emotions, found in them weapons he wielded in coarse humour. Only when Teudolfo nudged him did Alaric remember to release Rekiberga's hands. Was it his imagination, he wondered, or was there a faint trace of colour on her cheeks as she took them back?

She turned to her father, and Alaric lowered his head to hide his discomfort. "*Liefs*," said Sunifred, clearly enjoying Alaric's discomposure, "it appears the Count of Aurariola would like to see us honour our betrothal with his son. What say you to such a plan?"

Rekiberga lowered her head demurely, but not before Alaric saw a flash of something he could not read flare in her eyes. "I am yours to command in all things, Abba," she said softly.

"Hmph." Sunifred eyed his daughter's bent head suspiciously. "Well, since you are here, you may listen to what I tell your would-be husband. It may be that you will need to remind him of it."

It is just his way, Alaric told himself again, aware that his fists were clenched. He pushed away the unwelcome thought that his own father would never dream of treating Alaric's sister thus. *They are different men.*

"I will allow you to marry my daughter." Sunifred's words were so unexpected that Alaric's head snapped up.

"You will?" he said, unsure he had heard correctly.

Sunifred nodded. "I will," he said. "On three conditions. One, that you bring the men of Emerita to my cause. Two, that you convince Paulus to bring Illiberis with them." As Alaric began shaking his head, Sunifred held up his hand. "I haven't finished. My third condition is that you bring Theodefred, Duke of Corduba, to support my rule."

"The Duke of Corduba?" Alaric stared at him in disbelief. "Theodefred is a son of Chindasuinth. He is one of the most powerful men in Spania, every *stade* of his land sworn to the Crown, and he with it. He cannot go against Egica."

"That might be so. But Theodefred is also bound to Illiberis by marriage. His wife, Riccilo, is kin to Paulus's wife, and if what I hear is true, she wields as much power over her husband as any woman ever has. Theodefred's own brother, Favila, already stirs in rebellion, north in Gallæcia. Theodefred will have to choose his allegiance eventually, as will all the lords of the south, your father included. So here is my promise to you, Alaric of Aurariola." Sunifred drew his daughter forward. "Find a way to bring the support of these southern lords to my side, and you will marry my daughter, as agreed. Will that make you happy, *liefs*?" He smiled down at Rekiberga with avuncular affection.

"Yes, Abba," she said, colouring and lowering her eyes.

Alaric was so absorbed in looking at her that his mind turned away from the unspoken ultimatum Sunifred had left hanging in the air.

If Alaric could not bring the southern lords to Sunifred's side, he knew the duke meant to marry his daughter to someone who could.

It was war, after all, Alaric thought, pushing his distaste aside. And in war, men must at times be ruthless.

"Yes, Fráuja," he said grimly. "I understand."

Alaric was storming away from Sunifred's domus, heedless of the people in his path, when he heard his name called.

"Alaric!"

He swung around to find Rekiberga facing him, her face flushed and breath short. She was not clad for the street; a shawl barely covered the thin sea-green gown that showed more of her form than was decorous in public. She reached for him, her hands on his arms both delicate and somehow strong, as if the heat within her were a solid wall of reassurance holding him at peace.

"Forgive me following you," she said, trembling. "I could not bear to let you go without explaining –"

Alaric's hands clenched at his side in the effort not to reach for her. "You should not be here," he said roughly.

"Few will recognise my face. I so rarely leave my father's house." Rekiberga's tone was bitter as she waved dismissively. "I have tried to find opportunity to speak with you, but we are never alone." Her touch on his arm seared like fire. "I have begged my father," she said, "implored him, to let us marry. I would not have you think I support this game he plays."

"I know you do not." Alaric brushed a long strand of auburn hair away from her face, his heart aching. "And it is war, so I do not judge him too harshly. But I do not know how to give what he asks. My father will never join this rebellion."

"And mine will never give it up." Despair clouded her face. "My mother says I should forget you. They do not care what I wish for."

Alaric found he could barely breathe. "What is it that you wish for?" He searched her face. "We were betrothed once, but I do not now know what is in your mind, or your heart. I see you from a distance only, or at meat in your father's hall. I would not wish for you to feel bound to me against your will."

"Against my will?" Rekiberga's voice was low and fierce. She stepped forward, so close he could smell the faint scent of citron from her hair. "From the moment I saw you in my father's hall," she said, "I knew it was you. I knew it then, Alaric, and every day since." Her mouth curved in a smile Alaric thought might make his heart stop. "I know it now," she whispered, "with you standing in front of me."

Alaric stared at her, taking in the long line of her neck, the brilliant blue eyes that always reminded him of the summer seas at home in Aurariola; and without thinking, with barely even an awareness of what he was doing, he lowered his head and took her mouth with his own, groaning as she surrendered beneath him. He kissed her on and on, fingers twined in the scented weight of her hair, pressing her hard against him until there was nothing but her mouth and the feeling of her beneath his hands, the soft sound as she moaned against him.

It was this that brought him back to some realisation of where they were. With an effort he broke the kiss and found they had become an attraction for a group of children who pointed at them from a distance and giggled, hooting when they broke apart. Putting

an arm protectively about her shoulders, he whispered, "Come –
you should not be outside."

Rekiberga's face was flaming and her lips were still swollen from
where he had bruised them with his own. Alaric could barely
restrain himself from taking her there, in the street, and be damned
all who looked at them. Instead, he drew her close and hurried her
through the alleys to a low dwelling with a wooden door. He
knocked twice, and Teudolfo opened it. Seeing who Alaric was with,
he frowned. He was less than a decade older than Alaric, but it was
enough that he felt a certain responsibility for the young man he
had known from birth.

"This is a dangerous game I will have no part of," he said
sternly, looking between them. "My lady" – he addressed Rekiberga,
taking in her dishevelled appearance and the way she clung to
Alaric – "I will get you a cloak. I am taking you home." He glared at
Alaric. "Stupid as you are, *magula*," he said, "I thought you had
more sense than this."

"It was I who sought him." Rekiberga had gained some of her
composure. She drew herself up and faced Teudolfo. "Please allow
me in for a time. I can send word to the villa that I am safe and will
return presently."

Looking between the two, seeing the grim set of Alaric's face
and the concern on Rekiberga's, Teudolfo sighed and opened the
door. "Your father is going to kill us all," he said resignedly, showing
them in.

They sat at a low wooden table and drank rough *posca*.
Rekiberga sat close to Alaric. Her presence beside him was both
calming and intoxicating; he drew her close to him, and when
Teudolfo frowned, he glared in return. Alaric had ceased, he
realised, to care what any man thought.

"We have to speak to your father," he said.

"He won't listen." Rekiberga shook her head.

"Still." Alaric cupped her head, drawing it gently down to his
shoulder. "We must try, Rekiberga."

Alaric's eyes met Teudolfo's across the table. Teudolfo shook his
head. "I do not see it," he said bleakly. He rose, his face stern as he
eyed Rekiberga.

She held up her hand. "Wait," she said, and there was a note of command in her voice that made Teudolfo pause and Alaric look up. There was a shadow in her eyes that made Alaric's heart clench as she drew away and faced him.

"Don't say it," he said. "Whatever you are about to say – do not say it."

"I must." One hand came up and touched his face. "I do not wish you to speak to my father. No," she said firmly as Alaric started to speak. "Listen, Alaric. I know you, just as I know my father. You will not be able to live with yourself if you do his bidding and drag others into this rebellion against your own conscience." A fierce light flashed in her eyes. "And I will not suffer the indignity of being the bait used to lure men and swords to a cause I believe flawed."

Taken aback, Alaric looked instinctively to Teudolfo, who was watching Rekiberga intently. "If you do not believe in your father's rebellion, my lady," said Teudolfo, "then what would you have Alaric do?"

"Leave my father's court." Rekiberga met their eyes in turn. "Go now, to your father, while you still can." She swallowed, and when she continued, her voice shook slightly, but there was no doubting the sincerity in her face. "And if you will take me," she said, "I will go with you. I will marry you, Alaric, whether my father sanctions the match or not."

Her words fell into the stillness of the small room like a turbulent current, stirring the dust about them. Alaric felt the ground shift beneath him, a gulf opening within that he did not know how to fill.

Rekiberga searched his face. Awareness dawned slowly on hers, the fierce light fading from her eyes. "Despite it all," she said dully, "you believe in him still, don't you?"

Teudolfo swung to Alaric, frowning.

"My brother was attacked." Alaric shook his head, the words dust in his mouth. "Oppa and his father have wrought horrors upon my family, and others, that I can hardly think of without needing to strike something. Your father may not be perfect. But he acts, at least. And we must act, Rekiberga, or see Spania fall to men without honour or conscience."

"But how can you be certain," she whispered, "that the men who seek to take their place are any different?"

"*Magula.*" Teudolfo met his eyes. "Listen to your lady. This rebellion is doomed – you have said as much yourself. It is not too late. Your father's door will never be truly closed to you. He will take you in, protect your wife as his own –"

"Protect her?" Alaric's voice was rough. "As he protected my own mother – as he protected Theo? By hiding in Aurariola and leaving the work of revenge and war to other men? No, Teudolfo." He shook his head, staring at the table. "If I run with Rekiberga, I have betrayed not only my father but the man I chose over him, and to whom I am sworn. How many times must I betray my word?"

"You made a mistake, *magula*. A mistake any man could have made." Teudolfo's tone was urgent. "But there is time still to undo that mistake. You are not reneging on your word, Alaric. You are returning to your homeland, to your father. Following a man whose heart you know, even if you do not agree with his way."

Alaric was quiet for a long time, feeling the gulf opening wider before him. In it, he saw Theo's face, the day his brother had asked him to care for Lælia if he did not return. He recalled Theo's quiet resignation, his acceptance that he must do the duty his father and uncle had asked of him. He saw Laurentius's cool mask as he faced Egica in court and pretended diplomacy when Alaric knew his uncle despised the king and all he stood for. He saw Athanagild's gaunt face as he spoke of the Church's own divided allegiance. So many sacrifices – and yet what had Spania gained from all that suffering? What true change had they wrought, with their secret plots and diplomacy?

The memories swirled in the black gulf before him, and Alaric felt how easy it would be to blind himself to those complexities and return to the house of his father. He could release himself from the burden of choosing a path and instead follow Suinthila's way, blindly trusting in his father's direction and ignoring all he had seen and learned.

When he finally spoke, his voice felt rusty and old.

"I can no longer follow my father's way," he said. He stared at the opposite wall, upon which it seemed he could see his brothers' faces. "His world has fallen. It fell long ago, whether he wishes to acknowledge it or not. It fell when the king's family attacked and killed my own and were allowed to flee with impunity. What price must we pay for the Spania of my father's dreams, Teudolfo? What, or who, will be sacrificed next time?" His eyes slid to Rekiberga, who stood abruptly.

"Am I not already being sacrificed, Alaric?" Her eyes searched his. "What do you think it is when my father wields my hand as currency in his war?"

He caught her hand with his own. "You know I loathe his actions," he said roughly. "I do not love the man, Rekiberga, and I despise that he plays with you, with us both. But I cannot say I disagree with his cause." He turned to Teudolfo. "Just as I cannot say that because my father's heart is honourable, I agree with his cause – for I do not."

"Then you will stay," said Rekiberga dully.

Alaric forced himself to meet her eyes. "I must," he said simply.

"This is a mistake, *magula*." Teudolfo's face was dark. "You cannot split the heart of a man from his cause. Sunifred has neither honour nor integrity, for no man with either would play with his own child's life." He looked apologetically at Rekiberga. "Forgive me, my lady."

"No." Rekiberga's colour was heightened, but she spoke clearly. "You are right, Teudolfo." She looked at Alaric. "A cause is only as strong as the man who leads it," she said quietly. "And my father does not have the strength that men will follow. Your father, however, is renowned for the integrity and strength that mine is not. It is why my father seeks to hold you at his side. He hopes men will follow the son of a man they respect."

"She is right, *magula*." Teudolfo's face was grim. "In Sunifred you find a man concerned only with his own self-interest, one who will return us to the savage days your own father fought to bring us out of. Sunifred does not care for Spania. He cares for enriching his own pocket and gaining revenge on those he believes disrespect him. Is such a man worthy of a crown?"

"Perhaps not." Alaric felt tired as he spoke. "But though he may not be worthy of it, he will not, I think, stoop to murdering women and children – and that is more than can be said of Egica. And perhaps, too, if I remain at his side, I might be a voice of reason to him, save him from his worst excesses." He met Teudolfo's eyes. "You may leave, if you wish." Alaric felt the words catch in his throat. "I will not hold you here, Teudolfo."

The older man made a rough sound of dismissal. "You know it is more than duty that holds me," he said bluntly. "I cannot leave you, Alaric. I will not. Though I will say I think your dreams of acting as wise counsel to be whimsical. Sunifred is not a man to listen to counsel with which he does not agree."

Alaric had no answer to that. Rekiberga stared at him for a long moment, then she sat down slowly on the stool opposite Alaric. She bent forward and their foreheads touched, their breath mingling in the silent room. "Nor can I abandon you," she whispered softly. "But I beg you think on what I have said, Alaric. And remember this: if you decide to leave, I will ride with you, no matter how hard the road, nor the risks upon it."

They remained like that, inhaling the strength of each other, until Teudolfo finally stretched out his hand and led Rekiberga away.

9

LÆLIA

SEPTEMBER, AD 690

Montibus Awras, Mauretania
Aures Mountains, Algeria

The adwwar lay in a shallow depression amidst soaring mountains of red rock. In the early morning, the stone glowed like fire, and even in the late months of summer, dew sat on the foliage. It was this time Lælia enjoyed the most, before the Jerawa stirred, when she had the dawn to herself.

She was surprised by how much she loved the desert. The way each night erased the tracks of the previous day, leaving the sand rippled in perfect symmetry, as if it had never known human footprint. The deep silence of the nights, and the strange isolation of the days when wind threw sand into the air. Each mood seemed to Lælia perfect in its own way, finding an echo in her soul. Here she had no need to be the heiress of Illiberis, but was merely another Rider on the sands, swathed in material and following in silence through the vast spaces.

The adwwar, though, where the women and children of Dahiya's army made their home in low mud huts, was different.

"*Lalla!*" It was one of the women, calling her into the hut to eat. As far as Lælia could make out, *lalla* was a term of affection and respect. She hoped so. All of Dahiya's companions called her by it.

After she had eaten the flaky bread with almond paste that was a treat from the clay ovens of the adwwar, the women led her away to make henna patterns on her feet. Lælia inwardly sighed as she submitted to their ministrations. She had learned the hard way that such decoration could take all day, but also that it was useless to protest that she didn't want it. Just like the women of the Toletum court, the young women of the adwwar took every chance to make themselves beautiful and gossip amongst themselves about the men. Lælia did not need to understand their language to know the manner of their conversation. It left her feeling just as lonely and bored as she once had felt listening to the women at court.

Jadis, her cat, lay at the rear of the hut, eyeing the activities with profound disinterest. As footsteps approached, the cat's tail began to thud gently on the earth. Lælia was relieved when Dahiya entered the hut and the other women fell silent, then left them alone.

"You do not, I think, enjoy the talk of women," Dahiya said by way of greeting.

"I do not judge them." Lælia gestured to her feet and the intricate patterns the women had spent hours delicately tracing on the skin there. "I just cannot imagine thinking the making of these patterns an important use of my days." She gave Dahiya something of a reproachful look. "When you mentioned, in conversation with Ilyan, leaving me with the women to have henna made, I confess I had thought you joking."

"It is the safest place for you," said Dahiya bluntly.

"Safest?" Lælia was not smiling. "Is that what you have sought for yourself – the safest course?"

"I might have been wiser had I done so."

"But you did not. You wanted more."

"More comes with a price." Dahiya stood restlessly, moving to the opening of the hut and looking out at her people going about their day: driving herds of goats to feed, weaving dried *sabay* grass into baskets, pounding grain with long wooden poles. Jadis growled softly. "A price I would not wish you to pay."

"The women told me of the revenge you took, long ago." Lælia saw the other woman's back stiffen, but Dahiya did not turn around. "They say you killed your father's murderer with your own hands, then fed him his own private parts as punishment for ravaging you." She could not hide the admiration in her tone.

"The women speak too much. You should not listen to their gossip."

"It is not gossip," Lælia said with certainty. "You wanted more, and you took it. Why do you think it so strange that I would want the same? Or that I would want my revenge on those who have wronged me – and my family?"

"This vengeance you speak of and think you want." Dahiya still did not look at her. "Tell me about it."

"You know what Giscila did to my parents." Unconsciously, she put a hand on Jadis's large head. "He attacked our home when I was barely a month old, with an entire thiufa of men. Most of ours were north fighting with his brother, King Wamba. He murdered my father and the household guard. Theo's mother was visiting us and died in the attack. My mother escaped, taking Theo and I with her. She died later, in the caves where she hid us. If men of the tribes had not found us, Theo and I would also be dead." Lælia told her story in short, hard sentences. The cat butted her gently, curling into her side.

"You tell this story as if it belongs to someone else." Dahiya's face was shadowed by the brilliant daylight beyond the doorway. "Is it for this story that you seek vengeance?"

Lælia swallowed a growing feeling of resentment. "My grandmother told me that when she met you in Septem long ago, Giscila was in her grasp. She came to kill him, and she would have done so had your wars not intervened. She left with her revenge undone." Lælia tilted her chin proudly. "Now she has given the task of vengeance to me. I intend to see justice is done."

"My wars," said Dahiya, a small smile on her face. "This is what you call the Arabic force that even now bears down on us, determined to take Africa for the Caliphate. You think these wars do not concern you, that they are no more than an obstacle to be overcome on the pathway to exacting your revenge?"

"I think you have won the right to fight whom you choose, as you see fit. I ask for the chance to win the same right."

"And you believe that finding Giscila, and killing him, will give you this 'right'?" Lælia nodded, feeling foolish, though she did not know why. "Tell me this." Dahiya folded herself smoothly into a cross-legged position on the cushions opposite Lælia. "When you think of pushing your sword into Giscila's belly, of watching him die, what do you see? What do you feel?" Then, as Lælia opened her mouth to answer, Dahiya went on: "No. Close your eyes. Tell me what you see, what it is you feel."

The sounds beyond the hut faded away, and Lælia saw a man before her. She felt the weight of steel in her hand, the short, lethal dagger her grandfather had trained her to wield with deadly dexterity. She saw herself approaching the man, unbalancing him, causing him to fall to the ground, his eyes staring up at her. She stood over him, the sword in her hand.

"What do you see?" urged Dahiya.

Lælia stared at the face in her vision, her arm raised high, feeling the rage and bitterness course through her. *Not you!* she thought furiously, as she stared into the dark eyes of her imagined enemy. Jadis made a long, low sound beside her, of warning and hunger.

"What do you feel?" Dahiya's voice tugged at her, and Lælia's eyes flew open.

"I feel rage," she spat, staring angrily at the other woman.

"Ah." Dahiya's mouth curled in a knowing smile. "But anger at what? At whom?"

Lælia paused. *I could lie*, she thought. *Dahiya could not know.* But she knew, somewhere inside herself, how futile a lie it would be.

"Oppa," she said dully. "I saw the king's bastard in my mind – and I wanted to kill him."

"Oppa." Dahiya sat back, nodding in satisfaction. "Yes. He, I think, has wronged you."

"So has Giscila," said Lælia furiously. "He murdered my parents. He left me for dead –"

"Yes," Dahiya cut her short, "but you did not know your parents. You were a baby. This tragedy, it affected you, of course.

Such events have their impact, leave indelible scars upon our souls, in ways that forever mark and change us. The murder of your parents is part of who you are. But the pain of their loss is your grandmother's revenge to take, not yours. It is she who sees Giscila's face in her dreams, who knows a dark, visceral rage when she thinks upon him. Not you. Yours is reserved for Oppa, for the man who hurt Theo and tried to take you against your will. For Oppa, you have the dark rage of grief, the deep passion from which comes power. One day, it is Oppa who will create the warrior you may be. Not Giscila. Giscila is no more than a faceless symbol of what you have lost. Killing him will not bring you the power of which you dream. It will simply be killing, which alone does no more than stain the soul and weaken it. To kill Giscila would be to follow the false lead of your own pride, which seeks to make its mark and sees in his death a trophy that others might admire. There is no honour in such killing – and no justice."

Lælia wanted to protest, but the words tasted like dust in her mouth. Jadis stared at her, tail swinging low and slowly. "How are you so certain?" she said finally. "Did you allow any to tell you what revenge was yours to take? Acantha passed this task on to me. I will not fail her in it."

"I did not need anyone to tell me what revenge was mine to take." Dahiya's eyes flashed deep amber. "I stared down at the face of a man who had taken my body by force and who I had watched put steel through my father, and I knew he was mine to kill. I could not live whilst he did, and he could not be permitted to walk the earth again. My revenge was uncomplicated, and I do not regret it.

"But in the days since that man died, I have taken many lives. Most in the heat of battle, where revenge plays no part and steel will take what Ghurzla, the god of war, wills. But some lives I have had to take in the cold light of day and reason. Lives of men who betrayed me, or those captured whom it was too dangerous to allow to live. Such deaths I take with my own blade, that the deed will not stain the souls of my men, for I am their leader and such tasks must be mine alone. Often the deaths are well deserved. I mourn the men dead at their hands, or I loathe them as enemies on my land. But when my blade runs their flesh, it is not the savage heat of revenge I taste, but the cold, sickly flavour of death. There is no satisfaction, no justice, in such killing. Only the darkness of the deed itself, a darkness I must make room for in the home of my soul and carry with me all my life, for no light can ever truly take it away."

Lælia felt a secret relief that her soul did not yet carry any such burden. Then she looked around at the earthen walls of the hut, and she felt the frustrated impotence of sitting there, inactive, whilst events swirled around her.

"Tell me." Dahiya looked at her curiously. "When Theo returns, what life do you imagine at his side?"

"Theo will learn to administer justice in Illiberis, as my grandfather does. I will manage the herd as the women of our family have always done. We will marry." She coloured. "Have children."

"And what if there is no Illiberis?"

Lælia stared at her. "Illiberis is mine," she said flatly. "It will always be mine."

"Perhaps." Dahiya shrugged. "Perhaps not. Wars change things. And Spania will soon be at war. What will you do, Lælia, if war comes for Illiberis? Will you fight?"

"Of course I will fight."

"And if you are defeated – what then?"

"Then we will fight again."

"You say 'we'," said Dahiya quietly. "After you are married, is it you who will lead the men of Illiberis to battle, or Theo? Who will care for your children?"

"Theo knows who I am. He knows I can fight and that I will defend Illiberis with my last breath." She met Dahiya's eyes defiantly. "You have children," she pointed out. "And yet you fight."

The ghost of a smile crossed Dahiya's face. "I met their father as an equal, fought beside him as such, and bore his children alone in the sands. My ways are not yours, Lælia of Illiberis." Her use of the title emphasised the difference between them. "You do not wish to sit in the adwwar with the women," said Dahiya quietly. "You think yourself separate from them, destined for something more than the life of wife and mother."

The conversation was uncomfortably reminiscent of that Lælia recalled having with Acantha when she first learned of her betrothal to Theo: *When you have found the courage to face the challenges life already offers you, we might discuss again the great deeds you think yourself destined to accomplish…*

"Acantha once said something similar," she said slowly. "Since then, I have proven my worth. Won the right to come here, representing Illiberis. I may not have faced men on a battlefield as you have done. But I have faced my enemies – and won."

"You have won nothing." There was no malice in Dahiya's tone. "Proven nothing. You are the same girl you were when Theo left, still waiting for him to return, for your dream life to begin. You live beneath your grandfather's roof. Soon you will live beneath your husband's." She stared evenly at Lælia. "Even as you disdain the chatter of the women, you are preparing for the life they lead, not the one I do. You came here wrapped in the protection of the legacy you were born to and the one to which you are now betrothed. And if you think any man such as Theo will stand by and watch his wife, the mother of his children, lead men to war, you are deluded."

The words hit Lælia in the place far within where inadequacy lived and no lie could stand the glare of truth. "I cannot do nothing," she said tightly. "I will not."

Dahiya inclined her head. "No," she said evenly. "And perhaps it was wrong of me to expect that of you."

She stood, extending a hand to Lælia and pulling the younger woman to her feet. "Acantha once taught me the secrets of working with your Illiberis horse," she said. "But whilst there are none to compare with the women of your family when it comes to training horses, there are none to compare with my Riders when it comes to fighting on the back of them. Perhaps, whilst you are here amongst my Riders, I might train you to ride as we do."

Lælia felt excitement surge through her veins. Beside her, Jadis prowled restlessly, her tawny eyes gleaming in the dim light.

"I would like nothing more," she said, trying to retain at least a semblance of dignity.

"Then come." Dahiya moved decisively toward the open doorway. "After you learn a little, we will ride into the sands together. When you come out, we will discuss your future again. For now" –

she cast Lælia a wry smile – "we will occupy ourselves with lessons on the best ways to kill. For these are always of use, whether for enemies or for those on a battlefield one is forced to call enemy."

"Are they not the same?" said Lælia, following her into the daylight.

"Oh, no." Dahiya walked away toward the horses. "In war, all men are brothers, all women sisters. There are no enemies on a battlefield. Only the dead, and those who live still."

10

YOSEF

OCTOBER, AD 690

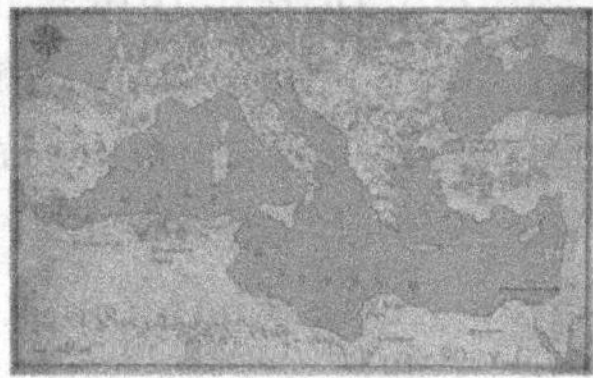

Ægyptus–Ilya
Egypt–Jerusalem

Yosef's dreams had grown deeper as the nights had grown colder.

"*Yosef.*" He felt the strands of Sarah's thick, lustrous hair stroke his face on the desert night. "*Yosef, I am still here.*"

"I know you are there!"

Yosef tossed restlessly on the hard ground.

"I cannot return to you, to Garnata. You do not know the man I have become."

"*I know you, Yosef. You will come back to us. You must come back…*"

Yosef's eyes opened. He lay in the still night, drawing deep breaths of crystalline air.

They had reached the great, red-banded fortress of Babylon on the banks of the Nile. They paid their toll to cross the canal that led to the famed Erythra Thalassa, the inland sea the Arabs called Qeyyih Bāhrī. "Now," said Bagay, "we reach the end of the lands we know." The three young men looked at each other. Yosef felt an odd stirring of excitement and fear, a strange exhilaration after the long months of isolated desert travel during which his dreams had sometimes seemed more real than the air around him.

"In less than one turn of the moon we will reach Jerusalem," said Khanchla. "The place of your people – and where the new caliph, they say, has his winter palace."

The road from Babylon was walked by people from every corner of the Circle of Lands. The trio heard Aramaic, Hebrew, Arabic, Greek, Latin, and a dozen other tongues, many utterly unknown to them. Some were traders and merchants; others were pilgrims, travelling either to the great monastery of St Catherine in the south or to Jerusalem, which the Arabs called Ilya, an adaptation of the Roman name, Ælia Capitolina. The three travellers tried to keep to themselves, but it was a sociable road, and many nights they found themselves sharing a fire and food with their companions. The indigenous people themselves were the tall and handsome Nabateans, darker than the Arabs who now occupied their land, and unfailingly courteous. They met travellers with respect and a deep, quiet dignity. It seemed to Yosef that they watched the quick-tongued Arabs move through their country with guarded reserve, neither liking nor disliking. Yosef had the sense that the Nabateans occupied a different frame of time in which the coming and going of men mattered little to their lives and internal reflections.

He found their measured pace and guarded eyes a stark contrast to the ambition and haste of the Arabic conquerors. It was the first time Arabs had surrounded them, and it had taken some time for Bagay and Khanchla to relax when companies of the caliph's army passed, which they did often. The Nabateans spoke their own language, a low, mellifluous sound Yosef found soothing and intriguing. By comparison, the clicks and chirrups of Arabic seemed alien and strange. In reality, the caliph's forces were a polyglot of men from conquered lands – Persians, Nabateans, Armenians, and, Yosef observed with not a little disquiet, a considerable detachment of slaves drawn from Bagay and Khanchla's own desert tribes.

Bagay's fists clenched the first time a group of these slaves was marched by them. Men stumbled along in chains, thin and exhausted, pulled angrily by an armed man on a horse and whipped from behind by his companion.

"They are Imazighen." Bagay stopped so abruptly his brother walked into him.

"Yes," hissed Khanchla. "And it is better the men driving them do not realise we are, also. Move."

The brothers lowered their heads and continued, trying not to look as the long, miserable column passed them. Clad in robes they had purchased in Babylon, Yosef and his friends looked much as the other merchants on the road did from that city, and if their features were not Nabatean, they took care to speak only Greek amongst themselves, and there was nothing to mark them as extraordinary. But alongside the weary column of beaten slaves, Bagay and Khanchla's identity was unmistakable to any who cared to look. They kept their heads down, but Yosef, watching his friends' tight lips and anguished faces, could only guess what it cost them to do so, confronted with the suffering of their own.

In Jerusalem, they ate in a narrow alley facing the Temple Mount. Having been raised on his father's stories of the magnificent Greek church that stood on the ground of his ancestors, Yosef was still reeling from the sight of a great dome being erected in its place. It had been more than six years since the Arabs had conquered Jerusalem, and yet still Yosef felt a strange shiver at the sight of an Arabic place of worship growing on the very ground beneath which, according to the beliefs with which he had been raised, the Holy of Holies dwelt still.

"Why do your people venerate this place?" asked Bagay, eating the warm unleavened bread and rich paste served by the stalls about the Mount.

"According to the first teachers of my faith," said Yosef softly, "it was from this place that the world as we know it was created. Here, the divine presence of God gathered the dust used to create the first human, Adam." He paused, but despite the profound nature of his words, the prosaic scene before him did not change.

"My people built temples here," Yosef continued. Looking at the swarm of men carrying stone and tools up the slope where the new building was taking shape, he added: "It is said that we will, one day, build a final, third temple – which will celebrate the coming of the Jewish Messiah."

Khanchla squinted at the light shining from the new stone construction. "It looks to me, my friend, as if you may be waiting some time for that Messiah," he said, grinning at Yosef.

Yosef felt as if he should have some kind of deep revelation, here at the place where so much of his own history had taken place. Instead, the evening shadows grew long, and they sought a bed for the night. In the morning, they walked from the city with little more than a backward glance, toward the palace of the caliph.

THEY ENTERED the fortress of the Al Sinnabra *qasr* upon the Sea of Galilee, which the Arabs called Kinneret, in the late afternoon when a cool breeze rippled the olive leaves and rustled the date palms. The great walls of the *qasr* ran a mile or more about the palace and surrounding settlement, more than twenty feet thick, studded with round and rectangular towers. Even after the magnificence of Carthage, Yosef had yet to become accustomed to the sheer scale of the castles and fortresses he entered, and Al Sinnabra, the winter palace of the caliph Abd al Malik, was the most magnificent he had yet seen.

They entered through a tall, arched gateway made of basalt and brick and passed a granary large enough, Yosef thought, to feed an army. Houses were packed tightly together in the outer part of the complex, prosperous dwellings from which robed women bustled to and from the market to the east, from whence he could hear the calls of the sellers.

They continued along a paved road lined with date palms until they reached the entrance to the palace proper. A guard, clad in pointed helmet and chain mail, raised his spear to guard their way and glared at them.

Yosef stepped forward and, clearing his throat, bowed.

"I am here to see Khalifatul Mu'mineen, Abd al Malik," he said, in halting Aramaic.

The guard looked at his fellow and laughed. "Indeed," he said, grinning. "And I am here to make love to his daughters."

Yosef remained bowing. "Please accept this." He handed one of the scrolls to the guard. "We have travelled far, from Spania itself, and at great danger, to meet with the Khalifatul Mu'mineen."

The guard's smile faded, and he eyed the good-quality robes and shoes of Yosef and his companions, his eyes narrowing thoughtfully. "Wait here," he said abruptly, and he turned into the palace.

They waited as evening grew and the call to prayer rang out from the minaret high above the palace. Since Babylon, it was a sound they had heard at every settlement, but they had yet to become accustomed to the strange, wailing song, though it had a plaintive beauty that touched something in Yosef's soul. It was odd, too, to see people halt in their daily tasks and roll out their prayer mats, turn to the east, and bow their foreheads to the ground every time the *mu'addhin* made his song.

In the chill of the evening after prayers, though, the streets were alive and festive, and people watched them curiously when the guard returned, this time with a well-dressed man in tow who bent his head in an expression of apology. "I did not mean to keep you waiting," he said, the deference in his tone in marked contrast to the guard's earlier disdain. The guard opened the wrought-iron side gate, commanding them to follow.

Beyond the inner wall, the palace gardens were thoughtfully laid out, reminding Yosef of those at Septem. Water trickled through fountains placed amidst marble columns. They walked through the central courtyard and beneath intricately carved arches, finding themselves in a small antechamber topped by a rich dome, threaded with gold and painted in careful geometric patterns. Beneath them, the tiled mosaic depicted, to Yosef's fascination, the signs of the zodiac, carefully laid out in a circle.

Presently they turned to the sound of footsteps coming down the corridor. The palace guard marched in full mail about a group of palace officials clad in rich robes with turbans wound about their heads, curled slippers on their feet. At their centre was a tall, strongly built man with dark, keen eyes and the hard look of command. He stepped forward and eyed them with interest.

"You will bow before Mohammed bin Marwan, brother of

Caliph Abd al Malik, general to his armies, and victor in the name of Allah," ordered the guard.

Yosef and his companions duly bowed.

"You are from Spania," said Mohammed bin Marwan, without preamble. "But you do not come from the king." He held up the scroll. "My clerk transcribed your document. He tells me of your journey to Serica and your request for aid. Shall we take refreshment whilst we talk?" He held out an arm politely, but with no less an air of command, and they followed him into a room that held a number of carved wooden chairs about a low table. Mohammed indicated they should sit and waited until they had done so, swirling his robes with an efficient flourish and settling into his chair with one knee crossed over the other, long fingers stroking the pointed beard at his chin.

"You are Jews," he said. Yosef, feeling it impolitic to refine his statement, nodded. "Jews, I am to understand, are not well liked in Spania."

Yosef hid his surprise. "You are well informed, Sidi."

Mohammed did not react to the honorific but watched him with shrewd interest. "In the Caliphate of the Umayyads, people of the book are welcome to live in peace under the One True God. They are *dhimmi*, protected persons under law. Taxes are paid, this is true; *jizya* is paid by all those who do not follow the law of Mohammed. But as Jews you are equal beneath the law, able to trade, hold property, do business, and worship according to your own custom. It is not thus in the Spanish kingdom of the Goths, I understand."

A sudden memory of his father burning in the square flickered through Yosef's mind, and he smelled again the sick reek of oil and flesh. "No," he said shortly. "It is not."

It seemed that Mohammed had perceived something of the nature of his thoughts. He sat back in his chair and stroked the short beard again, watching Yosef with a faint glimmer of a smile.

"And so, you come here to make alliance with the Caliphate. You have heard, then, of our progress, *Alhamdulillah*, across Africa?"

Bagay and Khanchla stiffened beside him. Mohammed's eyes flickered to them, then back to Yosef.

"Yes," said Yosef, trying to keep his voice as steady as possible. "I have heard of your victories."

"Victories we have had, yes. But losses, also. No matter. *Sabr*, patience, is a gift from Allah. Indeed, *Allah is with the patient*."

"*Salla Allah alayhi wa salaam*," murmured the palace guard.

"And when the forces of the Caliphate come to the gates of Spania," Mohammed continued, "the Jews there, you will rise in support and welcome us."

He said it as a statement, nodding his head.

"For that," said Yosef quietly, "I cannot answer."

Mohammed looked up in surprise. "You cannot answer?" He frowned at Yosef. "You stand here in the court of the caliph, begging for his mercy and indulgence upon your road, but yet you cannot pledge the allegiance of your people – who suffer beneath the corrupt yoke of rulers who oppress you?" He held out a hand, palm upraised in question. "Why?"

Yosef felt colour flood his face and tension prickle beneath his skin. From the corner of his eye, he saw the guards' grip on their spears tighten infinitesimally. He suspected his would not be the first blood to flow without ceremony on the floor of the magnificent council chamber. Urbane and benevolent Mohammed might appear, but Yosef sensed he was also ruthless as a sharp sword. Beside him, Bagay and Khanchla were taut and still, and Yosef knew they were thinking of the short knives concealed beneath their robes. For the first time, he doubted the wisdom of allowing them to accompany him. They stood in a chamber in front of a man sworn to destroy all they knew. How long could they hold their peace?

"Your armies work to conquer Africa," Yosef said, trying to keep his voice steady. "They may or may not succeed. I have seen much of the desert and its people, and I know they do not wish subjugation beneath another foreign power." Mohammed's eyes narrowed, but he did not interrupt, gesturing with an abrupt flick of his fingers for Yosef to continue. "In Spania, it is the same for the Jews," Yosef said slowly, trying to find the words to express what he wished to say. "We suffer under the laws of King Egica and the Church, it is true. But so we suffered before first we came to Spania. Such is the fate of our people – to be oppressed, to live apart from others. We do not seek to foment rebellion or start war. We seek only to trade in peace, to pursue our business, and worship in our own way."

"And this is what I offer you," said Mohammed, spreading out his hand.

"But we do not know what kind of society you will make," said Yosef. "Will subjugation beneath you benefit or hinder us? As yet, we do not know. And Jews know also the virtue of patience: *Many are the purposes in a man's heart; but the counsel of Jehovah, it standeth.*"

For a moment, there was silence. Mohammed watched him closely, the guards watched Mohammed, and Dahiya's sons watched them all. Finally, a reluctant smile broke across Mohammed's face. "So," he said. "You are here to decide whether the caliph is a man to your liking – to judge our society, no? You, a Jewish boy from a state in which you are oppressed and persecuted, have travelled halfway around the Circle of Lands to pass judgement on those who have conquered the armies of the emperor. We should, I suppose, be honoured by your presence."

The guards laughed. Yosef allowed himself a smile, feeling his heart begin to beat once more. "In fact," he said, "I come simply to beg passage through your lands, and to make known my people's wish to trade freely amongst them. I have neither the political understanding nor the authority to enter into any kind of official alliance. If I have mistakenly given that impression, I hope you will forgive it as the error of a boy not yet wise enough to manage his mistakes."

Mohammed regarded him for a moment; then he nodded briefly and flashed a quick, short smile. "I know many Jews," he said. "But I have never met one from Spania. I would speak with you more – you will dine in my home tonight, with your friends, of course." He glanced at Bagay and Khanchla and his smile twisted slightly. "Although I suspect their conversation is better on the topic of camels than the Torah." He raised an eyebrow quizzically when the young men looked up warily. "I do not command our armies in Africa," he said, "but I have received enough recruits from there to know faces from tribes when I meet them. Jews you clearly are, if you protect this one." He nodded at Yosef. "Spaniards, though, you are not. Nonetheless, you are welcome in our court. Perhaps what you learn in your time here may alter your opinions on my people."

Bagay and Khanchla, disconcerted, mumbled their thanks, colouring at the visible amusement of the guards.

Standing abruptly, Mohammed addressed his guards. "Take them to guest quarters and show them every courtesy." Glancing at Yosef, he said, "You will wish to bathe before we eat. My guards will show you." He nodded dismissal, then left.

Mohammed's home was within the palace walls but far less formal than the great reception chambers. Slaves served them whilst they sat on comfortable cushions on the floor, about a low wooden table inlaid with ivory. Yosef was conscious that he had not yet seen a woman in the palace, though he had heard their soft laughter through the lattice screen that separated the women's section of the palace from the men's. It was, he knew, *haram* — forbidden — under Islam for women to meet and talk with strange men. He found it strange to be aware of their presence yet forbidden to speak with them.

"I would like to learn Arabic," said Yosef.

They were eating delicate pastries of pigeon meat cooked with spiced fruit and almonds, drizzled with honey. Yosef could not recall ever eating something so exquisitely flavoured. It was served with a salad of pomegranate seeds, cucumber, and mint, washed down with goat's milk spiced with honey and cinnamon. The absence of wine at a meal was odd to Yosef, but it was something he was rapidly becoming accustomed to in the lands of the Muslims. Although the *dhimmi* communities could drink alcohol and trade it as they pleased, the Muslims he encountered did not touch a drop.

Mohammed nodded. "Whilst you are here, we will speak together. You will need, also, to learn some Persian, if you are to travel through the lands of Eran. That, too, you may learn at my brother's court."

"Your brother — Caliph Abd al Malik — is he here, currently, in the palace?" Yosef asked curiously.

Mohammed nodded. "But his time is heavily weighted," he said. "We have, only this past summer, ended a long war that has divided our people for many years. Now my brother is caliph, and he must work hard to unite the lands we have already won, and to win more."

"Where will you go?" It was Bagay who spoke. There was a challenge in his voice, and he coloured slightly as he met Mohammed's eye, defiance on his face.

Mohammed laughed softly. "We have already troops in Africa, my little nomadic friend," he said, smiling not unkindly. "But myself – I go into Persia, and Armenia, to subdue those who would contest the caliph's rule."

"And why can those countries not rule themselves?" Bagay persisted. "Why must they submit to your rule?"

"If they could rule themselves, they would." Mohammed shrugged. "But it is the will of Allah that all should live in peace, brethren in His name. And they submit, as is their destiny and the destiny of all men. The corruption of the old regimes rotted them. The persecution of peoples like your own" – he nodded at Yosef – "is wrong, and cruel. All those who accept the One True God should be united, sharing their culture and learning, creating a more prosperous society in which all – not only the few – can thrive."

"And what of those who do not accept the One True God?" Khanchla, emboldened by his brother, interrupted. "What of those who serve other gods?"

"They are pagans," said Mohammed flatly, "and little better than the animals they ride. Worship of pagan gods is the root of human ambition. To believe there are gods who act on behalf of men, savage gods who delight in cruelty and war, this is to deny the magnificence and benevolence of the One and to revel in the corruption and ego of man. Accept Allah and become equals beneath our laws, marry our women, and share in our prosperity. Allah is almighty and will conquer all. Our role is merely to worship Him and live in accordance with His law."

They continued to speak until late into the night. Once their questions were unleashed, Bagay and Khanchla found an unceasing flow of them, all of which Mohammed answered with patience and respect – but nonetheless, Yosef noted, with implacable certainty in the rightness of his words.

Yosef wondered, as he listened, why his own people had never felt the same urge to conquer and rule. His entire knowledge of his own history, he realised, was one of escape and persecution, one where his people survived rather than conquered. When they had taken up arms, it had been for survival rather than conquest. Even in Spania – where his own people had settled long before anyone in the Empire had even heard of the Goths – when Visigoth invaders came, defeating the old Roman regime, his own people had simply adapted rather than fighting for the land. *Could we have ruled Spania?* Yosef wondered. For a moment, he allowed himself to imagine the possibility: his own father ruling in Illiberis rather than Lælia's. A Jewish king sitting upon the throne.

Immediately he felt a stab of guilt, and the colour rushed to his face. He imagined the harsh words his father would speak if he knew of such a thought. *Such ambition is unpleasing to God,* he imagined Arun's stern voice saying. *It is not glory, or thrones, our people seek; it is true wealth, that of the soul, and family.*

Yosef looked about him surreptitiously. Even here, in Mohammed's own quarters, the sense of luxury and opulence was unmistakable. From the intricate carvings in the plaster walls to the mosaics inlaid in the floor, the silver ewer from which water was poured over his hands before eating to the delicately wrought plate from which they ate, everything spoke of riches and prosperity. He felt a sudden surge of resentment that his own people should hide their wealth, should need to bury it in a secret cave in the hills near Garnata. Should have to send their children in supplication to beg the assistance of other, more powerful men in order simply to conduct trade.

Why do we not take what we desire? Yosef thought. *Why not take up the sword and command our own armies – take a land for our own and demand other men kneel before us?*

But even as he thought it, he knew the answers, knew no Jew who followed the path of God would ever consent to conquering another people, to willingly take up arms.

And Yosef, to his own discomfort, felt anger and contempt for his own people and himself, for the fatal weakness that meant he must leave his home and travel the length of the Circle of Lands merely so his people could acquire wealth that would never become riches. It seemed to him that on a linear scale, where success lay at one end and failure at the other, in all things that truly mattered – protecting Sarah, his friends, his family – he sat firmly on the side of failure. Success, he imagined, was already gone from his grasp. Success belonged to the man who could have found a way to defend those he loved from harm, and who would know what lay ahead and how to manage it. Success belonged to the man he could never hope to be.

"You are very quiet," said Mohammed, smiling at him. "Is our conversation so boring?"

"Mohammed is to lead his armies into Persia and Armenia," said Khanchla. "Did you hear, Yosef? More than twenty thousand men he will command. I have never seen an army of such a size."

Bagay and Khanchla had dropped all traces of timidity, and they were now flush faced and smiling, perfectly at ease in the company of one they both recognised as a warrior worthy of their own respect. The fact that those very same armies could just as easily be deployed against their own people seemed not to matter to them at all. It was war, just as the wars they fought, and war was their business.

"I was thinking," said Yosef slowly, "that I have a very long way yet to go. And that I must keep moving if I am to reach Serica."

The faces of his companions fell. "Must we leave so soon?" Bagay asked. "There is much here to learn."

But Mohammed was watching Yosef's face. "Perhaps," he said gently, "your friends might care to remain here for a time. I think, beyond this point, the road is your own, my young friend, is it not?"

Bagay turned to Khanchla, frowning, but Khanchla's eyes could not meet Yosef's. Yosef remembered Dahiya's words, and he knew his friend must also be thinking of them: *If we are to defeat them ... we must also understand them.*

"It is better, I think, for you to stay," said Yosef, trying to force a smile. "From here, my work becomes more difficult – and I must become invisible."

"At least," said Mohammed quietly, "allow me to help with that. Will you stay the turn of a moon or so – until my armies march out?

Like this, I can help you." He smiled at Yosef, genuine warmth softening the hard face. "I would enjoy your company," he said simply.

Yosef felt the road before him yawn like a lonely cavern of dark unknown, the daily effort of pack up, move, find shelter, and sleep; a sudden wave of exhaustion swept over him.

"Yes," he said, unable to find a smile. "I would like that."

11

THEO

NOVEMBER, AD 690

Sebastopolis, Anatolia
Elauissa Sebaste, Cilicia, Turkey

"Where is bastard's dromon?" When Theo didn't answer, Leofric nudged him. "I cannot see from here. Can you see it? He is here?"

Theo did not turn his head, and his voice was flat when he answered: "He is here."

"*Xristus jap Tyr*," muttered Leofric.

"I doubt appealing to either will help." Theo's face was expressionless when he turned back to face them.

"We should have tell Apsimar to cut throat in Gortyn," said Leofric. "Or done ourselves." He directed this last at Silas, who made a low noise of annoyance.

"And what would that have achieved, *wenkai*?" He nodded at Theo. "What the boy told us we have seen to be true between Gortyn and here. Oppa has made a deal with Leontios. His coin bought horses, and men to ride them, all in the name of the Spanish king, and all under Leontios's command, at no cost to the emperor."

Silas spat through the oarlock, his face dark. "How do you think it would have aided us to kill Oppa, after that?"

"I think one look at *schnecke*'s face is good enough reason," said Leofric stubbornly.

"We have argued it enough." This time it was Theo who spoke, and both men subsided at the ice-cold anger in his voice. "Leave it – and Oppa – to the gods." *And to me*, he thought but did not say.

"We will land soon." It was Leofric who spoke again, this time in a low tone. "You can give me death stare all you wish, boy. I was there when he lay those stripes on your face. How you can sit here and tell me to leave to gods? *Ne*," he said, glaring and pushing back at Silas's restraining hand. "He meant to kill, and not only Theo. You think he does not come here to finish job?"

"He may not know we are here," said Silas.

"Ah!" Leofric made a furious noise of dismissal. "He know. You know it as well as I."

Neither contradicted him. Theo stared out of the oarlock at the merchant ship pulled into the harbour alongside the long, bustling dock that ran before the defensive wall. He knew Oppa's dromon by now as well as he did his own feet. He had watched it at every camp between Gortyn and Sebastopolis, could pick it out easily amongst the dozens of vessels in the harbour. Even if the low belly, built to hold horses, had not given it away, Oppa alone amongst the fleet flew his own standard – the bright red Chrismon insignia of Spania, the same emblem Theo had trained beneath in the grounds at Emerita, where his father had once overseen the king's military headquarters.

Theo instinctively touched the coin at his chest. Geila, his grandfather, whose face the coin bore, had fought beneath that flag. Had been king beneath it, as had his brother before him.

Raised his whole life to revere the Chrismon and peacock as the twin symbols of Spania, the very thought of Oppa carrying it as if by right made Theo want to rend the corrupt king's bastard from limb to limb, then feed every part to one of the mountain cats high above Illiberis.

He took a deep, shuddering breath and pulled the oar with unnecessary strength. He did not answer Leofric. Both men fell silent. Theo knew they were worried. He couldn't help them, nor make it easier for them. The fact was that Theo wanted to kill Oppa so much he could taste the copper of blood on his tongue at the thought. Yet if what Apsimar had said was true, Oppa played games that had wider implications than his own need for revenge, which meant that he could not kill him, or at least not yet. The knowledge goaded him and made him feel disloyal to Lælia.

It wasn't only Oppa's continuing existence that made him feel disloyal to Lælia. In Sebastopolis, Athanais would open a new tavern, one Theo must establish a pattern of visiting if he was to play his part in Apsimar's schemes. Every time he thought of visiting it, unwelcome recollections of Elpis crept into his mind, until the soft curves of her body as he had seen it on the docks in Gortyn had begun to haunt his waking moments as much as Lælia did his sleeping ones.

"Ease oar!"

Theo closed his eyes and lowered his head to his arms, feeling the slow, steady beat of his heart. It was only in his dreams, he thought, that Lælia was real. So real that he often woke sweating and trembling, her deep bronze eyes seared like fire on his soul. In his dreams he saw her riding hard, a large animal of some kind at her side. Her figure was vague. It was the emotion within her he remembered upon waking, a wild, almost savage loneliness and longing. The answer it prompted made his whole body ache with the need to both comfort her and seek his own comfort in her presence. When he woke, often to darkness and the sound of others sleeping, he would lie in the quiet and imagine what she must look like now, who she might be. He would take the memories out, one by one, and examine them privately, turning them over in his mind and wondering if he had imagined their power.

Doubts lurked in those dark hours, doubts Theo knew were unworthy of himself and unfair to Lælia. Fears that his memories were deceptive, the emotion between them a fantasy belonging to a time now past. But the thought made him so furious and sick he could barely breathe, and so he would pack the tumult away again beneath the careful layers of self-control so that when the others woke, he would row and train and fight harder than any of them, for there was one thing Theo knew above all else: one day he would return to Lælia and know the truth for himself.

And what manner of man would he be, Theo thought grimly, when he returned to her? With every day that passed, it seemed he must compromise another part of the man he had been. Sometimes, Theo feared that when finally he returned to Spania, all trace of the boy who had once been Theudemir of Aurariola would have been sheared away, his flesh left rotting on the tails of Oppa's whip, his heart lost in the darkness of a sordid tavern, and his soul spent wielding his sword for more powerful men.

"Stroke!"

"Pull your oar, damn you," grunted Leofric beside him. "Since you decide you want us all suffering that evil bastard's attentions again, the gods dock us beside him." He glared at Theo, but it was a glare tinged with concern, and Theo saw Leofric's hand touch his knife as if to reassure himself that it was still there.

As the boat glided into port, Theo squinted through the hard sunlight. The sun glittered from something, and Theo saw Leontios walking toward him along the dock. Heavyset, with none of Apsimar's lithe grace, the gleaming gold on his breastplate and tunic nonetheless proclaimed his seniority. It was not Leontios who held Theo's eye, however. It was the man beside him, head bowed in polite attention, clad in the rich green robes of a wealthy lord – or a king's son.

Theo's heart slowed to a thick thud. Oppa's dark, venal eyes raked the fleet from stern to bow, as if he were looking for something.

I'm here, you bastard, thought Theo savagely. The eyes swept the fleet once more. Theo stared out over the water, almost willing Oppa to look his way, for Theo had learned something about himself during the long months he had fought in the Karabisianoi.

He had learned he liked the game of war. Liked playing it – and winning.

Perhaps, he wondered as he watched Oppa and Leontios converse, it was his experience under Oppa's lash that had truly birthed his love for war, and his talent for it. Perhaps it was the torture he had endured that made him determined never again to be helpless, to do what he must to ensure victory for himself and his men. *And if I must fight in wars I do not understand,* Theo thought, *for men I do not know, then so be it.* He had decided, in the days between Gortyn and here, that he would play Apsimar's game. Whatever plot Oppa contrived with Leontios, Theo thought bitterly, there was none more experienced in the man's ways than he, none better placed to uncover it.

The dromon shifted slightly. Oppa's eyes fell on Theo at the same moment Leofric and Silas noticed him.

"*Wenkai,*" murmured Silas urgently.

"Kill him," Leofric muttered.

Theo did not hear either of them. His eyes were locked with Oppa's, a strange dance occurring in the space between them.

I know you want to kill me, said Oppa's eyes. *Yet still I am here, showing myself to you.*

I know what you are, said Theo's. *Today, tomorrow, it matters not. I will discover what you mean here. And one day, though I may not know when or how, I will watch you die.*

Perhaps. Oppa raised his shoulders in a curious gesture, as if acknowledging Theo's fury but not meeting it. His eyes cut sideways to Leontios. There was something almost conspiratorial in the small smile on his lips. *There are things you do not know,* his eyes seemed to say.

"Theo!" Leofric's voice hissed in his ear. "I do not like the look on the bastard's face, *schnecke.*"

Oppa held Theo's eyes, then, as Leontios made a gesture of dismissal, very deliberately he turned his back. For longer than necessary, he stood with his back bared to Theo's dromon, an open target.

One stray arrow. Just one, and Oppa would be gone forever. Theo's hand tightened on his bow. Then he thought of Apsimar's words: *It is my experience that such men, bearing such gifts, have ambitions beyond doing the bidding of their masters…*

"Oppa is up to something." Theo's words sounded rusty to his own ears, and he felt the twin astonishment in Silas's and Leofric's eyes as they turned to him.

"What does it matter what he is 'up to'? Kill the bastard, Theo, or I will." Leofric raised his bow, the swarthy face grim and set.

"No."

At the sharp command Leofric relaxed his arm, though his face was dark with anger. "Give me one reason why not, *magare*. And it had better be a good one."

"If Oppa intended to kill me," Theo said, "he would not have shown himself on this dock. He certainly would not have insinuated himself with our new commander. He is here for other reasons — reasons of his own." He tore his eyes away from the retreating figure and met the accusation in Silas's and Leofric's. He bent his head and lowered his voice. "Apsimar believes Oppa has plans with Leontios. Plans that may not be in the best interests of the fleet."

Leofric frowned. "What do you care what Apsimar believes?"

"Because he asked me to care." Theo met their eyes. "The day will come when I watch Oppa die," he said quietly. "And when I do, he will know from whom the death blow comes. It will not be a stray arrow on the dock. I pray it will be my steel in his belly and my face he sees. But if Oppa is dealing with Leontios, it is certain to mean trouble. Apsimar knew that."

Leofric and Silas stared at him. "And Apsimar expects you — the same man Oppa tortured and left for dead — to discover what that trouble is?" Leofric made a harsh noise and spat into the water. "Need I remind you, *schnecke*, that Apsimar has been recalled to Constantinople — which means we are no longer under his command?"

Theo made an impatient noise. "We know Oppa. Leontios does not. We do not know what he has already put in motion — but I intend to find out."

"I hope you know what you are doing, *magare*." Leofric scowled and spat overboard as he watched the retreating figure. "I would see the bastard dead, and worry about his plots later."

Theo did not answer. A part of him knew Leofric was right. Another part, one he did not quite understand, knew it was not yet time for Oppa to die.

Lælia's face, fierce and beautiful, made his heart clench. In his mind, she rode wild and free in the Illiberis mountains, untouched by the evil of Oppa's sinister plots or the dirt of war. Theo had to believe that she, and the life he had once dreamed of, waited for him still.

Somehow, Theo resolved, he must try to hold on to the man she had put her faith in. Even if that meant allowing the one man who had sworn to destroy her live for a while longer yet.

12

LÆLIA
NOVEMBER, AD 690

Montibus Awras, Mauretania
Aures Mountains, Algeria

The arrows came at Lælia from every direction. Holding the hand shield over her head with one hand, spear held low at her side with the other, she guided her horse with her legs and bent low over its neck across the undulating ground, riding in a line of men toward a cloud of dust. From the centre of it came the thundering of hooves, then a hail of arrows.

"Throw!" called the man next to her, and Lælia hurled her spear overhead as she had been taught.

Then the attackers were upon them.

Lælia found herself amidst a whirling, shrieking mass of chaos. Arrows whistled past her, one catching the side of her head with a glancing blow. Had they been steel tipped instead of blunt practice arrows, she would be dead.

"Sword!"

Lælia fumbled as she reached for steel. She was wrenched from her horse, tumbling hard to the earth. She looked up to find Dahiya standing over her, the tip of her spear piercing Lælia's throat. "Dead," Dahiya said, not unkindly. "Too slow."

Scrambling to her feet, Lælia trudged back to her horse, Jadis prowling silently at her side. Around her the mock battle continued. The Riders who had charged toward her were the clear victors. They rode in tight concentric circles, releasing a never-ending hail of arrows that unhorsed most of the opposition before ever they released a spear.

"These Riders." It was Tosius, the little Illiberis tribesman who had come with Lælia to Africa and who rarely left her side. "They take our horses and make of them a weapon so lethal none can stand against it."

Lælia nodded. "A weapon that may one day prove valuable, if we can learn it," she said.

Tosius looked worried. "I fear your grandfather would not like you here, far in the desert, learning such things."

"My grandfather is not here." Lælia winced as she swung herself onto her horse. "And he would like it even less if I wasted such an opportunity." Tosius tilted his head in acknowledgment, but his face remained dark.

Realising Dahiya had heard the exchange, Lælia said, somewhat tartly: "As you once pointed out, women in Spania do not fight as you do here."

Dahiya's bark of laughter was as hard as it was unexpected. "Do you think it is custom for women of the Imazighen to fight?"

"Is it not?" It was Lælia's turn to look surprised. "But there are many women training amongst your forces."

"Because I encourage them to. It is not our custom. There are many still who would prefer their women at home in the adwwar, making henna." Dahiya shrugged. "But some women are made for steel, just as some men are made to make henna. I prefer to understand what a man – or woman – is best inclined to, then help them master it. Like this, we are all better."

She gave Lælia a sidelong smile, there and gone. "And I need all the fighters I can train. If your cat came to me and offered her teeth, I would train her."

Lælia laughed aloud. It was a good feeling, to laugh, and

something she had done more of since joining the Imazighen than she could remember ever having done before. The Imazighen, she sometimes felt, would find humour in even the darkest moment. To them, the gravest sin was to show misery, anger, or impatience in conversation with another. Every grievance was laughed away, every hurt given to their gods and released. Emotion was saved for the haunting songs and passionate dancing around the fire, for the paintings done on rock or for ballads of tragic love.

It was oddly peaceful.

"You have had some training." It was not a question.

Lælia nodded. "My grandfather taught me to use a sword. Tosius" – she nodded at the little tribesman who ran silently at her side – "taught me to string a bow before I could walk."

"Yes. You taught her to shoot well," Dahiya said. Tosius ducked his head, looking absurdly pleased with himself. "But not well enough." The smile vanished. Dahiya turned back to Lælia. "You would not stand more than the first battle-rush. Your swordplay is clumsy, you cannot throw a spear with any force, and you do not use your shield correctly. Being good with a bow is the easiest thing you will master. Staying alive on a battlefield is quite another. And as for strategy – well." Dahiya glanced at Jadis, who stared back at her with malevolent yellow eyes as if she took every insult personally. "You attack with the same lack of tact as your animal – riding straight at your enemy, hoping you will take him in your rush. You know nothing of how to think through a battle, how to plan it. This is what we will learn whilst you are here."

Lælia swallowed hard on her hurt pride. "Thank you."

"Ah." Dahiya waved dismissively. "My sons gave me worse looks than that when I trained them. You will live to be grateful, and who knows what destiny holds? Perhaps you may be of use to me, one day, and my time will not have been entirely wasted." She began to ride away, ordering her Riders back into formation.

"Wait." Lælia coloured as Dahiya glanced back at her, one eyebrow lifted politely, but with the humour of a moment earlier gone. "I overheard men saying a messenger had come." Lælia stumbled clumsily on the words. "From Carthage."

"If there was news I thought you should hear," said Dahiya, "I would have given it to you."

"Then you have not heard if Giscila is there?"

"I did not say that." Dahiya met her eyes steadily. "I said that if there was news I thought you should hear, I would give it to you."

"But if Giscila is in Carthage, that, surely, is news I should know of." Lælia could not disguise her impatience.

"I do not agree. Nor, for that matter, does Ilyan."

"You had news from Ilyan?" Lælia felt heat rise in her face and fought to keep her temper. "Then is there word from Spania? Why didn't you tell me?"

"I lead an army of many thousands, Lælia of Illiberis. I have an army of Arabs intent upon making my home their own. Your concerns, whilst undoubtedly of grave importance to you, are not always my priority. If I had a direct message for you, you would have it by now. All other news is for me to determine how best to use it."

"But Giscila is in Carthage."

"Yes."

Lælia drew a sharp breath. She felt her face darken and felt powerless to stop it. "Then that is where I will go. Come, Jadis." Turning the horse, she began to ride back toward the camp.

"You will do no such thing." Lælia halted at the steel in Dahiya's tone, but she did not turn. "Why do you think Giscila has come to Carthage?"

Lælia lifted one shoulder in a non-committal gesture.

"No." Dahiya strode to Lælia's side and turned her, not gently, to face her. No trace of humour remained in the older woman's face. "You do not know, Lælia, and neither do I. What I do know I will share with you. Not because you are performing like the most childish infant in the adwwar – and you are – but because we may need to ride soon, and when we do, there will be no time for conversation. The messenger brings word that Giscila has come to Carthage, yes. But there is more." She looked gravely at Lælia. "He brings word, too, that the king's bastard son was with him. He has sailed east, in the company of Leontios, a commander in the Karabisianoi."

"Oppa?" Blood drained from Lælia's face. The desert wind sounded hollow in her ears. "Sailed to the fleet? He has gone to find Theo," she said flatly. "To kill him."

"Perhaps." It was Dahiya's turn to raise her shoulder. "Perhaps not. That is the point, Lælia: neither I nor Ilyan knows. Has Oppa gone in search of Theo? Had word of Yosef?" The amber eyes pinned Lælia like twin rays of fire. "Or," she said quietly, "has Oppa heard word that you are here — and sent his kinsman to take you captive?"

"He could not know I am here. Nobody knows I am here."

"I am sure Oppa believes the same of his presence on our shores. The messenger tells me he took great pains to remain hidden and move swiftly until he was far from Ilyan's shores." Dahiya's short laughter was contemptuous. "Fool that he is. Nothing sails the Circle of Lands that Ilyan does not know of."

"If Oppa sails for the fleet, then that is where I must go." Lælia began to walk determinedly toward the camp. "He enslaved Theo once. He killed Yosef's father and ordered the rape of Sarah, the girl Yosef was to marry." The terrible memories assailed her in a series of dark images. She had never seen Sarah since that day, knew nothing of what had become of her, though she had searched hard enough. The memory of Sarah's bleeding flesh, however — and Yosef's gaunt horror — she recalled with a clarity she wished she could forget. Her dreams of Theo during the time she now knew he had been enslaved, though indistinct and felt in a dream rather than actually seen, were even worse than the memories. She shuddered at the recollection of the stark terror she had felt on waking from them, the sickening pain she had sensed through the veil of sleep.

"Enough!" Dahiya ordered, loud enough that men stopped their work and turned to look at them. "You will stop, Lælia. You will listen and do as I say. And if you dare countermand my orders another time, I will tie you to a camel myself — yes, and gag you, so I am not forced to listen to your stupid pride making you its servant."

"I came to Africa to discover what I could of Theo, and of Yosef," Lælia countered, feeling all the pent-up frustration of the long years that had passed since Theo and Yosef had gone, of the silent nights she had stared into the darkness and wondered what had become of them. "Yet you have told me next to nothing. Only that Theo was enslaved, and that he fights now for the fleet. That Yosef's journey to the east continues. Both things I knew already from the messenger who came to Illiberis before I came here. You tell me I cannot seek revenge on Giscila, the man who killed my parents and Theo's mother, although he is barely the turn of a moon's ride away. All because you wish to wait – for what? If Oppa is gone, we can take Giscila without him knowing of it."

"And then what?" Dahiya countered. "Question Giscila? Torture him until he tells us what Oppa plans? What, then, do you think would happen to those plans? At the very least, Oppa would discover the disappearance of his kinsman. That fact alone would alter whatever plans he might have. But the longer we allow Giscila to sit at Carthage, the more questions he will ask, and the more visible he will become. With every day that passes, his frustration will grow. His questions will become less subtle, his purpose more clear. He will become clumsy, and we will be closer to learning exactly what game he and Oppa play on these shores." She gripped Lælia's shoulders. "If we ride to Carthage now, we lose that precious time. Did he come to capture you? To use you as bait for Theo or Yosef? You cannot know what he plans. If you ride straight to him, will it give him an unexpected gift that can be used against both Theo and Yosef? No matter how you turn it, Lælia, to show your-self to Giscila now takes away any power we hold. It would be the most foolhardy of acts."

Lælia's rage had calmed as she listened. "Why did you not simply say as much? Why keep his presence a secret from me?"

"Because I know the rage you feel and the revenge you seek. I understand it, child." Dahiya reached out, an odd expression on the hawkish features. Then her hand dropped away, and the hard mask returned. "There is more at stake than your own petty revenge," she said brusquely. "You are not a fool, nor is there time for you to be a child. You, of all people, should understand the importance of the mission Yosef undertakes, the sacrifices that have already been made, by more than just your Theo, to ensure he succeeds." A fleeting expression of pain crossed her face, and Lælia remembered that Dahiya had sent her own sons to ride at Yosef's side.

She felt a surge of shame at her own selfish ambition, then an answering stab of anger that she, Yosef, Theo – all of them – must ever sacrifice their own interests for those of others.

When will it ever be our turn? she thought savagely. *Will we always live to serve others – our country, the fleet, Illiberis itself? Will Yosef ever find happiness again, or Theo and I ever reunite?*

Hidden beneath the last question was one she had never even dared ask herself: *Is it still me of whom Theo dreams when he closes his eyes?*

Dahiya was momentarily forgotten as odd recollections swirled in her mind. *It has been months since I knew him in my dreams,* she thought, realising as she did that a part of her had been aware of this for some time but reluctant to face it. *When I feel his presence it is distant, angry. And there is something standing between us: a woman…*

She spun away from Dahiya, feeling a strange, proud anger she could not bear the other to see.

When Dahiya spoke, though, the older woman's voice was uncharacteristically gentle. "I know it is not easy to love from afar." Lælia felt the briefest touch on her shoulder, there and then gone, comforting nonetheless. "I know it better than you might imagine. I know, too, the difficulty of doing nothing when action seems the only antidote to the pain. But this, too, is part of war, child. The waiting. Watching. Patience. It is everything. There is a time for action, and when it comes, you will know there is no choice. In that moment, blood will spill – and you may find you wish, very much, it had not. You may find the moment takes more from you than it gives, and that you wish you could take it back. That is why I know the value of patience, Lælia. When that day finally arrives, I wish for you to understand what sacrifices you suffer, and to know they were not endured for foolish pride or insignificant ends. When finally you know the deep pain of blood and loss, I hope that you, at least, do not regret the price."

13

LETTER FROM ATHANAGILD TO SHUKRA
DECEMBER, AD 690

Toletum, Spania
Toledo, Spain

S*hukra –*
To do nothing in these times feels harder than any war could. All that happens does so in the shadows, and whilst I wait and watch, it feels that the entire world crumbles around me.

Trouble stirs on the northern border with Francia. So far, Egica's men hold it for him. Should trouble worsen, however, he may himself need to ride north. He forces those he does not trust to remain close. Theodefred, the Duke of Corduba, remains in the capital. His son Roderic has become the favoured companion of Egica's own son Wittiza. I suspect it is an intentional ploy by Egica to keep Theodefred close. It is whispered that on the northern border, Theodefred's brother, Favila, stokes the trouble Egica seeks to quell. They are sons of Chinda-suinth, and all know Egica has no love for them. I do not like how close he keeps Roderic. Theodefred is pale and drawn, and his wife keeps to the house.

I have visited Liuvgoto and built some measure of trust with her, as we discussed. She has a fine mind and a refreshingly blunt manner. Sunifred is her

cousin. Egica is her son-in-law. I believe she plays a dangerous game between them. But then, we live in dangerous times.
    —Athanagild

LETTER FROM SHUKRA TO ATHANAGILD

Athanagild —

Liuvgoto does indeed play dangerous games. She tells Sunifred of Egica's movements, and Alaric says Sunifred grows ever more arrogant. He receives much correspondence from your archbishop, Sisebut, also. Can it be that Egica truly does not know that Sisebut plots against him? I am knowing men, aziz-am, and I do not believe Egica so very blind. Nor does Laurentius. He wishes to see Sisebut for himself. I know your feelings on this, aziz-am, but Laurentius is as stubborn as you and your brothers. If he chooses to come, I cannot stop him.

I do not wish to interfere in matters private to your soul, aziz-am. But I might wish you would see Laurentius if he comes to Toletum.

More than all the news you send, aziz-am, I am concerned for your own self. I fear Sisebut is a dark master. If you will not confide in me, I wish you would in Laurentius.

—Shukra

LETTER FROM ATHANAGILD TO SHUKRA

Shukra —

Please tell Laurentius not to seek me out. It is not wise. Toletum is a hotbed of gossip and whispers, and the monastery is the centre of it. Sisebut grows ever more fearful and suspicious. A visitor would serve only to stoke his fears and make our communication more difficult.

As to your comments on Sisebut's nature, there is nothing to confide. What I do is done for Spania, my brothers, and my duty. It is done so that men like Laurentius might perform their duty.

It is my choice and I do not wish to discuss it.

Particularly with Laurentius.

—Athanagild

14

SHUKRA

DECEMBER, AD 690

Hispalis, Spania
Seville, Spain

Shukra folded Athanagild's letter, staring unseeing into the darkness of the River Bætis. He was waiting in the shadows beyond the Hispalis monastery. His four years in Spania had developed in Shukra a certain dark fascination with Spania's Church. He had found little to admire and much to despise in those who rose in its ranks. He had only recently begun watching Felix, bishop of Hispalis. Thus far, his clandestine observation had shown nothing more than a somewhat overzealous man of God, but Shukra was not yet convinced. It was no wonder the Church emphasised God's forgiveness. Never had Shukra found more men in need of it.

Perhaps the Church had been thus corrupted in Constantinople. Shukra, who had always taken comfort in the fires of his own faith, had never before had cause to ponder it. But that was before he met Athanagild and had reason to care how so-called men of God wielded their power.

He recalled the day, long ago in Illiberis, when he and Athanagild had both signed the contract of betrothal between Theo and Lælia. Shukra, accustomed to identifying those who might possess unique talents others overlooked, had returned after the room emptied.

"I BELIEVE you see a great deal, Athanagild. More than most."

Athanagild looked at him curiously but gave no answer.

"Your brothers are both warriors, in their own way. But you, Athanagild – I am believing, *aziz-am*, that you may yet be the most dangerous of them all."

Athanagild frowned. "How?"

Shukra leaned close and spoke very quietly. "At the Toletum monastery to which you are bound for training," he said, "I am believing there is much you might observe that could prove helpful."

"Helpful how?"

"Your Sisebut," Shukra said, "the bishop under which you will study – he is an ambitious man. He is also a talkative one. You will be well placed to listen to him."

He had watched the boy closely, seeing the long hands still, a faint narrowing of the eyes.

"What will that do?" Athanagild asked.

"Ambitious men like powerful friends," said Shukra. "They try to impress them, usually by doing favours and placing such people in their debt. Perhaps you might be seeing some of these powerful people."

"And listening to them," said Athanagild, a barely suppressed excitement in his voice.

"Ah." Shukra rocked back on his heels and gave Athanagild a half smile. "You are already understanding me."

"But what should I be listening for?"

"You are being more smart than most," said Shukra. "You will know when words are important. And if you doubt – you may ask."

"Ask?" Athanagild frowned in confusion. "Will you be in Toletum, then?"

"I will visit," said Shukra. "Soon. But we might be keeping this visit between ourselves, no?"

SHUKRA'S HAND clenched hard enough to crumble the edge of the wall against which he leaned. He had not known then what he asked. It had only been much later, after he overheard a conversation between Alaric and Athanagild, that the dark suspicions had begun to rise. When Athanagild had summoned him to the bathhouse next, he had questioned him directly.

"Your brother asked you a question, *aziz-am*. He asked how it is at the monastery."

Athanagild did not answer.

"You said it would not interest him to hear it." Shukra watched him. "But I am interested, *aziz-am*. So, let me ask you: how are the good brothers in Christ?" His words were light, but he examined Athanagild closely.

"It is nothing. I don't wish to burden my brother."

"No," said Shukra slowly. "But lying to him is no better, *aziz-am*."

Athanagild swallowed. "I am very grateful to serve God."

Shukra had spent enough of his life in the shadows to hear what was not said. "What are they doing to you?" His hand closed hard around his knife. Shukra was also a killer, and it was the latter who spoke now.

"Nothing I cannot endure." Athanagild turned to face Shukra and, for once, the wary veil fell from his eyes. "There is much I am able to learn." His voice was tight and hard, but he held Shukra's gaze without flinching. "If Sisebut did not… favour me, I could not learn what I do."

"This is not a burden you will carry."

"And if I do not," said Athanagild grimly, "then someone else must. More importantly, I know the value of the information I can gather to others."

"By 'others', I assume you are speaking of Laurentius?" Flushing, Athanagild nodded. "Then, *aziz-am*," said Shukra flatly, "you should know that Laurentius would never accept such sacrifice from you. And would probably kill me for even listening to you speak of it."

"But it is my choice," said Athanagild stubbornly. "And besides — he need never know."

"You cannot ask this of me." Shukra rose abruptly. "This is against my own feelings, *aziz-am*. It is not good feeling." He tried and failed to soften his expression. "You are brave. But no man would ask this of you, nor want you to offer it."

"I'm not asking your permission." Athanagild had returned his gaze evenly. "If you will not hear me, I will find someone else who will. And if you say anything to Laurentius, I will deny it."

Shukra looked at him for a long moment. When he finally spoke, the words tasted like ash in his mouth.

"I will keep your secrets, *aziz-am*."

Bishop Felix emerged from the interior of the monastery and moved into the darkened street. Shukra followed the cowled figure, but Felix went nowhere more interesting than into the church to pray before returning to his bed.

The acrid taste of disgust on Shukra's tongue had nothing to do with the bishop and everything to do with his own guilt. He thought of Laurentius's grey eyes and hidden pain, of Athanagild's terrible, haunted loneliness. Tomorrow, Bishop Felix would ride for Toletum. Laurentius planned to accompany him and, Shukra knew, to visit Athanagild. Shukra knew he could have prevented his friend from going, could have honoured Athanagild's wishes. He knew that Athanagild's secrets could not withstand Laurentius's scrutiny, and that when they were shown the light, Laurentius's rage at Shukra for concealing them might well undo even their long friendship.

In Toletum, Shukra knew, he would finally face Laurentius's inevitable rage. He paused for a moment and leaned his head against the rough stone. "I do not seek your forgiveness," he whispered, and he did not know if he spoke to Laurentius, Athanagild, or Ahura Mazda, the One who saw all. "I will never seek forgiveness, for there is none for the man who knows evil and yet sends an innocent to face it. I will not shy from my guilt as do those hollow men before their crosses. I will mend what I may and carry the rest, for a man's shadow is not a thing that can be left behind with prayers in a church, no matter how magnificent the roof above it."

15

LAURENTIUS
DECEMBER, AD 690

Toletum, Spania
Toledo, Spain

L aurentius paused at the wicket leading to the monastery. Taking a deep breath, he pushed it open, trying to ignore the slow, dull thud of his heart.

He was halfway to the great wooden doors when a voice spoke from the darkness by the trees.

"If it is me you search for, you have found me."

Laurentius swung around, his hand automatically reaching for the sword at his side. He relaxed his grip on it when he saw the slender, pale-faced figure who stepped into the faint light cast by the moon.

"Athanagild." He smiled involuntarily in welcome, a smile that faded as he saw the drawn tension in the boy's face. "Ilyan has sent word," he said, the years of discipline making his tone coolly impersonal despite the emotion warring within.

Athanagild waved impatiently. "Our own messengers brought word already that Giscila has been seen in Carthage."

"You know Lælia will be in danger, then." Slightly taken aback by the harsh response, Laurentius stepped forward, an arm outstretched; then he checked himself, suddenly grateful for the night's shadows that hid the stain he could feel on his face.

"I know." Athanagild had not moved away from his arm. He stood beneath the wide branches of an old holm oak, staring at Laurentius through cavernous eyes that held secrets Laurentius could not read. "I know, too, that Oppa is gone – sailed east toward Theo, we must presume." Tension flickered in his jaw. "Of course, I should know none of this, so I cannot speak of it to any." He said the last in bitter accents, his face tight and closed. Laurentius felt his heart twist in sympathy.

"It is not your responsibility to listen to such whispers," he said roughly. "I know you feel you should help. I would not have you listen at doorways, nor risk your own life, simply to pass me the gossip of churchmen and politicians."

"Gossip?" Athanagild gave a short, humourless bark of laughter. "Is that what you think I do here, Laurentius? Listen to gossip?"

His face was entirely devoid of colour except for his eyes, which glittered a strange, hard gold, visible even in the grey shadows of night. His voice held a brittle, mocking tone that pierced Laurentius to the core. Reaching out, he gripped one narrow shoulder, surprisingly firm and hard for such a slender young man.

"Athanagild," he said gently, "I have always known you to be more perceptive than most. But you also have much in common with your brothers. Your loyalty, your sense of duty; all of these matter to you just as they do to Alaric or Theo. I know your loyalties must be torn between the Church and your family –"

"You know nothing!" Athanagild flung the words at him and Laurentius stepped back, shocked by the barely suppressed fury in his voice. "You think you understand the truth of the Church? You know the barest fragments of it. You have no idea of the evil of these men. No concept of what corruption they conceal, what dark ambitions they hatch in the name of God. Sisebut's support for Sunifred's cause is only the beginning." He glared at Laurentius, fists clenched into hard balls at his side, looking so very much like Alaric in a rage that Laurentius forgot, for a moment, that the two were not blood-born brothers. "Do you think all that is at stake here is soil and coin? Or that I care only for the blood my family will spill trying to win it?"

"I think," said Laurentius quietly, trying not to betray his shock, "that I know very little indeed, Athanagild, of what your true sufferings are." He studied the face before him, the high jaw and glittering eyes, and for a moment he saw the naked agony in the back of them and felt his body seize with such longing and pity that he would have crushed the boy to him had the doors of the monastery not flung open at the same moment, casting a sickly yellow light on the flagstones beyond.

"Athanagild – are you here?"

Sisebut stepped out into the night, frowning into the shadows where they stood. It was not his face, though, that Laurentius noticed, but the possessive, almost petulant note in the priest's voice.

It was not the stern tone of a master to his student, Laurentius thought, with a sudden roiling of disgust in his belly. It was the caressing note of a lover.

"I am here," said Athanagild, his voice low and quiet, submissive. "I am fortunate, Father. My uncle, Laurentius, has just this moment arrived."

"Your uncle!" Immediately the tone changed, assumed the haughty note of authority, and Sisebut stepped into the darkness, holding his hand with its heavy ring out for Laurentius to kiss.

Swallowing his revulsion, Laurentius stepped forward and bent over the pudgy flesh, which bulged obscenely over the thick gold. When he pressed his lips to the fat ruby at its centre, he noticed that the priest's hand smelled of lavender and something else – something that made his gut churn.

When he raised himself again to standing, Athanagild was at Sisebut's side, his face composed and showing none of the wild emotion of moments ago. It was disconcerting to see how readily the blank mask descended – and how complete it was.

"You are far from Hispalis, my dear Severianus." From the coldness in Sisebut's tone, it was clear he did not find the fact a welcome one. Laurentius did not smile.

"Indeed," he said levelly. "And yet – as you may recall, Your

Grace – I have a library in Toletum. One the Church has freely availed itself of in my absence, I note."

"All knowledge belongs to God." Sisebut eyed him disdainfully. "You did not, I think, object when Julian perused your library. Are you now to dishonour his memory by withholding that which belongs, by right, to God?"

"Julian was a friend to my family." Laurentius felt a faint catch in his throat at the memory of the old patrician. Stern though he may have been, the archbishop had been his last link to Laurentius's own father. He felt the loss keenly.

"And I, I take it, am not considered as such by you – or those who follow you."

"Those who follow me?" Laurentius smiled coldly. "You flatter me, Your Grace. I lead no thiufa. Nor, as you are well aware, do I sit on the king's council. I wield far less influence than Your Grace appears to believe."

"I doubt that." Sisebut stepped closer, reaching out as he did so, a faint movement of the arm that drew Athanagild to his side. It was a subtle gesture, but one of ownership, nonetheless – and of challenge. If Laurentius had needed any more confirmation that Sisebut suspected what he himself was, the light, gloating smile that passed over the archbishop's face was enough. He felt his stomach lurch in loathing and rage, and he bit down hard on it, refusing to give Sisebut the satisfaction of confirming what he obviously suspected to be the truth.

Ignoring Athanagild, he forced his face into a more amenable expression. "Perhaps, Your Grace," he said in a milder tone, "we may come to some kind of arrangement that suits us both. In the meantime" – he bowed courteously – "please feel at liberty to avail yourself of any works in my library that may assist you in your contemplations. Athanagild" – he nodded carelessly at the young man, who stared at him from hollowed eyes, turned now to the rich hazel of a pond at midday, eyes destined to haunt his every waking moment now that he knew the burden they carried – "please ensure your father receives the news I brought about the progress of our training, as I will not have time to visit him in person."

"Of course." Sisebut's fat lips pursed in a sneer. "You persist still in this folly of yours – this fleet?"

He said the last words with a delicate emphasis that clearly conveyed his belief in the inherent futility of any such force.

"I am aware of the king's disdain for our efforts," said Laurentius calmly. "But, yes, nonetheless, I do. Unless the Arabs cease their somewhat relentless progress across the sands of Africa, I intend to ensure I do my best to train the men of Spania to defend her."

"Arabs!" Sisebut laughed contemptuously. "Heathen fools who follow a false God. They will perish beneath His hand and suffer beyond death for their heresy, as will all those who turn their face from His wisdom."

"Indeed," murmured Laurentius, clenching his fists behind his back so the priest did not see the knuckles turn white. "I am certain you are correct, Your Grace. But until that happy day arrives, it is my duty to ensure the readiness of our men – just as it is yours to ensure that their souls are clean and free of sin." He let his eyes slide to Athanagild at Sisebut's side, and a faint sneer entered his voice. "It is well," he said, injecting his tone with a contempt that cost him dearly, "that your father is unaware of your benefactor's... desires, Athanagild. Suinthila, as you know, feels strongly that every man's duty is to his country first. I fear he would not agree with His Grace's opinions." He looked at Sisebut with hard eyes and had the satisfaction of seeing the archbishop look disconcerted and, more gratifyingly, suddenly unsure as he looked between his young charge and the tall, grim-faced figure of Laurentius. "Do not think," said Laurentius softly, "that you know me well, Archbishop. I have been away from Spania many years. Both manner and custom are different in other places. But there are certain proclivities that are universally despised. Particularly when they are indulged by those who have sworn themselves to God." Laurentius could not bear to look at Athanagild. He knew he could not hold to his grim facade if he did. And everything, he knew, depended on Sisebut believing his lie. He knew, suddenly, why Athanagild had been so loath to meet with him. He had not wanted Laurentius to see this, to know the truth of what he suffered. And one glimpse into the dark desperation Athanagild was living had told Laurentius everything he needed to know about the danger Athanagild would be in should Sisebut suspect anything but the most distant connection between them.

Sisebut drew himself up stiffly, but he could not hide the note of anxiety in his voice, nor the fear lurking in his eyes when he spoke. "I fear I miss your meaning, Severianus. Neither my loyalty nor my... piety... would ever fail to be the highest exemplar." He stepped a little away from Athanagild. "I ensure all those in my care know their duty." Laurentius looked at him with hard eyes, and Sisebut shrank slightly from the coldness he saw there.

"I have no doubt," said Laurentius softly, "that you take great delight in showing my nephew his... duty." He could see Athanagild's stricken face from the corner of his eye, but he did not trust himself to meet the betrayal and hurt he knew he would find there. Instead he gave Sisebut a curt, contemptuous nod, turned, and strode from the grounds.

The final expression of doubt and serious discomfort he had seen in the archbishop's face did not, for a moment, eclipse the terrible pain he had seen in Athanagild's.

"I HAD NO CHOICE." Laurentius paced the floor of his father's Toletum study. "If that bastard Sisebut realised what I am, or thought for one moment he could use me as a pawn in his game, Athanagild would not only have been exposed but his very life put in danger. As it is, I have not entirely convinced Sisebut, only put doubt into his mind. Enough, I hope, to make him tread cautiously." He stopped pacing and turned to stare at Shukra. The little Persian leaned against the corner of the bookshelf, his arms folded in a deceptively nonchalant posture, dark eyes inscrutable as he watched Laurentius. "Well?" Laurentius demanded. "Spit it out! It is unlike you to remain silent when you have such a spread of sins with which to tax me."

"With which to tax you?" Shukra spoke quietly. He lowered his head and shook it once, slowly. "I have been knowing for many long months what this animal is doing to that young man. Months,

Laurentius. And I am staying silent, *aziz-am*. Azura Mazda has watched my silence."

"Months?" Laurentius stared at him. "You knew this – and did nothing?"

"I knew this and did nothing." Shukra raised his eyes to Laurentius and opened his hands in a gesture of surrender. "I am being yours to kill, *aziz-am*. There is nothing you can say to me that I am not already saying to myself."

"But… he confided in you? Athanagild?" Laurentius felt the colour drain from his face.

"He did not need to."

"How could you have let it continue? Allowed that sick bastard –" Laurentius broke off, the unspoken words mixed in his mind with the stricken pain on Athanagild's face. He gripped the back of the chair so hard the wood forced its design onto his palm. "I made what he is a sin," he whispered, the words rasping painfully in his throat. "I thought that if Sisebut believed me disinterested in Athanagild in that way, believed I didn't share his proclivities, that he might lose interest in the boy and better guard himself. I let my disgust show." His head felt heavy and thick. Laurentius lowered it into his hands. They were cold, the shape of the chair forced into the bloodless flesh. "God help me," he whispered. "I all but told Athanagild he disgusts me. What have I done?"

"Nothing that cannot be undone!" Shukra came to his side, concern on every line of his face. "You must be telling him, *aziz-am*. What you are – what he is. That this is not the sin your foul Church must insist upon it being. That you are understanding, my friend."

"Why?" Laurentius spoke as if he had not heard Shukra speak. "Why would he tell you and not me? Am I so dreadful a man – is what I am so very plain? Was he afraid?"

"Oh, *aziz-am*."

Laurentius spun from the sympathy in Shukra's face, and his own expression hardened. "And do not think," he said harshly, "that my own sins expiate yours. That you knew this all the time, Shukra, and did not stop it, that you allowed that twisted, sick bastard to defile that beautiful young man. Yes, I hope your Azura Mazda is a benign, forgiving God. Because I must tell you, Shukra, I am not."

A tense silence was broken by a servant at the door. "Fráuja," he said, looking between the two men curiously. "Bishop Felix is here to see you."

"Bring him in," said Laurentius tersely, not taking his eyes from Shukra's.

The servant cast them another curious glance and backed away, leaving the door partly ajar.

When Laurentius spoke again, his face was bleak, his tone flat. "I forbid you to approach Athanagild again, Shukra. I do not know what games or whispers have brought you to his door, but you will desist. I can do little, but I will ensure he feels no burden to endear himself to Sisebut on your behalf. And for the time, at least, remove yourself from my house and from my sight. I cannot look at you any more than I can look at myself." He turned, putting his back to his friend.

Shukra, seeing the rigid tension in the hard shoulders, swallowed the pain in his chest. "As you wish, *aziz-am*," he said softly.

Turning, his heart heavy, Shukra met Felix's quiet figure in the corridor. The bishop stared at him with the austere distaste with which he always regarded a man he considered little better than a pagan heretic, and Shukra's mouth twisted in a hard smile. "Indeed, my good father," he murmured as he passed, "for once, I fear your judgement is well deserved." He walked away, feeling Felix's eyes bore condemnation through his skin as he went.

16

THEO
JANUARY, AD 691

Sebastopolis, Anatolia
Elauissa Sebaste, Cilicia, Turkey

Sebastopolis, Theo soon came to realise, was a hotbed of multicultural tension – and warring ambition.

They had been billeted in a series of low buildings near the agora, the once-great marketplace. It was bound by a thick defensive wall with a grand entrance, guarded by two great lion fountains, long dry and beginning now to crumble. The wall itself was in a state of disrepair not helped by the townsfolk plundering it to build yet more dwellings to house the ever-increasing flood of humanity. But the agora still served as the central commercial district. It was surrounded by taverns catering to the thousands of soldiers who now found the port their temporary home. Theo and Silas were drinking wine in one of them, waiting for Leofric. With them was Boric, who had once been enslaved beside them and whom Theo had seen freed, long ago in the market at Carthage. They had fought side by side ever since. Boric was a good man.

Night had fallen, and the town had grown raucous. After his

victory in Thrace, Emperor Justinian II had inherited a force of Leofric's countrymen, over thirty thousand Slavs. They were hard fighters, bitter at the loss of their lands and sovereignty. Their mood had not been improved by being forced to fight for Leontios, the same *strategos* who had led the force that conquered them. Leofric had once fought alongside many of the Slavs housed in barracks they had built themselves, beyond the immediate port of Sebastopolis. Despite taking coin and grain from their Greek overlords, the Slavs maintained a lofty distance. They were hard men, and rough – recruits who followed old gods, and who had lived their lives fighting against an emperor they now found themselves reluctantly allied to. When Leofric entered the tavern fresh from an evening in their company, he looked rather the worse for the experience.

"The emperor made a deal with the Arabs," he reported.

"What kind of deal?" Theo asked.

"It seems that the Christian refugees," said Leofric, nodding at where a small group of lean, hard-faced men squatted against the wall of the agora, talking in low voices, "did not flee their homes as we thought. They are here because Emperor Justinian II gave their territory to the Arabs – in return for a share of the taxes from their lands."

Theo and Silas looked at him in surprise. "You are certain about this?" Theo said, frowning.

"*Ja.*" Leofric nodded sagely. "Come, I tell you more, away from this noise." He glanced uneasily at Boric, and even Silas frowned. Despite the months they had fought together, Theo knew that their conversation veered into territory too dangerous to risk to any but the most trusted.

"Boric stays," said Theo briefly. "He has put his sword between death and me more than once."

"Pah." Leofric gave a contemptuous sniff. "Death is having bad day if Boric's swordplay is winner." But there was no hostility in his tone, and he passed the wineskin to Boric as he spoke.

Silas gave Boric his slow smile. "Do not stand between Theo and death, *wenkai*. The boy has a knack for finding it." Jostling Boric good-naturedly between them, they moved out of the tavern.

Theo glanced at the men by the wall as they passed. The

refugees were followers of a regional priest, Ioannes Maronus, and were known locally as Maronites. Fiercely independent, when the Arabs had come to their Armenian mountain villages, they had banded together in their traditional clan groups, caught in a geographical pincer between the political machinations of Constantinople and Damascus, suspicious of both. Now some ten thousand of them lived in and around the port, alongside the same forces that frequently attacked their brethren.

They left the raucous noise of the market behind them and moved into the ruins of the theatre. It was a small place, popular for soldiers seeking privacy with local women. On the tiered benches, couples whispered together; behind large blocks near the old stage, relations of a more intimate nature frequently took place.

They climbed to the very back of the theatre and sat up high. Behind them the small port stuck out into the sea like a stubborn growth, connected to the mainland by a narrow strip of land along which men bustled at all hours, ferrying supplies, arms, and news from the boats that docked there. With the recent addition of both naval and land forces drawn from across the Empire, Sebastopolis was a seething pot of money, politics, arms, and people with competing concerns and hidden alliances. It smelled of danger and transience.

"The Arabs fight our armies to a standstill in the mountains," Leofric said. "My friends tell me there is no point to fight further east – the Arabs hold all, and they will not cede. But the same is true on this side of the mountains for the Greeks." He passed a wineskin to Theo, who drank and passed it to Silas, who in turn gave it to Boric. "It is the emperor who collects taxes from the mountains," Leofric went on. "My friends tell me they escort half of those payments to the Arabs on the other side of the passes – either by sea or by land. We are also here to subdue the rebels who would take the coin themselves – or who would bargain with Arabs to cede territory."

"And these rebels are many?" Silas asked.

Leofric nodded. "There is no loyalty in those mountains," he said, nodding sourly at the dark shadow on the horizon. "*Brarrhans minus* – my brudders – say the Christians who still hold fast are wicked fighters, fearless against both sides. Our time, they say, will be spent subduing the locals – and carrying money for emperor."

Boric spat on the ground in contempt. "This is not war," he said moodily. His eyes roamed the seething mass of humanity. "This is trouble," he muttered.

Theo tapped his leg with a restless hand, his eyes narrowed in thought. *And where there is trouble, men like Oppa find opportunity.*

"For this reason, my countrymen are stationed here." Leofric took a long pull on his wine flask. "We must hold the passes and ports on this side, or the Arabs have a clear route to Constantinople. It would not be first time they try to take those walls."

"But they have never succeeded," said Theo, remembering Laurentius speaking of the long years of the Arabic siege of Constantinople.

Leofric shrugged. "Does not mean they will not," he said simply. "We Slavs held our lands for years beyond count. Now we do not. Such is war."

They drank to this immutable fact. The sky was clouded with the scent from a hundred cooking fires, and people bustled through the streets whilst lanterns bobbed along the thin spit of land to the port.

"What of your brethren?" Theo asked Leofric. "How do they feel about doing the emperor's bidding?"

Leofric tilted his head. "Neboulos controls them. Neboulos is good man, and strong soldier, good leader. I like." He nodded.

"But?" Theo prodded him.

Leofric's face closed over, and he looked away as he pulled on the wineskin. "They will do as Neboulos instructs," he muttered. Theo, catching the undertone of defensiveness, suspected that Neboulos's instructions to his men would rely a great deal on his own conscience.

He sighed. The Slavs, he knew, were not happy. Neboulos, their leader, was no flag-waving puppet to be controlled by commanders he did not respect. And Theo was realising that nobody respected Leontios.

The commander seemed shadowed everywhere he went by Oppa's lean, dark figure, perpetually whispering in his ear. Theo had sent word to Apsimar, through Athanais, of their close alliance, but he had little to report beyond the fact that Oppa had brought horses to Leontios – and that could hardly be construed as anything other than a gift, in their current circumstances.

"So," Silas said, his deep voice somehow falling beneath the surface noise so it was both clear and yet unheard by others, "we are here to hold this port indefinitely?" His eyes narrowed as they scanned the terrain. "It is a bad place to stand," he said, nodding at the crumbling defences and wide-open plains beyond the city. All three contemplated the horizon for a moment, but there was little to say. Silas was right: it was poor country in which to make a stand.

"Come," said Theo, standing up. "Enough skulking in the corners, *ne?* We have armour to ready. We are to report to Leontios tomorrow – and I for one do not intend to do so with a sore head."

"Leontios!" Leofric spat in contempt. "He is a fool," he said. "I am missing that mad bastard, Apsimar."

"But it is Leontios's army," said Theo. "And Leontios it is we fight for now. Apsimar is gone to Constantinople. Even he must jump when the strategos commands. Leontios answers only to the emperor. Your brethren may consider him a fool, but do not forget, it was Leontios who conquered them, Leofric. No man likes to fight for the one who enslaved him."

"The man is a fool," said Leofric stubbornly. He looked at Theo and shrugged, a reluctant smile breaking out on his rough face. "But we have fought for fools before, *ne?*" He clapped Theo on the shoulder. "And no doubt, *schnecke*, we will do so again."

THE MOUNTAINS WERE HARSH, and they reminded Theo of the steep peaks near Lælia's villa. *Must everything come back to her?* he wondered, frowning as one of his men kicked a stone. They were scouting ahead of the main force, which rode into one of the mountain villages to collect their taxes, and should travel in stealth. Theo ran forward, spear in hand, staying low, eyes scanning the terrain with detached scrutiny, whilst his mind returned to Illiberis.

"Idiot!" hissed Silas fiercely as the man kicked another stone that went clattering down the path. He cast Theo a fearful look. Theo forced his face into something more approachable. He was aware that his temper was not kind, of late, and despite the man's clear remorse, he felt a sudden, unaccustomed rage within him at the small error. His fingers closed about the spear, almost willing an enemy to appear. He found himself longing for the fight, as he often had since they came to Sebastopolis.

He had not long to wait.

The Maronite rebels launched from the hillside in a sudden phalanx, taking the handful of Slavic horsemen who rode beside them in a rush of knife and spear, men rising seemingly from nowhere to take the horses first. The main body of fighters rushed the scouts with swords raised, shrieking their battle cries.

Theo felt the familiar dread rush through his body, followed by the immediate adaption of his physical senses. Time slowed, his body operating on instinct so that he must trust where it led. Now it called him to swivel; he did, and his spatha took the man behind him through the throat, just as he hurled his spear to take the one behind that.

He turned again to find Silas beside him and a line of men attacking them from the higher ground in front. Leofric was at his right, Boric beside him. In a small line, they hacked their way forward through the wall of swords coming at them. Silas whirled in front and to the left, both arms cutting his curved swords in fierce slices, taking a life with every movement. In lined battle, Silas must equip himself with spatha and spear as every other soldier did, but here, scouting in the mountains, such discipline was neither useful nor expected, and their small band of scouts had won something of a reputation for action that allowed them certain liberties. Theo was grateful for those now as he fought his way beside Silas and they cut down the men who appeared before them in a steady stream. There was something grimly satisfying in the carnage, in the fierce immediacy of battle.

"Retreat!" came the panicked cry from behind them, but none of their small band slowed or obeyed it.

"If we retreat," grunted Silas, slicing a man's throat so his blood sprayed the ground, "we are all dead."

"And," said Leofric, grinning manically as he fought close to them, "we lose money! Never forget the coin, African!"

"You," gasped Silas as he slammed two bodies together, "have your priorities very confused, Slav."

A shout of warning came from Boric, and Theo swung around in time to meet an evilly curved dagger meant for his neck. He deflected it with a quick dodge, and the man wielding it spun and leaped in the air. In a deadly, horrible flash, the steel was embedded in Boric's throat. He fell to the ground, his eyes wide with shock.

"Boric!" Theo fought around the fallen man with furious rage, cutting down any who would come near them; but it was almost over, the battered remnants of the rebel forces fleeing into the passes, beaten back and badly damaged. Theo threw his sword to the ground and grasped Boric, putting his hand to the wound to stem the bleeding. The man looked up at him through unseeing eyes, blood gurgling in his throat as he attempted to speak.

"Don't," murmured Theo, holding him close. "Don't speak, Boric. Rest now."

The man jerked in his arms, hands convulsively clutching his tunic; the eyes rolled once, toward the sea, visible on the horizon. He stiffened, then he let go, his body limp.

He was gone.

Theo stared down at the corpse. For an odd moment it seemed he was back in Illiberis, on the long-ago day when Sarah had been raped, staring down at Ilfric, the man Yosef had killed, the first corpse Theo had ever seen. Gently he brushed Boric's lids closed. It never became any easier, he thought wearily. No matter how many men he had seen die, still the finality of death had the power to shock him, just as it had all those long years ago.

He said a silent prayer for Yosef, as he did every time such memories came to him. *I hope you travel in an easier place than here, my friend,* he thought, staring at Boric's lifeless form. *And that your dreams bring more comfort than my own.*

He lay Boric's body on the hard ground and turned for camp.

17

YOSEF

JANUARY, AD 691

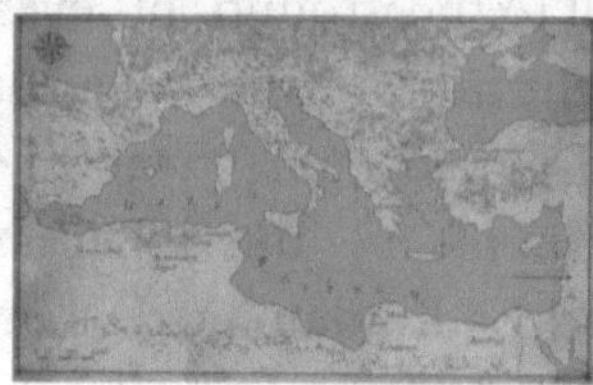

Al Sinnabra
Palace on the Sea of Galilee, Israel

"*Yosef!*" Sarah cried out to him, her face twisted in anguish. "*Yosef, help me…*"

Yosef tried to reach for her, but he couldn't break his captor's grip. A cruel voice whispered in his ear: "*You couldn't save her. You can't save anything.*"

"*Yosef!*"

"I'm coming," Yosef tried to say. "I'll save you. I promise –"

He woke, sweat cold and slick on his face, heart racing.

But I did not save Sarah, he thought dully. *I failed her.*

Rising from his bed, he washed and dressed hurriedly, trying to escape the ghosts that taunted his nights. Every day at Al Sinnabra had seemed to cast his journey more into stark parallels of success and failure, black and white. As his dreams became darker and the road ahead loomed more lonely, his ultimate goal yet more elusive, Yosef had begun to retreat from his emotions, finding comfort instead in his achievements.

Making good trade deals was success.

Making bad ones was failure.

Mohammed bin Marwan, brother to the caliph, had proved to be a tough ground on which to measure both.

It had taken Yosef the best part of the month in Al Sinnabra to have letters of accord drawn up, and in that time he had learned much about the Arabic mind and the manner in which business was conducted.

Mohammed was such an interesting – and interested – companion, Yosef would frequently become so engaged in conversation that he would forget the object he had set out to accomplish. Only at the end, after he had spoken exhaustively on a topic Yosef had not even considered important before they began speaking, would Mohammed lightly return to the figures they had originally been discussing, and Yosef would find he had somehow talked himself into a position that gave Mohammed the advantage in the debate. Such was the genteel urbanity of the brother of the caliph that Yosef rarely realised he was engaged in a negotiation at all – until it dawned on him that he had come out the worse off without understanding quite how it had happened.

As he became more adept in the language and in the style of conversation, spending long hours each day with Mohammed, he began to gain a sense of the nuances of speech and the meandering way in which the negotiations were conducted. Not least, this was because Mohammed himself had an equal fascination with the Western mind and so often shared experiences with Yosef to gain his opinion and perspective.

One of these discussions centred around a recent negotiation between Mohammed's brother, Caliph Abd al Malik, and Emperor Justinian II, in Constantinople.

"We fought the Greeks in the mountains of Armenia," Mohammed told Yosef. They were walking along a coastal path dotted with date palms, overlooking the bay, the horizon hazy in the late afternoon sea air. "Armenia is the passage to Anatolia and to Constantinople. The Greeks defend the mountain passes fiercely, and we were unable to cross into their lands. But we did take most of Armenia itself. The Christians there have proven stubborn and resistant. They follow their own brand of Christianity and have little allegiance to any outside their own clan. They withdrew to their mountain fastholds and attacked our settlements and rearguard, making government difficult."

Mohammed paused to cast Yosef a wry glance. "We may accept those who worship Christ to dwell in our lands, but we do require a level of co-operation. The Maronite worshippers of Armenia would not submit or negotiate. So we came to an agreement with Emperor Justinian II in Constantinople: he would relocate the Armenians to Anatolia, where they would be absorbed into his forces. In return, we would split the taxes of Armenia and Cyprus, sharing the income of those lands under a flag of truce. We neither of us had the heart to continue waging war in those mountains."

Yosef thought this over. "The Christians themselves," he asked eventually, "the Maronites. How did they accept their relocation?"

Mohammed shrugged. "This is not my concern," he said. "I believe they have joined those recently conquered by the Greeks in Macedonia – Slavs, and other rebels against the emperor's rule, now conquered and conscripted. The emperor's forces have been much enhanced by their arrival, and his strategos, Leontios, trains them now with his naval fleet at a place on the coast known as Sebastopolis, in Anatolia."

He trains them now, with his naval fleet…

Yosef thought of Theo. Would he be there? he wondered. Might he be on his way there now?

"What is it?" asked Mohammed, watching him. "It is unusual for a Jew to have such concern for conquered Christians."

"I have a friend," said Yosef. "From Spania. He is in the Karabisianoi, the emperor's fleet. I was thinking of him, wondering if he may be in the place you speak of."

"A Jew, fighting for the emperor?" Mohammed raised his eyebrows.

"He is not a Jew," said Yosef. "He is a Goth, a Christian. He… suffered a great deal, when first he left Spania. Much of it on my account. I would hope to see him well. I owe much."

Mohammed's face slipped into an understanding smile. "We are similar, you and I," said Mohammed. They had reached the edge of the cliff path. The sun was falling, and the dusk was purple and rose, hazy with dust and sea salt. The call to prayer would resound in a moment. Mohammed paused and took out his prayer mat, untying it as he spoke. "We have both been given tasks for which others must suffer, even those we care about. But nothing great is achieved without suffering, Yosef, remember that. For every negotiation you make, something must be lost for something to be won. You are about to go into the lands of the Persians, magicians and masqueraders all, men who follow pagan sorceries and beguile with words and beliefs as seductive as they are poisonous. And after that, to the land of Serica, where fearsome creatures live, and, it is said, they allow a woman to sit on the throne. If you survive all of this, to Constantinople you will travel − to the heart of the most corrupt regime in the Circle of Lands, rich in coin but destitute in moral integrity." He turned to Yosef and smiled.

"So it is good you are able to practise your negotiations with one as benign as me, is it not?"

The call to prayer wailed across the water. Mohammed raised his hands to the sky and began to pray.

"I DISLIKE YOU TRAVELLING ALONE." Bagay frowned worriedly as Yosef packed his meagre belongings.

"Then come with me," Yosef joked, smiling at him.

Bagay did not return the smile. "I would that we could. I tire of living amongst these Arabs."

"You do?" Yosef cast him a curious glance. "But you and Khanchla are welcomed, treated well, are you not?"

"Exactly." Bagay pursed his mouth. "Can I tell you something, Yosef?"

"Of course." Of the two, Yosef was closer in friendship to the younger brother. Khanchla had a hard edge that reminded Yosef somewhat of Alaric, Theo's older brother. Bagay had a softer nature and seemed to see more in situations, much like Yosef himself.

"Our mother sent us here to infiltrate the caliph's palace, learn what we could, and return to her. She believed that the Arabs would accept us as Jews, where they would not as pagan tribesmen."

"In this, she was correct, was she not?"

"Mohammed believes us to be Jews, that much is true. But he knows, too, that we are of the tribes. And he is too wily a strategist to think the tribes his allies." Bagay's face was grave. "Why would the Arabs be so willing to accept two of their sworn enemies into the highest echelons of their leadership, into their palace itself? They have shared with us their secrets of weaponry, of tactics and warfare, even training us amongst them, as if we were Arabs ourselves. Why would an enemy do that?"

"Perhaps Mohammed seeks to seduce you to his way of thinking – to his prophet and beliefs?"

"Perhaps." Bagay looked unconvinced. "I have a different opinion. Would you like to hear it?"

Yosef nodded, continuing to fold his belongings and put them away. He hated packing. No matter how many times he did it, it always seemed to be a lesson in sacrifice – this must go, this be left behind.

Much like the people in my life, he thought sourly. He was not looking forward to being without the company of Bagay and Khanchla. They had become his family in these strange lands. Now he would be alone once more.

"I think the Arabs do not concern themselves at all with any threat we may pose, because they know already that our defeat is guaranteed." Bagay's flat tone stopped Yosef cold. He turned to look at Bagay.

"Defeat guaranteed? What do you mean?"

Bagay shrugged. "I have watched them for months now," he said. "I have seen how they train, and fight. Together, like one body, just as my mother's Riders do. But there are more of them, Yosef. Many more than my mother could ever recruit or train. And this is but a small detachment of a far greater force. This is an army that fought the Greek emperor to a truce. That defeated the khan of the Persians. That rules, now, as much as half the Circle of Lands, with plans to take the rest. And the Arabs do not fight simply for coin, Yosef, though the gods know they care for it as much – more – than any man. They do so in the name of their prophet, and for the society they create in his name. When men truly believe, they will fight to the death in a way they will not for coin alone."

"But your people – the Imazighen – they fight also for what they believe, for their land and gods, surely?"

Bagay looked troubled. "My people will fight together when our home is threatened," he said. "But we are not united. We never have been. When the immediate threat passes, we disperse, return to our villages and the sands, to survival and family. To create a standing army, a system of government such as my mother dreams of – when I watch the Arabs, I see a people who can do that. I do not believe my own people capable of such cohesion. Not in their soul, nor their habit."

"Then you believe your people doomed to fall to the Arabs?"

Bagay shrugged. "The Arabs believe it. What does it matter what I believe?"

18

LÆLIA
FEBRUARY, AD 691

Montibus Awras, Mauretania
Aures Mountains, Algeria

Lælia was drilling with sword and spear when Dahiya sought her out.

"Now thrust," panted the Rider coaching her. To one side, Tosius looked on, the little tribesman's eyes gleaming as he watched Lælia whirl and duck beneath the onslaught.

"Spear," grunted the Rider, and Lælia came up from a crouch using her body to propel the spear into the target behind him. She whirled and ducked, thrusting the sword before her as she reached for the short knife at her side with her other hand. When she finished, the knife was held at the man's heart and his face wore a reluctant smile. Tosius leaped up from his customary squatting position, clapping and crowing his delight.

"You improve, child." At the sound of Dahiya's slow handclap Lælia swung around, hair stuck to her face with exertion.

"I have little else to do than train." Her attempt at a nonchalant shrug did little to hide her gratification, and there was no sting in her words. The long desert nights had given Lælia much solitude to ponder Dahiya's words, just as the long, hard days of training had served as a shield between her and the decisions that must, soon, be made. It had been almost a year since she left Spania, and many months since leaving Ilyan's court. It was a strange limbo. Dahiya's messengers brought word that Giscila sailed the coast, clearly seeking word of her whereabouts. She did not like his nearness and her own passivity. Nor would she do anything that played into the hands of Oppa – or Egica. Lælia knew that even now Theo's brother Alaric may be riding to civil war. Her grandfather might be riding beside him. She pushed the thought away, as she did every time it came.

"I said we would ride into the desert together." Dahiya nodded dismissal to the Rider coaching Lælia, and he left. "Be ready to leave before mid-morning." Tosius flitted like a shadow to Lælia's side, and Jadis curled between her legs. Dahiya's mouth twitched. "You have an army of your own, even here," she murmured, before fixing Tosius with a stern eye. "You will remain in camp." Seeing his face darken, she grinned at him. "Do you think yourself better able to defend her in the sands than I, little man?" Tosius glared at her and folded his arms, but his clear disapproval elicited no more than a low chuckle. When they rode from camp soon after, he was left staring worriedly in their wake, whilst Jadis ran silently at their side.

"A messenger came, from Ilyan, with news of Spania," said Dahiya as they rode. The air was not yet stirred by wind, and the desert lay silent and wide about them, mountains of ochre rock soaring in jagged peaks.

"What news?" Lælia asked.

"Little you do not know. An army gathers under a man named Sunifred." She glanced at Lælia. "It must be a significant force, though, for word of it to reach so far."

"Has Illiberis joined the rebellion?"

"That, I do not know." Dahiya looked at her curiously. "This king against whom they fight," she said.

"Egica."

"Yes. He is your enemy, no? Giscila's kinsman, and father to Oppa?"

Lælia nodded.

"Surely, then, your people will fight against him?"

Lælia paused. "It would seem simple," she said slowly. "But as you yourself once told me: 'There is more at stake than petty revenge.'"

"Ah." Dahiya's smile was a brief flash of humour. "I am surprised to hear you approve of such restraint."

"There was a time I did not." Lælia remembered her anger, in the dark days when all had thought Theo dead. "I wanted revenge. War."

"What altered your mind?"

"Theo," said Lælia simply. "And Yosef. The realisation that they were still out there, despite all that had befallen them. Fighting for Spania. Or the idea of it, at least. The dream of Mater Spania, for which my grandfather once wielded steel, and which my ancestors have fought for countless times." She met Dahiya's eyes. "You fight here for Altava," Lælia said. "An independent nation, ruled by the Imazighen, independent of overlords. Spania won that right. In my grandfather's own lifetime, our armies drove the Greek emperor's forces from our shores and united under the Chrismon-and-peacock symbol in Toletum. For almost a generation we have had relative peace, been a united nation with our own laws." An image of Yosef's father, screaming in pain as he burned alive, crossed her mind. "No matter how unjust some of those laws might be," she went on, "we have fought hard for the right to make them ourselves. Even Yosef, I think, does not wish to see Spania ruled by a foreign power once more. For this reason, his mission must succeed. And now that I am here" – she gestured around at the training men – "and see the force you fight against, I understand it even more."

"Your own soil," said Dahiya. "Illiberis, from whence your horses come. Acantha once told me that it is the women who hold this soil."

Lælia nodded. "We hold its secrets, yes. Illiberis is passed through the female line."

"Then you rule it as equals with your men? Your grandmother, she rules in Illiberis now?"

Lælia frowned. "Acantha rules the tribes, raises our horseflesh. My grandfather does not interfere with what she does."

"But it is your grandfather who is the Count of Illiberis?"

Lælia was quiet. Dahiya's questions raised uncomfortable memories. Of the day she had first learned she was to be betrothed to Theo, when she had felt as if both she and Illiberis were no more than horses to be traded at market. The deep, visceral sense of betrayal at the thought that it would be Theo who would one day bear the title of count. Oddly, though, Lælia realised she had never paused to think that Acantha, too, had suffered that same fate. Her grandmother had been born to Illiberis just as she, Lælia, had. Yet when Lælia thought of Illiberis, it was her grandfather's rule she recalled. Even if Acantha's teachings lived within her, Lælia knew her grandmother had never ruled, had never held control over the reins of Illiberis. Even now, as war grew, the choice to fight or not would lie with Paulus, not with his wife.

"It will be different with Theo and me," she said aloud. "Theo knows Illiberis is mine, that nothing matters to me more than my home. He will respect my decisions, and my ruling of it."

"I am sure he will." Dahiya turned a knowing smile to her. "Although I don't recall asking that question."

Lælia tightened her mouth and turned away, unwilling to let Dahiya see how much the conversation had unsettled her. "I meant to answer your earlier question, when you asked why we do not throw Illiberis into this war. Just as you do for Altava, I know that Theo and Yosef fight for Spania, for the future of our nation, not just for that of Illiberis. I know this is what my grandfather fights for. It is why he does not allow his 'petty revenge' to govern his decisions."

"And you, Lælia? Do you, also, put the future of your nation above Illiberis?"

In her mind Lælia saw the high peaks of the mountains that surrounded Illiberis. She smelled the figs, dusty with summer heat, and the heady scent of citrus. She saw the foals she and Theo had caught at birth, running high on the grassy plateaus in the early-morning light, the rush of mountain water fresh on the air.

She felt the dark caves and the wisdom held there, the old ways of water and stone and women.

"Illiberis is mine," she said fiercely. "It is my blood and my soul, what I am and what my daughters will one day inherit. Nothing can ever alter that."

"Ah." Dahiya was no longer smiling. "Then you do not fight the same war as your grandfather, or your betrothed, Lælia. You fight for your land, for your heart." She struck her chest, as Lælia had seen her do when she spoke of Altava with her men. "I believe in the dream of a nation, just as your men do. In the end, though, it is the sands for which I fight. They own me as I do them. I will die on them if I must. The desert belongs to me as I belong to it." They crested a rise and the ochre mountains disappeared, giving way to a wide, featureless bowl beneath. "Your grandfather, Theo, Yosef — they fight for Spania, for the concept of a nation and what it stands for. But if you belong to Illiberis in the way you say you do, then your war is not for Spania, Lælia." The darkness in the eyes she turned to Lælia made the other shiver. "It is for Illiberis — and it is a war that belongs to you alone."

They rode in silence for a time, Dahiya's words turning over in Lælia's mind, worrying at her like loose threads on a loom. Dahiya, too, was withdrawn for a time. As they rode through the valley, she finally spoke. "You said your family fight against the King of Spania because they understand the Arabic threat, and the king does not."

Lælia nodded. "Laurentius understood it, when he returned from fighting for the emperor against the Arabs. He, in turn, convinced my grandfather. Now that I have been here, I feel sure that Yosef, and Theo, too, must also have realised it. Why else would they have carried on against such daunting odds? Theo could have come home. There would have been no shame in it. But he did not. I thought, at first, it was out of loyalty to Yosef that he stayed. But now that I am here" — she shook her head, taking in the vast, rippling sands and the tired, scarred men who still laughed as they trained with grim determination — "I know it is more than that. I know that Theo and Yosef fight for Spania, for the future of our nation."

"This Giscila." Dahiya's face was grave. "Do you think he is loyal to the king and his bastard son? To Spania?"

"I know nothing of Giscila at all." Lælia's voice was harsh, even to her own ears. "Oppa, though, is a different matter." She frowned. "He is many things, most of them dark. He is not, however, lacking sense. If Theo and Yosef – and I – perceive the Arabic threat, then surely Oppa does too." She looked at Dahiya. "I've been thinking on it since news came that Oppa had left Spania again," she said. "Oppa is the bastard son of the king. Here, that is perhaps not so important."

She coloured faintly, not wanting to allude too obviously to the fact that Dahiya's own sons were widely considered to be the bastard sons of the Greek commander, Apsimar. Dahiya's faint smile said she knew exactly what Lælia was thinking, but the older woman said nothing, just waited for her to continue.

"In Spania," Lælia went on hastily, "Oppa's illegitimacy means he will never rule. Egica has his own, legitimate son, Wittiza. Even though our law states a king must be elected by the council, when the council is chosen by the king, such things are already certain. It is rumoured that Egica plans to name his son as co-ruler as soon as the boy can stand above his hip. Oppa might rise in the Church or become a powerful lord – but he will not rule."

"You think that perhaps he has ambitions beyond what his father plans."

"I think he is the most ambitious man I know." Lælia looked squarely at Dahiya. "Perhaps he has decided there is another way to take power. One not allied to his father."

"Do you think he would have shared this plan with Giscila?"

"Oppa is suspicious," Lælia said slowly, remembering the black eyes and hard, shuttered face. "He trusts nobody – not really. Whatever use he would have for Giscila, it would be to serve his own ends."

"I know a little of this Giscila." Dahiya's mouth curled in contempt. "He is a man without honour, one for whom only coin is king. I can believe he wishes to return to Spania – but not to serve, or save, his country. Rather for his own redemption, to see his pride assuaged, and to receive the riches he believes he deserves, to assume the position he feels was taken from him. When I met him years ago, he told me he was 'brother to a king'. I have never forgotten those words. No man of true worth would ever claim honour by association." She looked soberly at Lælia. "Giscila, too, trusts nobody. I think we must tread very warily whilst he is close."

Lælia thought of Oppa, edging ever closer to Theo and Yosef.

"Theo has been far from Spania for a long time," she said quietly. "And nothing unites men more than a common enemy. I hope he is not seduced by Oppa's lies."

"Theo knows Oppa better than you ever will," Dahiya said bluntly. "He bears the scars of Oppa's hatred, and he will all his days. I do not believe him so easily fooled – and nor should you." She looked closely at Lælia. "'Seduced' is an odd word. Is it only Oppa's lies you fear have entranced your lover?"

Lælia coloured. "He is not my lover. We are betrothed. Not married."

Dahiya raised her eyebrows. "It would be better, I think, if you had lain together."

Once, her words would have shocked Lælia. Now, however, remembering the dreams of Theo, the shadow form that turned away from her, angry and somehow shielded, a woman standing between them, her mouth tightened.

"Yes," she said shortly. "I think it would have been better, too."

Dahiya glanced sideways at her, then drew their camels to a halt. The wind had begun to pick up. The valley had widened into a large, featureless plain upon which Lælia could no longer discern any visible landmark. Dahiya muttered something and Lælia's camel dropped down to couch on the ground. "Dismount," Dahiya ordered.

Lælia obeyed. Then she stared in surprise as Dahiya murmured a command and the camel rose again. The older woman looked at Lælia over the folds of her turban, her eyes dark and distant. "Now," she said, "I will leave you."

"Here?" Lælia looked at her in astonishment. The wind was growing, and even the few paces between Dahiya and herself were becoming blurred. "Am I to find my way back to the adwwar?"

"No." Dahiya's face was disappearing, but her voice was still clear. "It is always easy to find what is familiar. I don't want you to find your way home, Lælia. I want you to track the camels and me. You will find me eventually, and you will have your camel with you when you do."

"But you have my camel," Lælia said, squinting into the sand gloom.

"Do I?" Dahiya's mocking laugh drifted through the sands. "Perhaps. I definitely have your cat."

"Jadis!" Lælia spun around, searching for her golden shadow.

Her cat, though, was gone.

The wind grew, sand obscured the sun, and Lælia was alone in the desert.

19

THEO
FEBRUARY, AD 691

Sebastopolis, Anatolia
Elauissa Sebaste, Cilicia, Turkey

Theo had found himself uncharacteristically withdrawn since leaving Boric's body to rot beneath a thin layer of rocks on the mountainside. His reticence had been hardly noted amidst the constant movement of collecting taxes and safely bearing them to the treasury in Sebastopolis, all the while fighting constant raids by those intent on stealing the coin they were charged with.

Money and blood. It seemed, to Theo, that this was all Sebastopolis was about. After the long months training beneath Apsimar's dynamic, single-minded focus, the drudge and rude bureaucracy of Leontios's army was depressing and somehow rotten at the core. Theo could smell the corruption from miles away, in the rubbish that burned on the edge of town and in the thin, starving women who camped at the outer perimeter, clutching their tunics and offering their dirty, ravaged flesh in exchange for a few coins.

Beneath his cool surface, Theo felt the emotions within him like the famous fire mountains of Greece, ready to erupt without warning. His disturbed dreams of Lælia left him frustrated with desire. His disgust at the manner of war they waged left him ashamed. And the death of good men such as Boric made anger surge through him in a red tide. He kept the volatility locked behind a disciplined, terse silence that occasionally escaped in an uncharacteristically sharp rejoinder. He snapped at Silas's efforts to cut through his mood, and he barely smiled at Leofric's bawdy humour which, anyway, had been notably muted in recent times. Leofric had spent more time in the Slavic camp recently, and Theo suspected he suffered some internal conflicts as a result.

One evening when they finished at the docks, Theo shook off Silas's offer of company as he watched Leofric walk away in the company of some of his Slavic friends. He turned from the watchful concern in Silas's eyes and stalked alone through the narrow alleyways. He knew where he was going, and he did not want company.

Athanais had established herself in a small, well-situated house far enough away from the agora that a measure of peace could be found. The interior was clean and welcoming, with frankincense rising from a brazier in the corner and tasteful hangings on the walls. The men who came here could afford more than a rough tumble – and they valued the more sophisticated company offered by Athanais's stable.

Elpis was employed by Athanais as a server. Theo knew the Persian woman did not like young girls to do anything other than serve as background colour. It was one of the things he liked about the whore keeper, as she laughingly referred to herself, and he was grateful that she cared so for Elpis and her sister, Pelagia.

The latter ran to him when he entered, leaping into his embrace and lightening Theo's heart. He rubbed his hand through her hair and grinned at her. "What mischief today, then, child?" he said, reaching into his pocket.

"What did you bring me?" she demanded, the bright blue eyes glittering despite the dim light, her white-blonde hair almost as brilliant as his own.

"This." Theo handed her a rock. It was white quartz, run through with a rare streak of fool's gold, beautiful but of no real value. He had taken it from the cliffside where Boric now lay, and his smile faded as he looked at it.

Pelagia turned it over in her hand, delighted. Then she saw the expression on Theo's face, and her excitement dimmed, replaced by a look of understanding and a wisdom too old for her years. She reached out, cupping Theo's face with her own hand. "Did people die?" she asked quietly.

Theo nodded and found that his voice had deserted him temporarily. His arms tightened involuntarily on the little body, and Pelagia hugged his neck with her thin arms. For a long moment they stayed like that, the young, scarred soldier and the tiny child; then she patted him on the head with one small hand and pinched his ear. "Devil!" Theo swung her down, grinning, and she poked her tongue out at him, racing through the door just as her sister appeared.

"Theo," said Elpis softly, his name a caress on her lips. Theo felt his heart pause momentarily. Elpis was clad in a thin gown cut in a low V to show the curve of her breasts in the Grecian style, her arms bare beneath the clasps that held the fabric at each shoulder. The material was gathered at her sternum and fell in a sheer skirt through which the ripe curves of her body were clearly delineated.

She leaned over him to pour wine, and Theo inhaled a delicate floral scent, mingled with a slight musk that made his senses reel. He caught her hand as she moved the jug, and she let him hold it, her eyes downturned and her breasts rising and falling rapidly against the material. Theo tried not to stare at them. "Are you happy?" he asked her in a low voice. "Are you safe?"

"Yes." She peeked through her lashes at him, soft curls falling enchantingly about her face. "I know you asked Athanais to take us," she said haltingly. "We owe you everything. Your men keep this tavern safe, and us with it."

"Good." His hand tightened on hers, and she stepped a little closer so she stood between his knees. Theo felt his whole body tighten at her nearness.

"You have fought hard," she said softly. "Let me help you forget, for a time." Her hand rested in his hair. Theo ached to pull her closer, onto his leg, and take the soft lips that pouted so invitingly, but even the thought of it felt like a crevasse from which he would never again climb out.

"I cannot," he said roughly, putting her aside. Undeterred, she cupped his jaw with one hand, her eyes knowing. "Elpis," he said roughly, when a cool voice interrupted them.

"You are being asked for in the other room, Elpis, and I would speak to our guest alone, *aziz-am*. Go, now." Casting him a last, regretful look, Elpis bit her lip in a way that made Theo clench his thighs hard together beneath his tunic and swallow a large mouthful of wine, his eyes following the sway of her hips as she glided from the room.

"I have told you before," said Athanais drily. "Pay your coin for the girl or leave her be. Your self-denial is more potent than bedding her could ever be."

"Are my men taking care of you?" Theo hid his discomfort with an abrupt tone, gulping more wine to mask the flush on his face. He had ordered some of their newest recruits to keep a close eye on Athanais's tavern. She had taken into her protection a number of the youngest, most vulnerable children who haunted the port town, and Theo had no intention of allowing them to fall into the hands of Athanais's biggest competitor: Oppa.

"Have you seen… him?" Theo raised his eyes to her face, which darkened when he asked the question. Athanais sat at the table beside him, pouring herself a small cup of wine and sipping it thoughtfully.

"Oppa's friendship with Leontios has gone beyond horses," she said, watching him.

"You have seen him, then." Theo frowned, all thought of Elpis fleeing his mind. Athanais nodded.

"Oppa keeps a brothel beyond the village, close to the Slavic camp, tailored to their tastes." Theo knew of it. Oppa's brothel was famous throughout the settlement, known for its coarse company and cheap whores. Theo knew many of his peers frequented it, though he forbade his own men to do so. "It is not the only one he owns." Athanais watched him. "Oppa is keeping his other, more exotic offerings for a different house, one not so easily found, nor entered. Here it is that he entertains Leontios, away from interested Slavic eyes and the censure of his own men."

Theo's lip curled. "Leontios shares Oppa's sick proclivities?"

"No." Athanais shook her head. "Perhaps he is knowing of the children held there – I suspect so. But it is not this, I am thinking, that is the appeal. It is the luxury and privacy, and the lure of being cosseted in the manner to which our strategos believes he should be accustomed."

"Leontios is ambitious," said Theo, watching her.

"Just so."

"Ambition is dangerous."

She smiled. "Ambition is weakness."

"So," said Theo, "you are watching our friend, then?"

"Of course."

Behind Athanais, Elpis crossed the room. As her eyes met Theo's, she flushed and bit her lip. Theo felt his body tense again, and he forced his eyes not to fall to where her gown dipped between her breasts. He wondered, not for the first time, why he tortured himself by coming here. He found Elpis's proximity an unsettling, delicious torment. Yet he could no sooner stay away than he could imagine simply paying his coin and taking a woman, as did Silas and Leofric. As they were undoubtedly doing right now, as they did every time their band returned from the increasingly violent forays into the mountains.

"It is time you took a woman, Theo," Athanais murmured, watching him with a faint smile. "Do not allow your own desires to become your weakness."

Theo stood up, his body hot and restless, his mind in turmoil. "Do not cease watching Oppa," he said abruptly. "The man means harm to more than just me – believe it."

"Sometimes the dangers we face," said Athanais softly, "are not those we see, but those we don't wish to."

"Enough." Theo cast Elpis a final look. Throwing a coin on the table, he turned without bidding her farewell. Crossing the room with hard, uneven strides, he thrust the door aside with a violence that nearly took it from its hinges and strode into the night, craving dreams of Lælia as much as he dreaded them.

OPPA

FEBRUARY, AD 691

Sebastopolis, Anatolia
Elauissa Sebaste, Cilicia, Turkey

"I do not know where you find such wine, Spaniard – nor such women." Leontios, strategos of the imperial army in Anatolia, inhaled the aroma of the wine and sprawled rudely on comfortable cushions.

"I am pleased to accommodate such honoured company." Oppa's smile did not reach his eyes, but Leontios didn't notice. His attention was captivated by a buxom, dark-haired beauty who approached at his gesture to rest in his embrace, sultry eyes promising much. Oppa made a mental note to congratulate Nicalo on acquiring her. It was Nicalo who acted as Oppa's chief procurer, for Oppa would never allow himself to be directly associated with such dirty work. Nicalo did not object. He was paid well, had all the women he could want, and had proven obedient.

Oppa's mouth twisted; she was not to his taste, but then, the strategos had tastes both coarse and shamefully predictable. Even the wine he deemed superior was, to any refined palate, harsh and lacking subtlety. Everything about the man, Oppa thought, lowering his eyes to hide his distaste, revealed his low origins and the stink of the military barrack.

Leontios had risen to his current prominence by being both ruthless and obedient, qualities guaranteed to find favour in the emperor's forces. He had a hard, square face with a brutal cast and favoured a clipped beard that grew a thick, coarse orange. The hand that rubbed it when he was agitated was equally heavy. He had found his way to Oppa's company because his favourite pastime was employing that same hand to pummel the spirit out of the women he bedded.

It fingered the girl lying against him now. She eyed him with undisguised avarice. Oppa ensured that the women he had Nicalo find for Leontios had no contact with the others in the house before meeting him. It was Leontios's preference to seduce them first, lulling them into the mistaken belief that he was a willing fool to be milked of his coin and led by the nose. Only when he had them exultant in their imagined power did he surprise them with a brutal fist. It was a game Leontios could eke out over days.

"You have, I believe, a countryman of mine in your ranks." Oppa spoke carelessly, as if making casual conversation, but Leontios, no fool, looked at him sharply.

"I have many Spanish Goths in my service," he said non-committedly. "Your country has been known to rid itself of those who do not share its views. Many exiles find their way to the coin of the emperor."

"Yes," said Oppa meditatively, "but few are men of good birth, and even fewer rise past the lowest ranks. The man I speak of is the son of a count, and he has risen fast and far in your service."

"And why would you show an interest in such a man?" Leontios caressed the round, olive thigh of the girl with one thick hand as he spoke. Oppa tried not to look. There was dirt beneath the round nails, and the fingers were so squat as to appear like short, fat sausages.

"I have reason to believe he seeks to undermine my father's rule." Oppa studied his wine cup, watching Leontios from the corner of one eye. "Spania is currently in a state of delicate balance.

Theudemir of Aurariola is a son of those opposed to my father's house. I do not believe he is here solely to serve the emperor."

"Whilst you, Oppa, a king's son, no less, are devoted to the emperor's service. Is that what you would have me believe? No." Leontios waved Oppa away, sneering. "Don't answer that." He didn't see Oppa's hand clench on the wine cup and would likely have been unimpressed had he done so. Leontios was first and foremost a soldier. Despite patronising Oppa's premises and taking the men and horses bought with Spania's coin, he held the bastard son of Egica in a light contempt he made no effort to hide.

Laugh now, Oppa thought coldly, dropping his gaze so Leontios did not see the dark violence lurking there. *I will see you undone before we are over here.*

"I know Theudemir," said Leontios. "What is it you want, Oppa? He is a good soldier, not an easy man to be lightly rid of."

"I do not wish you to rid me of him," said Oppa. He smiled coldly. "Not yet, at least. But I should like to know where he goes, and who he meets."

Leontios looked at him quizzically. "I had thought you adept in collecting such information."

"In Sebastopolis itself, yes," Oppa said. "Here, I have the eyes I need. But when he leaves port on the business of the fleet, I am blind."

"And if I should do this thing for you," Leontios said, looking at him through narrowed eyes, "what might I expect in return?"

"You are aware that I own several houses here," said Oppa. "All of which serve a different audience." Leontios inclined his head. "I have one catering to the more affordable taste. It is close to the Slavic camp."

"I know of it."

"Usually, the Slavs monopolise that establishment. It is rough, crude, and most of all, cheap. But recently, a small group of Slavs have been patronising one of the more exclusive of my houses. One not within the financial reach of a common soldier. And when they pay, they do so with coin of a most interesting type."

Oppa held up a shining coin and flipped it through the air. Leontios caught it in his outstretched palm and held it up to the light. "Now, my sweet," he murmured to his companion, who was eyeing the gold with interest. "What do you notice about this coin?"

She leaned closer. "It has pretty decorations," she giggled, tracing the odd characters around the edge of it. "I like the way they curl. What is it that they say?"

"I do not know what they say," said Leontios. "But I know well where they come from. The script is Arabic, my pet – the language of the savages we fight to the east. Of those you know, I believe?"

The girl nodded, eyes wide. "But how do those coins come to be here?" She nestled suggestively against Leontios. "I thought you kept us safe from the Arabs?"

"A good question indeed," said Leontios, "and one with a simple answer. There is only one way Arabic coin finds itself here, in territory held by the emperor." A muscle worked in his jaw, and the thick hand tightened on her thigh. "It arrives in a chest brought from the lands in which Arabic citizens pay taxes to their caliph, which the caliph then sends here as part of his agreement with our emperor. A locked chest carried by soldiers of the emperor's forces, and never opened by any other than the highest of the emperor's officials." He looked at Oppa thoughtfully. "There is only one way coins might escape that chest," he said.

Oppa nodded once. "I believe you may have some renegades amongst your tame Slavs," he said. "Men who exchange information for coin of their own before the chest is sealed."

Leontios looked at him shrewdly. "And you offer to inform me when these renegades pay their coin?"

Oppa spread his hands wide. "Of course," he said smoothly. "That is what good allies do, is it not? Protect one another against those who would betray their interests?"

Leontios sat back and stroked his beard, smiling lazily at Oppa as he pulled the woman closer to him, rucking the material of her gown higher so he could thrust one thick hand between the dark curls at the apex of her thighs.

"Indeed, it is, Oppa Kingson," he said slowly. "Indeed, it is."

. . .

Later, after Leontios had gone and the tavern become still and quiet, Oppa sat in the darkness, turning a cup of wine on the table before him.

"Fráuja." Nicalo's figure materialised in the darkness. Oppa looked up in annoyance.

"What is it?"

"Theudemir of Aurariola." Nicalo shifted uneasily. "Would it not be safer to kill him?"

Oppa turned the cup meditatively. "Perhaps."

"Then why let him live? The mountains here are unpredictable. It would be an easy enough task." Emboldened by Oppa's silence, Nicalo went on: "You narrowly escaped accusation last year, when the Illiberis bitch came to court. If Aurariola should survive and return to Spania, you will face worse than suspicion, Fráuja. Should any discover we were behind the attack on the fleet we will both swing, king's bastard or no."

"That is true." Oppa watched his cup.

"Then why?" The cup stilled.

"Tell me, Nicalo." Oppa's voice was dangerously soft. Nicalo blanched. "Do you enjoy the coin you earn, and the whores I allow you to enjoy?"

"Of course, Fráuja, you are very generous. I was merely saying —"

"Good." Oppa cut him short. "If you wish to continue enjoying both, I suggest you cease attempting to offer advice." Nicalo, who knew well his master's capricious temper, swallowed hard and edged out of the room.

Oppa watched him go, tapping the cup thoughtfully. Nicalo, for all his stupidity, was right. Should Theo return to Spania as Oppa's enemy the results could be disastrous.

And yet.

Accustomed to being always certain of his next move, Oppa was aware that, for once, that certainty was lacking.

Sending one of Leontios's men to watch Theo was sensible, as was keeping a close eye on him here in Sebastopolis. It was also, as Nicalo said, dangerous.

Amidst the bustle of ingratiating himself with Leontios and

establishing his various businesses, both shadowy and obvious, since his arrival in Sebastopolis, Oppa had watched Theudemir of Aurariola. Had watched him at the head of his men and amongst his superiors. At rest in the company of whores and at work leading the men of the fleet. And whilst Oppa might pretend to Leontios he watched Theo as one would an enemy, Oppa himself knew it was a lie.

Oppa was beginning to see Theudemir of Aurariola as his ally.

He could not rid himself of the vision he had seen long ago, of him riding at Theo's side, of them victorious in Spania together. At times over the past weeks, in the tense cesspool that was Sebastopolis, Oppa had found himself pondering things his former self could not have imagined. He had wondered, for example, how his life might have been if, instead of setting his bastard son to work bribing men in a backstreet brothel, Egica had sent him to train in his thiufae, as so many noblemen sent their byblows to do. Had put a sword in Oppa's hand rather than a whip. If Egica had made him watch sword drills rather than the torture of whores, Oppa wondered, turning the cup methodically on the table, would he even now be Theo's companion rather than his enemy? His hand clenched the cup convulsively. Oppa knew such thoughts were dangerous. The earliest lesson Egica had taught his bastard son had been never to hope for something he could not control. *Research, plan, and contrive.* Always remain in the shadows; never become so powerful that men noticed him; be what men feared rather than what they admired. Such lessons Oppa had imbibed with the rare coins his father had tossed his way, coins Oppa had always been certain to turn into more coins. He could not remember a time when he had not thought of impressing his father, of using his place in the shadows to ensure his father shone bright.

But with every day that passed in Sebastopolis, every corrupt scheme he uncovered, and every powerful man he lured into his web, Oppa was less convinced that his father was equipped to fight the world that was coming for him. The forces of the emperor and caliph did not fight with thiufae of one thousand men for the right to take this latifundium or that. They fought with legions of many thousands, for the right to rule entire nations. They fought with fleets and complex alliances and with the deadly war-fire that could decimate fifty dromons in a matter of moments.

Oppa had been sent by his father to train in the Spanish Church because Egica wished to have eyes and ears in the only institution he believed capable of undermining his rule. Being in the Church, however, had taught Oppa more than Egica could ever know: Oppa had learned the value of patience. Men of God, he had learned, did not think in terms of one lifetime, one king. They thought instead of the Church's power, of how the Church might rule in fifty years, or a hundred. They did not plan for the glory of their sons, but for the domination of the Church itself. They looked to the past to learn their lessons and to the future to find their direction. When they built a cathedral, men of the Church knew they might never live to see it finished.

Now, Oppa found himself thinking the same way. And when he did, it was Theudemir of Aurariola he saw in Spania's future. Theo, and men like him. Men who understood the enemies they faced and how to fight them. Men who spoke the languages of the future, knew today's ally could as easily be tomorrow's enemy, and understood how to turn course as needed.

Oppa knew he did not send eyes to watch Theo because he wished to harm him. He sent them because he was fascinated by him. But Theo himself, Oppa knew, hated him still.

He dashed the wine cup from the table in an uncharacteristic burst of anger, staring into the darkness. *I cannot continue in such a way,* he thought. *Eventually, I must confront him.* Oppa had seen the way Theo watched him, when on occasion their paths crossed. Had seen the vicious hatred in the faces of his two companions, who had also felt the lick of Oppa's whip in the long-ago days when they had been held captive by him on his dromon. Such men would not easily ally themselves with the architect of their humiliation. But Theudemir himself, Oppa suspected, just might.

For all he does, Oppa thought, *Theo does from duty. His loyalty to the Jew, to the fleet — even his betrothal to Lælia — all is done from loyalty to his family, his country, his commander. He is a man of duty. If I can make him see that Spania's way forward, now, is one that perhaps he and I are the only Spaniards to understand, then I might have a chance. But how to do it?*

A memory crossed his mind. "Nicalo!" he called. His companion entered the room after a moment, eyeing Oppa warily. "There is a girl," Oppa said curtly. "Her name is Elpis. She is owned by the Persian woman, Athanais." Nicalo nodded. "Buy her," said Oppa. "Find one of her customers and inform him that he has fallen in love with the girl and wishes to own her exclusively. Send him with enough coin to ensure the Persian will not argue, but not enough to make her suspicious."

"What if the girl does not agree?"

"She has a younger sister. Make it clear to her that should she object, the child will be taken in her stead. And without any coin to sweeten the blow." He gestured to the door. "Do it soon," he said. Nicalo nodded and left, too long accustomed to Oppa's capricious temper to question the order.

Even as he planned, Oppa felt doubt corrode the edges of his resolve. He would try to make Theo see things his way. The girl should certainly help matters. His informants whispered that Theo, who was renowned for never taking whores, could barely take his eyes from her. But Oppa would also send word to Giscila, discover if he had found the Illiberis heiress. Theo was one plan. Oppa, though, would never settle for one plan alone. He was far too careful for that.

Outside, the sound of the Slavs singing their savage war songs rumbled over the hill. Inside, Oppa sat in the darkness and planned to make an ally of his enemy.

LÆLIA

FEBRUARY, AD 691

Montibus Awras, Mauretania
Aures Mountains, Algeria

Lælia had thought the desert her home. Surrounded by Riders and camels, the means to make camp and to shelter from sand, home had seemed simple and ever present. Without them, she was a stranger in a strange land. In the hours after Dahiya left her, as the wind grew and sand swirled so she no longer knew where the land ended and sky began, Lælia knew herself truly lost.

She wandered until she grew thirsty, and then she ceased wandering and hunkered down in the sands. Her *guerba* contained some water and she clutched it close to her body, reluctant to drink lest she find herself with none at all. Her logical mind told her that Dahiya would not leave her alone in the sands to die. But as the hours passed and the storm grew, her logical mind faded. As the orange world of day faded into a starless night of wind and sand in which she could neither hear nor see, Lælia found herself in a strange state somewhere between sleeping and waking. It was not the deep dreaming she had once experienced in the caves with Acantha, where visions had come to her as if she lived them. Instead, the wind scoured her clean and brought snatches of past and future to her conscious mind. The incessant gale howled through her, tearing away control over her thoughts and dredging up those that had dwelled deep within, in the places she had chosen not to see.

Dahiya's face: *Tell me. When Theo returns, what life do you imagine at his side?*

Lælia remembered the shattering betrayal she had felt the day she found the contract of betrothal in her grandfather's study. *I forgot myself,* she realised, *when I met Theo and became part of what we are together.*

Now, as the desert wind raged, she heard Acantha's words to her on that long-ago day: *All learning begins with sacrifice, and women must master the art of sacrifice early … You do not see that for women, battlegrounds come disguised as harmless things such as love or a betrothal.*

I thought my sacrifice was playing the games of the Toletum court. Lælia did not know if her eyes were open or closed in the blackness, if the thoughts were within her or without. They seemed at once on the wind and in her mind. *I thought my battleground was facing Oppa across a room.*

Now, lying amidst the wind and sand, she wondered if she had truly understood Acantha's meaning.

She felt shadows from her dreams tugging at her. Instead of waking from them, she allowed herself to walk toward them, to the distant shore where she felt Theo, the dark turbulence of his soul churning like the wind. In front of him was a girl, no older than Lælia, with a sweet face and eyes the colour of a morning sky, shining as they fell upon Theo, her lips curving in a tremulous smile of hope and welcome.

Lælia felt Theo's desire as hot and fierce as her own. She reached for him, felt the moment he turned to find her, but they were no more than shadows across a dim sea, whereas the girl was flesh and blood before him.

No, she thought savagely. *He is mine and I am his, and nothing can come between us.*

But even as she felt it she knew the futility of her thought, and she knew the sacrifice she must already make. Rough sand cut across her face like a whiplash and she did not know if the shriek on the wind was her own or the storm, but it rent the air and split her away from Theo, cutting him adrift so that the last things she saw were the two shadows meeting on the shore as she drifted away from it, back out to sea.

Theo was gone and she was alone in the storm once more. The only thing that felt real was the earth beneath her. It felt warm and alive. When Lælia dug her fingers into the sand, it was not the desert she felt but the rich soil of Illiberis, pulsing around her like a living thing, calling her home.

She glanced back across the dim sea and felt the savage bolt of longing pulling her toward the shadowy figures there. *Women must master the art of sacrifice early,* whispered the wind. Lælia drew the hot desert air into her body and with it the fierce desire back into herself, away from that dim sea. With an act of will, she turned her back on the shadowy figures and her face toward the pull of her homeland. Thrusting her hands deep into the sand, she felt desire shift inside, pulling her not to Theo now but toward the land she had sworn to protect.

I am yours, Theo, she thought, *but first I was of Illiberis, and it is to Illiberis I will forever belong.* The amulet at her neck pulsed with the heat of the desert, but whilst she could feel the coin beneath it, now it seemed the metal was warmed by the amulet itself.

Lælia lay in the sand as the wind howled overhead, and she knew it was time to find her way home.

When dawn came, the wind was gone and the sand lay in perfect ripples, all trace of Dahiya and the camels gone from it.

At first Lælia stared at the unfamiliar ground and knew only that she was lost with no means of finding her way. But the wind had taken all that did not belong in her mind, and as dawn grew, she found the emptiness left behind allowed her to perceive details that had previously escaped her. She saw where the sun rose on the horizon and recalled where it had risen the day before, and the day before that. She looked at the sand beneath her and saw the direction and flow of the ripples, seeing that in their pattern lay a story. She noticed an acacia tree in the distance that seemed to call her, though she could not say why. She took a sparing mouthful of water and set off.

Only as she drew close to the tree did she see the bare branches that had been stripped by camels, the recent droppings partially covered over by sand. She felt a surge of strength. *I am not helpless,* she thought fiercely. *I can survive, and I can find my way.*

From the tree, she found a crop of *sabay* that had been trodden down. Further, in a depression between small dunes protected from the worst of the wind, she saw where an animal had couched. Each new discovery unfurled a seed of self-reliance inside that fed her, empowered her to find another sign, and another. To know herself as part of the world and the world itself as a benign thing that could help, if only she knew where to look.

She found her camel by mid-morning, snatching feed from grasses as it wandered. It took her longer still to catch it, but when she did, she thought she knew, if not where exactly she was, at least where she should be going.

Her *guerba* had barely two mouthfuls of water left.

It was mid-afternoon when she saw the first tracks, and long shadows fell across the sand as she crested a dune and looked down upon Dahiya chewing a stalk of grass, Jadis lying peacefully at her feet. She paused for a moment, savouring the warm glow of triumph within, then slowly approached. Jadis flicked an ear lazily in her direction but did not stir.

Lælia couched her camel. Squatting in the sand by Dahiya, she returned the woman's greetings courteously, then removed the top from her *guerba* and passed it to her, as was the custom.

"The gods have given me enough," replied Dahiya quietly, but there was a light in her eyes that gave Lælia a warm sensation inside. They sat in silence for a short time.

"I must go home," said Lælia finally. "To Illiberis." Jadis stretched and rolled onto her belly, staring unblinking at her mistress. Dahiya nodded but did not say anything. "If war is coming," said Lælia slowly, "it is my responsibility to fight it."

"What do you need from me?" asked Dahiya simply.

"My grandfather will never let me take command of his forces." Lælia shook her head. "I fear that I will return to find I have no part to play."

"Then," said Dahiya, "I shall teach you how to become the part around which the play revolves. It is a story we tell ourselves, that the game occurs and we must find our place in it. The reality is that our part determines the play – no matter what the game. You have been training in your part for long enough. It is time, I think, that you make this game your own." She stood decisively. "It is time we met with Ilyan."

22

LETTER FROM ATHANAGILD TO SHUKRA
APRIL, AD 691

Toletum, Spania
Toledo, Spain

S hukra –
My letters to you have gone unanswered since Laurentius's unfortunate arrival at the monastery.

My position as Sisebut's clerk allows me unprecedented access to his affairs. Access that may prove invaluable in the days to come, for I fear it is behind God's walls that Spania's fortune will be decided. I implore you not to cease communication now. I must know I do not risk all in vain. This information is the only gift I have in my power to help you all. Do not take that from me.

Sisebut grows daily more anxious. He drinks late into the night, and his tongue becomes careless. As yet, all believe him Egica's creature – all, I suspect, but Egica himself. Egica is no fool. He comes rarely to the monastery and says little of importance to Sisebut himself. With every indiscretion of Sisebut's I become more nervous that he will be discovered. He conspires with priests in the north, men drawn from the tribes who are barely literate themselves. He pays coin to these men to launch attacks on Egica's nobles in the mountains of Gallæcia. They attack all but Favila, the youngest son of Chindasuinth, and now the nobles begin to whisper that it is a rebellion made by Favila, in support of Sunifred's. Soon it will not matter who began it — Favila will be forced to war. Egica sends men to support his allies, strengthening his forces in the north whilst Sunifred prepares in the south. Sisebut believes he acts in secret, imagines himself the mastermind of all. I do not believe Egica so gullible, but I have yet to know his games. Meanwhile in Toletum, Egica chastises Theodefred, Duke of Corduba, for his brother's seeming rebellion and holds his son Roderic close to ensure he does not join it.

It is clear Egica must eventually ride north himself. When he does, Alaric tells me that Sunifred believes he will march into Toletum unchallenged, be anointed by Sisebut, his tame archbishop, and take Spania for himself.

None of it feels real, or possible. And amidst it all, Liuvgoto writes her letters and rallies her supporters. She is not forgotten. There are those who remember her father was the greatest of Spania's kings, the man who united our nation for the first time. King Suintila was our own father's uncle and namesake. Even his name evokes patriotism in the hearts of men, a memory of a more innocent time. Liuvgoto plays on this. She does not intend to die in that monastery, a shadow of the queen she once was. She is the grandmother of the king's son. Her daughter Cixilo might be cloistered at Liuvgoto's side, but she is still the king's wife, and mother to his son. In these gifts Liuvgoto sees her path back to power. Whether that path lies with Sunifred, her cousin, or Egica, her son-in-law, I believe she has yet to decide. I write this to you now because I know Sunifred corresponds with her and heeds her advice. Warn him not to do so. Liuvgoto plays her own games.

Sometimes it seems all in Spania at this time play their own games.

You are the only person to whom I may tell these things. I hope you may find use for them, even if Laurentius, I know, is disgusted by my manner of gathering them.

—Athanagild

LETTER FROM SHUKRA TO ATHANAGILD

Athanagild —

You know Laurentius less than you think, aziz-am. But on this I can say no more.

On your role as Sisebut's "clerk" I will say, again, that I cannot accept your suffering. I will hear your news, but I do not like these games. I fear for all the children lost amidst them. But for you, aziz-am, I fear most of all.

My heart is heavy.

—Shukra

23

YOSEF

APRIL, AD 691

Eran
Iran

By the time he left the palace at Al Sinnabra, Yosef felt wearied by the games of men and trade. He had learned much from Mohammed, but he had grown tired, also, of the endless cut and thrust of their conversation, which always left him feeling he had been bested in a game he did not quite understand. He left in the predawn, before the call to prayer woke the palace. He had said his farewells the previous night and had eaten lavishly in the palace, surrounded by musicians and friends and merriment. He had not slept after. The prospect of the road ahead kept him taut and awake, calling him from his bed and urging him away. Yosef had learned that to slip away was best. Farewells only dragged out the inevitable and became wearisome in the end. People, he was learning, came and went. If he was meant to see them again, he would.

He turned his horse eastward and joined the steady flow of

humanity on the road toward Damascus. He would pass through there into the lands of Persia and onward, to Serica.

At Damascus he paused before the great stone walls, watching people pass through the giant arched gates. Once, he thought, he would have felt a surge of excitement at the delights of the city before him. Now, though, he simply gritted his teeth, hunched low in his cloak, and handed over to the guards the paper from Mohammed that ensured not only his safe passage through the city but his right to negotiate with the merchants there.

He stayed with merchants who were distant relatives of his family, bargaining politely – and seemingly endlessly – for the fabrics and goods in which they traded. Accustomed now to the variety of hands through which any negotiation must pass – the Jewish merchant, Arabic official, Greek importer, and any other number of steps on the ever-turning wheel of commerce – he found himself switching between languages and manners with an ease his relatives found disconcerting.

"You are a strange Jew," said a cousin one night, looking at him over wine with a not altogether friendly eye. "Even the dress you assume distinguishes you from your people."

"It is necessary, on the road," said Yosef quietly, "to become invisible – to be unseen – rather than known for what one truly is. Not everyone is disposed to help a Jew."

"For you are a holy people to Hashem your God, and God has chosen you to be his treasured people from all the nations that are on the face of the earth," quoted his companion. "We have a duty to be who we are, Yosef – even when to do so rests uneasily."

Yosef slipped away from the conversation with the diplomacy he had mastered during his travels, but the conversation left him uneasy. Part of him admired such uncompromising faith, even mourning the loss of it in himself. But the traveller in him had become the greater voice, and that man knew that in rigid faith lay a man's weakness.

Yosef nonetheless recalled the conversation as he rode onward through the dry, rocky wastes and sudden lush valleys toward Persia. It was now a wilderness of lawless men without rule, subdued in theory by the Arabs but where resentful mutterings lingered in the streets and men still worshipped at the fire temples Yosef passed on his way. Through it all, he considered what his relative had said, and his own home, now so very far distant.

I do not feel chosen, he thought. *Nor do I believe God cares much at all that I should proclaim my identity so, amongst those with whom I ride.* His thoughts became bleaker and more frightening as he went. After so long abroad, Yosef found miles no longer seemed to have the same meaning, nor the places he arrived at very much appeal.

In the shattered streets of Ctesiphon, the once-magnificent city of the Sassanids, he found others of his kind and negotiated for carpets and rugs with a detached cynicism that surprised even himself. He saw no point in staying any longer than he must. Telling stories of his homeland had lost its novelty value. Yosef was tired of being amusement for men who would wake up tomorrow knowing who they were and what they worked for. He began to feel that to give up the stories of his own life was to lose it piece by piece, and he had already grown so thin that he no longer recognised the bearded, thin-faced stranger with hollow eyes he saw when he washed in the rivers and puddles he passed on the way.

The language of trade in Ctesiphon, which marked the true beginning of Persia, was Sogdian. When trade with his own people was done, Yosef made enquiries that in turn led him to a quiet district in an old part of the city, where he handed over one of the scrolls he had carried from Spania to a man who served him delicate pastries and spiced hot wine in a richly decorated townhouse close to the River Tigris.

The man, whose name was Farzin, studied the document carefully and looked at Yosef through deep-set eyes that gleamed with intelligence over sharp cheekbones. He was a tall, proud man who spoke with dignity and reserve – nothing like the quick-eyed traders to which Yosef had become accustomed. "I will write you another," said Farzin in his calm, cultivated tones after reading it. "This one will ensure you are not killed in the passes my people ride. Arabic rule does not extend there. It is my people who will determine what you are. The scroll will not ensure your safe passage to Constantinople when you return, however. You will need to navigate that yourself." His mouth twitched slightly. "*If* you return," he said evenly, holding Yosef's eye.

Yosef nodded politely but didn't react. So many had given their warnings before now. So many times, already, he could have died.

"You laugh," said Farzin, eyeing him curiously. "You are not afraid of death, then, my young friend?"

Yosef took a date from the silver tray and chewed it meditatively. Beyond the walls of the garden a donkey and cart clattered past, the scent of cut mint from its load wafting to where they sat. Night was falling, and the tempting smell of cooking meat permeated the air, dotted with spices as yet unfamiliar to Yosef.

"You are wondering how to answer without insulting me." Farzin nodded. "This I understand. But you must not concern yourself. I am not a man inclined to take offence."

Yosef gave a half smile, which he knew did not reach his eyes. "It is only that men easily fear that which they do not know," he said quietly. "And – forgive me – men in cities seem to fear the unknown more than any other. I have seen merchants tremble with fear to spend a night only miles from the city gates, certain they will be set upon by marauders. And yet the truth is, the greatest dangers to man are faced in the cities themselves, and usually by those they know. Once on the road, and away from the familiar, all men are companions and brothers in arms. I have found nothing to fear in the wastelands I travel but much of which to be wary once I return to the places of men."

Farzin sat back on his cushions and considered his words. "It is true," he said at last. "My own father, who hailed from the very passes you will attempt to cross, was wont to say the same thing."

He moved the tray, and an engraving on its base caught Yosef's eye. He leaned forward and touched it – an eagle, wings outstretched about a blazing sun, legs streaming away. Athanais had shown him the same symbol before he left for the sands. "That symbol," said Yosef. "Where did it come from?"

Farzin touched it. "My father brought the tray back from his travels," he said. "From a place called Pir-e-Sabz, in Yazd. He said it lay beyond a wasteland and that it brought him hope when he had none within."

Yosef recalled Athanais showing him a scroll with the same symbol: *This one bears the mark of Ahura Mazda, of the Zoroastrian faith. It will be trusted by the Sogdian merchants who control the passes.*

The memory forged a comforting connection between past and present. For a moment at least, Yosef's journey felt less lonely.

Farzin, ignorant to his thoughts, looked at Yosef with a somewhat wistful smile. "I shall never see such wastelands as you cross, or as my father travelled," he said. "And nor will most. Perhaps, then, it is easier for men to disparage that which they cannot understand."

"Perhaps."

They sat together in silence, and in the morning Yosef was gone.

24

LÆLIA

APRIL, AD 691

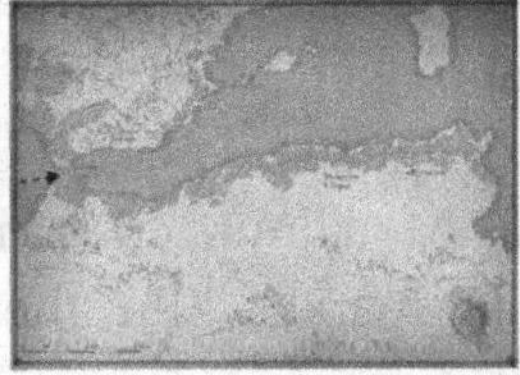

Septem, Mauretania
Ceuta, Morocco

Septem, Lælia thought as she rode through the tall gates, felt different to her after so long in the desert. People hurried in a way they did not in the sands, their faces tense and suspicious. The scent of coin permeated everything. She could see it in men's eyes and in the scrutiny of a hundred avaricious faces as they passed, each weighing the new arrivals for what opportunity they might present. She saw it in the fine embroidery of robes that had never seen desert sand, and the soft hands that had never tied a rope. She saw coin in the fat man served by thin slaves. After the desert simplicity, Lælia felt, as she inhaled the mingled stench of rotten waste and fine cooking, that the city showed her man's greed and cruelty in stark relief.

The bulk of the Riders they left camped outside the walls. Dahiya entered with Zdan and Igider, her two oldest lieutenants, on either side. They were dark-faced men with wary eyes who rode silently behind their *amgar*. Lælia rode behind them, swathed in turban and pantalons as Dahiya was, through busy streets teeming with merchants and wares. People whispered as they passed, staring at Dahiya with barely disguised awe. Dahiya and her men rode through the crowd without looking right or left, untroubled by the stir they caused. None looked at those who rode behind her. In Septem, there was none more famous than Dahiya, Queen of the Jerawa, the warrior Arabs called Al Kahinat, the Sorceress.

Lælia enjoyed the anonymity. She took a cup of water from the water seller in his garish-coloured robes, his body hung in gourds and metal bowls, and shook her head when an old woman tried to push bread into her hand. They rode past a wide square surrounded by wine and food stalls. Men lounged beneath canvas coverings, drinking and eyeing the market. On the far side, the human merchandise sat in dirty pens beside those holding livestock. Looking at the hung heads and blank, beaten expressions of the slaves, Lælia felt a wave of pity.

"We found your Theudemir in a market just like this one, in Carthage." Startled, Lælia glanced at Dahiya and realised she was serious. She turned back to the pens, revulsion rising in her at the thought of Theo amongst such filth and despondency. "He had been holding an oar for many months by the time we found him," Dahiya said quietly.

"Did you… buy him?" The words tasted wrong on Lælia's tongue.

"Apsimar did. It was a delicate matter. Theo had escaped Oppa, and Giscila was searching for him." Dahiya nodded at the far corner of the market, where horses stood in a pen finer than that of the slaves. "Theudemir was smart. There were Illiberis horses in the market, and he sent word to us to buy them. Then he made some kind of signal, and the horses led us to him. Like this, it seemed unremarkable that he and his men were noticed by Apsimar and bought for the fleet."

Lælia stared at the pitiful creatures chained together inside the pen, feeling sick inside. "Did he look like that?" she said, nodding at them.

"Much the same." Dahiya looked at her consideringly. "Do you know why I brought you here, Lælia?"

"I'm certain there is a lesson in it." The long ride across the sands had given Dahiya much time to instruct her young charge, and not a moment of it had been wasted. However much the hours of training with sword and bow may have hurt her body over the past year, the last few months of talking of strategy and negotiation had hurt Lælia's mind even more.

"I brought you here as a reminder that the lessons you truly need cannot be taught." Indifferent to Lælia's sarcasm, Dahiya nodded at the slave pens. "Your Theo did not escape slavery through dumb luck. He escaped it because he saw an opportunity and took it. He combined instinct with opportunity and action – against seemingly insurmountable odds." She turned to Lælia. "You are going to enter Ilyan's palace alone. I have brought you to Septem. Because of who you are, Ilyan will see you. Beyond that, Lælia, only you might create what happens." She took the reins of Lælia's horse. "Dismount," she said. "From here, you are on your own."

ILYAN, governor of Septem, had his back turned to the door and was staring out of an arched window when Lælia was shown into his council chamber. He stood with his hands twisted in his robes behind his back, motionless as a statue.

"Lælia of Illiberis," announced the guard. Lælia found herself standing uncertainly in the vast chamber, the only sound the faint trickle of the fountain at the centre, two guards immobile and impassive at either side of the door.

"I trust your time in the desert was instructive." Ilyan spoke without turning around, his tone no more than mildly interested.

"Very." Lælia took a hesitant step forward. "Thank you for seeing me."

"Surely Dahiya taught you better than that." The face Ilyan turned to her was remote and disinterested, with none of the warmth and courtesy she recalled from her time in his palace. "Only a beggar gives thanks for admittance. If you come here to beg, heiress of Illiberis, you should know I am not charitably inclined."

"I do not come to beg."

"Your second mistake." Ilyan crossed the floor with unsettling swiftness and mounted the dais, leaving Lælia standing awkwardly below. "Protest is a weak alternative to action."

Lælia swallowed. "You need eyes in the Toletum court."

The corners of Ilyan's mouth twitched. "Ah." He tilted his chin at Lælia and indicated the cushions opposite him on the dais. "You have earned a moment of my company. Use it wisely."

"You have many daughters," Lælia said. "It is said that many of them are rare beauties, and also that you employ the best tutors to instruct them."

Ilyan's eyes narrowed slightly. "My daughters will marry men from every port in the Circle of Lands. Such alliances are useful to me. Men in foreign lands expect their wives to speak their language and be of use. I ensure my daughters are useful."

"I can place one of your daughters in the court at Toletum, at the side of the king's legitimate heir." Lælia met his eyes steadily. "Ensure she is accepted into the king's own chambers and has access to those who govern Spania."

Ilyan clapped his hands and a slave appeared. "Bring wine," Ilyan ordered. There was a sparkle in the eyes he turned back to Lælia. "And tell me," he murmured, "why would I be better served sending my daughter to the Toletum court in the company of a traitor's granddaughter than simply sending her myself, as a guest of the king?"

"Because the daughter of Ilyan, governor of Septum, would be highly visible, and as such would be no more than a pawn in Egica's games. But a lady in service to the wife of a duke will be both protected and invisible." Lælia took the cup the slave offered. "My aunt Riccilo is married to Theodefred, the Duke of Corduba, and, next to the king himself, the most prominent man in all of Spania. Riccilo, however, is of Illiberis, as I am. Her son, Roderic, is of an age with Wittiza, Egica's own, and is kept at court to ensure Theodefred's ongoing support. Riccilo stays close to her son. I can ensure your daughter stays close to Riccilo. She, in turn, will ensure your daughter goes wherever the king's son does."

"I have eyes in the Toletum court."

"No. You rely on second-hand sources and foreigners with limited access. I am offering you the chance to place your own blood at the heart of the Spanish court."

Ilyan sat back and regarded her over his wine cup. "Interesting," he murmured. One finger tapped the rim of his cup slowly. Lælia waited. The silence drew out. She sipped her wine, willing her hand to remain steady, aware of Ilyan's eyes taking in her every movement. When next he moved, it was with such swiftness she was startled despite herself, and Ilyan was right in front of her, his face only inches from her own, staring at her with a stark scrutiny that was as disconcerting as it was penetrating. "And what is it," he said softly, "that you think you might ask in return for such favour?"

"The Karabisianoi have left a detachment in Septem. As allies of Spania, they dock in our ports with impunity." Ilyan inclined his head but did not answer. "In the coming months, I may need men brought from Africa's shores to Illiberis."

Ilyan raised his eyebrows. "The Karabisianoi are here to patrol the seas west of Carthage, not to fight petty wars amongst the Spanish nobility."

"I do not ask them to fight. Only to carry those who will, should I send word they are needed."

Now Ilyan's eyebrows shot so high they disappeared beneath his hair. "Those who will? Do I take that to mean you have gathered yourself an army, Lælia of Illiberis?"

"Not gathered. Paid." Lælia met his eyes steadily. "I will send a shipment of horse to the port of Sexi upon my return to Spania, where they will be held in lieu for one year, so long as two hundred of Dahiya's Riders remain within easy sailing distance of Spania for the duration. If, by next spring, I have sent no message, I will make a gift of the horses to Dahiya, and her men may take them and ride where they choose."

"And if you do send a message?"

"You will ask the fleet to transport the two hundred Riders to the port of Sexi, in Spania, from whence it is but one day's hard ride to Illiberis. I will send men from the tribes to meet them and show them the way."

"There is much speculation in this proposition, and little certainty." Ilyan shrugged. "If you send for men, you are by definition a traitor. How then can you aid my daughter?"

"If you send her back with me now, I will ensure she is deeply enough entrenched at court that war will not shake her place." Lælia did not flinch from his nearness. "I can offer the opportunity," she said quietly. "But to paraphrase the recent words of a wise friend – beyond that, only she can create what happens."

Ilyan watched her for a long moment, and then his face stretched into a smile. Lælia took a deep swallow of her wine and tried to still the beating of her heart.

"Very well," he said simply. "I believe we have an agreement, Lælia of Illiberis. I shall introduce you to my daughter at meat this evening."

He sat back on his cushions. "Dahiya," he said genially. "You may join us, if you like."

The doors opened and Dahiya strode through, looking neither right nor left as she mounted the dais. "Ilyan," she said, accepting a cup of wine and sinking cross legged to the cushions.

Ilyan raised his wine cup and tilted his head in acknowledgement. "I see you wasted no time with our young friend," he said mildly, sipping his wine.

Dahiya shrugged. "The ideas are hers, not mine. And she pays well."

"I see." Ilyan looked between them. "Though of course, you have no interest in whether Illiberis survives this war or not."

Dahiya looked at him squarely. "Just as you have no interest in what happens in the Spanish court, Ilyan."

"Ah." Ilyan's mouth curved into a small smile. "We are a veritable oasis of disinterest, Dahiya, are we not?" He raised his cup. "To disinterest," he said softly.

"To disinterest." Lælia met each pair of eyes in turn. "May it ensure the survival of us all."

Dahiya's lips twitched.

They drank.

25

THEO
APRIL, AD 691

Sebastopolis, Anatolia
Elauissa Sebaste, Cilicia, Turkey

On a spring night after their return from a recent mission inland, Theo avoided the tavern, unwilling to face the scrutiny of either Athanais or his men. He knew sleep would not come easily. It never did now, his dreams haunted by the elusive figure of Lælia, tugging at his body and soul in a sweet torture he simply couldn't bear. She was far away, so far it seemed sometimes to Theo that she may never be real to him again. Now Elpis, too, was gone, bought for a fee as if she were no more than an animal, disappeared somewhere into the cesspit that was Sebastopolis. Theo was uncertain whether this was a blessing or a curse. He did not miss the turmoil Elpis had roused in him. Deep within he knew himself afraid that if he committed that final act, he would lose the sweet agony of Lælia's presence in his dreams and break the invisible connection he felt every time he touched the amulet and coin at his throat. His promise had been to return to her. By remaining in the fleet when he could have returned, Theo felt he had taken the first step into betrayal. To take Elpis had seemed tantamount to casting himself into the abyss. No, he told himself, it was good that she was gone. And Pelagia remained under Athanais's protection. That, at least, was something good and innocent he could still protect.

Now he strode through the darkened streets, his body restless and his mind in turmoil, seeking the tedium of work to ease his irritation. He was nearing the docks when a shadow slid from the darkness and a voice from the past said his name: "Theo."

Theo had a knife at the man's throat in an instant. "Speak," he said tersely.

"Not here." Oppa met his eyes. "I know a place we can talk. You can kill me afterward, if you so choose." His half smile was disconcerting. Theo lowered his knife and Oppa slipped back into the shadows, turning into a narrow alley without looking back. Theo hesitated, then followed the narrow figure up the hill, cursing himself for a fool as he did so. Oppa led him out of the town to an abandoned ruin beyond earshot of any lingering on the fringes. Inside the crumbling walls Oppa turned to face him, his eyes unreadable in the pale moonlight. Theo felt his heart trip in his chest.

"Give me one reason not to kill you," he said tightly.

"I have news of your betrothed. That is one reason." Oppa's smooth tone set every alarm tingling in Theo's body. "And second — I have news of Spania."

"What news?" said Theo grimly. He kept his sword trained on Oppa, his body half crouched and only a breath away from attack.

"She can speak now," said Oppa. "Lælia." The sound of her name on Oppa's tongue made something vicious leap in Theo's chest. "She spoke in court, in front of the entire council. Argued that she was betrothed to you, despite my efforts to prove otherwise. Successfully, I might add." He said the words blandly, as if they mattered no more than the weather. Theo stared at him.

"Why would you tell me this?"

"Because I need you to trust me." Oppa stepped forward. The moonlight gleamed on his face, showing his eyes clearly, but Theo still could not read them. "It seems we may have more in common than I had previously thought."

"We have nothing in common." Theo's voice was like a whiplash. "And Lælia would rather die than find herself married to you."

"Yes. She made that abundantly clear." Oppa's tone remained calm, but something flickered behind his eyes, there and then gone. "The heiress of Illiberis is not what should concern us, however."

"Then what?"

"Spania will go to war," Oppa said flatly. "My father will not tolerate the upstart Sunifred. He means to destroy the south – your family included." He moved across the uneven tiles of the floor to where a window had once been in the crumbling wall, looking down at the port below, lit by lanterns along the water's edge. "He will succeed," he said.

"I wouldn't be so sure of that."

"Oh, I'm sure. In such things, my father does not lose." Oppa turned to meet Theo's eyes. "In the greater matter of Spania's future, however, I believe him to be sadly deluded." Taken aback, Theo stared at him but didn't answer. "You have seen the Arabic armies." Oppa gestured to the water beyond. "I, too, have seen their strength. Seen what havoc they can wreak. Do you truly believe Spania capable of standing against such a force?" He shrugged. "I do not. I think that if the Arabic armies should reach Spanish shores, we will be overpowered in an instant. And I believe they will reach Spanish shores." He met Theo's eyes steadily. "Would you not agree?"

Theo's eyes narrowed. "Why speak to me of such things?"

"We are Spaniards, alone in a foreign land. Who else would I speak to?"

Theo shook his head. "You must have spoken to your father. Told him what we face here, what is coming for Spania." Against his own instincts, he found himself very interested in the answer. Despite everything that had passed between them, despite even Oppa's admission that he had tried to force Lælia to marry him, Theo couldn't deny he was intrigued to know what Egica thought of the Arabic armies so close to his shores.

"Oh, I told him." Oppa's voice was unusually brittle. "Let's just say he did not perceive the threat quite as I did."

Theo stared at him. "You mean he didn't believe you?"

"My father believes the Arabs pose no threat to Spania." There was something behind the flat tone and hard face that Theo couldn't quite read. He had thought he knew Oppa's moods. But despite the endless days as Oppa's slave, watching every flicker of the hand on the whip, acutely aware of any shift in tone or eye, still, Theo realised, he did not know the man before him now.

"But you do believe they pose a threat," Theo said, watching Oppa closely.

"I do." Oppa nodded. "And this puts me in the curious position of wondering if, perhaps, you and I might find ourselves allies rather than enemies."

Theo tasted hatred on his tongue like old bile.

"Ah." Oppa half smiled. "I see that perhaps you do not yet see it. And I cannot blame you. Those scars I left on your face are hard. Although I do not think it will matter to Lælia. She seemed very… *determined*… to remain betrothed to you." He watched Theo keenly, but whatever he was expecting, he was disappointed. "Have it your way," he said, stepping away with a light shrug. He moved toward the door. "But I'm not going anywhere, Aurariola. I do not intend to blind myself to what is coming, nor to find myself powerless when it does. If you wish, also, to survive your return to Spania, then I suggest you begin to consider the future also."

"What do you mean, survive my return to Spania?" Theo's voice was hard. "And consider what future? Speak plainly."

Oppa glanced back at him. "Your brother Alaric is in open rebellion against my father," he said. "Before long, your father Suinthila will undoubtedly join him, with Illiberis at his side, I imagine. There must be something coming, for Paulus has sent his granddaughter away. Across the seas, in fact." He studied Theo carefully, gauging the effect of his words. "And still you do not ask! You have learned restraint, Aurariola, I will grant you that. Let me answer what you do not ask, anyway: yes, I know where Lælia is. And I have sent someone to ensure she remains safe. But this is not what should concern you," he went on, his eyes glinting as he saw Theo's hand clench around the sword hilt. "What do you think will happen when you return, Theudemir? Do you think my father will welcome to his court the son of a traitor, the man betrothed to the granddaughter of another traitor? Do you think you will still be Theudemir of Aurariola after your brother has been dragged through the streets or blinded as punishment for his treachery and your father lies dead on a battlefield?"

Theo stared at him, unable to find words in the emotion swirling in his chest.

"I would advise you," said Oppa softly, "to think on what I have said. Ultimately, you may come to the same realisation as me: that you and I are better served by working together than we are as enemies. I know you protect the Jew, Yosef ben Arun. I know you work together on something that you hope will bring gold and power to the south, gold and power I assume you intend to use to build an alliance I suspect you will do anything to protect.

"But ask yourself this, Theudemir of Aurariola – will it matter what gold the Jew finds if you have no home left to defend?" Walking through the door, he called back over his shoulder, "I am not your enemy, Theo. The real enemy is out there – and unless we fight it together, we will both lose." And then Oppa was gone, swallowed into the night, only the faint, sickly scent of musk on the air a reminder of his presence.

Theo stood in the silent ruins, the pounding of his heart deafening, thoughts and questions swirling like a desert storm in his mind.

26

LÆLIA

APRIL, AD 691

Septem, Mauretania
Ceuta, Morocco

Septem was a thread on one side of the dromon, Spania a jagged line on the other, when a shout from the stern alerted Lælia to the arrival of another vessel. "That is not one of my father's dromons," said Safia's quiet voice at her side.

"Do you know to whom it belongs?" Lælia fingered the knife at her side.

Ilyan's daughter nodded. "The man who owns it is a Spanish exile named Giscila." She looked at Lælia through wide, almond-shaped eyes that seemed almost too big for her fine features. Safia was not yet ten years old, stood barely to Lælia's chest, and was so finely built she seemed sometimes to disappear into the background. Any initial misgivings Lælia may have felt at the girl's extreme youth, however, had been rapidly dispelled. Safia spoke seven languages fluently, knew when to speak and when to be silent, and had almost perfect recall. It was rumoured she was the daughter of Ilyan's favourite courtesan. She had been raised in the women's quarters and her face was not known, even to the men who transported them now, all of whom thought her Lælia's own servant.

"Giscila," Lælia repeated now, frowning at the dromon. "He is bold, to approach us in Ilyan's waters."

"He comes in a merchant dromon, not a fighting vessel. I do not believe you have cause for concern." Safia's perfect composure was at times unsettling.

"I see that." Lælia felt her heart beat faster as she watched the dromon approach.

"We can outrun them," said the gruff *prōtokaraboi* at the helm. "And we outnumber them easily." He nodded at the dromons on either side of them. Ilyan had taken no chances in ensuring the safe passage of Lælia and Safia to Spanish shores. The dromons belonged to the imperial fleet, the Karabisianoi, and were manned by hard men. "The dromon is hailing us," he said now. "It looks like our friend wishes to talk."

"Allow him to approach," Lælia ordered. "But be alert."

The *prōtokaraboi* shot her a sideways look. "With respect," he began, "this is my command. My orders are to take you to Spania —"

"With respect," Lælia cut him off without looking at him, "your men might hold the oars, but those who hold the swords are Ilyan's. I know this because I requested it. I have seen what can happen on these seas. So has Ilyan. The other dromons may belong entirely to the fleet, but the men on this one are sworn to protect me. I respect your command. But make no mistake, I will take it if necessary."

Casting her a resentful glance, the *prōtokaraboi* nonetheless gave the order to slow, and the dromon thudded with the sound of fifty oars being drawn in. Lælia stroked Jadis's head, and the cat growled low in her throat. "Remain close," Lælia murmured to Tosius, and the little tribesman took up position behind her.

The dromon pulled close enough for her to see the faces within, and the *prōtokaraboi* spat into the water. "They are putting out landing spars," he growled to Lælia. "If we take them, they can board us."

"There are barely enough men to pull oar," said Lælia, looking at the thin crew. "They are not here to take us. They are here to talk."

Lælia recognised Giscila almost immediately. His features were broader than Oppa's, less sharp, and lacked Egica's dark intelligence, but the similarity was there in the long nose and hooded eyes, the hard angles of his face.

You are the man who murdered my parents.

Lælia waited for a sense of enormity to sweep over her, but it did not come. She felt instead an odd combination of fascination and revulsion.

"You board alone," she called over the water. "And without weapons of any kind." She ignored the mutterings of the men around her. If she had learned one thing after more than a year in Dahiya's company, it was that when a woman commanded, men would mutter.

Giscila's eyes on her face were hungry and curious as the dromons drew near enough for him to board. Jadis stood at Lælia's side, rumbling as he approached, tense and wary, her tail low and dangerous behind her. Safia had moved slightly away and drawn her cloak over her face, in the strange manner she had of rendering herself invisible in any room.

Giscila made a clumsy bow. "I am –"

"I know who you are." Lælia stared coldly at him. "It was ill advised of you to hunt me on these waters, Giscila, son of Tulga. I have many reasons to kill you." His face tightened at the mention of his father, the long-ago king who had been tonsured and disgraced, torn brutally from the throne by Chindasuinth. The hardening of his features made his resemblance to Oppa more marked. For a moment, Lælia recalled a long-ago night in Toletum, staring down at Oppa's body asleep in bed. She felt again the savage desire to kill, remembered how her every instinct had urged her to slide her knife into him – and yet she had not. Had waited, until she could eviscerate him in court, humiliate him before his fellow men.

It had, she knew, been better thus.

But the temptation remained.

Something of what she felt must have crossed her face, for

Giscila licked his lips and looked sideways, then back at her. "I had hoped to meet in different circumstances."

"But Ilyan no longer tolerates your dromons in his port. Dahiya's Riders would see you dead before letting you close to their camp. And you are not bold enough to land on Spanish shores." Something moved in his eyes, and Lælia tensed. "Not yet, at least," she added, watching him closely.

"You are perceptive." Giscila smiled. His features were so reminiscent of Oppa's that Lælia had to force herself not to recoil. "But if – when, perhaps – I land upon Spanish shores once more, I would pose no danger to you, Lælia of Illiberis." Her name on his lips was like an unwanted caress. Lælia had the sense he had been waiting to use it, to taste it in his mouth, and the thought made her ill.

"What do you want?" she asked bluntly. "I have three dromons of trained men who need only my command to kill you. None would miss you, and Ilyan certainly would not question my decision. I must assume you have good reason for such an unwise approach."

Giscila inclined his head. "I understand your anger. I ask only that you hear my apology. Then, if you wish to kill me, you might do so." He held up his hands. "I am unarmed, as you see, and have no men but those on the oar. My life is in your hands."

"Your apology," said Lælia flatly. "There is no apology you can offer that I wish to hear."

"Nonetheless, I must offer it." He knelt on the damp timbers of the dromon. Lælia watched him narrowly, her hand on Jadis's head. "I was responsible for the death of your parents." Lælia's hand stilled on Jadis's head. "I was driven by love, though I do not plead that as an excuse." Giscila kept his head down. "Had I known I would lose everything in my bid to win your mother, I would never have done what I did. I have had many years to regret my decisions and to recognise that I was driven as much by greed and ambition as I was by love." He raised his eyes slowly to hers. "I do not expect your forgiveness," he said softly. "But I wish you to know my only desire now is to protect you – and I believe you might be in danger."

Lælia stared at him in silence until she was certain her voice would be steady. Then she said curtly, "What danger do you speak of?"

Hesitantly Giscila rose to his feet. "From my nephew, Oppa." He spat over the side of the dromon, watching her closely. "He fights now at the side of your betrothed – Theudemir of Aurariola."

"That is a lie." Hearing the anger in her own voice, and seeing the flash of satisfaction in the dark eyes facing her, Lælia brought herself under control and said more calmly, "Oppa may seek my betrothed for his own dark schemes, but Theo will never raise sword at his side."

"Perhaps not in the Spania you left behind." Giscila's tone was still conciliatory, but Lælia, watching him, sensed the dark thrust behind them. This, she knew, was what he had come for. "But in the world in which Oppa and Theudemir find themselves," Giscila went on, "such old enmities are soon forgotten. When last I met with your betrothed, he seemed more than willing to forge new alliances." He spat to one side, holding her eyes. "If what I hear is true, he is forging one with Oppa even now. That is why I seek you out. My regrets may mean nothing to you. But if you care about Illiberis as I know your mother did, then my warning should."

"You work with Oppa," said Lælia flatly. "You launched an attack on the fleet that nearly killed Theo."

Giscila bowed his head. "I did."

"Then what makes you think I would ever believe you – or make an alliance with you?"

"Because Oppa and Theo no longer fight for Illiberis. They fight for Spania. And if that means they must trade Illiberis, or the spoils from the journey your Jewish friend takes as we speak, then believe me, they will. Oppa and Theo may hate one another. But they have learned to fight on the same side. And neither of them will hesitate to sacrifice Illiberis to ensure their victory."

"And you come here to tell me that you, by contrast, care for my wellbeing, and that of Illiberis?" Dark rage rose inside her, and Lælia had to fight to keep her voice steady. "You have been too long at sea, Giscila. Your mind is addled."

"I come here because I am a man who has lost everything for his family and their ambitions, only to be exiled and repeatedly betrayed." His tone was no longer conciliatory but hard and unyielding, and there was an ugly gleam of old bitterness in his eyes.

"Because it was their greed that took your mother from you, and the only woman I have ever loved from me. I agreed to the attack on the fleet because I thought it would buy my return from exile. Had I known the attack would injure you, I never would have allied with my family once again – and it is the last time I will ever do so." He met her eyes, and try as she might, Lælia could not read what lay in the depths of his. "I said I do not come to ask anything of you. It is I who owe you a debt. My offer is the only means I have to repay it." He stepped closer, stopping when Jadis surged at him with a warning growl. "I have men, coin, and dromons. Should the day come when Illiberis is threatened, Lælia, you need only send word to the port in Sexi and I will come to your aid."

"You would offer yourself as ally to the same house you once tried to destroy?" Lælia's tone was scathing. "Even if I were deluded enough to consider such an offer, what makes you so certain that Illiberis will be threatened?"

"Oppa told me that the southern rebellion cannot prevail against Egica's armies. Theudemir's brother, I understand, has sided with the rebels. When they are defeated, he will be killed as a traitor. Theudemir will be heir to Aurariola in his place. He will also be considered a traitor – and Aurariola itself forfeit to the Crown."

His eyes were dark and cold, and his words cast a shadow over Lælia's heart. "Oppa and his father do not need Aurariola," Giscila said softly. "But they want Illiberis, and for such a prize, treason may be forgiven. Illiberis may well be the price of your betrothed's return to Spania."

"You draw a long bow," said Lælia, but she could not fully disguise the tremor in her voice.

"Only two years ago," Giscila said quietly, "your betrothed looked me in the eye and told me he was a man without country or allegiance. He agreed to betray Yosef ben Arun in exchange for gold." Despite her certainty that Theo was merely playing a part, despite her knowledge of the man who had kissed her three years ago, still Lælia felt a dread fear cold inside her. She stared at Giscila, not trusting herself to speak. "Theudemir bears scars that will never fade," he went on relentlessly. "He is not the man who left Spania. I do not believe he will place Illiberis above all else. And nor do I believe that he considers Oppa the enemy he once did. I will say it again, Lælia of Illiberis, that you may hear me clearly: if the day should come when you need aid, send word and I will come."

He turned as if to leave, then paused and glanced back at her. "Oppa has been fighting beside Theudemir for some time now," he said. "Before you dismiss my warnings, ask yourself this: if Theo is truly the man you remember, then why does Oppa still live?"

27

YOSEF

APRIL, AD 691

Eran
Iran

Home had long since become a distant concept to Yosef. Garnata and Illiberis were dark memories, filled with terrible images that still haunted his dreams. Africa and the sands had been home for a time, but they lay behind him now, fading with every passing step. Without the jocular company of Bagay and Khanchla, Yosef found his thoughts took strange turns, dredging up emotions and memories he thought he had long ago buried. Amidst the darkness, Sarah glimmered like a distant light. In his most private moments, Yosef knew that she, above all, had come to symbolise home for him. Yet as soon as he allowed the thought, he recollected the cruel circumstances in which they had parted and berated himself for imagining that Sarah could ever welcome home the man who had been unable to prevent other men from raping her.

After a day when no amount of miles had served to still the turbulent thoughts of what he might do, where he might go, when all this was done, Yosef lay down to sleep in the wilderness, far from any man. His body was tired if his mind was not, and he slipped into darkness.

"Yosef…" Thin wind blew over his face, and the ground was hard as he turned in his blankets. Stars glittered high above. Dawn was still far away. *"Yosef…"* The voice tortured him, full of such longing it made Yosef's heart twist. *"I miss you."*

He burrowed into the blankets. *You cannot miss me,* he thought, fighting the rise to consciousness, wanting to return to the dark sanctuary of sleep, the sound of Sarah's voice, her imaginary touch. *You are lost to me.*

"Come back to us…"

Yosef sprang into waking, sitting up in his blankets, heart tripping wildly. *To us?* He stood and stepped out of the blankets, the dream alive around him as if he could reach through it to touch Sarah as he once had beneath the almond trees in Illiberis before Oppa and his men had come upon them and ravaged the flesh that even now tortured Yosef's dreams. The whisper of the voice clung to the high mountain air around him, making him swing around, examining the still blackness with suspicious eyes.

Slipping his sandals on, he reached for the water skin and splashed his face, welcoming the cold shock despite the chill of the night. He was alone on this stretch, a rare solitude he had come to savour rather than fear. At times the incessant company of other travellers could become tiring.

He pondered the dream. Sarah's voice had become a constant companion, but usually it was just the whisper of his name, an entreaty to return. Yosef had given the dreams much thought as he walked. He had tried to tell himself they were no more than his own guilt. His father had wanted him to return, had made Yosef promise he would come back to Garnata. Some trick of Yosef's mind, he told himself, had made Sarah's voice the sound of that promise. And he could not deny that even the imagining of her voice was a delicious, secret pleasure, a comfort he could not quite bring himself to resent during the long, lonely miles he had walked alone. Whilst he knew in himself that they would never have a future, out here, so far from anything he knew, he could not imagine it a sin to allow himself dreams of what could never be.

Especially when those dreams came upon him when he slept. No man could be held responsible for their dreams. Except that a secret voice within Yosef whispered that the dreams seemed something more than a trick of the mind, stronger than illusion.

Normally it was just his name he heard.

Come back to us. Yosef shook his head, trying to clear away the words that clung there still. Was his mind trying to tell him his father lived?

A recollection of Arun's tortured, burned flesh, hanging in tatters where the oil had melted it from his body, hit Yosef with a savagery that made him wince.

No. Even he could not imagine Arun alive. No man could survive such horrors. He turned his mind from the image with a discipline born of long nights alone in strange places, where such memories could turn a man to insanity if he did not learn to master them.

It is Garnata, Yosef told himself firmly. *The community my father hoped I could save. Sarah's voice is the way my conscience reminds me I made a promise to save my community, even if I no longer imagine myself a part of it.*

The thought took him by such surprise it temporarily drove the memory of Sarah's voice from his mind. *Do I truly feel so lost to my own people?* he wondered. It made him feel indescribably lonely, a man with no home, either of the flesh or of the soul.

He dressed in the silent night and began walking before the dawn so much as lit the far edge of the eastern sky.

Persia was a bewildering land of extraordinary riches — and terrible decay. Yosef passed the abandoned ruins of mighty temples to the Fire God, Ahura Mazda, desecrated by the Arabic conquerors and the bitter wars that had ravaged the lands here for a generation. Peace was still a localised affair and very much dependent on the integrity of the individuals tasked with tax collection. The Persians themselves treated their new Arabic overlords with a polite disdain that often deteriorated into outright contempt. To those proud, fearsome horsemen, educated men of often extraordinary riches, their new rulers were little more than desert peasants. Obedience to Arabic rule was given with sullen resentment.

To visitors, though, the Persians showed a level of sophisticated hospitality that Yosef found almost overwhelming in luxury. Even the humblest home welcomed him. In the poorest hovel, he would still find at least one written work, and the inhabitants were able to quote many more. He spent barely a night on the cold ground, for no Persian would dare raise his eyes to Ahura Mazda if he allowed a stranger to go hungry or unwelcome. Yosef's pace was slowed by the endless welcome he found beneath every roof.

He found himself fascinated by the deep wisdom of the fire faith, though to follow it now was, unlike his own faith and that of the Christians, strictly outlawed by the Arabs. Those who pursued the teachings of Zoroaster were punishable by death. The headless bodies of those who persisted in publicly professing their faith were found at every crossroads, displayed as a deliberate warning to others who would continue their adherence to a philosophy the Arabs deemed corrupt pagan savagery.

But Yosef could not cease his interest. He found himself actively avoiding his own people, though he could not have said strictly why, only that he no longer felt himself one of them. His nights were restless, tormented by Sarah's voice, her strange entreaties to return to a world he also felt he was no longer part of. At times he thought only the endless walking kept him from madness. And though it was not on his path, he followed the directions of his genial hosts to one of the most revered fire temples – the shrine of Pir-e-Sabz, in the province of Yazd.

He saw the bodies long before the temple came into view.

They were left on high mountain plateaus, in towers Persians called *dakhmag*. Yosef knew that Zoroastrians did not bury their dead, believing any contact with dead flesh a corrupting and evil influence. Instead, they brought the bodies to these high places, where birds of prey would descend and tear the flesh from the skeleton, returning the material to the cycle of life.

Yosef no longer found *dakhmag* distasteful. He had passed too many of them to be disturbed by the carrion birds that circled above, the vague smell of corruption carried on the wind. He had begun to find a strange peace in their presence, as if the dead themselves hovered on the air, preparing to soar with the birds that carried their mortal remains high into the sharp blue sky over the mountains.

Pir-e-Sabz was a grotto, built into the cliffside. A great tree grew by a cleft marked with a jutting piece of stone of a deep red colour, brighter than the dull rock that surrounded it. Yosef approached cautiously, seeing nobody as he made the steep climb to the entrance.

There was something poignant in the silent dignity of the caves on the mountain. Perhaps, Yosef thought with a strange disquiet, they simply reminded him of his home. He touched the tree, and the rock beside it, and entered the low, man-made grotto.

Water dripped from the rock in a steady, almost meditative rhythm. Green fronds of maidenhair grew by the water leaching from the stone, and in the centre of the cave, a fire burned in a large brazier. It was surrounded by simple platters of food and candles, offerings from pilgrims. Yosef felt that he should pay tribute in some way but had no idea how to do it.

"Fire purifies."

Yosef swung around, his hand on the knife at his side. A lithe, dark-faced man smiled at him. He was dressed in the white shirt, *sudre*, and girdle, *kusti*, given, Yosef knew, to initiates of the Zoroastrian faith, and wore a covering over his head not unlike that worn by the Jews Yosef had grown up with.

"I am Jahan, keeper of this shrine." He stepped forward and bowed lightly to Yosef. "*Khosh amadid.*" Welcome. Yosef returned the greeting.

"You speak some Persian," said Jahan.

"*Bale, man fârsi harf mizanam.*" Yes, I speak a little.

"I, also, speak other languages. Greek, or Hebrew, if you wish it. Latin, too."

"You are a learned man," said Yosef. "Are you a priest?"

"In our faith, we are known as magi," said Jahan. "And, yes, I am. Or I was, once, when magi still mattered in our country."

"And now?"

"Now," said Jahan, leaning forward to tend the fire in the brazier, "I practise the rituals of my faith and remind myself of their true purpose. In a shrine such as this" – he indicated the humble walls of the cave – "I am reminded of what is important, of the gifts that made ours the faith of kings. Kings who ultimately became its downfall."

Unlike Shukra, no eccentricities marred his speech. Like Farzin back in Ctesiphon, he spoke Greek in cultured, even tones, with barely a trace of an accent. His face was smooth and unlined, his eyes clear.

"What is this place?" Yosef sat on the carpet indicated by Jahan, cross legged.

"Some claim it to be the hiding place of one of the last Sassanid princesses, a beauty named Nikbanu. The stories say she ran to escape the Arabic conquerors, and a cleft opened in the cliff to admit her within. The coloured rock at the entrance is the cloth of her dress, petrified forever that we may remember her."

Yosef raised his eyebrows but didn't comment.

"Long before a shepherd was given this story in a vision," went on Jahan, "it was known, to those of us who know such things, that Pir-e-Sabz was a place sacred to Armaiti, guardian of the earth, and Anahita, guardian of waters. Here, both are present, and people may come to be cleansed by fire and balanced by their energies. In balancing and purifying ourselves, we also return to Ahura Mazda, the One, and strengthen the One's presence on earth."

"I am not an initiate to your faith." Yosef looked at him steadily. "I am Yosef, a Jew, from Spania."

"Of course you are." Jahan seemed not at all disturbed by the disclosure. "But you are far from your land, and Zoroaster spoke to Jews as well. It is from him that you take much of your understanding of God – though it is an imperfect understanding – just as the Christians and now the Muslims do in their writings of the One."

Yosef nodded. "I knew a Persian once," he said. "In Spania. He told me that good and evil exist in all men, that the devil is not a force beyond us but within us."

"Just so." Jahan smiled. "And is it a desire to exorcise that evil that brings you here, Yosef? For if it is the company of your people you wish for, Yazd is a rich place of commerce, and Jews trade freely there."

"I don't know exactly." Yosef spoke slowly, looking at the fire. "My journey is for trade, yes. And I will continue to do as I must, for it was the wish of my father that I make this journey. The outcome of it matters to others more, perhaps, than it does to me. But I no longer know what it is that I journey for, nor what I hope to achieve by the doing of it." He looked up at Jahan. "I no longer know if I hope to return home at all. I stop in cities and meet my own people, but they are consumed by trade, by the daily counting of coin and the politics it takes to make such coin grow. They are so certain that they must continue, regardless of the obstacles. That they work for some higher and, it seems to me, as yet unknown purpose. That by building a web of trade and profitable relationships, they somehow build a defence against the common foe of prejudice and persecution." He was quiet for a moment, trying to find the words. "I love my faith," he said. "I have grown from the cradle without ever questioning where I come from, or how I worship God. For my people, it is inherent in everything we do: the way we eat and pray, even the way we bathe. But now I find myself in foreign lands where my faith is no more important, or understood, than any other. And here in Persia, I find that my own faith is considered new. Is considered with benign tolerance, as a poor facsimile of an older, richer understanding.

"I find myself lacking patience, with my own people and with the God and the practices that have underpinned my whole life. In so many ways, this should not matter, for surely I have greater things to concern myself with. But it seems to me, as I travel onward through empty places, that this is the only thing that matters at all." He was surprised to find his voice cracking. "I do not know what I believe anymore," he said quietly. The fire before him blurred, and he was lost in mourning for the simplicity of a life he had once accepted without question.

They sat in silence for a while, then Jahan spoke. "Zoroastrianism is not a religion," he said quietly. "Don't mistake me; it became one under the corruption of wealthy kings who made magi rich men and used their skills for their own power. But all things have balance in the One, and when the fire temples no longer truly served the One, the corruption they had become was destroyed. Nonetheless, those who adhere to the Gathas – the sermons of Zoroaster – are born to it, just as you, Yosef, are born to the word of Moses.

"My point," he said, "is that my faith can no more guide you to find God in yourself than can any other. Your answers do not lie in your understanding of an external God, Yosef. They lie in discovering how you understand the One within yourself."

"To do that, must I accept a new faith?" Yosef asked. "Must I leave behind the Torah, and my people, in order to become something new – someone new?"

"Not leave behind," said Jahan. "But perhaps for a time, at least, you may need to allow yourself to be free of what you know. It is not possible for any person to find the One within themselves when they insist that it has already been found."

"I have so long yet to go," said Yosef. He spoke more to himself than to Jahan, looking into the flames of the fire, the steady dripping sound calming his soul.

"And yet you have already come so far." Jahan leaned forward and tended the fire, his movements spare and deft. Sparks leaped into the air, and the flames brightened, as if given new life.

"You will find your way," said Jahan. "It is inevitable." He smiled at Yosef. "And it is simpler, really, than you think. All you must do is what you are already doing."

"All I do," said Yosef, "is put one foot in front of the other. That is it. No more, no less."

"Just so." Jahan smiled. "And this, *aziz-am* – this is all any of us must do. Just that. Put one foot in front of another – and allow the One to walk within us."

. . .

YOSEF PASSED through Yazd and across the great desert on the other side. He entered the chaos of Kabul, on the far side of the great wastes, and traded for carpets and silks such as he had never seen. He prayed with men of his own faith, but he also entered the fire temples of the magi, praying at the shrines he found there. Amongst the Hind of Kush, he prayed also to gods of whom he had never before heard, fantastic figures of exotic face and body, belonging to stories and beliefs he did not understand.

And if he had thought himself scoured clean by the sands of the Ténéré, or exhausted by the wastelands of Persia and Kush, it was only when he reached the Danfeng Gate at the great Daming Palace of Empress Wu in the remote lands of Serica that Yosef knew himself truly lost.

28

THEO
OCTOBER, AD 691

Sebastopolis, Anatolia
Elauissa Sebaste, Cilicia, Turkey

It was only in action that Theo found solace from the thoughts tormenting him. He and his companions climbed silently through the rocks. Dawn would come soon, and men would die. But for now the night was still, dew dripping quietly onto stone, the night a damp curtain about Theo's face. Above them loomed a Maronite monastery, cut into the rocky cliffs, dark and imposing like an immovable sentinel. In the tight focus of battle, Theo could, if not ignore, at least tolerate Oppa's unsettling presence in their midst. Over the past months, Theo's world had become increasingly complex. He walked a tightrope of diplomacy, and the strain was beginning to tell.

"I don't like this," Leofric muttered beneath his breath, the words barely moving the air by Theo's ear. Theo shrugged lightly in dismissal. None of them liked it. But Leontios had become increasingly paranoid about the collection of Arabic taxes, and Oppa had found fertile ground in his fear. Now every expedition that involved the collection of coin also involved men in Oppa's employ.

To attack a monastery – no matter if Arab heretics now occupied it – went firmly against every instinct. But their instructions were to prevent any Arabic toehold in the area recently occupied by Maronite Christians, many of whom now stood on the rocks beside them, eyes glinting as they fingered their weapons. The Arabic forces, it seemed, did not content themselves on their side of the Nur Mountains, despite what their diplomats said in the Constantinople court. The monastery above owed tribute to Emperor Justinian II, but the call to prayer rang now from the parapets, and its coin flowed to Caliph Abd al Malik.

A faint movement fluttered the air. Theo held up a clenched fist, and the men behind him halted. Far above, there was the hint of movement – a shadow, no more – but it was enough.

"They know we are here," murmured Theo. "Retreat."

"Retreat?" The man beside him scowled in confusion. He was a slender man with dark eyes and high cheekbones, a local Maronite fighter, and his name was Kyros. "Before an arrow has flown?"

"Retreat." Theo turned hard eyes on him. "If they know we are here, flying arrows are the least of your problems. Our position relied on secrecy. The secret is out. Retreat."

They had no sooner begun their stealthy descent when above them, from every crevice it seemed, men emerged, shaking their bows and hooting derisively at the retreating figures.

"Xristus," muttered Leofric, looking at them. "There are hundreds. It would have been murder." He cast Theo a look of grudging respect. "It seems even your strange choice of friends does not affect your thinking, *schnecke*."

"I told you." Theo's face was grim. "Kyros is not your enemy. Here, we must play by different rules."

Leofric cast Kyros a dark glance. "He is Oppa's creature, sent here to watch us. We cannot move but that he is at our side."

"Kyros is a good fighter, and he knows these mountains."

Leofric snorted. "Kyros knows the touch of Oppa's coin in his hand." He looked around them suspiciously. "As do half the men here. The bastard has his hand in too many pockets, *schnecke*. I do not understand how you so easily forget the touch of his whip on your skin."

Theo didn't answer. He stalked down the rocky path, his body taut with tension, the scars combined with his grim expression forbidding enough to prevent men from asking questions. Only Silas wasn't intimidated.

"You must have your reasons for tolerating the bastard," he said in a voice low enough that it escaped the others. "I hope you are certain of them, *wenkai*. Oppa plays many games. Be certain he does not play them with you."

Theo grunted, the closest he could bring himself to acknowledging Silas's fears. He walked back to camp thinking of the many messages he had given Athanais. Surely one of them, by now, must have received a response from Apsimar? He kicked a stone in frustration. Always certain of his next move, for once Theo did not know what to do.

He was still pondering when they reached camp. Theo shook his head once in response to the enquiring glance from Neboulos, the Slavic commander. "Not today," he said briefly. "They saw us coming." Neboulos was a burly, stolid man, gruff in manner. If he lacked Apsimar's golden brilliance and compelling urbanity, he was a strong warrior, brutal in battle and utterly fearless. Neboulos's command, Theo knew, was not an easy one, and it was one of the reasons Theo's own choices were not simple.

It had been a long winter of training and infighting in the hard country about Sebastopolis, during which Theo had come to respect the surly Slav. Only the rigid hand of Neboulos had kept the different factions that were co-existing in the bulging port from exploding into open chaos. Keeping thirty thousand disgruntled Slavs in a semblance of order was task enough. Added to that, Leontios had conscripted Neboulos's aid in helping to carve the ramshackle contingents of Slavic and Maronite refugees into some kind of fighting force. After dozens of men had died venturing into the interior, Leontios tasked Neboulos with the command of scouting parties made of men undaunted by the rugged mountains and equally rugged rebel forces found there. Neboulos in turn had searched for good men to lead them, and he found in Theo one such man. The frequent incursions by Arabs into Greek territory had served as a not unwelcome distraction for Theo and a good training ground for new troops.

Under Neboulos's leadership, dozens of squadrons roamed the coast, disgorging small parties and their horses into the mountains to the interior, where they gave succour to those refugees hiding in remote outposts, fought off local rebels, and engaged the Arab invaders who constantly tested the uneasy peace. Today Neboulos camped with Theo's crew. Their dromons were only three days' fast travel from Sebastopolis. The Arabs were closer than they should ever have been to the main force of Emperor Justinian II's army.

"They number more than several hundred," said Theo now, sipping at a cup of coarse *posca* by the fire. Their camp was quieter than the hectic hub of Sebastopolis, and despite the tense nature of their work, Theo was content enough to be away from the port and its endless sordid distractions. A brief flash of Oppa's face passed behind his eyes, and Theo willed it away, not without effort.

"There is other way in?" Neboulos asked, squinting up the mountainside.

Theo nodded. "I believe so. Kyros said there is a tunnel in from the other face. But we will not know if it is safe until we enter it. We will take our time, scout the area, kill any who might raise the alarm."

"You trust this man?"

Theo shrugged. "He is a Maronite, like the rebels. But his daughter and wife are settled in Sebastopolis, and he himself trades in wine, a profitable enough business. He has little reason to see us defeated, and many to help us."

Neboulos shot him a sideways glance. "I have heard he answers to the Spanish bastard."

Leofric made a contemptuous sound. Theo quelled him with a frown. "All men in Sebastopolis are bought by someone. Kyros might answer to Oppa, but he has reason enough to fight for us."

"A man who can be bought will sell to highest bidder," said Neboulos, unmoved.

Silas's white teeth shone in the daylight. "Ah," he said, smiling, "but when those paying him also escort his wine through the mountain passes – and ensure it reaches those who are prepared to pay for quality – they are hard to outbid."

Neboulos looked between Theo, Leofric, and Silas and smiled reluctantly. "You will take men scouting tonight?" he asked.

"With your permission." Theo nodded. "I have the men for the job." He gestured behind him. A murmur of assent came from the men ranged about the cooking fires.

"So." Neboulos stood and slapped the dirt from his bare thighs. Despite the chill in the air, he never wore more than the brief tunic of the Greeks, and his legs were broad, thick, and hairy beneath it, scarred with the marks of a hundred battles. "Now we sleep."

It was not a hot day, yet Theo found it hard to rest. Oppa's voice taunted him: *What do you think will happen when you return, Theudemir? Do you think my father will welcome to his court the son of a traitor, the man betrothed to the granddaughter of another traitor? Do you think you will still be Theudemir of Aurariola after your brother has been dragged through the streets or blinded as punishment for his treachery and your father lies dead on a battlefield?*

The thought of Aurariola lost, his brother humiliated as a traitor, brought a visceral surge of anger every time it crossed his mind. Theo, lying on his back and staring up as clouds chased across a cerulean sky, gritted his teeth, pounded the hard ground impotently with clenched fists, and wished he could ask Laurentius, and his brothers, for advice. He did not trust Oppa. But in Sebastopolis, a place where there was no trust to be had, perhaps duty to Spania might be the only thing to which his loyalty could truly belong. No man could remain unmoved by what they had seen. Not even Oppa. *My father believes the Arabs pose no threat to Spania,* he had said. Theo tried to imagine how it would feel to tell someone about the Arabic forces, to have fought against them and to be told they posed no threat. He made an angry sound aloud at the thought of it.

Would that not be enough to change a man? he wondered, as he had so many times since talking with Oppa. He thought of King Egica's legitimate son and the fact that Oppa, no matter how high he climbed, would never be more than a royal bastard, favoured but not honoured. His own time away from Spania had changed the way Theo thought of his home country, had made the petty squabbles and pretensions of the nobility seem irrelevant to the greater objective of saving Spania itself. If his own perspective had so altered, Theo wondered, was it not possible that Oppa's, too, had changed? And would it not make sense, so far from home, for him to wish to ally himself with those he believed understood the real threat Spania would one day face – and who endeavoured to build the resources to combat that threat?

For I can do nothing at all, Theo thought in frustration, *if my family are denounced as traitors, Aurariola is gone, and I no longer have a voice.*

Theo tossed restlessly on the hard ground. One hand touched the hard ridges of skin on his face, smooth and burnished with time and weather but forever a reminder to all men of the brutal lick of Oppa's whip on his skin. Leofric and Silas, too, had felt that evil touch, and Theo understood why they could not forgive the man who had wielded the whip. But for Theo it was different. He and Oppa shared a life, no matter how distant Spania was, nor how they had been on opposite sides of their country's affairs. Still, they were both Spaniards. And Theo, who had been raised above all to respect the Chrismon-and-peacock symbol of Mater Spania, could not so easily dismiss that shared allegiance.

He touched the coin at his neck that bore the profile of Geila, his grandfather, who had once ruled Spania, albeit briefly. Beneath it, the smooth bone amulet Lælia had given him was warm against his skin. He stroked it, not daring to recall the touch of her mouth under his on the day she gave it to him. His longing for Lælia combined with confusion over Oppa's suggestion of alliance. The agitation and tension of war seemed to have made his body eternally aflame, and even the most casual recollection of Lælia, the curve of her body, the supple heat of her, set him afire with longing he had no way of assuaging.

He slept beneath a flowering apricot tree, through which dappled sunlight played over his eyes. The shadows playing through the broad canopy entered his dreams. Unwelcome images of Elpis were chased by brief, tantalising glimpses of Lælia, her face hidden from him. Where Elpis appeared in his dreams in vivid, disturbing clarity, Lælia's figure was clouded and distant, unreachable. The two figures chased across his mind, one pulling him like a magnet, yet ever elusive, the other terribly present and available. In his mind

Elpis seemed entangled with Oppa, as if by taking one he accepted the other. Theo felt their combined pull tugging him away from Lælia's fading presence across a divide from which he feared he could never return.

He woke at dusk with his cloak tangled about his ankles, drenched in sweat, to find Leofric observing him with thoughtful eyes.

"You speak much, *schnecke*, when you sleep."

Theo turned away and busied himself with his weapons. "That is why I choose to sleep at a distance to the camp. You should, perhaps, not bother yourself with accompanying me."

His tone was curt. He bent his head to splash water over his torso, expecting to find Leofric gone. But when he raised his head, the Slav was standing unmoved, arms over his chest, still eyeing him.

"When we return, you will take a woman, if I pay the coin myself."

"It is not your concern." Theo tossed a stone across the ground with more force than necessary.

Leofric clicked his tongue. "In war, *schnecke*, the only concern worth having is for the man at our side. I do not like to see that man distracted. Especially when the distraction is an itch that is easily scratched."

Theo fixed him with a hard eye. "Have I ever given you reason to doubt my sword arm?"

Leofric huffed as he turned away. "Take a woman, *schnecke*," he said over his shoulder, eyeing Theo darkly. "Before your distraction becomes the sword you die on."

It had taken days for them to scout the monastery. Now Kyros led three donkeys about the narrow, winding, rocky path. A small detachment of soldiers surrounded him. They marched with the desultory interest of paid guards and gave the impression of dull muscle. Below them, hidden beneath the lip of the cliff, Theo's men crept along a second, even more precarious pathway, every step calculated not to disturb the dry shale and alert watchers to their presence.

It was doubtful any observed them, however. Few ventured to the eastern side of the mountain, and the Arabs themselves would have won the monastery from the south, the same way Theo had initially attacked. Their lookouts were focused on the western and southern approaches, with a few eyes scattered also to the barren plains in the north. The east was mountainous territory inhabited by rebels ill equipped to launch direct attacks on the caliph's formidable fighting forces. The occasional smuggler carrying wine was overlooked in exchange for a small fee. Kyros had paid his fee and more, many times. His donkeys were a familiar sight, as were his wares a welcome relief. His special brand of arak was prized amongst the Maronites. He brewed it in an old wine cellar amongst the ruins outside Sebastopolis, and it was whispered that more than one Arab contingent had purchased it also, despite the brew being made from fermented raisins and thus prohibited under Muslim law.

Now Kyros plodded silently along the pathway, head down, clucking to his donkeys as they picked their way surefootedly amongst the stones. At a particularly wide bend in the wall of the mountain, he halted, ostensibly to alter one of the donkey's loads. He moved along the small caravan, pushing and adjusting, and paused at one spot, seemingly absorbed in his task. "That is the place," breathed Theo in Silas's ear. They waited until the donkeys had moved on again and listened to the night air. A casual watcher would not have noticed that the man who led them away was not the same as the one who had led them there.

Little moved. The creaking of the donkeys' harnesses was audible far into the distance, the only sound discernible in the silent night. The moon was dark, and little moved in the stillness. Far away a bird cawed. The sounds of the Arab encampment were shut behind the mountain. Silently, Theo and his men crept up the steep hillside to the narrow opening in the rock by which the man had paused. One by one, they slipped inside, leaving two men at the entrance. Those faded into the large boulders close by, appearing to anything but the closest of scrutiny merely more bulges in the rock face.

Inside, the passage was tight and black. "No Slav was made to fit in here," grunted Leofric as he squeezed behind the slender form of the Maronite rebel leading the way.

Kyros chuckled beneath his breath. "No Slav who drinks that terrible ale you like so much, anyway," he said.

"Ale is good for the body," muttered Leofric. "And better it is, most definitely, than arak you savages drink."

"Ale is cow piss. And you are fat, my friend."

"Fat? I am Slavic," replied Leofric, with as much dignity as could be managed whilst squeezing between rocks and trying to remain silent.

"You will both be dead if you do not stop talking," came Theo's calm voice behind them.

"Ho," chuckled Silas richly, "hark the sparrow teaching the hawks how to fight."

Kyros held up a hand, and all sound subsided. He held up three fingers, then cut his hand three ways; silently the leaders split into lines, and the men followed them as they cut into the passages leading up to the monastery. Theo led the centre. He moved silently, intent upon the way, every inch of his body alert to sound and touch. A faint movement came from ahead, and a thrill raced through him, setting his skin on fire. It was a mad tension, the one of battle. Theo welcomed it. He had come to live with it as easily as he once had the waves of the ocean on the cliffs at Aurariola. It felt natural to him, and now he felt his body tighten with its call, readying for the moment when steel and death would dance.

He reached the end of the passageway and moved into a dim cave filled with crates of stores. From behind the wooden door ahead came the muffled sound of voices. This was it.

He waited until the men crowded silently into the room. They looked at each other in the faint light, mere shadows in the warm shelter of the cave. Theo nodded, and they raised their swords, faces pale and set. He pushed open the door, and hell itself was unleashed.

The Arabs had been taken unawares, but they were not unprepared. The men were clad in mail, their swords close by. They were battle-hardened troops, veterans of Abd al Malik's long campaign across Persia. Theo had a quick glimpse of pointed helmets and elaborate armour before the scimitars came swinging and he crouched to meet the attack. Then it was close fighting, hard and furious, just the grunt of men and the clash of steel. They met in the great hall of the monastery, but the fight soon spread to the terrace, where men fell from the dizzying heights to crash brutally on rocks below. In the courtyard to the west that led into orchards, men spilled in a bloody tangle, crashing into apricot trees, falling beneath olive trees planted before Christ walked the earth.

Theo cut his way through the men before him, feeling the familiar blood-rush take him over so there was nothing but the sing of his blade and the fierce, delicious tension in his muscles, his body revelling in the fight. He wheeled and ducked, strangely exultant, his blade like a liquid extension of his own being, knowing with an almost supernatural instinct from whence the next cut would come. He saw the fear in men's eyes as they faced him and felt it in their retreat before his attack, in the way they fell from his arm as if they knew it presaged their deaths.

"Theo!" Kyros's cry of warning came just in time for Theo to duck beneath the evil slice of a scimitar from behind. Snarling, he turned to retaliate. He saw the scimitar continue as the man behind it spun with the force of his own strike. Theo's mouth opened to yell, but even as he moved to cut the man down, he saw the scimitar come down across Kyros's chest, slicing him from shoulder to waist in a bloody gash no man could survive.

With a roar of fury Theo cut the man down in a single blow and fell to his knees beside Kyros, who stared up at him with the startled awareness of his own impending death. "Theo," he said, and amidst the heat of battle, his words seemed to reach Theo as if they were the only two men present. "I have to tell you –"

"No," rasped Theo, gathering up his bloody body. "Rest, now."

"Oppa." Theo heard the urgency in the other man's voice. "He paid me to watch you."

"I know," said Theo, shaking his head. "It doesn't matter now."

"I did not betray you." Kyros grasped Theo's arms, trying convulsively to raise himself up. "Coin is being stolen from the taxes we collect. Oppa wanted only to be certain you were not involved."

Despite the roar of men, the air around Theo seemed to still. He leaned in close. "Why?"

"Oppa does not wish to see the treaty with the Arabs fail. But there are those who do, and one of them fights at your side." Kyros's eyes swivelled to Leofric, defending Theo's flank. He slipped something into Theo's tunic. "Your friend paid me for wine with this. Do not trust the Slavs," he breathed. "Friend or no."

Seeing the last spark fade from Kyros's eyes, Theo felt the battle snap back into focus around him at the same time as he heard Leofric's cry of warning. With a savage snarl of rage and frustration, he leaped to his feet, sword in hand. A man was coming at him on the terrace, a tall Arab clad in rich armour. Beneath the helmet his face was lean and hawkish, and he strode at Theo with the lethal intent of a man accustomed to the business of killing. Theo met the man in a crash that jarred his every bone, and as they clashed again and again, he felt rather than saw men fall away, giving them space.

They wheeled about each other cautiously, the mad battle-rush retreating in place of a cold, deadly calculation. Theo meant to kill him. Leofric's face swam at the periphery of his sight, driving his battle rage into a dark place hitherto unknown. Even as he balanced steel in his hand and faced his enemy, he felt doubt and betrayal corroding all that carried him into war and a vicious desire to kill rising in its place.

His opponent drove Theo backward, his curved sword flashing in rapid cuts that took Theo every ounce of his ability to counter. Rallying, Theo whirled beneath a stroke and came up with a savage thrust that lanced the man's leg, eliciting a grunt of pain. Theo forced his retreat, his sword flashing in deadly, relentless pursuit, the man he fought barely managing to hold him off. The killing desire rose hot and hard inside him, all the fury he had felt since arriving in Sebastopolis flowing through his sword arm so he fought with bitter intent, the man's face no more than a haze before him.

Then the curved blade rose from nowhere, and Theo knew, as he saw it, that he was too late to counter the stroke.

He contorted his body, twisting just enough to ensure the cut, though deep, was not lethal. He felt the searing cold lash his side, cutting through leather and linen to slice the skin. The pain served to cut through the final shred of restraint, touching something deep and visceral within. A furious snarl ripped from his belly. Theo rose from a crouch to leap through the air, his sword high and swift, whirling as he himself turned, cutting through skin and bone with cold ferocity. It seemed to Theo that the sweep of his steel sheared away more than life. It was as if his blade cut away the boy he had been, the Spaniard who had been raised to the dream of noble alliance made with men of honour. Theo cut through flesh and bone and with it cut away the last of the child he had once been.

When he landed, catlike on the balls of his feet, the man's head lay on the ground, his body crumpled, lifeless, beside it.

Theo barely paused to take it in, his sword flying now with deadly accuracy, about him men falling like stones in a river of blood. He ceased to be aware of the battle as a whole. His own sores were forgotten. Theo leaped and danced as if it were the sword that commanded him to do its bidding, and he knew no more where he was, knew only the triumphant thrill of the cut of steel and victory over the man before him.

"Enough!" he heard dimly through the mist of blood in his mind. "Theo, stop. It is done, by God! Xristus! Hold him!" It was on the last that he realised the arms binding him were Leofric's, and he was calling Silas to help; Theo threw them off with a savage growl. It was only when Silas bore him to the ground that he looked about him to see the dead littered all around and his own men leaning on their swords, panting and staring at him with something akin to awe – or fear.

"It is done, *wenkai*," murmured Silas in his ear. "Stop now." But though Theo subsided, he pulled himself angrily from Silas's grasp and turned his head from Leofric's view until he regained control. The blood-thrill had not left his body. He felt oddly detached from the men about him. Even as he issued curt orders and managed the aftermath of the battle, he remained remote. The fury of death and betrayal within him was a lick of lightning that at any moment, Theo felt, could spark a blaze he could not control.

He moved like a man possessed, driving his men ruthlessly to clean up the mess before dawn, organising a detachment to stay, leading the others back to the camp without permitting so much as a barrel of the wine to be opened.

At camp Neboulos was waiting. "It is good you are returned," he said. "A message has come from Leontios; we are needed back in port." His face was dark. "I cannot keep leaving Sebastopolis," he said in an uncharacteristic admission. "My people are not happy. They talk when I am not there. Too many, there are, who stir trouble. I am afraid how it will end."

Theo frowned, trying to assemble his thoughts. He would have sworn Neboulos was an honourable man. But how could he know? Theo thought of all the times he had misplaced his faith, and he questioned his own judgement. "Do you think you have rebels in your midst?" he asked instead, watching Leofric from the corner of one eye as he did.

Neboulos's face closed over, the rare moment of vulnerability gone. "My people will do what I say," he said stolidly. He followed the direction of Theo's eyes, and his own narrowed. "They may harbour little love for this war," he said. "But the men are loyal."

Theo turned away before his face could betray him further, wanting only to welcome the mindless task of rowing ahead.

29

THEO

OCTOBER, AD 691

Sebastopolis, Anatolia
Elauissa Sebaste, Cilicia, Turkey

Theo and his men left the shores that had seen Kyros's death before dawn, when the water was still and greasy. The sky hung low with cloud, and insects hovered over the shore. Theo pulled away hard, looking up at the mountainous wall where death still lay upon earth soaked with blood he had spilled. He forced a hard pace. Men cast him sullen glances, still covered in gore from the battle, wanting rest and succour, wine to soothe the pain in their minds. Theo rowed uncaring. Wine they would have soon enough. There was a favourable wind for port, and he meant to capture it. They put up sail and moved quickly. Theo felt the weight of Silas's and Leofric's eyes, but he could not meet them nor answer the questions he saw there.

They docked late that same evening, doing three days' journey in less than two. The men stumbled from the dromons onto shore, legs and arms trembling, so grateful to be back in the comfort of their fellows and proximity to wine and women that they hurried to tidy the dromon with newfound eagerness.

Theo doused his torso in a barrel of water on the dock, rearing back from it so water flew through the air and mixed with the blood on his side, shaking off the exhaustion. When he opened his eyes, Pelagia was watching him.

"You are hurt," she said, her little face grave as she looked at the red rivulets running from his skin onto the dock.

"It is nothing." Theo knelt down and forced a smile.

Pelagia came closer, beckoning as if she would tell him a childish secret. "There is a man to see you," she said instead when Theo tilted his head toward her. "Come to the back door and knock twice. Tell no one." She held out her hand for a coin and ran into the night.

"You will finish here," said Theo curtly to Silas and Leofric.

He drew his tunic over his still-damp skin then strode through the darkened alleys until he reached the back door of Athanais's tavern. Pelagia opened it and showed him into a windowless room, which, beside the large bed that was its most prominent feature, had two stools and a table on which stood a jug of wine and a plate of bread and meat. A tall man stood by the fire with his back to the door, a cloak hiding his face. He turned as the door closed behind Theo.

"Apsimar," Theo said as the other man put back his hood. His voice was thick with more than exhaustion as he looked at the strong features of his old commander. "I began to doubt that my messages had found you."

"They found me." Apsimar gestured at the stool. Pouring two cups of wine, he passed one to Theo, taking in the dirt- and blood-covered figure before him without comment. Apsimar was a man who understood war. Theo tasted salty relief at the reassurance of his presence, drinking deeply to disguise his emotion. "I came as soon as I could." He leaned forward and eyed Theo keenly. "What news of matters regarding our Arab friends?"

Theo reached into his pocket and withdrew a coin, which he flipped into the air. Apsimar caught it neatly and frowned as he held it up to the light. "Arab coin," he said.

Theo nodded. "And there is plenty more of it to be found in Sebastopolis." Kyros's face swam behind his eyes, and he put his wine cup down with more force than necessary. "Particularly in the Slavic camp," he said tersely.

"Leontios's reports to Constantinople mention nothing of Slavic unrest." Apsimar turned the coin slowly in his hand.

"It is more than unrest." Theo met his eyes. "The Slavs do not like being used as coin collectors for an emperor they despise. I do not doubt Neboulos's loyalty, but nor am I certain that his men share it."

Apsimar looked up sharply. "Do you think it might come to rebellion?"

Theo remembered how Leofric had turned away when Theo had asked him about Neboulos, the way his face had closed over. He felt again the sting of betrayal. "I have a Slavic fighter amongst my men," he said, trying to keep the anger from his voice. "He once said that the Slavs like Neboulos and will do as he instructs. But one man cannot hold thirty thousand, if it comes to it, not even Neboulos."

"I remember your Slav. Do you trust him?" Theo was aware of Apsimar watching him closely.

"I did," he said shortly. "But now —" He broke off and shook his head. "He recently paid for wine using that coin."

"Does he know you suspect him?"

"No." Theo stared bleakly into the fire. "I thought it wiser to keep such knowledge to myself, for now, at least." His mouth tightened.

"No man can go easily into battle unsure if the man at his side is ally or enemy." Apsimar looked at him soberly. "Who else knows of your suspicions?"

Theo turned the wine cup in his hands. "The man who told me was in the employ of the Spanish bastard."

"Oppa." Apsimar nodded thoughtfully. "And he is close to Leontios, I think."

"They are rarely seen apart. But I am not certain what game he plays." Briefly he told Apsimar about his conversation with Oppa some months earlier. "Oppa understands the Arab threat," he said.

"I may loathe him, but that much I do not doubt. He has no reason to undermine our position here."

Apsimar sat back and stared at the fire. "Whispers have reached Constantinople," he said. He glanced sideways at Theo. "It is a city of whispers, make no mistake, a cesspool of politics and games no man of honour has any place in. But these whispers persist, and Emperor Justinian II begins to heed them. They say that Leontios has not been as careful as he should be to ensure that the terms of the treaty negotiated four years ago with the Arabs are adhered to. The Arabs, it is said, complain that they are being cheated of the taxes to which they are entitled. If both the whispers and the Arab discontent are true, there is a real danger that the peace might break." He looked grimly at Theo. "And I do not need to explain to you, of all men, how precarious our position here is. That treaty cannot fail, do you understand? If it does, Armenia is lost to us."

Theo nodded. "What would you have me do?" He felt a rush of relief as he asked the question and waited for a command. He had not realised until he spoke how heavy a burden it had been, trying to decide what he should do alone with no other voice to consult.

"If Leontios indeed plays a double game, then we must discover what it is and put a stop to it before everything we have achieved here is lost." Apsimar's eyes were dark as he looked at Theo. "Let your Slav continue as he will. Do not alert him to your suspicions. Watch him, see what you might learn."

Theo stiffened. "Spy on him? On my friend?"

Apsimar shrugged. "I did not say you would like it. But it is what must be done."

"And Oppa?"

Apsimar hesitated a long while before answering, and when he did, his voice was quiet. "It is one thing to ask you to watch your friend. It is another to make an ally of an enemy. I will not tell you how to proceed with the Spanish bastard, Theo. That is a choice you must make yourself."

"I cannot make an ally of Oppa." The words tasted foul in Theo's mouth. "And nor can I fight beside a man I thought was my friend and who may instead be plotting to betray me." His relief of a moment ago was gone as fast as it had come, disappeared into a dark pit of loneliness in which he could see no glimmer of light. "This is not a war I want any part of."

"But it is war." Apsimar's voice was harsh. "We none of us may like it, but wars are fought by men, Aurariola, just as they are fought over coin. If we are to have any hope of winning this one, we must understand the men who fight it, what drives them, and who might betray us."

"And if I discover that the whispers are true, that Leontios betrays the emperor himself – what, then, am I to do?" Exhaustion rose like a tide inside Theo as he spoke.

Apsimar's eyes were not without sympathy when he answered. "If there is time, I will send men to aid you. But I must warn you, Theo – Constantinople is a clumsy ship that takes much time to change its direction. And war, as we both know, is a fickle wench that turns in a moment. Send word as soon as you can, and I will do what I might in Constantinople. But we both know Sebastopolis cannot be defended." He looked soberly at Theo. "If it comes to open battle here, Theo, there will be little to do other than run."

"If I run from here," Theo said hoarsely, "it will not be to Constantinople. Not after this." He met Apsimar's eyes. "Spania is at war, my family and lands threatened. I cannot stay away forever."

Apsimar's mouth tightened. "Keep me informed," he said curtly. "And hope to Xristus the treaty holds." He stood and put out his arm. After a moment, Theo took it. Apsimar nodded, then he turned and left without farewell.

Theo sat for a long time, staring at the coals glowing in the hearth, seeing only the dark spaces between them until their light faded and the fire became ash.

30

LETTER FROM ATHANAGILD TO ALARIC

OCTOBER, AD 691

Toletum, Spania
Toledo, Spain

A laric —

The news that Sunifred still withholds his permission for your marriage saddened me. We should all be free to love as we choose. You have not sought my advice, so I will not offer it, other than to say I believe it a vile snare in which Sunifred holds you, one I pray you find the strength to endure.

Teudolfo — it was wise that you sent him, brother, for none suspected him to be anything more than a passing peasant — tells me Sunifred prepares to ride when the winter has passed, and you at his side. You will be pleased, I hope, with the news I send with Teudolfo's return. I pray it may, perhaps, help you. Our father sends word that he will not order the men at Emerita to hold against Sunifred. He will not guarantee them, mind, but he will not order them to oppose you. You will know what to do with this, I think.

Might I suggest that if Teudolfo comes again, he should adopt Shukra's disguise and meet me in the pleasure house by the river we both know? It is, surprisingly, the safest place for a man of God to hide his true business. It is also *a good place to hear dark whispers from the palace. Egica, the whores whisper, relishes Favila's rebellion in the north. He takes his revenge by keeping Theodefred's son at the palace, close enough that Roderic might be called hostage. Theodefred grows dark, and war closer.*

I am grateful for your queries as to my wellbeing, but please do not be concerned for me. I find myself well able to navigate the complexities of my situation. At least I am able to aid Laurentius and our father by passing information on Sisebut's plans, and in this, I believe I can at least be of service, even in a small fashion.

I pray for you, my brother. Every day. In the midst of this darkness it is thoughts of you, and Theo, that light my heart.

—Athanagild

31

ALARIC

NOVEMBER, AD 691

Hispalis, Spania
Seville, Spain

Alaric had avoided Rekiberga's presence since his choice to remain at Sunifred's side. A thousand times he had questioned that choice. The mere thought of Rekiberga being married to another man made Alaric's fists clench, his heart thud with fury, and every muscle in his body tense to carry her off there and then, and be done with it. Teudolfo, Alaric knew, believed he should go, and every day that passed proved in a new way that his assessment of Sunifred was well founded. The man was as self-centred as he was impatient with either intelligence or the opinion of others. Alaric, long accustomed to his father's calm manner of gathering counsel and assessing each man's opinion, found Sunifred's fractious dismissal of any counter-argument to his own ideas both frustrating and capricious. Sunifred was a true product of Spania's privileged aristocracy, raised during a time of relative peace, when the only battles he had fought had been against a weaker foe with the full might of his wealth and privilege behind him. He had complete faith in his own instincts and a remarkably thin skin when it came to criticism of any kind. And yet still Alaric could not stomach grovelling at Egica's feet and recasting his allegiance to a man who had not only killed his mother but sent his son to kill Alaric's own brother.

It was an impossible choice, but the third – to run with Rekiberga at his side – seemed to Alaric the least honourable of all, for in so doing he would abrogate all ability to give her a life of honour and pride. To leave her father because he did not live up to the ideals of manhood to which Alaric had been raised seemed to him both childish and unsophisticated. Should a man's moral character determine his right to rule? It was a question Alaric could not quite reconcile in his mind.

As they walked now into Sunifred's villa on the outskirts of Hispalis, Alaric wished, as he had every day since the decision had been made, that he could seek his brothers' counsel. Theudemir, he felt sure, would know exactly the right course he should take. And Athanagild would advise him soberly and wisely. But Theo was all but lost to them, and Alaric could not bring himself to lay his decision upon the younger brother he had always felt bound to protect. Instead, he wrestled alone with his conscience, to no satisfying end.

They found Sunifred pacing the œca. He gave Alaric an impatient glance but did not pause. Rekiberga, seated at her father's table, met Alaric's eyes, her own so fierce they made Alaric's heart twist under the knife of his own indecision. Gathering himself, he turned to Sunifred. "I have men to offer your cause," said Alaric bluntly.

Sunifred stopped pacing at that. "What men?"

"I have news from my father." The words tasted foul in Alaric's mouth, and he avoided Rekiberga's piercing gaze. "He will not order the men of Emerita to fight at your side. But he gave his word that he will not stand against me when I do."

Sunifred's eyes narrowed greedily. "And you will do this?"

"I led the men of Emerita in all but name for several years. They know me. They knew my brother, Theudemir, also, and they know it was Oppa behind the attack in which he was almost lost to us. They have reason enough to fight even if I were not to order them. But I will command them, Fráuja, and they will open the gates to you." He nodded at Teudolfo, who stepped forward and bowed.

"I have served in Emerita Augustus under Alaric," he said. "The men know what manner of man they follow, and they will ride behind the son of Suinthila, no matter whose banner he follows. If Alaric asks, they will follow yours."

Alaric nodded and turned to Sunifred. "If his men ride," he said, "my father will not long stand to be left behind. And if Emerita rides, Paulus, also, will. You will have Illiberis."

Sunifred gave a short bark of laughter. "If you think that, lad," he said, "then you are even madder than I. Paulus hates treason even more than he hates me. He won't give so much as a *tremissis* for our 'cause', as you call it." He looked calculatingly at Alaric. "And what of Theodefred, the Duke of Corduba? It is a son of Chinda-suinth I truly need. With Theodefred at my side, none will stand against my rule in Toletum." When Alaric did not reply, Sunifred's smile faded. "I made my terms clear," he said, looking between Rekiberga and Alaric. "And yet you stand before me with nothing more substantial than vague promises."

"I bring to the marriage the title of Aurariola, my own thiufa — and my loyalty." Alaric held Sunifred's eye and kept his resentment under tight control. "I have defied my own father to support your cause," he said quietly.

"But you have not yet brought him to heel," Sunifred snapped. "I told you once before that my daughter will marry whom I choose, at a time of my choosing."

From the corner of his eye, Alaric saw the blood drain from Rekiberga's face and her mother's hand close over hers in a silent caution.

"Yes, Fráuja, you did." Alaric kept his tone calm with an effort. "But war is coming. I have fulfilled the bulk of your conditions. And I would not ride from here without settling the matter."

Sunifred moved as fast as a serpent strike, pushing Alaric hard against the wall. "I tell you this again, and hear me well, boy, for it is the last time I will say it: bring Paulus and Theodefred to my cause — yes, and your father too — and we will talk about you wedding my daughter. Then, and only then, do you understand?" He stared at Alaric with a hard eye, then stalked from the room, leaving Alaric staring wordlessly at Rekiberga's pale face. She half rose from her chair, remaining there despite her mother's forceful tugging at her arm.

"Will you do his bidding, then, my lord?" Rekiberga spoke in a low, hurt voice, her eyes raking Alaric's with a raw, proud fire that twisted the knife even deeper into his soul.

"Your father is right." His voice was harsh in the empty œca. "With Corduba and Illiberis behind him, he has a real chance to take Toletum and sway the northern nobles. Without them, his cause is lost."

"And you would see those men join you." It was not a question but an accusation, one cast with enough heat to scald Alaric's blood. It was only when he met Rekiberga's blazing eyes that he saw the pain behind her contempt and felt the horrible chafe of the bind in which they were caught. "It is not too late," Rekiberga whispered, her eyes searching his face, seeking the sign that would tear her from her mother's grasp to flee her father's house, placing her faith in Alaric and her life in his hands.

Glancing briefly at her mother's drawn, fearful face, Alaric knew that life to be too uncertain, and himself to be unworthy of such faith.

"Yes," he said, meeting Rekiberga's eyes bleakly. "It is too late. I am sworn to your father's course, Rekiberga. I will not dishonour us both by disavowing him now."

She stared at him, the last vestiges of colour leaching from her eyes and cheeks.

"Then go," she whispered finally. "And remember that this decision was yours, Alaric – not mine." Pulling herself free of her mother's grasp, Rekiberga turned and stalked from the œca, straight backed and proud.

Alaric watched until she had gone. Then, under the watchful eye of Sunifred's men, he turned and left, shame and resentment warring inside him.

32

LÆLIA
NOVEMBER, AD 691

Illiberis, Spania
Granada, Spain

Lælia could see Theo on a distant shore, his back turned to her. She felt the sharp edge of danger close by, and she sensed many men, a dark undercurrent of violence.

"Turn around," she tried to say, but the words wouldn't come, were choked in her throat as they had been for so many years, and then his figure was fading from view, sucked into the mists of a dream.

She woke drenched in sweat, her blankets crumpled at the foot of her bed, the blazing Illiberis moon lighting the mountains beyond the villa. Striding to the window, she leaned out and dragged breath into her body, shaking her head. Coming back to Illiberis had brought a return of the dreams that had tortured her youth and which, she realised belatedly, she had been blissfully free of in the desert sands. Here, she seemed bound by worlds beyond the immediate one, connected to an invisible force she both craved and ran from.

She missed Safia. Ilyan's daughter had felt like her last link to the desert and the freedom she had felt there. Safia would already be in Corduba with Lælia's aunt Riccilo. Lælia suspected the girl would do well at the Toletum court. She had her father's mercurial nature, powers of observation, and ability to meld into the background of any room, welcome but unobtrusive.

Dawn was coming, a thin crest of gold on the horizon. Lælia dressed and left the villa, welcoming the crisp air on her face as she rode onto the low plateaus where grass was still plentiful, Theo's figure still vivid in her waking mind. Lælia knew her dreams held a reality. She had lived too many of them to doubt they had meaning. She knew, too, that their meaning was indiscernible in practical terms. Separating impression from reality was impossible, for the world of dreams was where souls roamed in the mists, free to speak truths beyond human rationale.

Her mind kept returning to the sense of resignation she had felt, as if Theo had given up on something in himself, had withdrawn not only from her but from a part of himself. *I am still here!* she thought fiercely, digging her heels into the horse's side and cantering up the last of the narrow path. *I do not relinquish you, Theo. Even if we must turn from each other — we are bound, you and I.*

She forced the dream from her mind, knowing she could learn nothing more from it. She turned instead toward the drill ground, craving the mindless discipline of training. By mid-morning, three young horses were breathing hard and Jadis raced at her side as she galloped the final stretch on a fourth. Lælia leaped from the horse in mid-stride, as she had learned to do in the sands, tumbling and coming up with arrow drawn. There was a comfort in performing the skills she had spent so many long months mastering, even if here, on her home soil, it seemed none cared for them at all.

The sound of a slow handclap startled her and she swung her bow, ready to release. Her grandfather, Count Paulus of Illiberis, moved from behind a clump of holm oak, holding his hands up in surrender.

"Hold your arrows, child," he said, a crooked smile on his grim features. "There will be time enough for them, I suspect."

"It is early for you to be riding." Lælia lowered her bow.

Paulus inclined his head. "That presumes I rode out from the villa this morning. I did not. I am come from Gaius."

"Gaius?" Lælia frowned; the town was more than a day's ride north. "I was not aware you had left Illiberis."

"No." Her grandfather raised his eyebrows sardonically. "You seem aware of little other than the herd and training since your return."

"If war is coming, little else matters." Lælia met his eyes steadily. Paulus had yet to grant her a formal audience. She had the sense he was taking her measure from afar, assessing who she had become in her time away. Her grandmother, too, had been uncharacteristically quiet, leaving her mountaintop abbey only once, to welcome Lælia home, before returning to her solitude.

Lælia herself had felt uneasy since her return. Everything seemed different, yet entirely as she had left it. She was aware that what had altered the most was herself, but she did not have the words to explain what had changed within her, and neither of her grandparents were of the disposition to enquire. Perhaps as a result of her disturbed night, she felt an uncharacteristic urge now to try to explain herself.

"There is much of which we should speak," she said, then she stopped abruptly, wondering why it was that she felt entirely in control of her words on a dromon of soldiers, yet unable to so much as form a sentence in the presence of her grandfather.

"It is normal." Her grandfather's voice was gruff. "Men come back from war much the same. We long for home, then reach it and find ourselves lost." Paulus gave her a sideways glance and then, as if regretting his words, made a dismissive gesture. "Enough of this. I rode to Gaius to meet Theodefred, but he sent a messenger in his stead. And before you ask, the servant girl, Safia, arrived in Corduba. I have news of her."

Theodefred was the Duke of Corduba. He was married to Riccilo, whose mother had been Acantha's sister and whom Lælia called Aunt. Theodefred himself was the youngest son of the great king Chindasuinth, who had once taken the throne from Egica's grandfather, Tulga, and whose rule had brought Spania into the longest peace it had known. He was also one of Paulus's oldest friends. Theodefred's position at court, Lælia knew, had become increasingly precarious since rumours swirled that his younger brother, Favila, rebelled against Egica in the mountains of Gallæcia.

"Egica has taken Theodefred's son, Roderic, and sent him with his own, Wittiza, to his family lands in Tuy, far to the north west," said Paulus. "He says he is to be companion to Wittiza, but none are fooled. Roderic has been taken hostage. And it is not only Roderic he has taken." He moved restlessly in the early-morning sun, looking out over the valley below. "Theodefred's younger brother, Favila, left his own son Pelayo in Theodefred's care some months ago, when rebellion broke out in the mountains of Gallæcia. Now Pelayo, too, has been taken to Tuy. The children are held in a fortress under strict guard, and Egica has named Favila traitor to the Crown."

"Riccilo must be distraught," Lælia said. "Roderic is her only son."

"She is also smart – and ruthless." Paulus smiled grimly. "When Egica took the children from the Toletum court, Egilona of Aurariola was with them."

"Egilona? Theo's sister?"

Paulus nodded. "She has been a companion to Roderic since they were infants. Riccilo saw an opportunity. She sent your Safia to Tuy with Egilona." He gave Lælia a wry smile. "The messenger tells me Riccilo was very impressed with your gift."

Yes, Lælia thought, her mind racing. Riccilo had always been astute in the ways of court, and in reading people. She would have perceived Safia's skills immediately. Ilyan, she thought, could not have hoped for anything better. His little spy was even now positioned beside the future king and his closest companions.

Paulus was watching her closely. "I suspect a bow is not the only weapon you learned to wield in the desert sands," he said dryly.

Lælia ignored his comment. "What does Favila do?" she asked instead. "What does he mean by this rebellion in Gallæcia?"

"It is not Favila's rebellion, though it is likely to soon become his." Paulus's face darkened. "The men who attack Egica's holdings in the north are not Favila's. They are from the tribes, allied to no lord, men who fight for coin. The messenger says that Theodefred believes Egica plots to destabilise his brother's rule in Gallæcia and ensure that neither Favila nor Theodefred join Sunifred's rebellion in the south. I believe he is right."

"Declaring a son of Chindasuinth traitor is a bold move, even for Egica."

"Indeed. Taking his son hostage even more so. But by naming him thus, he forces Theodefred to his knees, taking the one ally Sunifred needs to take Toletum."

"What will Theodefred do?" Lælia asked.

"Theodefred is Duke of Corduba, possibly the most powerful man in Spania next to Egica himself, and he is sworn to the Crown. Egica has demanded Theodefred send the Corduba thiufae north to fight alongside Egica's forces – even if that means taking up arms against Favila." Paulus's face was dark. "Theodefred's messenger told me hundreds have ridden north under the Corduba banner, as Egica commanded."

"You do not approve," Lælia guessed.

"I cannot." Paulus strode restlessly, first this way, then that. "I do not like Sunifred," he said bluntly. "But the time comes when we may have to join him. If we take up arms against our own blood, our own brothers – where does it end?" He met Lælia's eye gravely. "We may not be able to remain out of it now," he said. "None of us. Egica wants a war. He has already tried to take Illiberis, and you, once. We must assume he will do so again."

Lælia did not flinch from the unspoken question in his tone. "I am not yet a proven warrior," she said. "I have not led men in battle and I do not pretend to know how to do so. But I have not spent this last year in the sands learning to lay down my sword." Feeling the weight of what must be said between them, she chose her next words carefully. "Illiberis does not have the strength to defend our own boundaries and also fight a rebellion. That is why I made an agreement before I returned. I have two hundred men, trained warriors from the desert sands, whom I can call upon and have here within a matter of weeks."

Paulus looked at her closely. "Might I ask what you have traded for such bounty?"

"Two hundred horse," answered Lælia promptly. "And a favour."

"Two hundred," repeated Paulus flatly. "Impossible."

"Not at all." Lælia met his eyes directly. "We have over five hundred head in the mountains. Ten different herds. More than half of those are at least partially trained by the tribes. Your men are already mounted, and you need less than a hundred to mount any others you can find. We can spare the others. The horses will remain in Sexi for one year, as surety for Dahiya's men, after which time they are given whether we need the men or not. It is a light bargain for the service of good warriors, and you know it."

Paulus's eyes narrowed. "And the favour?"

"Nothing that has a cost to Illiberis, to you, or to me." She met his eyes. "Beyond that, I can say no more."

Paulus raised his eyebrows. "And if I agree to this, who do you propose will lead the defence of Illiberis?"

"With the Riders from the sands and the Illiberis tribes with Tosius, we will have the men to counter any attack. They need only command. And I can command, Grandfather." She spoke quietly, without boast. "I have learned much from Dahiya, not least how to listen. You have men here who have seen war: your thiufadis, Gratimo, and the ten men of your personal thiufa. They are hardened in battle and know the ground here. I may not have wielded sword on a battlefield, but I can learn from those who have and take their counsel. Egica and his men might try to take me, it is true. But first they must take Illiberis. And in our long history, Grandfather, that is a feat none have yet managed."

Paulus watched her face as she spoke. When she finished, he drew a deep breath. "I have watched you since your return. I do not say you cannot do this, but nor am I convinced you can, and there is not another man in my position I know who would let you try."

"If you had planned for me to stay out of this, you would never have sent me into the sands to train with Dahiya." Lælia held his eyes steadily. "I have men amongst the Riders who know me, Grandfather. They trust me. And they are not unaccustomed to riding behind a woman."

Paulus gave her a half smile and nodded briefly. "You will join

Gratimo and me in my study this morning," he said. "We will wait a time before we send for your desert swords. But even if we do use them, Lælia, if it comes to that, if Illiberis falls and Egica comes for you, then you must promise you will ride for the coast, and for Ilyan." He stepped forward and cupped her face, looking at her closely. "Do not die for Illiberis, Lælia," he said roughly. "We have lost too much already. Live – even if it is on a foreign shore."

He released her and turned away, his eyes looking restlessly to the horizon. "I had not thought Theodefred so quick to give up." Lælia, seeing the gaunt expression on the rugged features, thought it was the first time she had seen her grandfather look old.

33

YOSEF

SEPTEMBER, AD 691

Chang'an, Serica
Xi'an, China

The wind was freezing, and dust whipped from the plains against the great walls surrounding the city. Yosef endured the admonitions of the Sogdian merchant who headed the caravan with his head down, standing by the double-humped, long-haired camel that had carried him across wastes already growing icy with the coming season.

"We do not enter the Danfeng Gate." The merchant was stolid and implacable. "The Daming Palace is the seat of power of Sheng-shen Huangdi, the most powerful of the powerful. It is no place for merchants and trade. We go to Chang'an, where we can trade our goods peaceably."

"But I must enter the gates to find the family I seek. Perhaps Empress Wu can help." Yosef was too tired for his customary circumspection. He had ceased, many miles ago now, to think of anything but making the connection his father had dreamed of. His destination was Serica and the family connected to the silk tree. Beyond that, Yosef no longer knew, nor cared, what would happen to him.

"Shh." The merchant put a finger over his lips and frowned. "Do not say that name aloud. The person of whom you speak has assumed the title of Huangdi — what your people might call emperor, or empress. To refer to her by name is punishable by death."

Yosef clicked his tongue in frustration. "I have a letter of introduction." He was generally more careful; experience had taught him that those who knew of the scrolls would find him, or at the very least, find a way to make themselves known to him. To speak openly of his business went against everything he had learned since leaving Spania. But to stand less than a handful of miles from his ultimate destination after so many long years of travel and be refused entry seemed to Yosef a frustration beyond endurance.

"I am entering those gates," he said fiercely. "With or without your consent."

"If you will permit me?"

A quiet, well-modulated voice speaking Greek broke into their conversation. Yosef and the Sogdian swung around to find a hooded figure wearing simple black robes. Yosef could not see his face, and nor could he understand where the man had appeared from — the plains were wide and deserted, and the caravan had drawn to a halt for this discussion long before they neared the main entrance to the palace.

"Who are you?" The Sogdian merchant's hand was on his knife, and he glanced around uneasily.

"My name is unimportant." The figure let a small fragment of material unravel in his fingers. "This, perhaps, will help you understand." The merchant took it and examined the symbol painted there. Yosef's heartbeat, which had for months now felt oddly weak, seemed to shift and jump in his chest. The symbol was the winged sun of the Zoroastrians, a symbol every merchant through Persia knew and understood. The merchant bowed deeply.

"I would speak to your friend alone," said the newcomer, his face still hidden. Yosef moved closer, and the two stepped slightly aside, out of hearing.

"Are you a merchant?" Yosef asked. "I have a family I need to find –"

"What is needed," said the figure, in a surprisingly stern tone, "is for you to stop talking and start listening. Your words have already sung to the wrong ears. Now you do as I say, and the letter you carry will find the right hands. Do you understand?" He flicked back his hand, and on the white hem of his sleeves, Yosef saw the mulberry tree symbol, delicately picked out in silk thread.

Yosef swallowed and nodded. His new companion turned back to the Sogdians. "This one will come with me." The figure bowed low to the merchant. "He is wanted for questioning by Huaiyi – Buddhist monk and adviser to Shengshen Huangdi."

"Ah." The Sogdian merchant took in the austere robes and bent head, and a new tone of respect entered his voice. "We are honoured to serve those who serve Shengshen Huangdi," he said humbly. Returning the messenger's bow, he inclined his head to Yosef. "It seems you had the right of it, friend," he said, smiling. Putting his hand out, he shook Yosef's. "I wish you well. You know where to find us should you require anything."

Yosef barely had time to untie his meagre belongings before his new companion prodded him with somewhat painful urgency in the side. "Move," he hissed, and Yosef found himself walking away from the caravan in the direction of the gates. "Do not speak." His companion spoke with his head down, hood still covering his face. In the distance, the Sogdian caravan swayed on its way, gradually disappearing into the bitterly cold dust haze. A moment later, Yosef found himself pushed to the ground into a slight hollow, and his new companion's cloak was drawn over them.

"What are we doing?" he asked, bewildered.

"Waiting," came the implacable answer. "Do not speak. We will move at night."

Yosef was cold, hungry, and exhausted, and for a moment he felt indignation swell in his chest. Long years on the road, however, had taught him the necessity of endurance, so he bit his tongue and closed his eyes, trying to block out the bitter cold and the tired, sad despair that crept through his blood.

It was late, and Yosef had dozed when he felt his companion's hand on his shoulder. "Now," said the voice in his ear, "we move." Yosef stumbled to his feet, and the man clicked his tongue in annoyance. "You are loud as a monkey," he hissed in reprimand. "Follow me, and try to do it quietly."

It began to snow. All through the night they moved, silent and fast, and when dawn broke Yosef squinted around at the colourless landscape in confusion.

"The gates of the city are nowhere in sight," he said, frowning. "Where are you taking me?"

"If you entered the Daming Palace, you would have been killed – or imprisoned – before half a day was out. I am taking you somewhere safe."

"Somewhere safe?" Yosef stopped and put down his roll of belongings. He felt a weary, tired anger rise through his body. "I understand that you are trying to help," he said, trying to maintain an even tone. "But I must enter the palace, and I must find the family I am instructed to meet. If you just tell me where to go, I will enter the palace myself and tell none we met."

"No." His companion picked up the roll with surprising ease, given he was slight and reached barely to Yosef's shoulder. "You will walk where I tell you and cease arguing such nonsense."

Yosef stiffened. Stealthily, he slid one hand inside his cloak, reaching for the knife he had long carried strapped to his thigh. "I appreciate your concern," he said carefully. "But our ways will part here."

His fingers had no sooner touched the hilt of his knife than the slender figure in front of him moved in a series of lightning-fast movements. Yosef felt a blow like a hammer in his chest and found himself on his back in the snow. When he touched his thigh, the knife was gone.

"How did you –" he began, frowning.

"I told you to cease arguing."

"At least," said Yosef, squinting against the snow glare, "tell me your name."

His captor pushed back the hood of the cloak, revealing pale ivory skin, midnight hair tied in an elaborate knot, and features at once delicate and determined.

"I am Jiang Fei Hong," she said. "And you have been a long time fulfilling your father's promise, Yosef ben Arun."

34

THEO

DECEMBER, AD 691

Sebastopolis, Anatolia
Elauissa Sebaste, Cilicia, Turkey

Theo found Pelagia on the dock at twilight and handed her a coin. "Go to the Spanish bastard," he said, "and tell him to go to the ruins above the port." He cupped her chin. "Tell no one, do you understand?" The child nodded solemnly. Theo cleared his throat awkwardly. "Your sister," he said in a low voice. "Do you have word of her?"

Pelagia looked around, to ensure nobody was listening. "Elpis is safe," she said, but her face was troubled. "She said to tell you she thinks of you."

Theo felt unaccustomed colour flood his face. He was suddenly very aware of Leofric and Silas behind him. "Well, go on then," he said roughly. "Off with you. Don't spend it all at once."

Pelagia looked at him through wide eyes that hurt his chest, then turned and ran into the night. Theo walked back to where Leofric and Silas were coiling rope by the dromon.

"Your heart is too soft, friend." Leofric cast him a wry smile. "It is a wonder you have any coin left, *ne?* You are generous with that child." Undeterred by Theo's lack of an answer, he went on: "Will you not join us at the tavern tonight and find better sport upon which to bestow your coin?"

Theo knew his absence from the nightly drinking in which his men indulged had begun to be marked. He kept his distance primarily to avoid conversations such as this with Leofric. Even the slightest thought of Leofric's possible betrayal was enough to send him deep into a blackness that threatened to swallow him.

"That is the advantage of so long an abstinence." He kept his tone light, and loud enough for the rest of the men to hear. "I have spare coin to buy a prettier face than yours for company, Slav." His men guffawed, and Leofric clapped him on the shoulder, grinning appreciatively. Only Silas did not smile. Theo turned from the older man's dark scrutiny and moved quickly uphill, turning until the dock was behind him and keeping his face hidden beneath his cloak.

Silas alone had grown concerned at his continued absence. Theo knew his friend was worried. But it was unfair, Theo felt, to alert the other man to his suspicions. And despite what he had told Apsimar, Theo could not bring himself to truly believe Leofric a traitor. Nor could he bring himself to follow him in order to discern the truth. Somehow, doing even that felt like a betrayal. And from the moment he had shared knowledge of his suspicions with Apsimar to the conversation he was about to have, Theo knew he had already betrayed far more than he had ever, in his worst nightmares, imagined himself capable of.

From the ruins, he could see anything coming up the hill. He settled into the shadows and took a pull on his wineskin, feeling a strange calm descend.

Oppa appeared soon after, melding himself to the wall opposite and keeping his own hood raised over his features.

"Kyros is dead," Theo said without preamble. Oppa nodded but said nothing. "He told me the Slavs are stealing the Arabic coin."

"Not stealing," said Oppa quietly. "They are being paid."

Theo looked at him sharply. "For information?"

Oppa shrugged. "For information. And, perhaps, for more than just their loyalty."

"Does Leontios know this?"

"Leontios knows. He doesn't care." Oppa said it simply, without emotion.

"But you do."

"I care about the treaty with the Arabs. About ensuring it holds. Leontios likes to know which of his Slavs are traitors. Eventually he will use the information against them, make a show of force intended to humiliate them and bring them to heel. I fear that when he does, his actions will have the opposite effect."

"You think he will push the Slavic forces into open rebellion," said Theo.

Oppa nodded. "It was I who told him there were traitors amongst the Slavs. I thought he would act upon the information and shut it down. But he did not." Oppa moved restlessly away from the wall and shifted his hood so the moon lit his features. Theo suppressed an involuntary shiver with an effort. The sharp features had been hated for too long for him to look upon them without instinctive revulsion. "The mutterings in the Slavic camp grow daily worse, their treachery more blatant. I take as much Arabic coin in my taverns as I do Greek. Not only does Leontios turn a blind eye to their dealings; he sends small parties such as yours to collect taxes without so much as a clerk to record it. Such carelessness is no accident."

"My men do not steal," Theo said flatly.

"If you were sure of that, you would not be here." Oppa's response was hard and sharp. "But it is not theft that should concern you. Leontios is sending a detachment of Neboulos's army to Cyprus." He met Theo's eyes. "He will use the missing coin as grounds to take Cyprus back in the name of the emperor, reneging on the agreement to render it neutral ground with all taxes split evenly."

"He plans to break the treaty," breathed Theo.

Oppa nodded. "I believe he does."

"If it comes to war," Theo said, "Sebastopolis cannot be held."

"And now you see why I seek you as ally, not enemy. Neither of us wishes to see the Arabs gain another toehold." A short silence fell, in which Theo heard Neboulos's words: *I am afraid how it will end.*

Neboulos knows, Theo realised. *He knows that if it comes to war, there is no guarantee the Slavs will remain loyal.*

"Why tell me this?" he said aloud. "What is it that you want from me?"

Oppa made to move closer and Theo's hand flew to his sword. "Do not come close to me," he growled. "I will hear you, Oppa Egicason, but never make the mistake of thinking I trust you."

"Very well." Oppa's mouth twisted. "I will speak plainly, then. I believe you might have certain… allies… who would not agree with Leontios's current actions. Who may yet be able to make him change his mind. Firstly, I would like you to make contact with those allies and see if there is a way to avoid the crisis."

When he was met with nothing but Theo's blank face and silence, he went on. "There is also the matter of what happens if, or when, we both return to Spania." Theo remained silent. Oppa made an impatient sound. "You have been at war long enough to know that nothing will come of this rebellion in the south. My father will crush it. He has already sent word requesting that I return and help him to do so. When I do return, it will be with enough men and coin to ensure my father's victory." He spoke with flat certainty, and Theo felt a cold dread in the pit of his stomach. "My father will not be content with peace. He will take the lands he has conquered and treat his enemies mercilessly. You know, as do I, that Spania cannot afford such squabbles." His eyes gleamed unpleasantly in the moonlight. "Nor," he said softly, "do I wish to find myself accused of crimes such as the attack on the fleet. Or of anything else that might result in my father's displeasure." He looked pointedly at the scars on Theo's face. "So I propose that you and I make an arrangement between ourselves, here, to which we adhere in the event that we return to discover our homeland rent by open war. An agreement that safeguards us both and helps us to ensure Spania itself is best prepared for what might come."

"An agreement," said Theo slowly. "What kind of agreement?"

"Your father's lands in Aurariola are on the eastern coast. Precisely the point where a foreign force might invade. At present your father has ensured that entire reach of coastline is well defended and protected. I wish that to continue, and I believe you are the right man to do it. I will guarantee you keep Aurariola, and I will extend your lands around it, as far south as Cartago Nova.”

“You do not have the power to do so.”

“You would be surprised by what coin might achieve. And coin I have. More than my father would ever have dreamed of.”

“Very well.” Theo folded his arms. “And what do you ask in return?”

“I need a stronghold in the south. I need to give my father a prize, and I need horses. I will take Illiberis in my father’s name.”

“And now you show your face.” Theo stood and began to walk for the door, shaking his head. “You will never have Lælia. You will never have Illiberis. And I should never have come here.”

“I don’t ask for Lælia.” Oppa’s voice was uncharacteristically rough. “I would never ask such a thing again.” Theo paused in the crumbling door frame and glanced back, curious despite himself. There was a raw emotion in Oppa’s face that took him aback, something almost like regret. “You forget,” said Oppa harshly, “that I faced your betrothed across my father’s council. I looked into her eyes. I know she will never be mine. And I know that in taking Illiberis, I will make of her an enemy even more dangerous than she already is.”

“If I traded Illiberis,” said Theo equally curtly, “then so would I.”

“Lælia does not need to know,” Oppa said quietly. “The south will be defeated. She will either be your wife, and the Lady of Aurariola, or she will be given to whomever my father chooses.”

“You,” said Theo. “She would be given to you.”

Oppa nodded. “It was, always, my father’s intention.”

Theo stared at him. “You disgust me,” he said softly.

“Perhaps.” Oppa’s mouth twisted. “But you have been at war too long to ignore what I say. One day soon we will face one another across a Toletum court. Your family and Lælia’s will be traitors. I will be the son of the king who defeated them. I offer you an agreement that can save both you and Lælia from my father’s games.”

“Even if I agreed,” said Theo, the words like ash on his tongue, “I would never trust you to keep your word.”

Oppa withdrew a roll of parchment from his tunic. "You would, if it was written and witnessed."

Theo stared at the parchment as if it were a snake. "A contract," he breathed. "You have drawn up a contract?"

Oppa shrugged. "I have come to respect the power of the written word – and to be wary of it. There are two copies of this contract. If we agree upon terms, we will sign it in the presence of men who cannot be bought, and who will stand witness should they be needed."

Theo's mind seemed split in two. On one side, he could see Lælia's accusing eyes, horrified at his betrayal. On the other, he saw his father lying dead, Alaric dragged through the streets, and, perhaps even more painfully, Lælia standing beside Oppa in a church, forced to marry against her will.

"It is an impossible choice," he breathed.

"It is war." Oppa moved toward the crumbling wall, readying to leave. "Whilst you think on my offer," he said, "you might wish to visit the brothel near the Slavic camp. The whore, Elpis, is there. I bought her from the Slav who wanted her, for more coin than he could refuse." Seeing Theo's face darken, he held up a hand. "Do not slice me with that sword arm. She is safe. I have ensured she does no more than pour ale."

Theo stared at him. "Why would you do that?"

"Do not mistake my interest as compassion," said Oppa dryly. "I assure you, the gesture was entirely motivated by self-interest." He cast Theo a slightly amused glance. "The Slav wanted to keep her under my roof. I have learned enough of you and your damned honour," he said, "to know that if you found her in such circumstances, any conversation between us would be over. It seemed a bargain worth my coin."

"Elpis is not mine." Theo winced at the defiance in his tone. Oppa shrugged again.

"If that is the case," he said mildly, "then I shall put her to work. An idle whore is nothing but trouble." He turned to leave, seemingly oblivious to Theo's clenched fists. "Whilst you consider my offer, I suggest you ask your Persian brothel keeper to send one of her messages to Apsimar, warning him of Leontios's intentions." He smiled grimly at the flare of surprise Theo could not quite conceal. "In the game of war, you might well be a master. But when it comes to the games of men, you can never hope to be my equal. Remember that, Theudemir of Aurariola." Pulling the hood of his cloak over his face, he moved away through the fallen wall at the far end.

Theo waited until the hooded figure was gone.

When he finally left, he took the way past the brothel outside the Slavic camp. He stood for a long time in the shadows beyond the entrance, watching men come and go, his stomach churning at the brief glimpses he caught of Elpis when the door opened and closed.

35

YOSEF

WINTER, AD 691–692

Wudangshan, Serica
Wudang Mountains, China

Deep in the Wudang Mountains, behind a temple devoted to the dark warrior deity Xuanwu, lay a small valley of fertile ground. On one side of the river, tea grew on terraced fields. On the other, hidden by a seemingly impregnable wall of rock, lay a small plantation of mulberry trees.

In the early-morning mist that swirled above the river like celestial smoke, Yosef moved in silent imitation of Fei Hong whilst her grandfather, Jiahao, watched from his seat on a wooden chair nearby. Jiahao had not walked since his legs were cut off nearly twenty years earlier, when he had helped a Jewish merchant named Arun Radhan escape those who did not agree with opening Serica's trade to foreign interests.

Now, two decades later, Arun's son Yosef moved through morning air scented by the delicate white flowers of a stewartia tree, which grew alone by the platform at the monastery where they trained. On the steep slopes of the ravine beyond, kudzu and kiwi vines coiled amidst the tree canopy, and only the bleak caw of crows broke the silence.

Yosef inhaled, arms moving across his body, balancing on one foot as he turned and exhaled, lowering himself gently, feeling the minute extension of his muscles, the infinitesimal changes in the air about him. He followed Fei Hong into the deep, poised crouch that had taken him weeks to master, uncoiling with slow precision, heat burning through his body. It always amazed Yosef how strenuous such graceful, slow movements could be – and how hard he must focus to execute them.

"Today," said Fei Hong, when they had ended the sequence, "the eggs will hatch, and you will learn." Yosef's heart lurched with excitement. He glanced up to where Jiahao watched them with features as inscrutable as the deep forest. "My grandfather has ordered it," added Fei Hong, following his gaze. "Time passes. Normally, you would spend many years tending the mulberry trees, understanding the five elements, before working directly with the silkworms. But you are not Han. Not one of us. We owe your family a debt, one that must be repaid. Today your training in the art of silk begins."

Yosef bowed his head, swallowing the response on his lips. Several months in the mountains living the rigorous life of discipline and obedience demanded by the Daoist tradition of Jiahao and his granddaughter had taught him caution in what he said. Now he followed Fei Hong along the narrow path that led to the mulberry plantation, picking his way carefully so as not to disturb the plants that grew alongside the path. Nothing here grew by chance; all was constructed to enhance the growth of the mulberry trees themselves, every plant contributing to create the perfect environment amidst which the trees could flourish.

They picked the tender new mulberry leaves in the early-morning light, whilst moisture hung still in the veins. The catkins of previous days had given way to the juicy new leaves. They were ripe and full of goodness. They must be perfect for when the eggs hatched.

Near the temple was a specially constructed building, enclosed on all sides with openings both high in the walls and at the base of them, which allowed the correct flow of air and moisture. The building itself faced east, toward the rising sun, though no rays fell directly upon the trays made of twigs and paper.

Morning was still fresh in the air when they entered the home of the silkworms. Fei Hong carefully laid the widest of the mulberry leaves across the paper on the round, woven trays, keeping the other, richest leaves to one side.

There were no eggs on the trays, and Yosef looked around in confusion, wondering where they were. It was the first time he had been permitted in the hatching area, and he did not know where the eggs were kept.

Fei Hong leaned over the round tray and opened the side of her robe. Carefully opening the material, she gently removed a large roll of material, placing it on the tray. Yosef's eyes widened. Clinging to the material was a mass of eggs, clustered together. "You keep them inside your robes?" he asked, fascinated. Fei Hong nodded. Her face was still, her movements studied as she spread the eggs over the tray. Moving to one side, she took a sharp knife with a silver hilt and began to chop the remaining mulberry leaves with fine precision.

"In the days leading up to the hatching, the eggs must be kept close to the body," she told Yosef as she cut. "It is better for a woman to hold the eggs than a man, for it is women who are mothers. The eggs know they are safe with her. Soon the worms will emerge," she told Yosef. "They will be hungry. When they are hatched, we will feed them for the first time. It is very important."

Day was high when the first worm poked its head from the translucent egg. Yosef watched in fascination as one by one the eggs broke open and the tray became a mass of wriggling, bemused silkworms, heads poking blindly into the air as they sought food. Fei Hong took the sliced leaf fragments and spread them through the tray, tilting it this way and that to nudge the infant worms to eat. Eagerly they fastened onto the rich mulberry flesh, and within minutes, the leaves were gone.

"Now what?" asked Yosef.

"Now," said Fei Hong, giving him the unguarded smile that was so rare it always took him by surprise, "now we do not sleep, or rest, for the turn of a moon. The worms are our only job. Over the next few days, they will all hatch. We harvest leaves, feed them when they hunger, and watch them when they sleep. Five lives, the worms have, before they spin their cocoons and transform. We must be their god for all of the five lives."

"We do not have mulberry trees in Spania," Yosef mused, frowning. "How will I feed our worms when they hatch?"

"You cannot carry them to Spania," she answered bluntly. "In Constantinople, the emperor makes silk beneath the palace in strict secrecy. There are people of your own there, people you can trust, who have access to trees, though they lack both the worms and the knowledge to make the cloth themselves. It is impossible to smuggle worms from the palace, and the secrets are so tightly kept that for decades none have penetrated them, which is why your father came to us. But you can stay there for a season, until the eggs have hatched, and take trees with you when you leave. You always planned to go to Constantinople, did you not?"

"Yes," said Yosef hesitantly; he turned away, ending the conversation, but inside he felt an all-too-familiar disquiet. *Will I ever reach home again?* he wondered, looking at the worms. *Is my father's dream no more than a fantasy?*

They were thoughts he had lived with for too long, and so in many ways, Yosef was grateful for the unceasing labour of the following days. He trudged to and from the mulberry plantation, cutting the best leaves, shaking them into the wide tray. He got to know the caterpillars, watching them for hours. "You must know them like your own children," Fei Hong said. "For when they go into the cocoons, you must choose which will live to be your breeding pairs. The others will die in their cocoons when they are steamed. Only the strongest will live to lay your next harvest, and you cannot afford to choose wrongly. Watch them carefully, and see which are the survivors, the hardiest of the crop."

In the dawn they exercised, Yosef following Fei Hong's different sequences of movement, one for every age of the silkworms. At the beginning the worms were hesitant, finding their way into the new air.

"This is the time of feeling," said Fei Hong as they trained on the open terrace of the monastery. "Just like the silkworm, we practise strength, understanding the flow of energy through the body. We demand little and listen to the messages in our blood, noticing our weaknesses, feeling our strength." Yosef trained blindfolded during these days, learning to anticipate Fei's movements by the faintest stir of air, feeling where his own vulnerabilities lay.

After several days of eating, the silkworms went dull and, one by one, sank into a deathlike sleep. "Now they change," said Fei softly. "They disappear into their own underworld, to allow their skin to fall away." That night Fei and Yosef sat out beneath the growing moon, cross legged in meditation.

"Feel the river far below." Fei's voice guided Yosef onto the night breeze so the river's noise became one with his own breath and the night flowers filled his senses. "Allow your mind to die and, with it, all that Yosef was. Follow the river to the stars and become one with its path."

Yosef followed her voice, upward and inward, so the river became one with the stars and both seemed to exist within him in an infinite expanse. He ceased to be Yosef of Garnata, Yosef the Jew, or even Yosef the traveller, instead becoming something else, another part of himself hitherto unknown. In that place of peace, he became aware that all those lives were simply parts he chose to play, whilst the piece of himself that existed amidst star and river was eternal, a different being altogether. When he emerged from the deep state of peace, he knew himself as if for the first time and the world around him as a place of wonder.

"Now," said Fei Hong in the hatching room, "after the first moulting, the silkworms hunger. We must feed them regularly and observe any who sicken, removing them from the rest to prevent the spread of disease." She looked at Yosef. "We ourselves learn now about the enemy," she said.

"What enemy?" Yosef asked.

"The one within." Fei Hong raised a teapot. "This is our discipline for today."

Yosef frowned. "Making tea?"

Fei Hong nodded, smiling at his confusion. "All that a person is can be observed in the manner in which they consume tea. In order to defeat an enemy, one must first understand how to control one's own behaviour, and this begins from within."

The tea they used was particular to the terraces behind the monastery. It was clear and sweet, made by the monks themselves in a ritual older than any could recall. Fei Hong prepared it using water heated on coals, her utensils laid out on a specially prepared tray. It had taken Yosef many weeks of fascinated observation to understand even the basic sequence of tasks involved in preparing tea; but today, Fei Hong expected him to actually make it.

"See how your hands shake," she said as he poured the leaves into the funnel through which, in turn, they fell into the pot. "You are not thinking of the tea. You are thinking of me watching you. The tea is the river; become the stars. In making tea, cease to be Yosef and become the process. When you are the process itself, you are no longer showing your enemy Yosef. All that exists is the tea. When you yourself are serene, the tea becomes perfectly clear."

During this stage, they fed the silkworms every six hours. Every time, after they had finished laying the leaves over the trays, Fei Hong would lead Yosef through a sequence of movements, often outside beneath the clear night sky. Only when his breath had stilled to a slow calm, and his movements become like liquid, would she lead him to the fire in the next room, where he would make tea.

"To a mind that is still," she said, watching him, "the whole universe surrenders."

After several days, the silkworms became still once more.

"See," Fei Hong said, pointing to where the first worms had gone still, sitting up, legs folded before them, heads bowed. "Now the worms begin to pray, for once again they must die a little, lose their skin. They surrender who they are for who they must become. This, too, we must do."

That night they sat beneath the stars again, breathing in the scent of the river, and Yosef felt himself flowing as the tea itself had done. In his mind he saw the amber liquid, inhaled its clear fragrance, felt each tiny fragment of tea expand to give the liquid exactly the right amount of flavour.

The next day, before the worms began to eat, he made tea for them both.

Fei Hong sipped from her bowl, her eyes never leaving Yosef's face. Yosef met her gaze with clear ease. He had felt the tea within himself and knew it to be perfect.

They drank in silence. Behind them, a soft rustling betrayed the stirring of the worms from their second death.

"My grandfather," said Fei Hong as she finished her bowl, "would not detest this tea."

THE WORMS WERE STRONGER NOW; their appetites were voracious. Yosef and Fei Hong no longer slept an entire night through, their sleep disturbed by feeding times. They harvested branches from the mulberry trees and divided the silkworms onto trays, as they had become far too big, now, for only one. The worms devoured each leaf with gusto, leaving only the veins behind.

"The worms must eat now, for when they make their cocoons, they live off their own fat," said Fei Hong as Yosef scattered yet more leaves over the trays. "Notice how their faces have changed, grown bigger. The more they grow, the more they must consume, and they adapt to allow themselves to eat. They become strong, believe themselves invincible."

She looked at Yosef. "When we believe ourselves invincible, we become vulnerable."

That day, they sparred on the terrace outside the hatching room, in between feeding the worms. "You must move faster," said Fei Hong, catching him on one side with the bamboo pole. "Like the tea, like the river − flow with your breath and leave your skin behind, as the worms do. Do not cling to what you once were, for if you do, you cannot learn what you must. Allow your skin to shift and change. Give your body permission to become something new, something you may not believe yet that it can. None of the silkworms know why they eat, or why they shed. They simply trust that they must, that the changes in their bodies are necessary. Trust in change, Yosef. Trust your body to adapt, to carry you where it must.

Be at peace with your own skin and allow your instincts to guide your movements."

Over the following days, they fed the worms and sparred. When they did neither, they meditated on the high terrace or prepared tea. As the silkworms' appetite grew, Yosef's own disappeared, and days passed where he drank only water and tea, his body alive on the mountain air alone. Time became a distant concept and his mind and body a new, agile being closer in nature to the inner being Yosef sensed in meditation. He moved in harmony with Fei Hong and felt the movements of the silkworms as his own.

When the silkworms began to retreat into their posture of prayer again, Fei Hong halted their sparring.

"We must be attentive now," she said. "Nothing must disturb this final changing. If the worms become stuck or are interrupted – if they fail to make the change, for any reason – then they will die. If any sicken, they must be removed immediately. Nothing can threaten the silkworms as they shed their final skin. This is the death through which they must all pass."

They sat through the night, watching, Fei Hong removing any worm that appeared to be struggling or ill. When dawn broke, only a handful of worms had shed their skin. The others lay in a death-like state, preparing for their own battle.

"I will watch them," she said to Yosef. "You will spend today with my grandfather."

Jiahao did not speak Greek, and nor did he smile. Instead, Yosef sat before him, cross legged, as the old man made a tea that smelled heady and oddly disturbing. When Jiahao handed him the bowl, Yosef drank, masking his instinctive reaction to the bitter taste. He must not have been entirely successful, for Jiahao laughed, a sudden, harsh cackle that jolted Yosef's nerves just as the liquid itself seemed to set his mind quivering.

Later, he recalled little of that day, other than Jiahao's face above him and the acrid scent of the incense the old man burned in the house. Yosef was aware he had fallen into a deep haze, but little remained with him. He had the sense of travelling along pathways upon which he found those he had left behind and faces he knew he had yet to meet. He saw his parents, as they had once been, laughing together and with him. He saw Sarah, healed and whole once more, playing in the sunlight with a small child, her face soft with love.

Then he saw Fei Hong, naked beneath the moonlight, her ivory skin glowing a soft invitation. She reached toward him, and it seemed to Yosef that for a moment he touched her, feeling the dewy softness of her skin beneath his hand, his body filled with a sweet ache of longing.

When he woke to the sunset, he was weak and tired, but a flame had been lit beneath his skin and to his embarrassment, he was stiff and hard beneath his robes.

Jiahao stroked his chin and opened his mouth in silent laughter at Yosef's discomfort. He nodded in the direction of the hatching room and Yosef stumbled from the monastery, stopping to wash and change his robes before rejoining Fei Hong.

They sat the rest of the night in silence, Yosef not daring to look at her lest she guess at what he had seen in his vision.

For days the worms struggled through their changing, and as they emerged, Fei Hong and Yosef moved them to new trays, fewer to each, so they had more room to move.

"Look how they seek food now," said Fei Hong, smiling as they watched the silkworms rear up, waving in the air eagerly, searching for food. "Now we can place the leaves further away, and still the worms will find it. They are curious about the world now, seeking their own destiny." She looked up at Yosef, and her eyes held something new, a strange uncertainty. "They prepare to spin their cocoons," she said, and Yosef thought he heard a note of shyness in her voice.

They went down to the mulberry plantation and stood close together in the dawn, cutting whole branches of leaves.

"Now, in their last age before transformation, they feast with abandon," Fei Hong said, her hands moving close to Yosef's on the rich, moist leaves. "We must cut plenty. They will eat all they are able and lust for more."

As she said the last words, her eyes slid to Yosef, and he saw the tip of her tongue reach out and touch her lip.

Yosef felt lust rip through him with an almost unbearable ferocity. One hand on the silver knife trembled, and he touched the thin stuff of her robes with the other, feeling the warmth of her flesh beneath. "When I drank your father's tea," he began, his voice not quite steady, "I saw —"

"I know what you saw." Fei Hong's head was bent, but through the loose strands of hair against her face he could see faint rose colour her skin. "It is necessary, if you are to understand their urges, for you to feel as the silkworms do." Her tone lowered, and she said: "I, too, drank the tea. We are taught to do so."

"But" — Yosef drew her face up, his hand light on her chin so the dark almond eyes met his own — "it is more than just the tea, Fei Hong."

"No," she said softly, drawing a hand down his face. "It is not more. It is simply your body, your skin, and what is meant to be learned. But I am content to be part of that, Yosef. I learned long ago to become one with these cycles." The colour grew deeper on her face, and her eyes dropped to one side. "Although," she said softly, "I have never longed for this fifth life so much before now."

That day, as the worms ate and ate, their sound like a distant sea stroking the shore, Yosef fell into Fei Hong's body, devouring her flesh with his mouth and hands until the tide took them both in a storm that consumed them for days. As the silkworms voraciously consumed whole branches of leaves, so Yosef and Fei Hong became consumed in each other. Yosef found in himself an endless appetite for her body, the silken taste of her beneath his mouth, the sinuous entwining of her limbs about his own. At times he thought of Sarah. When he moved above Fei Hong in the pale dawn, for a moment he saw Sarah's face in his mind, felt her lips beneath his, and when he did, he surged into Fei Hong with a fierce longing that left him both sated and hungry.

"Who is she, the girl you see in your dreams?" Fei Hong's voice came through the darkness on the third night, and Yosef was grateful she had not asked when daylight would have exposed him.

"Her name was Sarah," he said quietly.

"Was? Does she no longer live?"

"I don't know." Yosef moved restlessly on the thin pallet. "After I drank the tea, I saw her – but I also saw my father, and he, I know to be dead."

"How do you know your father is dead?"

"I saw him tortured." The words brought the scene back in all its horror, and once again Yosef could taste the foul stench in the air, hear his father's screams above the roar of the crowd. He trembled, and Fei Hong put a hand on his thigh.

"Tortured," she said slowly. "But did you see him die?"

Yosef swallowed, tasting acrid smoke as if it were real. "No man could survive his wounds," he said. "My father is dead."

"But," said Fei Hong, "you did not see this."

Yosef frowned, turning on his side, trying to read her features in the darkness. "Why do you ask?"

She was quiet for a time, her hand on his thigh stroking lightly, meditatively. When she finally spoke, she did not answer Yosef's question directly.

"When I was a child," she said slowly, "I lived with my father in Chang'an, near the Daming Palace. My father was a merchant of silk; his family, my grandfather Jiahao, were well-known and respected Daoist silk gatherers. They lived up here, in the Wudang Mountains, near a Daoist temple of which my uncle was the *daoshi*, the head priest. For centuries, we had studied the ways of the silkworm, learning their rhythms, cultivating their silk. Our product was one of the most highly prized and sought after by merchants, used to make the royal robes, and my father was a well-respected merchant and visitor to the court of Emperor Gaozong and Empress Wu.

"It was in the last days of Emperor Gaozong's reign that your father arrived at the Daming Palace and was given to our family's care." Yosef froze. "I remember him," said Fei Hong softly. Yosef could feel his heart beating, heavy and painful, in his chest. "He arrived with the Sogdians, just as you yourself did. He was older than you are now, but he was also broken, just as you were when you arrived. His father had died on the road to Serica, and Arun mourned him deeply. He may never have received a welcome to the palace had it not been for the horoscope he cast for a certain Buddhist monk by the name of Huaiyi."

"He stayed with you?" Yosef's voice rasped, and he cleared his throat. "You knew him, then?"

"I was a child," said Fei Hong, "no more than ten years old. But, yes, I knew him. He was kind to me. It is because of him I speak Greek. He taught me my first words."

"Then, if he stayed with you, why did he not learn as I am learning now? My father knew nothing of how silk is made. I know this."

"To understand the answer to this, you must first understand Serica," said Fei Hong. "We are a people who do not share our secrets. Your father was a foreigner, an outsider. He did not understand our ways and did not speak our language. He would never have been allowed to stay as long as he did had it not been for the monk, Huaiyi, and the favour Arun found by casting his horoscope. Huaiyi, you must understand, was a favourite of Empress Wu."

A note of bitterness entered her voice.

"This friendship – it did not last?" Yosef guessed.

"No," said Fei Hong softly. "It did not."

"After the death of Emperor Gaozong, Huaiyi gained immense power at the court of Empress Wu. It was a tumultuous period, one when many competing factions sought power. But Huaiyi, it was rumoured, had the ultimate bargaining piece – the ear of Empress Wu herself, listening to his whispers from the comfort of her own pillows." Fei Hong glanced at Yosef. "They were lovers," she said bluntly. "All knew of it, and all feared the power such alliance would give Huaiyi, for he was not a humble monk.

"At this time, Buddhism had not the influence in Serica that Daoism did. Huaiyi resented this. He also resented the wealth controlled by the silk monasteries in the Wudang Mountains, which grew and traded not only the rich cloth but teas that are prized throughout the East.

"So Huaiyi asked your father, Arun, to study his horoscope to determine if his religion would, one day, supersede that of the Dao."

"But that is impossible," said Yosef, shaking his head. "No horoscope could determine such a thing."

"Your father told him as much," said Fei Hong. "Huaiyi flew into a rage, claiming your father lied to protect his Daoist masters, that he was no more than a foreign tool of insurrection employed by traitors to Empress Wu's court. He denounced my father, and my uncles, as traitors to the throne and enemies of Empress Wu herself.

"You must understand that, at this time, the Daming Palace was awash with rumour and counter-rumour. A foreigner at such a time was naturally suspicious, and the wealthy Daoist monks who profited from their seemingly arcane knowledge of silk making – well, the combination proved an irresistible target for the empress's counsellors."

"What happened?" Yosef could not imagine his own father in such an environment. To think that he had lived amongst the same people Yosef now found himself, had struggled in isolation and fear just as Yosef had, seemed incomprehensible.

"The empress's assassins came late at night with orders to kill all in our household and to ensure your father was amongst the dead." Fei Hong spoke in a cold, clinical tone. But Yosef, who had experience of violent death, recognised the device as one covering deep trauma. He put a hand on her hip, stroking the skin there gently, and felt her tremble faintly beneath his touch.

"Your father died?" he guessed.

"Not then," she said. "Not right away. But my mother, my brothers, all my uncles – they were killed instantly. My father had taken Arun and me into the gardens near the palace, where tea grows, to begin to teach Arun. He had an insatiable appetite for knowledge, and my father had begun teaching him the secrets of herbs and how to decoct them into potions that heal."

"My father never forgot those lessons," Yosef said. "He was the most renowned physician in our village."

Fei Hong nodded. "He had a gift – and because he was fond of me, and I him, my father would take me, also, on these lessons. We returned to blood in the streets and the sounds of death."

Her voice trembled, and Yosef could envisage the scene in his mind: the palace soldiers storming the low house, thrusting steel into every living being they found within.

"They saw us," she said, "and my father made to fight; but Arun stepped in front of him, ordering him to take me, to run." The words caught in her throat. Yosef remained silent, waiting, until her breathing returned to normal.

"An arrow caught my father in the chest as we ran," she said, her voice low. "He never made it here to the mountains. Arun found me on the edge of the city, and somehow, using only the stars and what he knew from my father's stories, he led us both into the mountains, travelling by night, until we came to the monastery of my family. My grandfather, who was also caught by the palace soldiers, eventually found us both. We left the monastery and came deeper into the mountains to here, where Grandfather knew of an old temple. We began again – with barely any silkworms, and with mulberry trees nearly dead in the soil, far away from the eyes of the court."

"And what of my father?" Yosef asked. "What happened to him?"

"Your father returned to the Daming Palace," said Fei Hong. "Against our wishes. We believed they would kill him, but your father wanted official sanction of his presence here, to negotiate on behalf of his people to buy silk. Huaiyi, I believe, would have killed him. But he was not at the palace when your father arrived, and Empress Wu was in a benign mood that day. She had also heard that Arun cast horoscopes. She asked him to draw hers and was gratified when he saw that she would rule, alone, for some years to come. She gave your father a letter that stated he could enter the city of Chang'an."

"Then why did he not stay?" Yosef asked, confused.

"Because that same night," said Fei Hong grimly, "Huaiyi returned, and he sent his men to where your father rested. Arun escaped only because there were those in the city who knew what he had done for us and sought to warn him. He left in the dead of night with barely the clothes on his back, escaping the city only by hiding in the baggage of Sogdian merchants. Had he dared return, or dallied at all, he would have been killed on sight."

There was a silence during which he digested her words. "But why," Yosef asked, "if my father knew only danger awaited us, did he not at least warn me?" He thought of his arrival at the Danfeng Gate. "Had you not met me that day," he said, "I would have been killed."

"No. Your father ensured his safe return — and yours." Fei Hong turned to him in the darkness. "Three years after your father was here, a messenger came to our temple in the mountains. A messenger carrying more money than we had ever dared hope would find us again. Enough money to buy more silkworm eggs, and to plant tea." Yosef felt her smile in the darkness. "Enough money to re-establish our family business, albeit in secret." She turned to Yosef, putting a slender hand on his chest. "That money came from your father," she said. "Sent via a hundred different hands until it reached ours. Money he could ill afford, I believe, but which he found, nonetheless. Not because he wanted anything. Because he was worried for a small girl, and her crippled grandfather, to whom, according to his writing, he felt he owed his life."

A hard heat blocked Yosef's throat.

"He told us he would return one day," said Fei Hong softly. "That he hoped we lived still. And that his small offering could, perhaps in part, repay the debt he felt he owed us. We sent a reply."

"I don't think he received it," Yosef said hoarsely. "He never spoke of it."

"Yes," said Fei Hong, "he did receive it. Last year — barely six months before I found you at the gate of the Daming Palace — we received a letter from him."

"He must have written it before he died," said Yosef, feeling again the stab of grief in his chest.

"I know only that he was alive when he wrote the letter," said Fei Hong. "It came by sea. In it, Yosef, Arun wrote that you would be coming — and that we must teach you what you need to know. I have met every caravan since."

Yosef felt a roaring in his ears. The sound of the silkworms feeding was so loud, it felt as if they were about to consume his own flesh. "It is impossible," he said, his voice seeming to come from a long distance. "It must have been someone impersonating him – or writing in his stead."

"No." Fei Hong's tone was definite. "The hand was different, but I know the letter came from him. That is why I waited beyond the gates, day after day, through the coldest months of the year, for you." She withdrew a small piece of cloth from the robes by their bed. "When I was a child, I gave your father a gift. He said he would cherish it always, even though it was no more than a childish trinket, a fancy of mine. When the letter came, my gift was wrapped inside it. No other would have known what it meant to me but Arun."

Opening the material in her hand, Fei Hong held it up to the moonlight, so the thick, black strokes in a childish hand were clearly visible.

Instantly, Yosef was transported back to the night in the cave, the last night he had shared alone with his father: *That was a gift from a dear friend. If her gods and ours will it, one day you will meet her.*

"My name," said Fei Hong softly, touching the black ink, tracing the childish strokes. "These were first characters I ever wrote – and I gifted them to your father."

YOSEF LIVED through the cocoon phase of the silkworms feeling as if he, too, were shrouded in a silken haze.

In the early-morning mist, he moved through the sequences he had learned, feeling his own body as if it belonged to a stranger. A new awareness seemed to live in his veins. He moved like water, flowing with his breath, his mind seemingly cast adrift on the wispy cloud that floated below.

Odd fragments of memory passed across his mind as he moved: the night in the caves, where he had held in his own hands the piece of cloth that held Fei Hong's name.

His father, screaming in agony.

Is it possible?

Yosef felt his body tremble, his balance falter. *Do not think. If you think, you cannot be as water must be.* He inhaled, exhaled. Felt his mind clear. Spun on one foot, his other striking high; then again, changing feet. Felt the sinuous strength of his body moving before he willed it, the delicate push of air on his skin as he slipped through it. He ended in a crouch and put his hands together, bowing to the three Pure Ones and the Way within himself.

When he rose, his mind was still, and he pondered the questions from a steadier distance.

I must return, he thought. *If there is even a chance my father lives, I cannot ignore it. I must do all that I promised.* There was a strange relief in his mind. For now, at least, his course seemed clear.

"If you are to leave us, you must do so before the summer comes." Yosef swung around to find Fei Hong standing behind him. Her eyes glittered, but her chin was strong, her expression clear. "The eggs will travel if you carry them through the cold months. But when late spring arrives and the weather warms, they must be stable in order to hatch. You cannot travel with them through the heat – or if you do, it must be done with great care, and only for a short time."

"Fei Hong –" he began, reaching out to touch her. Fei Hong stepped neatly out of his reach. The half smile she gave him was genuine, but it did not mask the pain in her eyes. "We owe your father our lives," she said quietly. "I have always known how the debt was to be paid; when you leave here, and take the silkworms with you, a piece of me will live forever in your world."

Yosef cast about for a response, but he could find none. Any words he found seemed inadequate, unworthy of the honour she had shown him. The half smile twisted her face again, and this time, her eyes softened as she saw his struggle. "I know you dream of her," said Fei Hong softly. "Sometimes, in the night, you say her name: Sarah."

Her pronunciation tinged the name, so it sounded to Yosef's ears like "Salah".

"Even if she lives still, I do not know if she would want to see me," he said quietly. "We were children when I knew her. She endured… terrible things."

"We are none of us children any longer," said Fei Hong. "And terrible things are what birth our souls. Lao Tze, the great master, said: *Difficulty and ease produce the one, the idea of the other.* You have not become who you are through ease, Yosef ben Arun, and nor has she."

She looked at Yosef, and in her eyes he saw both bravery and sacrifice, and he knew that if they both lived a hundred years more, the ravine between them opened by awareness could never be truly spanned again.

"Go home, Yosef," she said softly. "Take your silkworms to the Jews in Constantinople as your father wished; then go home, to your Salah."

36

THEO

JANUARY, AD 692

Sebastopolis, Anatolia
Elauissa Sebaste, Cilicia, Turkey

When finally Theo received a reply from Apsimar, it was both too late and not encouraging.

Leontios had grown increasingly paranoid. Men and coin were disappearing with worrying frequency. Leontios believed the Slavs were stealing part of what they collected on his behalf. And now that payments were made in the new Arab currency rather than that of Constantinople, Leontios began to suspect that in addition the Arabs themselves were cheating on their payments. In retribution for this suspected treachery, and goaded by his emperor's own ill judgement, he had recently mounted an expedition to take the province of Cyprus, in direct breach of the emperor's treaty with the caliph, under which the Cypriot taxes were to be divided equally. Apsimar could do little other than caution the emperor against such action. Theo, facing increasing resentment amongst his men, unable to tell anyone of his communication with his old commander, was left in the unenviable position of defending actions he privately believed reprehensible, to men of whose loyalty he was uncertain.

And worse, the only person he felt he might possibly speak to was the one he trusted least of all.

Now Theo stood amongst his men on the Slavic drill ground and watched Oppa, dark eyed and inscrutable, standing just behind Leontios. He was ever present at Leontios's side, and he was trusted, Theo suspected, more than the strategos's closest advisers. *And yet,* Theo thought, his eyes narrowing, *still Leontios invaded Cyprus.* If Oppa was as opposed to breaking the treaty as he claimed to be, why had he not strongly counselled the strategos against doing exactly that? Why ask Theo to enlist Apsimar's support when he, Oppa, was right beside the man making such decisions? Surely, Theo thought, he must know there was little Apsimar could do to influence a superior's command and tactics.

As he watched Oppa, his thoughts churning, an incensed, manic Leontios stalked in front of the Slavic ranks, his face ruddy with rage. He had gathered them to address the matter of the missing coin, convinced the thieves would be found amongst the Slavic forces he did not trust.

"One of you will die every minute until I have names!" Spittle flew from the corners of his mouth as he glared at the men.

"If you allow me time," said Neboulos calmly, "I will find those responsible and bring them to you."

"You have had time enough!" One fat finger jabbed the air, and Leontios turned menacing eyes on the Slavs who sweated beneath a hot sun, eyeing him sullenly. "Kill another one!" Leontios ordered his guard. The man raised a curved sword in the air and brought it down with violent precision. A Slavic head rolled forward, blood spurting from the stump before the body toppled with mundane finality to lie beside four similar corpses.

"Five turns of the sand – five dead!" Leontios raised the minute glass and turned it again. "Before the sand runs a sixth time, who will stand forward and tell me of the coin stolen from our ranks? Or are all of you traitors to your emperor?"

"He is not our emperor!" a Slavic voice called from the rear, and an answering rumble of assent joined him. "Why should we fight for you?" came another voice. "We have no lands to defend. And we owe no allegiance to Constantinople."

Leontios glared at the sea of faces. "You take the emperor's coin. You eat his grain and ride his horses. You live because the emperor deigns to have it so – and, by God, you will fight with him, or be cut down as I did your own barbarian masters!" He turned to the guard. "Kill another one!" The sword swung again, and this time, a roar of protest rose from the ground.

"This is folly," muttered Silas to Theo, glancing at Leofric's red, furious face on Theo's other side. "These men will turn on Leontios any moment now, and all will be lost. Is the man insane?"

Leontios certainly looked it, Theo thought. The strain of recent months, added to by the increasingly aggressive attacks closer to the port, had made the strategos both volatile and vicious. Never a man to tolerate even mild criticism with equanimity, the thought that he might be facing renegades in his own ranks had made Leontios paranoid and vindictive, willing to kill however many it would take to re-establish his ascendancy.

"My lord." Theo tensed as Oppa stepped forward. His tone held the perfect blend of deference and authority designed to calm Leontios, and the strategos paused and looked at him.

"Speak, Spaniard!"

"My lord – perhaps we should honour Neboulos's wishes," said Oppa quietly. "He knows these men better than any. It is he who has led them into the mountains these months past." He glanced at Neboulos. "As he says, nothing happens in his camp without him knowing of it."

Neboulos paled.

"Tyr!" cursed Leofric, tense beside Theo. His fists clenched, and he took a half step forward. Theo saw Oppa's eyes flicker between Leofric and Theo and something gleam in their depths. It triggered something inside him that made him instinctively grip Leofric's arm with an iron strength.

"Do not move," he muttered through clenched teeth. "Whatever you think to confess, do not."

"Confess?" Leofric turned startled eyes to him. Theo, grim faced, stared straight ahead. For a moment he thought Leofric would speak. Hoped, even, that he might. But then his old friend stepped back quietly, his arms folded and face impassive, and Theo felt the last of his hope flee.

Leontios was staring at Neboulos, his face creased with the same dark suspicions that had churned Theo's gut these past weeks.

"The Spaniard is right." Leontios stared at Neboulos. "You must know who it is who betrays me. You must have known before this!"

Neboulos was white faced, but his voice was steady when he answered: "It is true that I have my own suspicions, Strategos. But I would not condemn a man without proof – and this, I do not yet have."

Theo could not look at Leofric. Every word, he knew, condemned his own actions.

"Do I understand that to mean you are seeking such proof?" demanded Leontios. "What do you do to ensure the loyalty of your men?"

Neboulos inclined his head. "I do not wish, any more than you do, to face an Arab army with thieves – or traitors – at my back."

Oppa stepped forward again. "Perhaps, though," he said in a low voice to Leontios, ignoring Neboulos's presence, "you could make an example of these men." He indicated the white, set faces of the men who knelt behind them, waiting for the executioner's blade. "Do not kill them," Oppa said softly, fingering the whip at his side. "Make it clear, though, what awaits any who dare to steal the emperor's coin." He nodded at Neboulos. "And begin with making it clear that even the highest rank is not immune from your power."

Surely, Theo thought, Leontios could not be such a fool as to whip Neboulos. He felt rather than saw Leofric go rigid at Oppa's words, his fists clenched.

The men moved uneasily, eyeing one another, fingering their weapons. Neboulos looked out at the restless ranks, then up at Oppa, who watched him with a small, unpleasant smile on his face. Neboulos stepped forward. "If there is treason in my ranks," he said, in a voice that carried across the field, "then the fault is mine alone. And I, alone, will take the punishment." He met Leontios's eye. "I will swear on my men's loyalty," he said quietly to the strategos. "And you may whip me so they see I will swear on it." He tore the shirt from his back and turned, passing it to Oppa in a curiously insolent gesture. Leontios, looking suddenly disconcerted, glanced uneasily between Oppa and Neboulos.

"Do it," muttered Neboulos through his teeth.

Oppa stepped forward and raised the whip. "Behold," he said, dark eyes glittering across the field, "what happens to those who would betray our emperor." The lash came down, and the Slavic ranks watched, their faces dull with resentment.

THE MOON WAS SICKLY yellow on the horizon when Theo made his way to the tavern high on the hilltop. He had left the drill ground the moment it was over, unwilling to face either Leofric's explanations or Silas's questions. Leofric's betrayal sat inside him like an open, festering wound, one Theo doubted would ever truly heal. He had known Leofric to be many things: uneducated, crude, occasionally shockingly brutal. But he had never imagined him a traitor. Not even for his own countrymen.

I am a fool, Theo thought despairingly as he climbed the hill to Oppa's tavern. *I did not see it because I did not wish to believe it possible.* How many men had died, he wondered, for Leofric's loyalty to his homeland? He thought of Kyros, dying in his arms, and rage and pain surged through him in a bitter torrent.

The man who opened the door to him narrowed his eyes suspiciously when he recognised Theo. "What do you want here?" he asked rudely. "All know your coin is spent in the Persian woman's house."

"I do not want what you sell." Catching sight of a girl no older than Pelagia bearing a wine cup, Theo's face twisted in distaste. "I am come to see your master."

"My master will have nothing to say to you."

"That is not entirely true." Oppa's voice interrupted his slave smoothly, and the man stepped back, bowing his head deferentially, his eyes on Theo no less hostile. "Perhaps you will join me, Theudemir?"

With every appearance of courtesy, Oppa gestured Theo inside, walking him through the rooms to a private chamber at the rear of the house. Seeing Theo's expression of distaste as he took in the extremely young age of the girls there, Oppa smiled as he closed the door. "You do not approve," he said, nodding. "*Ja*. I understand your revulsion. You are a man with normal appetites, cannot fathom the darkness that drives such desire. But I was raised in a whorehouse, not a villa. I learned long ago to suspend judgement on such matters and instead derive a profit from them." He waved Theo to a seat. "The more depraved a man," he said conversationally, "the more vulnerable he is. Every desire he sees fulfilled is another debt he owes. Over time his desires become darker until eventually he finds himself in a place where no coin can pay for what he does. That is when he becomes my creature." He shrugged. "It is an art form I mastered early. One I have had much opportunity to practise since coming here."

"With Leontios, you mean." Theo's voice was harsh. "He comes here. Is this how you twist him to do your bidding? Is it young girls?"

"Ah." Oppa turned his wine cup between long fingers, looking at Theo with detached interest. "It began with young girls, yes. But it appears Leontios has a rather more… violent turn of mind. He enjoys suffering, you see."

"Is that why you whipped Neboulos?" Theo stared at him, unable to hide his revulsion. "For titillation?"

Oppa tilted his head to one side. "Not entirely. Although it did serve to excite Leontios. It took several of my best girls, and two whips, to satiate him afterward." At Theo's grunt of disgust, Oppa's face grew hard. "Leontios was intent upon making a show of strength. Whipping Neboulos saved the lives of a dozen men, maybe more. Had I not intervened, the entire Slavic army might well have rebelled today."

"You cannot truly believe that was the only course."

"It was the course I saw, and I took it!" Oppa stood and strode restlessly across the room. "As it is, we may still have a chance to salvage this. And if we can, we must, Theo." He pulled out a parchment and handed it to Theo. "I have news from Spania. From my father." He nodded at the parchment, which bore the unmistakable seal of Egica Rex, a seal Theo had himself seen often in his father's study. Theo unrolled it, almost unwilling to read the familiar hand upon it, whilst at the same time terribly conscious that he held in his hand the writing of Spania's king – of his king.

"Sunifred's army marches upon Toletum," he muttered, as his eyes travelled down the page. Then he froze. He raised his eyes to find Oppa's resting on him. "And my brother rides with him," Theo said hoarsely. "With the men of Emerita – my father's men."

Oppa nodded slowly. "It worsens," he said quietly. "The north is in open rebellion, under the command of Favila, a son of Chindasuinth. My father believes that Favila's brother, Theodefred, Duke of Corduba, may be plotting to betray him." He held Theo's eyes. "With the Count of Illiberis."

"Tyr!" Theo pushed the parchment back into Oppa's hands and gripped the chair back so hard it marked his hands as he stared into the fire. It was all he had feared, and worse. His brother in open rebellion, Illiberis not far behind, and his father forced to commit both Emerita and Aurariola to a war he had never wanted.

"You see, now, why we must act decisively." Oppa's voice was relentless. "Sebastopolis will fall, Theo, sooner or later. Before we are lost with it, we must both return. Or there may well be no Spania left for us to return to."

Theo barely heard him. *Alaric.* He closed his eyes and his chest seized in pain at the thought of the choices his brother must have had to make, at the agony his father must be feeling.

Then he thought of the choices he himself had made, was making even now, standing in the room with the very man who might well be held responsible for his brother's rage, and he knew, more than at any time in his life, that he was unutterably lost.

"Do not forget what we discussed." Oppa's voice drilled into Theo with painful precision. "When we return, I can ensure you survive, Theo. I will ensure my father knows what we did here to help one another. But you must be prepared for what is to come. For Illiberis to be lost."

Theo made a harsh noise and pushed the chair hard enough to topple it. "Leofric," he said roughly, staring into the fire. "The Slav who fought at my side. You were right. He was taking the Arabs' coin."

Oppa nodded. "I thought as much. I am sorry, though. Betrayal is never easy when it comes from those closest."

"He was my friend." The words rasped in his throat.

"Do not judge him too harshly. You of all men know the curse of a choice between friendship and country."

"You would defend him to me?" Theo stared at Oppa. "Why?"

Oppa's head tilted. "You see the world through the eyes of the past," he said quietly. "Through the tales of the victors. You see the Spania your father's father helped win. You have been raised the son of a legend." He stared into the fire. "I was born the bastard son of a disgraced line," he said quietly. "The lowest of creatures, with only shame as his lineage. Your world has been one of clean lines. Black and white. Evil and good. Honour and betrayal. Mine has been one of shadows, of nuance. I have not the luxury of judgement, Theudemir of Aurariola. I know too well that all men walk both sides of the line at some point in their lives. You look at your Slav and see a traitor. I see a man caught in an impossible pincer between his heart and his soul. I do not judge him, no. Perhaps you, also, should not."

Theo met his eyes, reading the unspoken rebuke there: *perhaps you should not judge me, either.*

"We no longer have time to live in the past, Theo." Oppa laid two rolls of parchment on the table beside the letter from his father. "Read them," he said quietly. "I will leave you to make your decision."

He left the room. Theo stared at the parchments side by side on the table. He read King Egica's letter again, his blood racing at the thought of his father and brother, possibly even now fighting for their very lives. *I should be there,* he thought. And what of when he did return? Would Leofric have been at his side, even before this? Would Silas? He paused for a moment and allowed an even more painful thought to enter his mind: would Yosef?

He thought of landing, without money, army, or friend, on a hostile Spanish shore. To a land where he was traitor, where Lælia was held captive by Egica. He would have nothing with which to bargain, none to fight for him at court. Nobody would care for his story of Oppa's attack on the fleet. Those who might have stood behind him would have been defeated, part of Sunifred's failed rebellion. Even if he might wish to believe Sunifred could succeed, Oppa's blunt assessment had held the chilling ring of truth.

So absorbed was he in dark musings that he barely heard the door open behind him. It was only when a soft voice said his name that he swung around, his heart thudding.

Elpis looked frail and uncertain, her eyes wide and luminous in the dim light as she held her hands out toward him. Theo found himself holding them tightly before he thought of what he did. "Have you been harmed?" He searched her face. "Are you captive here?"

Colour washed her cheeks. "I am well," she said in a tremulous voice. "I believe it is you I have to thank for that."

"I would never have seen you brought here," said Theo fiercely. "It was Oppa's doing –"

"No," Elpis interrupted him, her voice low but sure. "You misjudge him, Theo. Oppa saved me. He could have let the Slav have me. All know the man to be a brute. But Oppa heard of it and intervened, at great cost, I believe. And I have met with nothing but kindness here. He has even promised to ensure Pelagia is safe, should Sebastopolis fall.

"Theo." One small hand came up and cupped his cheek. "I know you do not trust him. But, perhaps, is it not possible he has changed? Have not the years far from your homeland changed you?"

Theo covered her hand with his own, his heart thudding at her nearness, feeling the abyss beckoning. She stepped closer, the heat of her body so intoxicating he trembled. "I know your heart belongs to another," she said. "It is not your heart I ask for, Theo."

Her eyes fell to the table and the parchments there. She raised them to his again. "What do they mean?" she asked quietly. "What does Oppa want from you?"

Guilt twisted his belly. "He wants my help," he said curtly, stepping away from Elpis but forcing himself to meet her eyes. "And in return, he promises to protect the one to whom I am betrothed." He touched the coin and amulet at his neck in an unconscious gesture.

"Is it such a terrible thing?" Elpis asked gently. "To protect her, whom you love so much?"

Theo made a harsh noise. "It is a trade to which she herself would never agree. And if I make it, I am Oppa's ally. For that, too, she will never forgive me." He could not bring himself to name Lælia, here, in this place, to Elpis.

"And if you do not make it?"

"She will die defending her home." Theo made himself say the words aloud. They had swirled within him for weeks; they must be said. "And if she should somehow live, she will find herself captive of the king, forced to marry a man of his choosing – if she is fortunate. If not, she will be alone, penniless at court, with neither title nor power. She will have even less control over who takes her than –" Realising what he was about to say, Theo bit off his words and looked away from Elpis.

"Than a whore like me?" Elpis smiled gently. "You can say the word, Theo. It does not frighten me, nor make me ashamed. I live the life that a roll of the dice gave me, and I do not resent it. But this girl of yours, raised as a fine lady on a large estate – Theo, she cannot possibly understand what such a life would truly mean for her. Do you honestly believe she would make the same choices if she did?" She stepped closer to him once more, and this time he did not move away when her arms snaked around his neck. "How would you face her," she murmured in his ear, "knowing that you could have saved her from that fate?"

For a moment Theo imagined Lælia, the plaything of men drunken and triumphant after the fall of Illiberis, her wild pride beaten into sullen defeat and then into abject terror. He saw himself, standing in the great palace at Toletum, begging Egica to spare Lælia. *If,* he thought bitterly, *we both live long enough to make such a plea – and are permitted to do so.*

Perhaps, he thought, Elpis was right, and Oppa was changed. Even if Oppa had bought her as a means to ensure Theo's goodwill, was that in itself not some kind of evidence that the man was no longer the impulsive, angry boy he had once been? And was not his upbringing, by Oppa's own admission, reason enough for at least some of his behaviour? Oppa's battle to make his father see sense had undoubtedly changed him, just as Theo himself had been altered by all he had seen. And even if none of it was true and Oppa was the same monster he had always been, what choice, in the end, did Theo have? Any day now, Sebastopolis would fall. If it did not, Theo would have time to undo his agreement with Oppa. But if it did, and they both fled to Spania, he could not risk returning without some kind of surety. No matter the cost to his own pride or soul, he would not see his father's sacrifices, his brother's, or Lælia's, come to nothing.

"Elpis," he said, and now his voice was suddenly clear, once more the commander whom men had followed into battle. "Tell Oppa to return. And to bring his witnesses."

Elpis touched his cheek, her eyes soft with understanding. "They are lucky," she said quietly. "This girl of yours. Your family. To have a man who prizes them so."

The door had barely closed behind her when it opened again, this time to admit Oppa, followed by two black-clad priests. Theo recognised them both from his time in Toletum. They were from good families, had once been acolytes in the same monastery that his brother Athanagild now attended.

"These men have been in Constantinople these past years." Oppa made the introductions. "They came here because they heard word of my presence and thought to carry word of me back to my father. They leave tonight, on a merchant dromon. Do you agree to trust them to witness our agreement?"

Theo drew a deep breath. He nodded curtly, not trusting himself to speak.

The rest of it was done in a matter of minutes, his signature marking the parchment below Oppa's, the two priests fixing their own marks on the other side. The deeds were sealed, and Oppa handed Theo one of them. "Yours," he said quietly. "I will hold the other."

As if sensing he had pushed Theo to the limits of his endurance, he nodded at the men to leave and moved toward the door, where he paused. "The girl, Elpis," he said gently. "She does not need your coin. She was yours before ever I took her from the street, and I have ensured she has coin enough, now, to make her own choices. If you wish her to leave with you, she is free to go, or to return to the Persian woman, if she chooses." He did not wait for a response but went from the room, and when Theo turned, it was to find the door closed and Elpis in the room, holding a jug of wine.

She poured him a cup. Theo drank it, then another.

"Is that what you wish for?" Theo asked harshly. "To return to Athanais, and to your sister?"

"I wish to be with you." Her hand rested on his chest, a touch so gentle it broke something inside Theo. "For as long as we have, Theo, I would be near you." Her eyes slid to the low cot by the wall, and back to his. "But for tonight," she murmured, "can we not simply have this?" She took his hand and placed it over the curve of her breast, moving so she stood between his legs. "Can you not take this one night for yourself, Theo?"

His arm slid around her and she settled herself across his lap, her lips grazing his throat. "Let me be your comfort," she murmured in his ear. "You, who do so much for others and never ask the price – this once, let me be your comfort."

This time, when her mouth sought his own, Theo did not turn away.

But even as he sank into the welcome oblivion of her flesh, he knew himself lost finally to the abyss he had so long feared, gone far into a darkness from which he knew he would never again be truly free.

I made my choice, Apsimar, he thought bitterly as the night closed around them and Elpis's body drew him into the place where all sense was lost. *Gods help me, but I made it.*

37

ALARIC
APRIL, AD 692

Hispalis, Spania
Seville, Spain

A laric—
All men know that Sunifred marches north, and you with him.
I know you have no choice. From the moment, perhaps, that you saw Rekiberga, there was no choice.
I pray for you, my brother.
—Athanagild

ALARIC FOLDED Athanagild's letter for the tenth time, placing it inside his tunic where it gave him an odd feeling of comfort, as if his brother's hand on the page could steady his own heart. Taking a deep breath, he stared at the stone wall that surrounded the private garden of Sunifred's villa, shadowed in the dark of the moon. Tomorrow they would ride out. Alaric knew he could not leave without seeing her before he went.

He scaled the wall with the help of a low fig branch and found the servant he had bribed earlier waiting for him at the door. "Hurry," the woman breathed in his ear, ushering him inside and looking about fearfully. "If either of us are caught, it will be our lives."

Silently, Alaric followed her through the corridor to the arched wooden door. "Enter," said Rekiberga's low voice. The servant pushed him inside, then closed the door discreetly behind her.

Rekiberga sat at a low table, her back turned to him. Her hair was unbound, falling in fiery ripples to her waist, the brush still in her hand. She was clad in no more than a thin linen shift, through which Alaric could see the elegant curves of her figure. It felt almost terrifyingly intimate to be here, and it took a moment before he found his voice.

"My lady," he murmured. "Forgive me for coming to you like this." The brush fell from her hand and Rekiberga swung around, her mouth a perfect O of surprise, eyes gleaming cobalt in the low light. "Do not be afraid." Alaric put out a hand, then let it fall to his side. "Only your servant knows of my presence, and Teudolfo tells me she can be trusted."

Rekiberga's mouth curved. "Since the worthy Teudolfo has been enjoying my servant's charms for the best part of the winter, I imagine he would say that," she murmured, but Alaric, seeing the hectic colour at her neck, knew she spoke to cover her own discomfort.

"If you wish me to leave, I will," he said. Holding his eyes, Rekiberga shook her head slowly but did not speak. Heartened, Alaric took a step closer. "I cannot leave as you asked me to do," he said, and even to his own ears his voice sounded harsh. Rekiberga watched him but did not answer. "Not because I do not want to," he went on, "or because I believe in your father, or his cause, for I do not."

"Then why?" Rekiberga stood, and her form was silhouetted in the light of the fire beside her. It took all of Alaric's willpower not to cross the room and pull her against him. He forced himself to keep his eyes on her face.

"Because if we run now, we are fugitives forever, no matter which side of this cursed war is victorious. I would not have you condemned to that fate."

"And if we stay, you might be dead, and I taken by the king as a prize to be married as he chooses – or simply taken." She did not flinch from his grunt of hurt at her words. "All know that the daughters of a defeated nobleman are become no more than concubines at court."

Alaric's fists clenched at his side. "If we run," he said in a low, fierce voice, "I may still die and you be taken as you fear. But we will be without friends to fight for us, or recourse. Rekiberga –" He took a step toward her, and she to him, so no more than a few feet parted them. "I know you would face that fate without fear, for you are as brave, and more, than any woman I have ever known. But I cannot live with myself if I ask it of you, just as I cannot live with myself if I leave Spania now as it teeters on a precipice I have helped bring it to."

Rekiberga took the final step toward him, her hand coming up to hold his jaw, her thumb stroking the tension there. "I know," she whispered, her eyes holding his. "I do not like it, Alaric, but I know." Her hands gripped his face. "Promise me this," she said fiercely. "When this is done – no matter how it ends – promise that if we both live still, you will come for me, and we will leave all of this behind."

"I promise."

She stepped forward into his arms, and as they came around her, Alaric groaned. "I cannot bear to let you go." He kissed her, feeling the wonder of her lips opening beneath him, every inch of his body hard and longing for her. She moaned against his mouth and he drew her to him, the long lines of her body and the sweet crush of her breasts against him, kissing her on and on.

"Please," she gasped when he let her go. "I cannot say goodbye without knowing you are mine – truly mine."

"I cannot." Alaric's voice cracked, and he knew in another moment he would lose the last vestiges of control. "What if I should not live through this? How would you then face your father – and your husband?"

"If you do not live through this," she said fiercely, "then I do not wish to face either."

He kissed her again. All that existed was the feeling of

Rekiberga in his arms, the waterfall of bronze hair falling through his fingers.

"Alaric." She held his face, and there was something in her eyes that made him pause and frown. "I know my father will not prevail," she said softly. "I know he cannot. I saw your face the last time he gave you an ultimatum. I have known for a long time he is not the man you need him to be. When first I realised it, that knowledge broke my heart." She searched his face. "But it also set me free. Now I need you to set yourself free also."

"Rekiberga —"

"No." She pressed her lips to his with an urgency that made him groan, then pulled away and bent her forehead to meet his. "I know what he is, Alaric, and so do you. I will no longer be the bait he dangles to catch men and swords. I need your assurance that you will not needlessly throw your life away in his service. What happens after this farce of a war is done is beyond the control of you or me. For now, we must both play the parts he has set us, but I would face whatever the coming days bring knowing that I am yours. That if there is a future left to us at all, we will face it together."

He took her face in his hands. "If we survive this," he said roughly, "you have my word, Rekiberga: nothing — not your father or mine, no king or country — will ever divide us again. And if I cannot return to you," he said, stilling her protest with a finger on her lips, "then I will send men for you. If you are in danger, Rekiberga, go with them to Illiberis. You will be safe there, so long as it holds. Let my blood and my friends be your shield. I swear they will protect you, as long as they may."

She nodded, her tears threading through his fingers, and that was when he was lost, gathering her close and losing himself in the taste of her lips, the sweet fragrance of citron and jasmine that always clung about her. When she tugged with one small hand at the laces binding his tunic, he could no longer fight himself. He took her then, in the light of the spring fire, over and over, until the first streaks of dawn threaded the sky and the clamour of war called him as he kissed her goodbye.

38

YOSEF

SPRING, AD 692

Sogdiana
Uzbekistan and the Steppes

Yosef had approached Serica haunted by echoes from the past, exhausted in body and soul. Now those same echoes seemed to pull him forward with an inexorable strength as he crossed the great plains and the Roof of the World. He felt invigorated by the sense of being called by those he had once loved, and consequently he moved at a pace he could not have imagined on his way to Serica.

Every morning, long before dawn whilst the other men slept, he rose to perform the flowing sequence of movements he had learned in the mountains. As he moved slowly, feeling the energy course through his body, he felt the land itself seep into his bones. The morning ritual not only brought him back to himself. It made him part of the land he woke in, wherever that was.

The weary loneliness had left him. The changes wrought by his time in Serica became apparent to him when he returned to the company of merchant travellers. Yosef was no longer searching, for all he had sought was now contained within. He found he did not seek company or need it, though he found it easy to be in if he must. He did not delay at trading posts but sought the fastest caravans, moving on when they stopped to rest or trade. He covered ground far more rapidly than he ever had on the way to Serica. Knowing the route, he discovered, made its passing less burdensome.

For a time, he travelled with a merchant named Omar. An Arab diplomat from Damascus, Omar had been overjoyed to discover that Yosef not only spoke his language but had visited his lands.

"You are accustomed to this mode of travel?" He gestured disdainfully at the long, slow caravan of the Sogdians' double-humped camels.

Yosef inclined his head. "You find it uncomfortable?"

Omar clicked his tongue in annoyance. "These people are peasants. Their language is like the barking of dogs, and they have no God."

"They believe in the One," said Yosef. "In Ahura Mazda."

"Infidels." Omar's face darkened. "And they do not pay the tribute they should for the right to trade in the caliph's lands."

"No, they do not. The Sogdian lands are a bridge between the Circle of Lands, the world shared by the Arabs and Greeks, and Serica, a world apart, with its own traditions and history." Yosef waved behind him. "A bridge no Arab or Greek army could ever take, even had they the inclination. The Sogdians own the one thing we all need – access between the worlds that rule."

"You admire them?"

Yosef shrugged. "I can work with them."

Omar looked at him curiously. "You have been a long time in foreign worlds, my young friend, have you not?"

"I have."

"Then perhaps you may know of the man I ride to see now, to whom I carry word from our allies in Serica. Mohammed bin Marwan, brother of the Khalifatul Mu'mineen, Abd al Malik."

The name brought such a flood of memories that Yosef fell silent for a moment, allowing them to wash through him. Bagay and

Khanchla: *The Arabs do not concern themselves at all with any threat we may pose, because they know already that our defeat is guaranteed.*

Mohammed: *You are here to decide whether the caliph is a man to your liking – to judge our society, no? … Will you stay the turn of a moon or so?… I would enjoy your company.*

It was in Mohammed's company, Yosef thought, *that first I questioned my people. My God. My purpose on this journey. It was with him that my true journey began.*

"Yes," he said aloud, none of his thoughts showing on his face. "I was previously honoured to be in the company of Mohammed bin Marwan for some weeks."

"Ah!" Omar clapped his hands in delight. "Then you know the welcome that awaits us in his camp." Chattering eagerly, the discomforts of his journey forgotten in his delight at discovering common ground, Omar spoke of the great victories of Bin Marwan, and the miles drifted away just as Yosef's mind itself wandered across the sands.

THEY REACHED the Nur Mountains in late spring, when tamarind pods hung fat and heavy on the trees. They released a faintly rank cinnamon scent that mixed with the chalky soil and sea salt from far below, lending a thick pungency to the air.

The Arab encampment was on a plain near a lake. Arab forces occupied the nearby city of Antioch, barely half a moon's march from the famed trading port of the Greeks at Sebastopolis, where Yosef intended to pay his passage by sea to Constantinople. Mohammed himself disdained the city walls. The warrior Yosef remembered welcomed them instead from a voluminous tent, stitched inside with rich silks in a multitude of colours. His camp was as lavish as Yosef recalled his palace had been, yet it retained the efficient discipline of the military. Every item within was of superb workmanship and quality. No item was superfluous, grandiose, or a meaningless luxury. Mohammed was first and foremost a warrior, and almost as importantly, a man of God, a scholar of the Qur'an.

"Yosef!" His eyes widened in surprise and he paused in his

greeting, taking in the long, rich robes made in the Sogdian style, the pointed boots and carefully stitched travelling cloak. He kissed Yosef's cheeks lightly, the merest touch of flesh, his skin cool. His robes gave off the vague scent of musk Yosef recalled from Al Sinnabra. "You are much changed, my friend," he said, regarding Yosef thoughtfully. "I am glad indeed to meet you again after the journey you have had. We will have much to speak of, no?"

It was not for several days, however, that the opportunity came to speak together.

Skirmishes were a frequent occurrence in the mountains beyond the Arabic camp. Yosef, long accustomed to perceiving the subtleties in atmosphere, sensed trouble brewing beneath the surface. The men were tense and on edge, resentful of the forays they were forced to make into the mountain wilds.

"For every journey to collect taxes, we lose almost as many men as the coins we take." Mohammed was tired, his face drawn and lined. Despite returning that day from another foray into the mountains, he had nonetheless taken the time to wash, dress in white robes, and pray before joining Yosef for dinner. After his time in Serica, Yosef noted these small disciplines, the subtle habits rigidly enforced even when unobserved. It was these same habits, he understood, that made Mohammed the formidable commander he was. "These are Christian lands. The Greeks promised they would subdue them. Thousands were moved to make way for Muslim settlers. But the Christians remain – and they do not submit." Mohammed's face darkened and he ate in silence. When he had finished, he washed his hands and looked at Yosef. "The Greeks have not paid their share of the tribute," he said bluntly. "It was not skirmishing that took me into the mountains this time. It was a meeting with envoys of Emperor Justinian II under their commander, Leontios."

He sipped water flavoured with mint, served in a delicate glass cup encased in silver filigree. It was, Yosef thought, typical of Mohammed's attention to detail, and love of beauty, that the glass had somehow survived the rough roads from Al Sinnabra to here.

"We meet to exchange tribute every quarter," Mohammed went on. "The treaty between my brother the caliph and Justinian II states we are to share the taxes from Armenia. Taxes we risk both men and resources to collect from our respective parts of that nation." He sat cross legged on cushions, straight backed and upright, robes perfectly draped over his lean figure. His eyes beneath the carefully wound turban were dark and implacable. "The Greeks have defaulted on their part of the payment for two quarters now. Not only defaulted – they have retaken Cyprus, claiming that we have not paid the portion we owe."

Yosef willed his emotion not to show on his face. He was so close to reaching Constantinople, so close to bringing the secrets he had learned to those who needed them, to fulfilling the destiny his father had set for him. And now, it seemed, he had walked into a war. One in which he could not easily avoid involvement if he honoured his friendship with Mohammed.

"What will you do?" Yosef thanked his long months in Serica for his composure, the steadiness of his hand. He remembered a lesson he had learned in the mountains: To understand a man, watch him drink tea. And if you wish to keep your secrets, look to your own cup and the hand that holds it.

Mohammed was scrutinising his face closely. Seemingly satisfied with what he saw there, he leaned back against the cushions and rolled the filigree cup in his hands. "We will go to war," he said calmly. "In reality, we were always going to war. We conquered these mountains. We need Sebastopolis if we are to take Constantinople, and we will take it, Yosef. This treaty" – he waved his hand in contempt – "was never destined to last, on either side. But the Greeks, under that arrogant fool Leontios, have made a fatal mistake, one they still do not recognise."

Yosef raised his eyebrows politely. He allowed disinterest to flow through his body, felt it in his fingers and breath, allowed it to spread over the distance between them so Mohammed's musings became internal, less guarded.

"The Greeks believe that a conquered people are obedient servants," Mohammed went on. "In this, they are wrong. They believe that by adding conquered peoples to their own forces, they increase their numbers, their strength." His eyes had been staring over Yosef's shoulder into the distance. Now they returned, alight with a dark force. "But war is won not by those with great numbers. It is won by those who know for what they fight. The emperor's new forces have no homeland to fight for and no pride in victory. Justinian's Slavs and tame Christians, these savage forces he has bound in the sewer of Sebastopolis, these are people beaten and savaged, torn from their homelands and deprived of their heritage. They owe no allegiance to Constantinople. They have no allegiance that cannot be bought, for all they held dear has already been taken from them. They fight now for coin alone, whilst simultaneously resenting the hand that pays it."

"And in their resentment you see a fatal weakness?" Polite curiosity in every note of his voice, Yosef let detachment flow with his breath, through the windows of his eyes. He was present but not intrusive. He was no threat to Mohammed; he was a neutral observer, no more.

"Yes," said Mohammed, at ease on the bland sea of Yosef's neutrality. "But more than a fatal weakness, I see an opportunity. We will take Sebastopolis after Rabī' al-awwal, during Rabī' ath-thānī."

Yosef made rapid mental calculations. The lunar month of Rabī' al-awwal had begun a week earlier. It was a sacred month in Islam, the month of the birth of the prophet Mohammed; fighting was not forbidden, as it was in certain other months, but few Muslims would wish to break peace. Rabī' ath-thānī, however, was the second spring – and was considered a good time to make war.

Three phases of the moon, thought Yosef. *I have twenty-one days to pass Sebastopolis and sail for Constantinople, where I will find those I can trust with what I carry.* He raised his cup and bowed deeply to Mohammed. "I salute your insight, and your venture," he said calmly. "May Allah lend his blessing to your endeavours and ensure the fruit you reap is rich."

Mohammed returned the salute, and they drank. The cool night air moved through the open sides of the tent. Beyond the rich carpet, the stony desert ground lost its heat beneath the stars. Men moved on the outer periphery of Yosef's sight, feeding horses penned close to the tents. Donkeys, used here for most of the carrying, made raucous cries from their own pens. It was a neatly ordered camp, one with rigidly maintained discipline.

"You are much changed." Mohammed spoke abruptly.

"I have been a great deal amongst people not my own." Yosef returned Mohammed's gaze evenly. "It would say little for me if I were to pass those ways without any alteration."

"I have seen travellers before. Merchants, diplomats." Mohammed nodded to the door of the tent, in the direction Omar had taken after they had finished eating. "Omar has been gone from Damascus longer even than you. Yet he is still the man who left my brother's palace. His loyalties and ambitions remain unchanged. But you, Yosef, are not the boy who left my company. I believe I no longer know the man you have become."

"I am Yosef ben Arun, a Jewish merchant tasked with forging a route that may prove the only hope for his people. This I have done, in the name of my father, and of those to whom I owe much. I stand now on the edge of success, needing only passage to Constantinople to make it so. After that I am bound for Spania, and for the completion of the task I was given." *All truth is relative. Speak only that which must be spoken. To a mind that is still, the whole universe surrenders.*

"Ah." Mohammed uncrossed his legs and reclined gracefully on one elbow, one knee hitched up, toying with his cup. "So you have found your God once more, Yosef?"

"I never lost God." Yosef met his eye and smiled faintly. "I simply needed to know what God wanted of me."

"And you know this now?" Mohammed looked at him curiously.

"No." Yosef laughed softly. "But I know what I want of myself. I know what others need me to be. And between those two places, I know my duty."

"Your duty." Mohammed nodded slowly. "And if I should let you leave here and pass to Sebastopolis, knowing what we have discussed here tonight, does your duty lie with the Greeks to whom your country is bound or with my army, which is about to attack them?"

"I am a Jew." Yosef did not flinch. "I owe nothing to the Goths who rule Spania, nor the emperor to whom they claim allegiance. My duty is nothing to do with their ambitions." The eyes that met Mohammed's were clear. "And nor," said Yosef quietly, "does my duty have anything to do with you. The only thing I have of value to you is information about the imperial court in Serica. And that, I am happy to share – though I warn you, it will prove of little use."

Mohammed looked searchingly at him. "Omar has already shared information," he said.

Yosef inclined his head. "With respect, I may be able to add to that," he said. "The people with whom I passed time in Serica have spies at the heart of Shengshen Huangdi's court."

"And in exchange for these insights, you would leave my camp in order to pass to the port?" Yosef gave the eloquent shrug mastered during long days watching Fei Hong. Mohammed's mouth twitched. "Yes, you are changed indeed, young one," he said, but he was smiling. "You will stay a day or two and speak to me of what you learned of the pagan monsters' court. You will also be pleased to learn that your old friends remain in my lands, though they are not at present in camp."

"Bagay and Khanchla?" Yosef's delight was unfeigned, even as behind the mask of his eyes, new opportunities revealed themselves, showing him the way he might take. "They are well?"

Mohammed nodded. "They are. Though I hope never to face either of them on the field." He gave Yosef a crooked smile. "They will wish to see you." He looked away for a moment. "Then you may leave and carry out your 'duty'," he said quietly. "Though only Allah himself knows what lies in your heart now, Jew."

39

THEO

MAY, AD 692

Sebastopolis, Anatolia
Elauissa Sebaste, Cilicia, Turkey

On a close May night, Theo sat on a hillside far above Sebastopolis, tossing stones futilely down the hill. He knew he should be at his dromon. At least, he should be with his men. But since his meeting with Oppa, and Leofric's departure for the company of the Slavic barracks, Theo had found little solace in the company of his men. He fought harder and more desperately than ever before, seeking his escape in the fierce wielding of steel and, afterward, in wine and Elpis's skilled caress. He spent his spare hours in the closed walls of Athanais's tavern where he had, despite the Persian woman's visible disapproval, installed Elpis, taking the girl over and over in search of an oblivion that remained stubbornly elusive.

He missed Leofric's gruff company like a lost limb. It had taken time for him to realise that Leofric was not coming back from the closed ranks of his Slavic brothers. Theo could have ordered his return. But in the chaos that was Sebastopolis's preparation for war, none noticed that one Slav fought now amongst his countrymen rather than for his commander, and Theo did not have the heart to issue the order. Theo had relived the moment over and over when Leofric had realised Theo knew of his guilt. All he recalled clearly, though, was the devastation of watching Leofric walk away. Silas had said nothing of Leofric's departure, but his silence had been reproach enough. Theo avoided being alone with him. If Silas ever learned of the parchment he had signed in Oppa's presence, Theo knew silence would be the least of his concerns.

Theo hurled a stone viciously down the hill. The mere thought of his hand on the parchment sent cold ice through Theo's veins, just as it haunted his dreams every night. He knew that signing it was a sin so deep it could never be expiated. He knew, too, that faced with the same decision, he would sign it again. Somewhere between those two truths lay the dark abyss in which Theo now found himself, a place absent of every moral touchstone that had guided him since he left Spania.

Theo knew himself lost in the darkness. He had been lost before, he knew. The difference now was that Theo knew the abyss was of his own creation and that he did not deserve to be pulled from it. And so he ignored Oppa's messages, turned from Silas's scrutiny, and tried to drink away the memory of Leofric's stiff back as he walked away.

Four months after Leofric's departure, Theo still waited for his caustic comment every time he issued an order. In every battle, he turned to his flank expecting to find the burly Slav's reassuring presence. Each time, when he met only silence and empty space, the loss of his old companion stung like an open wound.

When Silas's dark bulk rose before him, Theo threw another stone with unnecessary force and glared into the purpling night.

"When a man climbs so far," he said curtly, "it is generally an indication he seeks peace."

Silas looked at him gravely. "If it is peace you seek, *wenkai*, no amount of solitary stone throwing is like to help."

Theo threw another stone. "Say what it is you came to say."

"I have much to say, *wenkai*." Silas settled his bulk on the hillside some feet away. "None of it pleasant."

Theo grunted. "Speak, then, and have it done. I have wine and a woman waiting for me."

"The girl Elpis," said Silas without preamble. "She is not for you."

"You climbed a mountain to tell me this?"

Silas shrugged. "Amongst other things."

Theo's eyes flashed. "After years of urging me to take a whore, when I finally heed your advice, you find fault with my choice?" The tone of his voice was one that his men knew well to tread cautiously about.

Silas, however, was not so easily cowed. "Those years of abstinence are exactly why I speak now. You know nothing of whores and their ways, so it lies with others who do to warn you when you make stupid decisions."

"Stupid decisions?" Theo's eyes narrowed.

"Yes, *wenkai*," said Silas, unmoved. "Stupid decisions. Adept you may be in matters of battle. Clever with a sword, fast-thinking on your feet. But when it comes to women, you know nothing. And when it comes to duty, and loyalty, you are blind. Elpis is not the innocent you imagine her to be. Leofric is not your enemy. And making an ally of Oppa is a mistake." He cast Theo a hard glance. "You are not the only one who spies, *wenkai*. I know about your meetings with the bastard."

"You know nothing!" Theo spat the words out and turned away from Silas. "Do not think I forget what Oppa is, what he did to you and Leofric, as well as to me. But we are at war, Silas, and allies are scarce. How are any of us to judge what is right in such circumstances?" He sent a stone careening down the hill. "I do not judge Leofric for his betrayal. But he betrayed us, nonetheless."

"We will discuss Leofric in a moment. First, your whore."

"Do not call her that." Theo turned smouldering eyes to Silas. "I do not pay Elpis coin. The choice to lie with me is hers alone. Elpis is not a whore. Not anymore."

"Elpis is not *your* whore. That does not change what she is. I would trust her more if she asked for your coin. I do not judge any woman for such, and nor, I think, do you."

"Then what?"

"Elpis is a gift on a string that the bastard may pull when he chooses. She does not look to give you solace from the goodness of her heart. She takes Oppa's coin and does his bidding. Such a nature has no allegiance. You are a powerful man in Sebastopolis, *wenkai*, whether you see it or no. Such a man must be careful of those he surrounds himself with. Even the whores he chooses. Perhaps especially the whores he chooses. Elpis may yet become a dangerous burden."

"Whether she was once Oppa's tool or not, Elpis is my responsibility now, and I will not see her hurt. She is a victim of this war just as any other. You do not know her as I do."

"I know her better than you do," Silas said bluntly. "Her, and a thousand girls like her. You credit her with honour she does not deserve – whilst turning your back on those who possess it."

Theo stiffened. "What are you saying, Silas? That Elpis is traitor, and Leofric innocent?"

Silas looked up at the indigo sky, his eyes tracking a colony of bats as they rushed overhead in a dark cloud. "I am saying that not only have you made alliance with the one man we know has committed evil, but you have, on no more than his word, also condemned another who has shown you only loyalty."

"It was not only Oppa who accused Leofric –"

"I do not care who it was, *wenkai*." Silas's voice held a hard note that silenced Theo. "Leofric of all men deserved more from you than your assumption of his guilt based on no more than the word of Oppa the bastard." The contempt in his voice caused heat to rise up Theo's neck and shame to coil in his stomach. "And I thought you were an educated man who knew the stories of Greeks who come bearing gifts. In one foul night, Oppa ensured you lost one of your greatest allies, sent his spy into your bed disguised as a gift, and forced you to sign away your allegiance."

At Theo's startled look, Silas nodded curtly. "I know you fixed your hand to a parchment of Oppa's creation. The Persian woman has eyes everywhere, even amongst the bastard's girls. Unlike you, however, Athanais does not judge before asking. So here I am, asking." The dark eyes stared implacably at Theo in the dirty light cast by the town below. "In your heart, do you truly believe Leofric to be guilty? And do you truly believe Oppa will not use that parchment against you?"

Theo swallowed hard and looked down the hill. "Whether I believe Leofric is guilty or not," he said tiredly, "he made his choice, and now he is gone. As for Oppa and me – what we are will only be known when I return to Spania." He threw another stone, this one further and harder than any other.

Silas regarded him soberly. "You know what Oppa is. Such a man does not change his nature, *wenkai*."

Theo frowned into the distance. "You do not know his past as I do, or what is at stake, for us both."

Silas made a harsh sound of dismissal. "I do not need to know the contents of that parchment to know that you believe the country you left is at stake, along with the loyalties that tie you to it still. You look at Oppa through the eyes of the boy you were and allegiances upon which you were raised. You touch that coin at your neck and feel the weight of duty. Such duty is admirable, *wenkai*. Such loyalty is the stuff upon which stories are made and ballads sung." His deep brown eyes were fathomless in the pitch-black face marked by the three parallel scars of his people. "Your mistake, *wenkai*, is believing that Oppa, too, acts from such loyalties. He does not." Despite himself, Theo could not look away, nor find it in himself to argue. So rare was it for Silas to speak his mind that Theo found himself compelled to listen. "In all the time we spent on that dromon," Silas asked, "did Oppa ever speak of Spania – of his concern for your country?" When Theo did not answer, he shook his head and went on: "And now he is here, close companion to Leontios. Yet did he accompany us on the dangerous missions to the interior? Did he wield steel at your side? No, *wenkai*. Whilst Leofric risked his life in your company, Oppa skulked in the whorehouses he made to cater to men's worst nature, bribing the vulnerable to do his bidding. He is a man who pays for his friends and extorts his enemies. Such a man is not an ally, Theo. He never will be."

Unable to sit any longer, Theo leaped restlessly to his feet. "What is it you want from me?" he flung at Silas. "You know nothing of the choices I face. You will never have to return to your homeland knowing you were offered the power to save everything you love – and threw it away from pride." His eyes were hot and dry with anger and sorrow. "Our time here is nearly done. We will fight one last battle together. After it, you will go on to fight on foreign shores – but I must return to Spania and the wreckage I will find there. Do not judge choices for which you will never have to pay the price. They are mine alone, and soon enough I will suffer their consequences. It is time you forgot the responsibility you feel for me. I free you from it, Silas."

"And it is time for you to forget the boy you were, *wenkai*, and become the man you must be in order to survive." Silas faced him, his voice deeper and more commanding than Theo had ever heard it. "If you do not, it may be more than you who pay the price for your blindness."

Theo kicked the ground in frustration and turned to walk away, only to find his way blocked. "*Wenkai!*" Silas's bulk was a wall before Theo. "Will you not at least speak with Leofric?"

"If you see him," said Theo dully, "tell him I was wrong to judge his guilt without question. In that, at least, you are right."

Silas nodded over Theo's shoulder. "You can tell him yourself."

Theo swung around. Leofric's swarthy figure stood just beyond hearing distance, solid and silent. "You told him to come," Theo muttered.

Silas shrugged, his face twisting in the semblance of a smile. "Someone had to. You are a foolish child, and he is stubborn as a mule."

"You know I can't make this right."

Something old and sad crossed Silas's face. "I do not care if you make it right, *wenkai*. I care only for right itself." He nodded to Leofric. "You owe him that, and more." He turned and walked away, leaving the two figures staring at one another across the bleak hillside.

Leofric remained still, arms folded across his chest, waiting.

Theo walked across the ground until he stood before the silent figure.

Leofric pulled his wine flask from his tunic and swallowed a large mouthful, then threw it to Theo, who unscrewed the cap and drank, holding the other man's eyes. "Say what you will," he said. "I deserve it."

Leofric did not take the flask back when Theo offered it. "I am Slavic," he said, looking meditatively at Theo. "I was a boy when the emperor's men tore my home apart and forced me to fight in his army. A man does not forget such a thing. My brothers – they do not forget this thing.

"Since then, I have fought on a dozen shores. I have been a slave. I have been whipped – just as my brother, Neboulos, was whipped. I, too, have felt the sting of the Spanish bastard's lash. And I do not forget, *schnecke*. I do not forget any of it." He stepped closer, his face barely inches from Theo's. "But in all that time," he said softly, "I have never betrayed the men beside whom I fight.

"My country may fall. My commander may leave. The world, it may end, and all I know with it. But this, *schnecke*, for me, this is all that matters in war and in life: the man at my side." He stepped closer to Theo, his eyes hard. "Ask your question."

"You paid Kyros in Arabic coin –" Theo began.

"Ask it!" Leofric pushed him with such force Theo stumbled.

Theo nodded slowly. "Did you take Arabic coin in exchange for information?"

"Ha!" Leofric's eyes glittered dangerously. "So. Now we come to it. And I will answer, for though I fight now in the Slavic ranks, technically you are still my commander, and a man must answer his commander, *ne*, lest he find himself on the end of a whip, it seems. So." He did not look away from Theo. "I drink in the Slavic tavern. Men there pay with Arabic coin. They gamble with it. I did not take the Arabic coin for whispers. I won it at dice. And before you ask – no. I do not know who takes this coin, or who speaks with Arabs. But if I were to make a guess – and I have, my old friend, I have made this guess many times – it would be that your Spanish bastard is somewhere behind that coin. For if ever I knew a man for whom corruption and coin alone are king, it is he." He finished speaking and stepped back.

Theo cleared his throat. "I know it is too late," he said quietly. "But for what it is worth, I am sorry, Leofric. I had no right to suspect you, let alone judge you. I was wrong."

Leofric met his gaze with hard eyes. "Yes, Spaniard. You were wrong."

Theo waited. After a long silence, he held out the wine flask. "This is yours."

Leofric's mouth curled, and when he spoke, his voice was cold with contempt. "Keep it. Some wrongs cannot be put right. With friends, I share wine. But you and I, Theudemir of Aurariola" – he shook his head, holding Theo's eyes – "you and I are no longer friends."

He turned and walked away, his back stolid and unyielding.

Theo watched him go for the second time, regret and shame curdling the wine in his gut.

40

ALARIC

MAY, AD 692

Hispalis–Toletum
Road between Seville and Toletum

"*Xristus jap Tyr*, but it's hot," Alaric remarked to Teudolfo.

"And now you know the delights of riding in full mail, *magula*." Teudolfo grinned and threw him a wine flask. "Not as you imagined war to be?"

"Not a *hairus* have we seen since we left Hispalis." Alaric squinted at the blinding haze on the horizon, heat shimmering off the pale ground. "And for what?"

Teudolfo cast him a droll look. "I thought perhaps you had forgotten the Gothic word for sword after all this time swinging the spatha with your little Persian master."

"I have not spoken so much of my own tongue since we rode out from Aurariola all those years ago. But Sunifred's army is perhaps the most" – Teudolfo's lips twitched slightly as Alaric searched for the word – "*rustic* company I have ever travelled in." Teudolfo burst out laughing. The trials of the past months had bound them together, the two becoming almost as close as the brothers Alaric so missed. Now they rode alongside each other behind Sunifred's broad back, the duke's vivid red hair so like Rekiberga's Alaric could barely look at it.

"Rustic is one word for it." Teudolfo cast a disparaging glance at the motley lines of men in front of them. "Terrifying would be another."

Alaric glanced around to ensure they were not being overheard. "Surely Sunifred does not intend to take Toletum with such a force."

"No." The humour faded from Teudolfo's eyes. "But he knows you will deliver the men of Emerita. With them, and with you leading them, he thinks he will have enough."

"My father has trained the men of the king's thiufae in Emerita for decades. And the men from his lands around Emerita are sworn to him, not I, even if he remains in Aurariola from ill health. Even if he has said he will not stand in my way, still I know he does not bless this campaign. He has made his desire for peace very clear." Alaric did not attempt to hide the bitterness in his tone. "The men of that city are bound to the king by every law we own. And to bid them follow my father's banner, without even his true blessing, transgresses the last vestiges of honour left to me." He shook his head wearily. "I do not like this, Teudolfo."

"The men in Emerita will fight for you anyway."

Alaric frowned. "Why do you say that?"

Teudolfo shrugged. "What choice do they have? Sunifred rides on the city with five thousand men. Trained warriors or no, with the forces Egica has already taken north, there are not enough left in Emerita to hold it against him."

"That is not reason enough to turn traitor, surely. They are the king's own guard – Emerita is the military headquarters for the Crown itself."

Teudolfo raised his eyebrows. "Those who will not fight against Egica have already left to fight with him. Those who stay know what is coming. They either fight against Sunifred when he arrives or they join his forces. Like as not, those still there have already lost faith in the king. Your presence will be the deciding factor, whether you wish it or not, *magula*."

Teudolfo was proven right.

Emerita Augustus might have flown the Chrismon and peacock, but it had been loyal to Alaric's family for three generations and more. The Chrismon-and-peacock symbol was, to them, synonymous with the great general Geila, Alaric's grandfather, and Geila's brother, the legendary King Suintila, who had first united Spania beneath that very symbol. The soft-handed politicians and those who hoped still to find favour amongst the *seniores* of Egica's court had, as Teudolfo predicted, prudently left as Sunifred's hordes marched along the wide, sweeping plains from Hispalis to Emerita.

It did not come to a fight. The gates instead were flung open in welcome to Sunifred as if he were already king. For who, after all, was to say that he was not? War was in the air, and alliances were fluid.

The army, to which Sunifred referred in the old Gothic manner as *harjis*, or host, camped beyond the walls of the city. Alaric and the men of Sunifred's own thiufa rode within and made the palace their home.

"I have never known a man more enamoured of a history he knows nothing of," said Teudolfo drily, the first night they sat at the rear of the great stone hall Alaric and his brothers had once known as their second home. "Since gathering his beloved *harjis*, Sunifred has begun to sound like a relic from the days of Theodosius. What is next – blood sacrifice to old gods and parading about in animal skins?"

Alaric stifled a grin.

It was true that Sunifred had grown in swagger with every man, no matter how baseborn, to join his horde. He had spared no expense on the passage north, paying good coin for what his *harjis* ate, keeping his followers drunk on mead and *posca*, slaughtering beasts every day for meat.

"Half the men here ride only to keep their bellies full and the wine flowing," said Teudolfo, casting a disapproving eye about at the raucous revelry in the hall. "Your little Persian would not approve."

"Do I detect a faint measure of respect for Shukra's tactics? Surely not!" Alaric speared his meat, openly laughing at his old friend. Teudolfo and Shukra, from the first day they met, had waged a cordial, if nonetheless pitched, battle over the best way to train young men.

"Say what I may about that conniving little *listeigs*," said Teudolfo, "I will never call him a fool. This one, on the other hand…" He cast a scornful glance at Sunifred, who held court from the dais, red faced and bold as ever, his arm around a plump serving wench, fingering her breast with his hand.

"*Aba dauhter minus!*" he called genially to Alaric, raising his wine cup in their direction. "Husband of my daughter! Enjoy the lovely women of Emerita whilst you can, my friend! For tomorrow we will take Toletum, and you may be dead!"

"Tomorrow?" grumbled Teudolfo beneath his breath, raising his cup with Alaric and smiling politely at Sunifred's exhortations. "We'll be lucky to get this lot moving before midsummer."

But Alaric wasn't listening. "Whether we take Toletum or not," he said grimly, "I'm marrying his daughter."

Teudolfo smiled wryly. "Well," he said, "you did deliver the men of Emerita, after all."

In the end, it was another week before they rode out from Emerita, and tempers were already flaring. They passed Castra and turned west to Toletum, men joining as they rode. They met no resistance and a great many deserted fortresses. Whilst Sunifred took each abandoned village as evidence of his inevitable victory, Alaric was unable to quell a distinct feeling of unease – not aided by Sunifred's unfailing arrogance.

As they entered the final approaches to Toletum, Alaric was wound tighter than a drum. The days were hot and still, and he feared for his men, the men of Emerita, who had rallied about Alaric's flag as Teudolfo had predicted.

"Your men believe in our cause!" Sunifred had said, the day after they arrived in Emerita, clapping him on the back with such force Alaric had almost stumbled. The duke was bleary eyed and red faced, as he seemed always to be since they had ridden out from Hispalis. He began drinking as soon as he woke, and he rarely fell into bed less than insensible. Accustomed to the abstemious discipline of first his father's household and then Laurentius's training, Alaric found the excesses and wild temper swings unnerving and his own contempt increasingly difficult to conceal.

"And he is wrong," Alaric said now to Teudolfo as they rode. "The men of Emerita do not believe in this rebellion any more than I do. They ride because I asked them to do so, and because I used my father's name to force their hand. I forced honourable men to fight a rebellion they cannot win." His voice was bitter. "I do not deserve their respect or their loyalty. I can barely bring myself to look them in the eye."

"Not true." For once there was no mockery in Teudolfo's voice. "Every man here could have gone north to Egica. They chose to stay and fight. How you lead them from here will decide whether or not they remain." He gripped the younger man's shoulder. "If I did not think you could lead them, I would have left your side long before now, *magula*. Give them a chance to know the temper of your steel, and yourself a chance to wield it. Men will follow strength even when they do not believe in the cause, Alaric."

"I wish I could believe in it," said Alaric bitterly.

Teudolfo looked at him askance. "Then you do not any longer?"

"I know only that my father does not. Nor Laurentius, nor Athanagild – nor any of the men I have been raised to follow. And the more I follow Sunifred, Teudolfo, the more I understand why they will not." He frowned into the sun. "I thought I could separate the cause from the man," he said quietly. "But without good men to lead it, no cause can stand. I knew Sunifred was not that man. Now I fear men will die for a cause that deserved a better leader. Worse, they will die because they followed me to that cause – and to that leader."

"Perhaps," said Teudolfo, "it is you who will lead them to victory."

"The only thing worse than a lost cause," said Alaric bitterly, "is a divided one."

Ahead, the final ridges bordering Toletum materialised through the shimmering light on the horizon.

"Unfortunately," he said, "the time for division is past. Now we fight together – or we all die."

A monk came to their camp in the night, sent from Sisebut's monastery in Toletum.

"Egica is still in the north fighting in the mountains against the rebel Favila. His Grace, Archbishop Sisebut of Toletum, says Toletum itself is poorly defended. He promises that if you pass the forces on the plains, he himself will see the gates open for you, my lord."

The monk's words bothered Alaric more than he cared to admit. He had hoped for communication from Athanagild, but the monk was an officious, portly fellow who had carried no word from his brother. *Can it truly be so easy?* Alaric pondered as Sunifred plied the visiting monk with wine and meat to which he looked unusually accustomed for a man of the cloth. *What game does Egica play?* His brother's warnings sounded in his mind, but Athanagild was not here, and Alaric knew there was nothing his brother could do even if he were. Alaric, though, seemed the only one of Sunifred's company who was concerned.

"That fool Egica has left his city open for the taking!" Sunifred gloated, drinking deeply. "Did I not tell you how it would be, Alaric?"

"You did, Fráuja." Alaric turned a frowning expression to the monk, who seemed remarkably unconcerned given the gravity of the news he brought. "But why has he left it so? Surely Egica knew we rode on Toletum?"

The monk bowed. "Perhaps, my lord. But the king" – he looked at Sunifred and flushed, realising his diplomatic error – "That is, Fráuja Egica, is far north in the mountains, with much of his forces occupied in putting down the rebellion there. Even if he wished to ride back to face your army, he would not have arrived before now. And I believe he thought your force significantly smaller, my lord," he added, bowing respectfully to Sunifred.

"There!" Sunifred turned a triumphant expression to Alaric. "You have your father's dour countenance, *magula*! Have faith! Has not the archbishop himself blessed our endeavour?"

"For one who invokes pagan gods at every turn and disobeys

every dictate of the Holy fathers," said Teudolfo as they backed out of the tent, "Sunifred bandies about the friendship of this archbishop with a deal of confidence."

Recalling Athanagild's dire warnings regarding the alliance between Sunifred and Sisebut, Alaric swallowed his disgust and made no comment.

He did not sleep at all that night.

He thought of Rekiberga as he had last seen her when they parted in Hispalis, of her blazing auburn hair and eyes the colour of the sea at midday. He thought of nothing but her during the long night before they rode for Toletum, so that if he must die, it would be with every inch of her flesh embedded upon his mind.

The memories lingered still as they rode across the wide, red plains, trampling olive trees in their wake, on the approach to Toletum. A paltry force rode out to meet them.

Sunifred's front line, led by Alaric, took them in the first rush, beneath a hail of spear followed by cavalry. The survivors gave up the bridge with little more than token resistance and retreated behind the gates to the jeers of the attackers.

Not all found it amusing. "The bridge is but the beginning," muttered Teudolfo, eyeing the city with misgiving. The walls of Toletum were high and wide, the city itself built on a hill. The bridge was narrow to deter a mass advance. Sunifred's army must first cross the broad reach of the River Tagus, then attack a city from which the defenders had the advantage of high ground and robust defences.

It should have been, at the least, a siege. Alaric's own father had helped plan the defence of Toletum. Alaric knew how hard it should be to take if it were properly guarded. But it was not, and in the end, it did not prove the great battle Alaric had expected, nor barely even a skirmish.

The city hid behind the walls for much of the morning, putting up no more than a desultory defence as Sunifred rode between his troops, directing ladders and bowmen, readying them to storm the walls. No more than a few desultory arrows had been loosed before a messenger wearing the brown robes of a monk was sent under a flag of truce.

"Fráuja – there has been a rebellion within our own walls," said the messenger, red faced and flustered. "The palace guard is defeated, and to prevent further loss of life, the archbishop has declared he will open the gates if you, in turn, guarantee the safety of all in the city." By early afternoon, Toletum was Sunifred's, with barely a hundred lives lost in the taking.

"Why?" Teudolfo mused, as they rode at the front of a vanguard through the city gates. "Why would Egica relinquish his own capital?"

Because he knows he will take it back, thought Alaric bitterly. *And because when he does so, it will be with all his enemies unmasked, revealed to him.*

Archbishop Sisebut met Sunifred in the great square before the grand portico of the basilica. His robes were blazing white trimmed in gold thread, and he appeared carrying both mitre and sceptre. Sunifred dismounted and prostrated himself before the ornaments of God, Sisebut intoning the holy words of the sacrament above him: "*In nomine Patris et Filii et Spiritus Sancti...*"

It was not a coronation – not yet. But it was the Church's blessing, and in Toletum they amounted to the same thing.

Alaric was not looking at the archbishop, however. His eyes were locked on his brother, who stood in a cluster of priests flanking Sisebut.

He saw Athanagild's eyes search the array of lords behind Sunifred. They passed over Alaric twice. The third time, however, the hazel eyes flared with recognition, and a brief, blazing look of relief and joy passed over the thin face, so fleeting it was gone almost before it had occurred. It left Alaric feeling warm inside and oddly reassured.

When did it happen, he wondered, *that Athanagild became what he is?* He remembered for a moment the quiet, thin boy who had hung back from his and Theo's games, watching always with a half smile. He recognised in the man before him the understated strength he had not noticed in those childish days, the calm intelligence that lay behind Athanagild's reserve.

He watched Athanagild throughout the long afternoon. His brother remained close to Sisebut's side, leaning in attentively when the archbishop spoke. Sisebut addressed a great many comments to Athanagild, Alaric noted. Once, when Athanagild had momentarily removed himself, Alaric saw Sisebut look around, a petulant frown on his face that only lifted when Athanagild's quiet, tall presence reappeared, bending again to attend his archbishop with a thoughtful, measured air. A passage from Athanagild's letter of several months ago passed through Alaric's mind: *Please do not be concerned for me. I find myself well able to navigate the complexities of my situation. At least I am able to aid Laurentius and our father by passing information on Sisebut's plans, and in this, I believe I can at least be of service, even in a small fashion.*

Alaric's hand clenched about his wine cup. *Is this how my brother has risen so high?* he thought, quelling the feeling of disgust in his gut. He thought of Laurentius, normally so urbane and controlled, uncharacteristically grim at any mention of Athanagild; of the clouds over Shukra's face whenever he returned from Toletum. Alaric had thought both no more than concern for the fate of Spania in such uncertain times. Now, watching his brother, he began to wonder if there had been more to both than he had previously considered. *Is it this that is the cause of Shukra's silence and Laurentius's grim demeanour?* He thought again of the boy his brother had once been, quiet and watchful – but stubborn, too. He was just as much a warrior as Theo or himself, Alaric realised. Even then. Athanagild, Alaric knew with a sudden surety, would no more step away from the duty he saw before him than either of his brothers would, no matter who asked him nor what he must suffer to carry it out.

"Sisebut depends upon your brother," Teudolfo remarked, watching the interaction. He turned to Alaric. "Just as Sunifred does on you."

Turning away so Teudolfo could not read his features, Alaric composed himself and grunted an answer: "Sunifred does not depend on anyone."

"You believe that?" Teudolfo looked at him shrewdly. "What do you notice about Sunifred's army, *magula*?"

Alaric made a disparaging noise. "Its total lack of preparedness."

"*Ja.*" Teudolfo nodded at the high table on the dais, at which Alaric had refused a place, citing his need to converse with his men as excuse. "The army contains no lords of Sunifred's own rank, or even approaching his own rank. He is not a man who is able to withstand the scrutiny of his equals. Instead, he chooses you – a boy whose future he holds by his daughter's skirts. Something in him knows that you have the qualities he himself lacks. Men may drink with Sunifred, but they will follow you. He needs you, Alaric. He always has. For once Egica turns his attention back to Toletum, no archbishop will hold the city for him."

Teudolfo's was not the only dour face. There was a subdued note to the revelry, despite Sunifred's best efforts. It was dawning on many that Toletum was simply the beginning of a much longer war. The older veterans amongst them were already fretting over what would feed the great host Sunifred had brought and how to best defend the city itself. At the high table, Sunifred talked of sending Alaric north to meet Egica's armies as they turned southward.

Alaric caught his brother's eye. From the dais, Athanagild raised his cup slightly, a faintly sardonic smile curling his mouth. Alaric allowed his eyes to move to the right, where Athanagild's hand rested on Sisebut's shoulder. Athanagild coloured faintly but held Alaric's eye, tilting his own face upward in both challenge and apology. Alaric tilted his own head in the direction of Sunifred. He shrugged, eyebrows lifting in a rueful gesture of equivocation, then raised his cup in salute.

Athanagild's face broke into an unguarded smile, filled with a mirth that recalled the sunlit days of their childhood, the understanding they had once taken for granted amidst the comfort of a life they had not known could end.

Alaric felt his own face return the grin, felt the warmth of it steal through him like the Illiberis sun.

Across the crowded hall of bloodthirsty men covered still in the dirt of battle, the two brothers stared at one another and felt the echo of the third smiling with them.

Silently, unnoticed by the rest of the hall, Suinthila's sons toasted one another and drank.

41

LÆLIA
JULY, AD 692

Illiberis, Spania
Granada, Spain

Lælia had thought she knew much of Illiberis. In the months following her return, however, her grandmother Acantha taught her much she had never known.

Acantha, like Paulus, seemed to accept Lælia's new place in the household with little opposition. "We have held Illiberis before," she said as they rode together, her tall figure as straight backed and austere as ever. "And in years gone by, our people have survived famine, plague, and pestilence by using the caves in the mountains, knowing how to survive on little and hide when we must."

Grain and dried meat were stored in the caves, enough to sustain them through a winter. Weapons were hidden in others, steel wrapped in suede. As Lælia and Tosius taught the men of the tribes and the Illiberis thiufae the methods used by Dahiya's Riders, Acantha taught Lælia other things of the land to which she belonged. The ravines in which an attacking party could hide. The places where rivers might safely be crossed, and those where horses would fall beneath the current. The shadowed parts of a hillside on which men could be concealed, and the ridges that afforded a view of what came.

Acantha seemed even more like Dahiya than Lælia recalled. At times when she spoke, Lælia felt the presence of the tall woman from the desert close by and wondered that two women could be so alike.

"You knew her," Lælia said to Acantha once. They were riding across the high ground to one of the cave stores where grain was kept. "Dahiya. She told me of the time you spent together in the sands."

"Did she tell you of the place of pictures?"

Her question took Lælia by surprise. "No. She said only that you had ridden together – and that you had sought Giscila."

Acantha nodded grimly. "Sought but did not find." She glanced sideways at Lælia. "I do not judge you for leaving him untouched," she said, and only the tight line of her jaw betrayed what it cost her to say that. "There is a time for revenge. If it had been right, you would have known it." She halted her horse and dismounted by a narrow creek. "There is something I must explain to you," she said. "I had not thought it necessary, but perhaps it is, now more than ever."

To Lælia's surprise, the older woman began to remove her pantalons, smiling wryly at Lælia's expression. "I have not yet lost my wits, child," she said dryly. "It is only to show you this." She indicated a faint scar on the inside of her thigh. It was worn silver with age but clear still. It consisted of two straight lines parallel to one another, a slanted line joining the two in the middle. "The two lines are the walls of Carthage." Acantha traced the scars. "The slanted line is a cord that must not break." She pulled her clothing on and touched the woven horsehair cord at Lælia's neck. "This, I knew the first time I saw it, is the cord that must not break," she said. "Carthage's walls must not fall, Lælia, and the cord must not break. Dahiya and I saw the same things in the place of pictures, many years ago. I saw things there that I did not understand. Some, now, I know. Others are yet to pass." She nodded at the cord, her eyes vivid gold. "I saw the horses, lying in blood, the day the foals were born. I did not know what it meant when I saw it, but I do now. Those foals bound you and Theo together, and both of you to Illiberis. That cord might be merely something you wove of horsehair, but it is a symbol of a far greater connection."

Lælia touched the cord. "Since I returned to Illiberis," she said, "I have dreamed many things. Things I did not see in the desert. I see Theo in my dreams. I always have. It is as if I know him, even if he is far away. Feel him."

Feeling her grandmother's scrutiny, Lælia coloured. "He lies with another," she said curtly. "I see them." She met Acantha's eyes briefly and turned away again. "I know that such things are not important," she said, striving to retain her detachment. "Who he lies with does not matter to me."

Acantha made an odd noise. It took a moment for Lælia to realise her grandmother was laughing.

"You find it amusing?" Lælia was unable to keep the hurt from her voice. "I saw it in my dreams, and yet I did not crumble, nor blame Theo for his actions. Was it not you who told me women must learn the art of sacrifice?"

"Learn it, yes. Not ignore it." Acantha's eyes on her were not without sympathy. "You have not accepted Theo's betrayal, Lælia. You have put it in a box and hidden it in a part of your soul you cannot see. You think that when he returns you need speak nothing of this woman, whoever she is, that you will carry this knowledge like a martyr does a cross. You do not forgive Theo his infidelity. You hold the knowledge of it as testament to your own nobility, a secret weapon you will one day hurl at Theo in anger. This is not sacrifice, Lælia, and nor is it noble."

"And what would you have me do?" Lælia flung the words at her. "Theo is not here for me to confront. I cannot blame him for taking a woman. Any man would have done the same. I have no right to anger, and it serves no purpose to feel it."

"You have no right to anger?" Acantha raised her eyebrows. "Anger is not earned, or justified, Lælia. It is experienced. If you have learned anything from our lessons together, surely it is that all emotion has a purpose to serve. Do not confuse logic with emotion.

It may be logical that Theo would take a woman. But ignoring the pain it makes you feel is not acceptance."

"I cannot think on it." Lælia struggled to push the words into the air. "When I imagine Theo… with her… it hurts so much I can barely breathe."

Acantha smiled gently. "And therein lies the challenge," she said softly. "It is in such moments that a woman faces her darkest battles. They are not against an external enemy, Lælia. It is not the woman he lies with who angers you, and nor is it Theo himself. The battle lies within yourself. It comes from your fear that you are unworthy of his loyalty, or his love. That is what you must reconcile within yourself. It is a battle no other can win for you, Lælia. Not if Theo told you a thousand times you are all that matters to him. It is one every woman must win for herself." She cast a sideways glance at her granddaughter. "If you do not confront it now, child, you will be forced to when Theo returns."

"What if he does not return?" Lælia struggled to get the words out. "What if he stays with her?"

"Theo will come back for you." Acantha's voice was strong and sure, reassuring. "Such things are not to be understood, only trusted."

"I cannot imagine what life we could have together after all that has taken place, for me as well as him." Lælia stared into the distance. "I have waited so long for his return. Now, though, I cannot even begin to see what that life might be."

"You do not need to see it." Acantha reached out and briefly covered Lælia's hand with her own. It was an unexpected gesture of comfort that touched her, and Lælia felt tears blur her eyes as Acantha went on. "Your destinies are entwined with that of Spania itself. Dahiya thought they were bound also to her own land, and perhaps she, too, is right." She shrugged. "I have lived long enough to know all we plan is like to change. We can do no more than know ourselves and do what is right in any moment. I cannot tell you how your fates are joined, nor how they entwine with those of Illiberis or Africa. I know only that they are. But I will say the same thing your grandfather did, Lælia: do not sacrifice yourself for Illiberis, or for Spania. Change is coming. The vision I had in the sands was clear

in that, if in nothing else. Change is coming. I may not live to see it
– but you will."

ILLIBERIS COULD BE HELD to the west, where a series of fortresses
were manned by men from Corduba, Illiberis, and Malaka. The
Count of Malaka had lost a son of his own in the attack that had
seen Theo almost drowned. He had been one of the first to join his
men to Sunifred's rebellion, and what men were left would hold
their fortresses until the last, under Illiberis command. To the east,
the vast mountains and desert beyond had repelled attacks for
centuries beyond memory. To the south lay fifty miles of steep
mountains between Illiberis and the port of Sexi, which was
patrolled by allies loyal to Illiberis.

It was from the north that they were most vulnerable. Lælia rode
with Paulus, Acantha, and Gratimo, the scarred, old Illiberis thiufadis, to visit their allies in Gaius and the closer town of Ipocobulcola. Both lay on the road north to Toletum and would form a
barrier before any army reached Illiberis. The lords there were
tense and wary. Thus far, they had remained apart from the battles
raging north of Toletum, but all knew war was reaching for them.
Lælia sat at their tables and suffered their cynical expressions when
Paulus told them his granddaughter would hold Illiberis if he were
to leave.

On their return, they rode to the fortress that marked the
northern border of the Illiberis latifundium. It was perched on an
impossibly steep mountain above a wide, sweeping valley. Stone
walls stood atop the shale descent that no army could climb.
Attackers must first fight their way around the mountain to the
southern side, then through tall wooden gates at the base, for the
only way to Illiberis lay on the other side of the fortress. The difficulty of the approaches was one of the reasons Illiberis had held
against invaders from time immemorial and was largely considered
impenetrable.

"But all fortresses can fall," Paulus said grimly, as they sat on
their horses at the base of the mountain looking up at the fortress.
"You must not allow any force close to the gates. Fight them on

the valley floor, where they have no choice but to spend themselves on the fortress itself, for unless they breach the gates, it will hold."

"And if it does not?" Lælia asked.

"Come." Paulus led them through the gates where men were at work reinforcing the ramparts. They rode down the steep, winding path to the bridge that led to the township of Illiberis, which lay several miles from the villa itself. The river beneath it roared deep and swift, the bridge the only means of crossing it for miles in either direction.

"If the fortress does fall," Paulus said, "then only this bridge stands between an army and the villa." He fixed Lælia with a stern eye. "The bridge cannot fall," he said flatly. "If it does, you have no choice but to run. Do you understand me, Lælia? If the bridge falls, Illiberis is gone."

Lælia nodded.

"Grandfather," Lælia said as they ate that evening. Paulus looked up. "You have said I cannot hold the bridge. Not with the forces we have. The fortress above that, on the mountain, we also cannot hold if a large force rides against us."

Paulus frowned. "What is your point?"

"If Illiberis falls, you have told me to flee to Septem," she said slowly. "And yet Dahiya has shown me another way. Acantha, too, knows such ways. Our women did not always flee."

"They were different times." Paulus's jaw worked tensely. "In decades past, women here were trained, as men were. They made bows of bone and wood and were taught the secrets of battle and land. But those days are gone, Lælia. And no matter your training, even if Acantha maintains the caves – and I am glad she does, for there are those who will need to eat, regardless of what comes with this war – you cannot hold Illiberis from there as the women of old did." He looked at her with hard eyes. "I have ordered you to leave here if Illiberis falls. If I thought you could hold it, I would not order differently."

"Would you not at least have me try?"

"No." Paulus pushed his plate away and stared at her across the table.

"If it falls, Lælia, the forces arrayed against us are too great for any army you might have to defeat. I would have you live to return here one day with your own children, who might in turn take it back. But they cannot do that if you do not live to see them born. Your life is more important than any ground upon which we stand. Land is land. Villas are no more than stone and wood. Illiberis is yours, Lælia; but you are the last of my blood, and I would not lose you to a vain hope."

A tense silence was broken by the sound of hoofbeats coming down the long approach. Not a lone horseman – the thunder of a force.

"Gratimo!" Paulus roared, pushing the table from him with such force the cups spilled onto the floor. He was already reaching for his sword, and Lælia for her bow leaning against the door. But when Gratimo's scarred face appeared, he was smiling broadly, waving at Paulus to relax.

"Did you truly think your thiufa would allow an unknown force to enter your own home unmarked?" He shook his head in mild reproof. "You insult me, *maists*."

Paulus was still frowning as he peered into the darkness. His face only relaxed when a tall, cloaked figure came close and pushed back his hood.

"Theodefred!" Paulus embraced the other man hard.

Theodefred looked terribly old, Lælia thought, but the eyes that met her grandfather's were lit with an odd triumph. "Paulus."

"Are you mad, man?" Her grandfather still held his friend's arm at the elbow, and his gruff tone belied the reprimand in his words.

"I am not staying." Theodefred gestured at the men who rode behind him; Lælia had never seen a force so great travel together in Spania. The dark mass of man and horseflesh filled the plains about Illiberis, a thousand or even more. "But my men will. And they will fight for you, Paulus."

Paulus dropped his head, and Lælia saw his throat working with emotion. "Why?" he asked eventually, his voice hoarse. "Why would you do such a thing?"

"Because," said Theodefred, "I cannot sit idly by and do nothing. Egica has taken my son; he has taken my brother's son. And now," he said bitterly, his face darkening, "he has taken my brother as well. Egica's games forced Favila to join his neighbours in rebellion against the Crown. Now Favila's forces have been defeated, he and his men taken captive. If I ride against Egica myself, I give him all he needs to condemn me forever. But you, Paulus, none will expect you to remain out of it forever, and if my men must fight beneath any banner, there is none I would entrust them to but you."

Lælia could not look at her grandfather; she knew he would not wish her to see what was on his face. Theodefred and he looked at each other for a long time, then Theodefred turned to her. The shadow of a smile passed over his face.

"Riccilo," he said, "bade me tell you that the servant you sent her has proved useful indeed. Safia has become close companion to Egilona of Aurariola and playmate to both Wittiza and Roderic. She has also found a messenger to bring word from Tuy. She is, it seems, a most resourceful young lady." He smiled. "If anything should occur – should you need us – Corduba is your home, Lælia, and Riccilo your blood. Do not hesitate to come to us." Lælia inclined her head gratefully, touched.

"And how," said Paulus, staring at the multitude of men on his fields, "do you intend me to feed this generously provided force of yours?"

Theodefred looked between them, smiling openly. "Riccilo also tells me," he said, grinning, "that Acantha has ways of feeding stray armies."

Paulus shook his head in mock exasperation, but he was smiling. "I will welcome your forces gladly," he said. "But I will ask that you drink a cup of wine and give me your company for the night."

Theodefred's smile faded. "I cannot," he said, "though I wish to all the gods I could. If it should be even marked that I am missing, Egica will not believe me innocent. My household servants believe me ill. The men of my personal thiufa have been gradually disappearing for weeks; as yet, none suspect them of riding south. I would keep it that way as long as I may, and that means I ride tonight, alone."

He came close to Lælia and touched her face. "Do not forget what I told you, Lælia," he said quietly. "Riccilo loves you, though she is not the kind to speak of such things more than she must. Be safe in the coming times."

Lælia had never been easy with physical affection, and she found, as the years progressed, that emotion made her lose the words she had found so late in life. She nodded mutely but said nothing. Theodefred looked as if he would say something else, but her face must have appeared cold and unwelcoming, as she knew it often did when she was uncomfortable, and he let his hand fall without speaking further.

Theodefred reached out and gripped her grandfather's elbow. The two men clasped arms tightly. Lælia thought there was more emotion in their silence than any words could have expressed. Then Paulus nodded, and Theodefred mounted his horse.

Her grandfather stood on the portico, watching the silent darkness, long after Theodefred's tall figure had been swallowed by the night.

42

ATHANAGILD

JULY, AD 692

Toletum, Spania
Toledo, Spain

"My men intercepted this letter." Sunifred's voice echoed around the deserted church, louder than any sermon. "Liuvgoto has been writing to that whoreson, Egica. Telling him every detail of our southern formations – who supports us, who has provided troops, where they are. Even as with one hand she writes to me and our allies in the south encouraging us to go to war on her behalf, with the other she informs Egica of our movements." Sunifred waved the piece of parchment in the air, face engorged with rage, red veins standing out in angry relief.

"Fráuja, please." Sisebut put out a placating hand, which Sunifred shook off impatiently. Sisebut cast Athanagild a worried glance. Surreptitiously Athanagild moved to the heavy doors, closing them on the curious ears beyond, as Sunifred paced.

"She is a dangerous, traitorous bitch, and I want her dead!" Sunifred hit the back of a pew with the parchment, which crumpled and tore in his hand.

"Compose yourself," said Sisebut, rather more sternly. "None must hear you say such things."

"I don't care if they do!" Sunifred strode angrily for a few moments, watched by Sisebut and Athanagild who stood silently to one side. They had both seen this mood before. In recent weeks, especially since Alaric had ridden north to face Egica's coming army with the bulk of Sunifred's forces, it had become all too familiar. Athanagild had learned to simply wait out the storm.

It did not take long.

"She has sent men to their deaths." The fury had faded from Sunifred's tone, and his voice was bleak. "Alaric has sent word that Egica mounts his defences with uncommon accuracy, seeming to guess their every next move. And all the while my vicious, double-crossing bitch of a cousin has been betraying us. Plotting with her feeble-minded daughter, Cixilo, to regain the throne. Liuvgoto's ambition has no end." He turned to Sisebut, who watched him with trepidation from the nave. "I have tried your way, at your urging. Egica locked them both in a monastery, whereas I promised to make allies of Liuvgoto and Cixilo, to treat them and Cixilo's son with generosity and indulgence. But only a crown will appease Liuvgoto. She knows her daughter does not possess the strength the take the crown as queen, so she plays both sides to ensure her grandson Wittiza gets it. We have no option now." Sunifred's face was dark. "You do see that, do you not?"

"I cannot countenance what you suggest." Sisebut's face was pale. "I cannot hear such things spoken, Fráuja. And certainly not in this holy place."

"You cannot hear! *You* cannot hear?" Sunifred's tone was derisive. "Everything you have asked, I have permitted. You may place whom you choose in the bishoprics and undo all those canons that would deprive the Church of coin. You may charge fees for christenings, or present churches to your relations and friends if it benefits you. You may exact a fee from those Christians who would trade with Jews – and fine Jews themselves if they are found not to have converted and be living under Christian faith. If men should leave and marry, they may be permitted to rejoin orders when they choose, no matter how short the marriage, and given only minimal penance.

"In short, Sisebut, I have given you license to undo every stricture placed upon the Church, its earnings, and its moral practices these last hundred years." His eyes narrowed, became calculating. "I have overlooked certain… *predilections*, shall we say, that a less tolerant man would not find so easy to overlook." He allowed his eyes to slide sideways to Athanagild, then back again. "And all I ask in return – the only thing! – is that Liuvgoto and Queen Cixilo be disposed of as the traitors they are." He stepped closer and glared at Sisebut, his tone lowering to become soft and insidious. "Or would you prefer to find yourself, several moons from now, attempting to explain those predilections – and your support for my rulership – to a council headed by Egica himself?"

Sisebut blanched and swallowed. "No," he said feebly. "That would be… unconscionable."

"Good." Sunifred nodded grimly. "Then we are in agreement, are we not?"

"But –" Sisebut was pale, his eyes darting like a trapped animal.

"Don't concern yourself." Sunifred's voice was rich with contempt. "I will see that no blame falls on you. Liuvgoto is old, and all know her daughter has been sick with grief since Egica took her son away. Their passing will come as no surprise and will occasion no comment."

Sisebut turned away. His hands trembled as he fingered his stole, and his face was ashen. "What would you have me do?" he said, his voice low.

"Laymen cannot gain entry to the monastery." Always a man of action, Sunifred was calm now that he knew himself in control of the situation. "A messenger from the court will bring you a gift, with instructions. All you must do is ensure that the contents find their way into Liuvgoto and Cixilo's wine. None dear to you will be implicated." He glanced over to where Athanagild stood unobtrusively against the wall, head turned discreetly. "You!" Sunifred beckoned him.

"Fráuja," said Athanagild respectfully.

"Alaric's brother, are you not?"

He bowed. "I am."

"Then you will serve your king – as does your brother?"

"Of course, Fráuja. Anything you ask of me." He cast a glance at Sisebut. "As long as my father in Christ permits it."

Sisebut nodded palely but didn't meet his eyes.

"Of course he agrees," Sunifred scoffed. "Everything he has he owes to me. He knows it can be taken as easily as it was bestowed." He glared at Sisebut. "Never forget that." He turned to Athanagild. "Someone will find you," he said brusquely. "Be ready."

Athanagild returned to his cell in the monastery, his mind whirling.

Laurentius and Shukra were both in Hispalis, ostensibly preparing the men of the fleet there to join Egica's forces, although, in reality, their charges had already scattered, joining the southern forces in the thiufae of their fathers. He could send for either of them – but for what purpose?

Athanagild paced the narrow confines. Two paces forward, turn, two back, turn. He sometimes thought he would one day find it difficult to think without that same steady motion. Rather than finding the cell's confines oppressive, he had come to welcome them. Within these walls, he found the only true peace and privacy he owned. But now he paced in agitation.

I cannot poison the queen and her mother, he thought, horrified at the detached manner in which he was forced to even consider such atrocities. But if he did not do as Sunifred commanded, he would be unmasked not only as Sisebut's whore but as a traitor to Sunifred's cause. And even Athanagild knew Liuvgoto's plots could no longer be ignored. They endangered not only his own brother but all those who risked their lives to fight for Alaric and Sunifred. The rebellion might well be doomed to failure, but Liuvgoto's treachery too easily discarded the lives of good men, made a mockery of their sacrifice.

Somehow, he must find a way to keep the two queens safe, the Church free of scandal, and Sunifred happy, all without raising Sisebut's suspicions that Athanagild was anything other than his loyal confidant. He paced, trying to think through the myriad of competing concerns.

First, he considered the Church itself. If Sunifred triumphed, he would forever own the archbishop, compromising the Church. On the other hand, if Egica was victorious, he would see Sisebut executed alongside Sunifred and appoint an archbishop who was his own slave. Both options would see the Church lose its integrity and role in Spania's future. Athanagild must find a way to circumvent both options. To do so, he must determine who might be deserving of the role of archbishop and see that man installed by his brethren before others took control.

With the rapidity of mind that had seen him rise so fast not only in Sisebut's affections but in the very fabric of Church politics, he mentally reviewed each of the prominent bishops, rejecting them one after another: too rigid, too weak, too pious.

Felix. He thought of the quiet, dignified bishop of Hispalis, an educated man of high birth, an acquaintance of Laurentius, and of the now-dead Archbishop Julian. He considered Felix's record. There was no taint of partiality there, and Egica would find in Felix nothing to threaten him. Likewise, if Sunifred should, by some rare chance, prevail, Felix possessed a calm nature able to both mollify the worst of Sunifred's excesses and preserve that which was truly important to the Church.

With that settled in his mind, Athanagild turned to the second problem: that of the two women he was tasked with murdering. *For let us not delude ourselves,* he thought bitterly. *Murder is what I am asked to do.* The two women must live. That was an absolute and incorruptible truth. Athanagild would not be responsible for their deaths, but he must also ensure they did not die at the hands of another. If the plot to murder them was ever known beyond the Church's own brethren, as Athanagild felt sure that one day it would, it was at Sunifred's door that blame must be laid, not that of the Church. To do that, Athanagild knew, he must be the sole person involved, the only one able to testify to the plot and its execution. He could not take this task to another. *Who,* he wondered, *do I know who is both assassin and confidant?*

Immediately, it was Shukra's mercurial, lethal figure he saw. Athanagild winced. Shukra, he knew, would not like either the task itself or being forced to keep such a secret. But he would,

Athanagild was certain, know how to circumvent the poison. And even if he loathed the secret, Shukra would keep it.

Athanagild stared at the wall, seeing in it blank parchment upon which his words would fall. Two letters, then, he must write. One to Felix, laying out his suspicions, the corruption he had been a part of and continued to witness. It must be a careful balancing act of diplomacy, a confession rather than a call to action. Groundwork laid for the day when stern, impartial judgement would be needed. Enough to inform, but not quite enough to condemn. Not yet.

He looked again at the blank wall. *Why, if I know what must be done, do I hesitate?*

The answer, when it came, was a third problem, one both confusing and unwelcome: that of loyalty, and to what, and whom, it was owed.

Athanagild knew that in Sunifred's plot to poison Liuvgoto and her daughter, fate had presented him with the perfect opportunity to expose Sisebut's corrupt ambitions to the judgement of his brothers. He knew, too, that it was what he should do, and without delay, if he himself was to survive the bloodletting that hovered on the horizon.

And yet again, I am bound by loyalty. Athanagild paused in his stride, frowning. He could not fathom why it was that he felt loyalty to a man who had violated him from boyhood in the most vile ways, taken his body with never a regard to the young soul within. A man who had done nothing but lie, scheme, and corrupt. He knew only that to betray anyone who believed in his loyalty seemed to his own heart an unforgivable sin, a betrayal of the code to which he had been raised. And yet he lived in a world where the same powerful men who claimed to live by that code sinned daily against God in their pride and ambition.

But despite his evil, he thought, *Sisebut and I share a secret that would see us condemned not only in the eyes of the Church but in the hearts of our own fellow men. For this alone, I feel a strange loyalty to him.* The realisation sickened him. *It is this that binds me to him, this shared, great sin that makes me now hesitate. Not because I fear exposure myself, though I know it would mean my death, but because I know that for all his evils, the sin of his sexual nature is the one that Sisebut is powerless over.*

To whom, then, did he truly owe loyalty? To what?

Laurentius's face, grim and closed, swam before his eyes. Laurentius, Athanagild suddenly knew, had sacrificed every feeling within in order to serve Spania. He would never allow personal considerations to take precedence over that loyalty. Laurentius was loyal to Spania.

And I, Athanagild realised with a bittersweet twist of his heart, *am loyal to both Laurentius and Spania, for in my mind, they are one and the same. They are the honour with which I was raised and the future I believe in.*

Whatever loyalty he felt to Sisebut or the Church, Athanagild knew it could not be allowed to interfere with what was best for Spania itself. Athanagild's own conscience was his burden to carry, not something he could allow to be an obstacle to what was right.

Athanagild left his cell and made his way to the writing room. In the early hours of the morning, two letters left in a messenger's satchel from the monastery in Toletum, one to Felix, bishop of Hispalis, and the other to Shukra, the magician.

Athanagild watched the day rise over the sleeping city, his eyes gritty with exhaustion. In the red and gold hues of dawn, it was not beauty that he saw, but the blood and money spilled for the dream to which his loyalty belonged – the nation that men called Spania.

43

YOSEF

SUMMER, AD 692

Sebastopolis, Anatolia
Elauissa Sebaste, Cilicia, Turkey

Sebastopolis was at once the same as any merchant port Yosef had passed and yet utterly different. Beneath the seething morass of trade and greed, desperation and avarice, lay the turbulent undercurrent of war, ready to erupt at any moment. Yosef had no business there other than to sail, and he wished to find none. But few ships were leaving for Constantinople, most traders wary of the increasingly volatile waters beyond the harbour.

"It is folly to sail unless under the protection of the fleet," said one merchant gloomily in a tavern by the dock. "And the fleet is going nowhere. Not at the moment, at least."

Undaunted, Yosef began to walk the back streets. His years as a lone wanderer had taught him to look far beyond the first negative. There was, always, a way from one place to another. The secret lay in finding those with motivation to travel it. Mention of the fleet made Yosef wonder if perhaps Theo might be found in the port. It was an outside chance, Yosef knew. The imperial fleet was large, their ports many. It would be well to enquire, but such enquiries must be done with subtlety. Subtlety meant taverns and the women within them who knew men's secrets.

He smiled as he approached a low, arched doorway in a back alley in the late afternoon. The faint sound of girlish laughter echoed from within, followed by the rumble of a man's voice. There was no better place to begin his search.

Will I forever seek the back alleys? he wondered as he pushed open the door. *After all my time roaming, after Fei Hong, is this what I am now? A man comfortable with whores rather than one who truly loves? Will there ever be a wife for a man such as I have become?* For a moment, an image of Sarah flitted across his mind. He took a deep breath, calming the sudden skip in his heart. The memories seemed more frequent now but no less jarring when they occurred. *A wife as Sarah could have been is not meant for such as me,* he thought as he stepped into the dark interior. *Only in places such as these will I ever find solace, and with that I can be content.*

I must be content.

A young woman opened the door. She was pretty, and Yosef smiled and paid her handsomely for the wine she poured. But he was unmoved by the blatant exposure of cleavage as she leaned over him, and one glance at her dull eyes told him she would not possess the answers he sought. He looked about the tavern, searching the faces for one that held the key.

Then his hand clenched the wine cup so hard it almost fell from the table. Athanais stared at him across the tavern, one long, slender-fingered hand going to her throat, fingering the winged amulet there, the Zoroastrian symbol, colour draining from her face. Yosef stood, his heart beating a flurried tattoo. Her face made the very air swirl with memory and doubt, so he was both the man who stood now in possession of a fortune and the boy who had last seen her after fleeing his home, alone and terrified.

The curtain behind her parted to reveal a tall, lean figure, and all sense, every fragment of the self-control hard won in the Wudang Mountains, fled from Yosef's mind. His cup dropped to the floor, wine spattering like blood on the stone. "Theo," he whispered.

The man looked up, eyes narrowing, one hand going instinctively to the spatha at his hip. Then he saw Yosef and froze, the tall body tense as a wound coil. Theo took a hesitant step forward. His hand came up in a half gesture, then fell to his side. Piercing green eyes searched the face before him: the rich foreign robes, the pointed shoes, the hat that spoke of lands far away.

"Yosef?" he said hesitantly.

"Yes." Yosef found his voice cracking on the word, and he paused, clearing his throat. He realised he was smiling, felt the odd sensation of emotion breaking through the careful mask, so unexpected and powerful that tears pricked his eyelids. "Yes, Theo – my God."

They stepped haltingly forward and then met in a fierce, almost violent embrace in which both felt the unknown years that lay between the boys who had bid one another farewell on a rocky desert shore and the men they had since become.

Yosef felt the corded muscle and steel strength beneath Theo's tunic, but more than that, he felt the tremor of emotion that had always drawn him to Lælia's betrothed, the quiet depth of feeling that made Yosef feel unaccountably comforted, as if he had, in some profound way, found sanctuary.

"Come," said Athanais, her voice not quite steady. "We will be more private in the back." She smiled at Yosef, her beautiful brown eyes misty. "*Khosh amadid,* Yosef," she said softly. "*Kheili vaghte ke azat khabari nist.*"

He reached out and took her hands, pressing them firmly. Drawing a deep breath, he drew from his memory the words he had memorised during the long miles he had walked, hearing them said by Sogdian merchants at every pause.

"*Zãmchã asmanemchã yazamaidé,*" he began.

"*Vãtemchã dare-shîm Mazda-dhãtem yazamaide.*

Taé-remchã harai-thyão berezo yazamaidé.

Bûmîmchã vîspãchã vohû yazamaidé.

Apãmchã frakhshao-strem yazamaide.

Vayãmchã fra-frao-threm yazamaidé.

Atha-uru-nãmchã paitî-ajãthrem yazamaide,

yoi yéyã dûrãt asho-îsho dakhyunãm.

Vîspãschã Ameshãn Spentãn yazamaidé."

We praise the earth and the sky.
We praise the strong wind created by Ahura Mazda.
We praise the peak of Mount Harîti.
We praise the earth and all its gifts.
We revere the flowing waters.
We revere the flight of birds.
We revere the return of priests
who go to remote countries to promote righteousness.
We revere all the eternal holy laws.
Athanais put a hand up and touched his face.
"Yegheh h ātãm ā-at yesneh paiti vangho,
Mazd āo Ahuro vaeth ā ash āt hach ā y āonghãm-ch ā.
Tãns-ch ā t āos-ch ā yazamaideh," she responded softly.
Ahura Mazda, on account of His Holiness, is aware
of all the acts of good worship of all the living beings.
We revere all such men and women.

The words of praise passed between them in a slow moment of murmured reverence, flowing like water from the sacred grotto at Yazd, like the energy Fei Hong had taught him to feel in his own body. To hear them again, to feel the power of Ahura Mazda and the ch'i he now knew in the very blood of his veins, seemed to connect all his past and future in a glimmering circle of power, and Yosef felt held by it.

"Come," she said and led them through the curtain.

"Then you are bound, now, for Constantinople?" Theo raised his wine cup, his eyes searching Yosef's face. Theo's gaze was both fascinating and unnerving, Yosef thought. When Yosef had last seen him, Theo had been a young man still, his face a mass of livid red welts. But now the scars were stark, white ridges, and the man he had become was fearsome, broad, and tall. With his piercing green eyes and white hair, Theo looked, Yosef thought, like the Titans of old, a mythical god with the coiled power of a wild beast.

I would not face him on the field, thought Yosef. *And I doubt he would hesitate once there.*

There was a shadow behind his eyes, an odd reticence in his

manner that Yosef did not recognise. War, Yosef knew, changed a man. He could imagine at least some of what Theo had endured. It was no wonder, he thought, that those experiences had left their mark.

And there lingered still a trace of the Theo he had known, in the gentle smile he bestowed on Athanais, the quiet understanding he shared with the tall, ferocious-looking man who came through the door in search of him. The man halted at Theo's brief gesture, looking at Yosef with open curiosity.

"Are you," Theo repeated, "bound for Constantinople?"

"Yes," Yosef said, trying not to be disconcerted by the close scrutiny of Theo's companion, whom he vaguely recalled from Africa, a man so big and black he was like a mountain in the room. "I have business there that cannot wait." He looked at Theo, an unspoken message in his eyes. "Do you know of any who will pass that way?"

The black man beside Theo shook his head and folded his arms.

"No ships will sail to Constantinople now," said Theo, and Yosef read the truth in his eyes. "No matter the reason. I am sorry, Yosef. The last left some days ago. We are treading perilous ground. At any minute it threatens to open beneath us." He looked at Yosef closely. "You will have passed through the mountains," he said. "Through the Arabic lines, if you came from Sogdiana. You must have word, then, of their number? Perhaps even knowledge of their plans?"

The room swirled and darkened. Yosef heard the teachings of the Dao in his mind: *It is easy to dodge the arrow of an enemy but difficult to avoid the spear of a friend.*

But who is my friend? Yosef thought. *Is it Mohammed, to whom I gave my word, or Theo, to whom I owe my life?*

"Yosef is tired," Athanais interrupted them gently. A girl came forward to pour wine, and Yosef saw her hand rest lightly on Theo's shoulder. It was the merest press, but he saw the colour steal into Theo's cheeks, the quick, surreptitious glance he threw in Yosef's direction.

So that is how it is, Yosef thought. He wanted suddenly to tell Theo all he had seen and been. But he did not know who Theo was anymore, nor how to begin explaining.

"Of course," said Theo, standing and pushing his chair back.

"And we have duties of our own at the docks. Athanais will give you lodging and food. We will speak again when you are rested, Yosef. You will be here?" He turned those disconcertingly penetrating eyes on Yosef once more, and Yosef found himself nodding even though he knew with everything in his well-trained mind that this was the very moment he should flee.

"I will be here," he said.

Theo nodded once. He leaned forward and gripped Yosef's shoulder with one hand. A sudden, brilliant smile lit the scarred face, so blazing it warmed Yosef to his toes and brought the same odd sensation of heat just below the skin. "It is good to see you, friend." And then Theo was gone, and the room seemed oddly empty without him.

Yosef looked up to find Athanais watching him, not without pity. "Rest," she said quietly. "I do not need to guide you in this." She smiled, a hint of sadness in her eyes. "You have all learned to guide yourselves," she said. "Although at what cost, I wonder?" She made to leave, but Yosef reached out and caught her hand.

"Theo is changed."

She turned her hand over in his, studying it, not looking at him. "As are you," she said softly.

"Is he bound, still, to Spania – to Lælia?"

"Ah." She smiled, but there was a sadness to the tilt of her mouth, and she did not meet Yosef's eyes. "Bound he most certainly is. Though the binds are no longer simple. And Theo, I think, believes himself unworthy now, both of her love and of the Spania he left behind."

"Unworthy?" Yosef frowned. "Because he took a whore to bed?"

"No." Something dark stirred behind Athanais's eyes. "Because he feels he has whored himself."

Though Yosef waited, she said no more, and eventually he left.

It was twilight when he walked into the streets, needing cool air to soothe the temper in his body, seeking a place in which he could find peace from the town. He walked from the port limits and found the hill beyond, climbing up a narrow goat track, passing an old ruin that clung to the side. He stopped there and sat, watching the hub of the port below, allowing his mind to still. He disciplined his breathing, bringing himself under control, feeling the gradual quiet steal through him with each breath.

A soft movement, a cry in the distance, made him turn his head. A group of men rode on a distant hillside. Their horses were fine, better than any Yosef had seen even in the Arabic camp. A man rode at their head, his horse clad in rich armour, the men surrounding him riding in a phalanx that was oddly familiar, though for a moment Yosef could not place it. Then they turned, and the dying sun lit their faces and the design on their shields, and Yosef gasped.

It was the Chrismon insignia of Spania on a blood-red flag. One only the King of Spania, and his envoys, might fly.

There was only one man arrogant enough to hoist that standard above his head, and the last time Yosef had seen him, that man had been watching with flat black eyes whilst one of his men raped Sarah.

Instinctively Yosef slipped behind the stones, becoming the water he had learned to be, invisible to all unknowing eyes. He examined the men before him, realising, as he did, that their phalanx was familiar because they rode in the Gothic formation – like a thiufa – with Oppa at the head of the diamond.

How? he thought savagely, his hand going to his waist, fingering the jewelled hilt of the knife Mohammed had once given him back in Damascus. *How is it that he lives? And how is it that Theo is here – and Oppa also?* He was gripped by a passion he had not known still existed within him, a rage so deep and visceral he felt the knife in his hand like it was his own skin. *I could take him from here,* he thought coldly. *None would know from whence came the knife, and I would be gone before they knew I existed.*

But even as he crept forward to throw the blade at the angle that would mean death, Yosef knew he would not.

No action born of such impulse could be right. To kill in such a mind would bring a balance unwelcome to his soul, and Yosef, hungry to feel Oppa's life flow from his body, almost cursed his knowledge of the inherent evil of his wish. He sank down behind the rock, watching long after the thiufa had passed.

Because he feels he has whored himself. Was that what Athanais had meant? That Theo had found common cause with Oppa, the same man who had taken everything from Yosef – his home, his family, his country, the woman he loved?

When finally he stood, night had fallen and Sebastopolis was coming alive. Yosef walked very slowly down the path. There were choices to be made. Choices between friends. Between his heart and his duty. Choices that would result in men dying. And despite all the miles he had walked, all the ways in which he had learned to understand God and his own soul, Yosef had no idea what the right choices now were – nor if he could even consider the options evenly.

The smell of his father's burning flesh hung in the air with the meat roasting below, and Sarah's violated body walked like a spectre beside him.

The waning moon hid in the night, and darkness filled his soul.

44

ATHANAGILD

JULY, AD 692

Toletum, Spania
Toledo, Spain

"To be sending a messenger directly to my quarters! Have I been teaching you nothing?" Shukra stood stiffly in the bathhouse, dark eyes flashing. "Even now, I am not being certain I was not followed!"

"Your quarters are in a brothel on the river in Hispalis." Athanagild raised sceptical eyes to his mentor. "I doubt very much a messenger would rouse suspicion by entering there after a long ride."

"Perhaps! But still it rouses suspicion when a man such as I leaves in a hurry. Perhaps you are unaware, Athanagild, but war has made spies of good men and traitors of friends."

"As if," said Athanagild drily, "I could forget."

"Hmph." Shukra eyed him. "Well, what is it that is so important you have me exchanging a perfectly nice pleasure house in Hispalis for this terrible one by the river in Toletum?" He cast a disapproving glance at the closed door separating the deserted bathhouse from the brothel, through which came the muffled sound of female laughter and the clatter of wine cups. "And with not even the distraction of the women themselves." He folded his arms and looked at Athanagild, his expression softening slightly. "What, *aziz-am*, is so urgent that I must lie to Laurentius – again?" He attached particular emphasis to the last word, and Athanagild noticed the lines about his mouth, the strain by his eyes. *Disloyalty comes uneasily to us all,* he thought, *no matter what form it takes.*

"This." Athanagild held up the vial. It was small and innocuous, made of pewter with a latched stopper easily removed with a thumb push. It was designed to be easily hidden and even more easily emptied into an unsuspecting wine cup. "I received it today." Gingerly Athanagild handed it to Shukra. "Be careful. It is dangerous."

Shukra thumbed the latch and wafted the open neck beneath his nose. He glanced up at Athanagild, his face dark. "Where did you get this?"

"Sunifred's messenger. I have been charged with administering it."

"Do you know," Shukra said quietly, "what this is?"

Athanagild tilted his head. "I know it can kill. What I need to know is if you can alter it."

Shukra frowned. "Alter it? You hold in your hand a decoction of henbane – one of the most swift and deadly of poisons – and you wish to know if it can be altered?"

"Liuvgoto and her daughter must drink it," Athanagild said. "They must be seen to drink it and to suffer. But they must also live. It must appear that the poison itself is inadequate. No suspicion can occur that it was not given. Nor can I apply an antidote. The poison must be rendered faulty."

"Liuvgoto and her daughter." Shukra stared at him. "You have been tasked with poisoning Queen Cixilo and her mother, the old queen, Liuvgoto?"

"Yes," said Athanagild, so caught in his thoughts he was oblivious to the shock on Shukra's face. "I have already written to Felix that I suspect Sisebut and Sunifred of conspiring to do so. After all this ends, when Toletum is fallen and a reckoning is made, he will know who plotted this."

"And the women themselves?" There was an acid note in Shukra's voice. "Are they aware they are to be poisoned – by Sunifred, their own cousin, and with the blessing of the Church itself?"

Athanagild's face paled. "Why do you think I called you here? Do you think I agree with this?"

Shukra searched his face. Gradually, the hard light in his eyes faded to resignation and then to a sadness that hurt Athanagild almost more than the deed before him. "No, *aziz-am*," said Shukra tiredly. "I know you do not."

Athanagild swallowed on the hard lump in his throat. He looked down at the vial, then back at Shukra. "Can you alter it?" he asked hoarsely.

"Yes." Shukra pursed his lips. "Yes, I can alter it. I add frankincense, a little mulberry leaf soaked in vinegar. Enough of the two and the poison will make them ill, very ill, but it will not kill them."

"Can you do it tonight?" Athanagild heard the relentless note in his voice but it was too late now to stop. "I do not know when I might be forced to use it."

Shukra's face seemed to grow even more tired, the lines at his eyes deepening. "Yes," he said resignedly. "I can do it tonight."

"Good." Athanagild turned. "When it is done, return here. I will wait; I cannot risk you being seen at the monastery."

Shukra walked to the door and paused. "Is there not another choice, Athanagild? For it is certain that Laurentius would not approve of this. Nor your father. Nor any true man of God, however God is understood to them. No man should be forced to such action."

Athanagild turned slowly, his heart thudding painfully. "I act now because if I do not, Liuvgoto and Cixilo will both die. If any know I thwarted Sunifred's wishes I, also, will die. And if I die, who is left to protect them?" He stared at Shukra. "When this is done, this rebellion, this chaos, who will see some form of order return? Sunifred? Egica? The nobles who squabble over every *stade* of earth?"

Shukra's eyes narrowed. "And so now you are thinking, good priest that you are, that it is the Church who is being the ultimate authority? That your bishops and monks will be Spania's saviours? After what you have suffered at the hands of Sisebut, how can you still believe so?"

"I have written to Felix, told him of Sisebut's plot with Sunifred. I may yet lose my life. But Felix is a good man. He will guide the Church, and Spania, without corruption."

"Did you tell Felix what Sisebut has done to you since first you entered his holy company?" Shukra's tone was uncharacteristically harsh. "No," he said grimly, without waiting for Athanagild's response. "I did not think so. And nor, I think, are you confessing that it is you who has been tasked with the poisoning. You know that if you said either of these things, your Church would intervene and Sisebut be instantly condemned, the matter made public." He stepped closer to Athanagild. "Why would you be protecting such a man as Sisebut? Or this Church of yours that thinks so little of debasing its young men?"

"Who else will see order restored to Spania when this is done?" Athanagild flung at him. "Who else will be the voice of moderation amidst chaos?"

"The 'voice of moderation'!" Shukra's voice was derisive. "I am coming from a country in which the priests believed so strongly that they were the only authority that they stood about the flames as their country and people burned, believing until the last that their wisdom would prevail. And now you would stand before me, you, who have been more a victim of the corruption of those who espouse God than any man I know, and have me believe that those same men will be the voice of moderation?" He stepped closer to Athanagild, his eyes burning dark fire. "This Church you so revere," he said, the concern in his voice hurting Athanagild more than his words, "would condemn you, and others you love, by your very nature. Would see you die for what you are. And yet you would poison two women at the archbishop's bidding and lie to protect him? Sisebut, a man from whom your God Himself must surely turn away?"

When Athanagild did not answer, Shukra's eyes grew dark with sadness. "I will do what you ask," he said heavily, "for I have sworn to protect you." He flung open the back door that led from the bath-house into the street, pausing for a moment in the frame. "But do not think I love you for it, Athanagild. For I do not."

He banged the door against the wall with violence and strode through the brothel into the night. Athanagild stared blankly through the open door after him.

It was only as Shukra's cloak swirled into darkness that Athanagild noticed the cowled figure standing in the doorway oppo-site, almost concealed by the shadows. Athanagild gave no outward sign of his awareness but instead closed the door slowly, turning away as if unaware of the watcher opposite. As soon as the door touched the frame, he moved swiftly to the thin crack at the side, invisible from the street but able to look out unnoticed. The figure moved from the shadows, and in the brief touch of moonlight on his face, Athanagild recognised the monk who had previously brought messages from Hispalis and Bishop Felix.

So he is watching, Athanagild thought grimly. *But what he searches for, I do not yet know, nor if he believes what I wrote or suspects more treachery.* He retraced his conversation with Shukra in his head, wondering how much of it the monk had overheard.

Finally, Athanagild turned for the monastery. He could not recall anything said that discredited the account he had sent Felix. But as he walked through the darkened streets, the recollection of the monk's cowled face left a cold foreboding in Athanagild's chest and unrest in his mind.

He was still pondering the matter when Sisebut sent for him later that night, anxious to hear of the plans he had made to carry out Liuvgoto's poisoning.

"I know what to do."

Sisebut, Athanagild thought, was unusually irascible, pacing his chamber agitatedly, picking fault with every detail of Athanagild's plan. "If anyone suspects you of Liuvgoto's death — or if you should fail — it will mean our end, do you understand? You can have no confidants! None must know even a breath of what you do. You are the only one I trust, Athanagild. You will not betray me?" He came close, taking Athanagild's face roughly in his hands, his body rank with sweat and tension. Athanagild forced himself not to recoil.

A knock came at the door and it pushed open before Sisebut moved. The monk from Hispalis who had but recently lurked in the shadows entered the room. Athanagild felt the earlier sense of danger clawing more urgently at his chest and strove to maintain a neutral expression as he moved away from Sisebut.

The monk looked between Athanagild and Sisebut, curiosity plain on his face.

"You are only recently come from Hispalis," said Sisebut harshly, turning away. "So I will forgive you not yet knowing our rules. But in future, if you wish to enter my chambers, you will wait until you are bid." The monk bowed respectfully, but a knowing expression lurked in his eyes, and he did not look at Athanagild as he presented some papers to Sisebut.

Athanagild watched the door close behind him with growing unease. "You must be more careful," he said curtly to Sisebut, shrugging on his cloak. "When this is over, men will look to you as the head of the Church in all Spania. You cannot afford any hint of corruption linked to your name."

Sisebut looked at him with a surprisingly hard eye. "Is it my reputation you are concerned with?" he asked abruptly. "Or have you found other ways to amuse yourself?" Athanagild felt his heart miss a beat. *What does he know?* He met Sisebut's eyes with the bland disinterest cultivated over years of practice.

"What is your meaning?"

"I know you are meeting someone. That friend of yours – the one with the accent." When Athanagild still looked uncomprehending, Sisebut gestured impatiently. "The one who trains men with your uncle."

"Ah!" Athanagild allowed comprehension to light his face. Not by the merest flicker did he betray the dread Sisebut's words struck in his heart. "Shukra."

"Shukra." Sisebut tasted the name as if it were an unsavoury dish. "What kind of friend is Shukra that you must meet him in a brothel? I saw the way you took this evening. That road leads to a low pleasure house by the river. And a guard I know told me this

Shukra frequents it when he is in Toletum – and that he is here now."

Athanagild laughed. "If you knew anything about Shukra," he said lightly, "you would know he makes his home in a brothel in Hispalis and craves the attention of whores wherever he goes. The brothel by the river here is his favoured house in Toletum."

"And you crave the company of whores?" Sisebut came closer. "Or is it," he said softly, "the attentions of the pretty foreigner you crave?" He reached out and stroked Athanagild's face possessively. "If it is the former, you commit a grave sin against the Church, and you will be punished. But if it is the latter" – his fingers tightened on Athanagild's face in a sudden, vicious grip – "then you have sinned against me. And that, I must advise you, will result in punishment far more dire than any the Church fathers may think up."

Athanagild's first thought was one of passionate relief: *He does not even suspect the reason for our meeting.* It was a measure of his obsessions and his arrogance, thought Athanagild, that Sisebut's only thought was for jealousy and possession. *And you must keep it that way,* he thought, with sudden realisation. He allowed a tremor to creep into his voice and dropped his eyes from Sisebut's.

"I admit that I have… curiosities," said Athanagild in a low voice.

"Curiosities?" Sisebut forced his face up, shaking Athanagild's head. "About women?"

Athanagild shrugged. "Women. And men."

"I knew it!" Sisebut threw his face to one side and strode angrily across the room. "Does this Shukra share your interests?"

"I don't know." Athanagild bowed his head as if in shame. "I don't even know," he whispered, "my own nature."

"You are a man of God." Sisebut waved a hand carelessly in the air. "What happens in these walls, with your brothers in Christ, occurs with God's understanding, and forgiveness, for we do God's work in all things. But outside these walls" – he gripped Athanagild's shoulders and shook him gently – "you lie with no one, do you understand?" He caressed Athanagild's cheek, his touch covetous and possessive once more. "Make no mistake, if the foreigner is meeting you in a brothel, he desires you. And I know, better than any, how desirable you are, Athanagild. For even now, all these years since you came to me, I desire you more than any man I have ever known."

He gripped Athanagild's face hard, turning it toward his own. "Do not betray me," he whispered. "For if you do, I will kill you. Do you understand? I will kill you."

45

THEO

JULY, AD 692

Sebastopolis, Anatolia
Elauissa Sebaste, Cilicia, Turkey

The new moon hung in a cobalt-blue sky, gleaming like a thin, curved blade above the violent flame of sunset. The night was warm, and the smoke over Sebastopolis was scented with roasting meat. It would have been festive had the city not been preparing for war.

Theo was surrounded by the crew of his dromon.

"It is certain, then?" one of the men asked. He and the others looked at Theo, their faces lit with the edgy excitement men felt when they knew they must face death. Silas stood slightly apart from them. He remained amongst Theo's men, but the distance between them was marked in contrast to their former intimacy, and Theo knew it would remain that way so long as Silas knew him allied to Oppa. It was no way to go to battle. Theo, who knew the schism was of his own making, had no more idea how to heal it than he did how to manage Oppa's shadowy presence and dark bargains. He had not met with Oppa again. The bastard, as if sensing Theo had been pushed as far as he might go, had not tried to find him. Oppa's shadow, though, lay over Theo's every moment. His dreams were haunted by images of Aurariola and Illiberis in flames, of his father and brother fighting a war they were doomed to lose, just as Theo felt his own was. Theo tried to imagine Lælia amidst it all and could not, for if he allowed himself to think of her defending the mountains of Illiberis, all he could see was Oppa's hooded eyes as he watched Theo sign an agreement that would trade Lælia away like horseflesh. Even the memory of that conversation left him rent asunder in such a way that he would wake from the dreams more lost than when he sought the refuge of sleep.

Elpis had been his last refuge from such dreams. But after Yosef's unexpected arrival, Theo had gifted her a purse full of all the coin he had and sent her away. He had said nothing to the querying look she had given him, for he did not know what to say. He felt guilty lying with her, and guilty leaving her. Yosef's arrival had brought Lælia's presence into his every waking moment. The potency of her memory had eliminated his desire for Elpis as effectively as if it had never been. Yosef's presence had done more than that. It had jerked him out of the abyss so abruptly that Theo felt as if he were waking from a dark, disturbing dream only to find the reality more terrifying than the nightmare. He longed to speak with Yosef as much as he feared it. He had gone in search of Yosef the day after his arrival, intending to lay his sins bare and damn the consequences. But Yosef had disappeared as abruptly and mysteriously as he had arrived, leaving Theo with the unnerving suspicion his old friend had somehow learned of his alliance with Oppa.

"Is it certain? Is battle here?" asked the man again, bringing Theo abruptly back to the present.

"It is certain." He looked at Silas as he answered the man's question. "The Arabs sent envoys today with a message for Leontios: 'Pay what is owed under the treaty, or Sebastopolis will fall.'" He shook his head, face dark. "Leontios laughed."

Silas made a low sound of contempt. "That man will see us all die – for what? A few coins?"

The first man frowned. "Surely we will prevail," he said, looking at Theo. "We have the numbers, do we not?"

"It would seem so." All eyes were on Theo, except Silas's. Theo tried not to feel the pain of his old friend's distance. "But Mohammed bin Marwan is no fool. The man has taken cities with far greater defences than Sebastopolis. He would not attack without certainty in his victory."

"So you think he knows something we do not?"

"I think he has a plan of which we have not yet been apprised, yes."

It was Silas who asked the question Theo dreaded: "What news from the Slavs?"

"I cannot say." Theo strove to maintain an even tone. "Neboulos I have barely seen, not since the lash bit his back and the Arab army made camp barely five miles from us." He met Silas's eyes. "I have no other friends in the Slavic camp to bring news," he said quietly. Silas stared at him for a long moment, then released a long, low breath. When he looked up, his face was tired and resigned.

"What of the Jew?" he asked. "Your friend? He knows the Arabs, no? What does he say?"

Theo shook his head, unwilling to confess that he did not know Yosef's whereabouts. He looked away from Silas, swallowing the bitter shame he carried as constant companion in the place where Leofric had once stood. He knew he could never forgive himself his betrayal of his friend. Time had served neither to dull the pain nor soothe his conscience. Every day that passed deepened a sense of loss and devastation unrivalled in all the time since Theo had left Spania, one made all the more savage by the knowledge that the loss had been both entirely of his own making and entirely preventable. Silas had not broached the subject again, but his silence spoke louder than any rebuke could.

His realisation that Yosef, too, was gone had jolted Theo to the core. He could not help but wonder if the two losses were linked. He wanted to ask Athanais, but to do so would mean confiding to her the details of his own deal with Oppa, and Theo could not quite bring himself to do that. Every time he thought of his signature on the parchment, his blood ran like ice through his veins and he felt a terrible, dark awareness that he had done wrong. The mere thought of Yosef brought the darkness closer, swirling about him until he could not see out.

"What will Athanais do?" Theo jumped, though Silas spoke in a low tone. The others were moving about the camp with the jittery movements of men who knew they would ride to face death: going over and over their weapons, sharpening steel that could need no further edge. Theo's mouth tightened.

"I have told her to stay close to the harbour." He looked at Silas. "If it comes to it, make certain she is aboard our dromon when it sails, with as many of the girls as we can take. She knows which it is."

Theo didn't mention that Athanais had seemed peculiarly detached when they had spoken of her leaving, barely heeding his instructions. Nor did Silas say the obvious — that if it came to leaving in the heat of battle, passengers would be the least of their priorities. Theo had sent word to both Pelagia and Elpis to come to the dock and remain there. He knew he could not abandon either of them. But if Elpis should sail with him — if he took responsibility for her — what then?

He shook his head impatiently. The eve of battle was no place for such thoughts.

One large hand settled briefly on Theo's shoulder, gripping it hard. Silas did not speak, and the moment was fleeting, but the gesture gave Theo more comfort than any of the preparations he had overseen all day.

As dusk grew, the Slavic camp was closed and uneasy. Leontios had summoned Neboulos to his quarters for a conference. Theo and his men saw the Slav pass from a distance. Neboulos did not hail them, though, and they respected his privacy. The Slavic commander walked with a slow, bowed gait, as he had since Oppa's whip cut him. Theo thought it was more than that, though. In recent days, all sounds of revelry had disappeared from the Slavic camp. They huddled behind their stone barricade in ominous, sullen stillness that reminded Theo of an ocean sky waiting upon a storm.

Theo had earned the rank of *komes* and commanded a detachment of three dromons. He captained one himself, with Silas *kentar-*

chos of another. Whenever Theo looked at the third *kentarchos* in his command, a man relatively new to his detachment, all he saw was the place where Leofric should stand, and he felt the now-familiar shame and loss.

When the strategos called a meeting, it was Theo, as komes, who attended. Leontios had commandeered the church that stood at the centre of the agora. Theo passed the lion fountains, touching the head of one as he did, a habit he had adopted from the local people. It felt smooth beneath his touch, still warm from the sun. The floor of the church had a mosaic pattern, which had been covered in sand to protect it from damage. Theo thought they might as well not have bothered. The church was so full of steel and armour he imagined the mosaic tiles beneath would be torn to shreds by the time it was done. Leontios sat on the lone chair in the church, the commanders of his forces standing about him.

Oppa stood close by the strategos's chair. His eyes narrowed when they found Theo. For a brief moment the two stared at each other.

First, we win this. Theo answered the unasked question in the black eyes.

Oppa's mouth curled. He lifted a shoulder in a careless gesture that sent a visceral fury coursing through Theo's body, accompanied by a sudden urge to stride across the room and thrust his blade to its hilt in Oppa's flesh. It was not the first time since he had signed the parchment that he had felt rage and frustration at the impossible choice Oppa had laid before him, the desire to lash out. But there was something about the knowing gleam in the dark eyes that sent a tremor of true unease through Theo. Then Leontios called them to attention, the moment was gone, and Theo moved to stand amongst the others of his rank, deliberately removing himself from Oppa's line of sight.

"Do not get too excited," muttered one of the other kometes as Theo moved into place. "Leontios's strategy is best described as: 'Don't worry, we'll win'." Theo's mouth twitched. He composed his features and kept his eyes away from Oppa. It would not do for any to know of their alliance. Battle was coming, and whether they won or lost it, Theo would give his men no additional reason to fear it.

"The cataphracts are ready," Leontios began, nodding at the heavily armoured horsemen. "None can match our horse and armour. Our men are well trained. They have had months to accustom themselves to the terrain and are well placed to hold off any Arabic attack beyond the walls of the city. They are backed by the horse archers, our well-mounted friends from Spania led by our ally." Oppa smiled in acknowledgement, inclining his head.

"Say what you will about the Spanish bastard," muttered the same komes who had spoken earlier. "Better horses than his I've never seen."

"Yes." Theo spoke grimly. "There is none anywhere in the world to rival the Illiberis breed; they are trained from birth to the bow and sword." It made him sick to see Lælia's beloved breed in Oppa's hands, knowing that he himself had signed the deed that might one day result in Oppa's owning the best Illiberis had to offer.

The kometes glanced aside at him. "You know them?"

Theo nodded once, swallowing his guilt. "I know them."

"The Arabs will try to negotiate." Leontios was drawing in the sand as he went on. "Their show of force is a bluff, and they know it. They cannot win against us. They have half our number. They will approach from the north, and that is where the Slavic army will focus both horse and foot. Our cataphracts will form the front line of each wing, and Oppa will lead his horse archers behind them. The Slavs at the centre will be flanked by their own cavalry and be headed by the *skutatoi*, ahead of two detachments of light foot. When the Arabs realise they are outmanned," Leontios said with satisfaction, "we will send our negotiators to them. The Arabs do not want war. They want coin." Theo and the other commanders stared at him, not daring to look at one another. Oblivious to their stunned expressions, Leontios continued: "Given that the Slavic forces will confront the Arabs from higher ground, with the city wall at their backs, I do not anticipate any skirmish to enter the city itself."

Theo waited with the other men of the Karabisianoi for the defensive plan of the city. But Leontios merely smiled at his commanders.

"We will triumph!" he said, pounding his chest and thrusting his arm out into the air. "For Justinian, for God, for Constantinople!" Obediently the men raised mailed arms and cried their approbation, but the cries had a hollow sound, and looking at the troubled faces nearby, Theo knew he was not the only one questioning the wisdom of assuming the walls would stand.

Theo stepped forward and knelt. "Strategos."

"Stand." Leontios's smile faded. He frowned at Theo impatiently. "Speak."

"Do you wish to order a formation within the city walls?" Theo indicated the men nearby. "The Karabisianoi will be idle through the battle. Perhaps we can be better utilised on the walls, and mounting a defence, in the event the Arabs close in on the city."

Leontios's frown grew heavy. "The Karabisianoi have already been instructed to remain with your ships," he said brusquely. "Should the Arabs attack by sea, we must hold the port."

"Yes." Then, knowing it was reckless but unable to stop himself, Theo went on: "But we know the Arabs will not attack by sea. We have had patrols scouring it in every direction for days. There are barely any ships accompanying Marwan's forces, only a handful of command dromons. Marwan's army is a land force. His dromons are directed elsewhere. The bulk of his attack must come by land. Please" – he nodded respectfully at Leontios – "allow us to man the walls, to be on hand should any trouble befall your forces on the field."

Leontios's eyes narrowed, and he looked at Theo with an unpleasant expression on his heavy face. "Do you doubt the skill of our forces?" he asked bluntly.

Sanyi, the *tourmarchai* who oversaw the fleet at harbour, stepped forward and put a restraining hand on Theo's arm. He was a quiet man and a good one, new to the port but not to war. "No, Strategos." Sanyi spoke respectfully, but he still met Leontios's eye. "God willing, it will be as you have planned. My komes seeks only to give to the emperor's forces what humble aid he may be able to proffer, in the event that losses become heavy."

"Pah!" Leontios waved a careless hand in the air. "These Arabic dogs will be brought to heel." He smiled unpleasantly at Neboulos. "They will learn obedience, just as the Slavs have learned. And when it is done, and we no longer indulge the Arab greed by sharing coin rightfully belonging to the emperor, the Karabisianoi will have the honour of shipping the profits home." He glanced dismissively at Theo. "That is the only true purpose of your presence here, boy. Do not think to overstep it." The men hooted, not a few of them casting triumphant glances in Theo's direction. Apsimar's approval of the young man had not gone unmarked, and nor had Theo's rapid rise through the ranks. Komes was a role much prized by those in the Karabisianoi. For a young man, and a foreigner at that, it was a heady height indeed, and there were those who were not sorry to see Leontios's sharp putdown of Apsimar's blazing prodigy.

Sanyi leaned close to Theo. "It is unwise to say any more," he said quietly. Theo himself was unmoved, though as they left the church and stepped into the chill night, his forehead was creased and his head bowed.

Late that night he sat on the stone benches in the abandoned theatre, listening to the banter of his men and ignoring the soft grunts and moans from the shadows all around. It was the night before battle, and all men craved the touch of a woman, lest it be the last time he enjoyed it. Theo, however, had avoided the one place he might find such comfort. Lælia's memory drew him, as it always seemed to when battle loomed. Even the slightest recollection of her had the power to suck the breath from his body. His interval with Elpis had seemed only to ensure the memories returned with an even more savage longing, and Theo found he could not, anymore, hide from them. He shook his head impatiently, frustrated that he was lost in such thoughts at such a time.

"All men think of the women they love before battle." Silas's dark eyes met his, wisdom creasing their corners. "Do not push such thoughts away, *wenkai*. They come to bring you power."

Theo was grateful for the darkness, as he was for Silas's unexpected kindness. It was the most the big man had said to him in weeks.

"It does not feel like power." Theo tossed a pebble down the stone tiers.

Silas smiled. "She is always with you, *wenkai*. Your child bride." He touched the twin amulets of coin and bone at Theo's neck. "So long as the cord does not break, she rides with you. Her heart is strong, as is yours." Seeing Theo's visible surprise at his warm words, Silas gave a low laugh. "The night before battle is not a time for enemies, *wenkai*. If we are to fight together one last time, as you say, then let us do so as friends."

Theo nodded, unable to find words. Eventually he cleared his throat. "I do not like Leontios's strategy," he said in a louder tone, changing the subject and including the wider group in his comment.

"He gives no instruction for the city?" one of the men asked. Theo shook his head. The man frowned. "But what if the Arabs breach the walls?"

"He does not believe that will happen."

"Does it matter what he believes?" Silas stood up, powerful muscles gleaming ebony where the light caught them, one fist smacking into the palm of the other hand. "If the Arabs enter the city, they must be fought." He turned to Theo. "What is your plan, *wenkai*?"

"The city is indefensible without standing forces at the weak sections of wall." Theo spoke slowly; he had given the defence of Sebastopolis much thought over the last months. Sometimes he wondered if he had always known it would come to this: the Arabs standing beyond the walls, the dromons of the Karabisianoi the only escape route should those crumbling walls fall. "I cannot order standing forces there, Sanyi either, and Leontios will not. Which means all we can do is guard our ships and be ready to sail if it goes against us."

"Pah!" Silas took a few short, frustrated strides, then turned to march back. "I do not like this! To remain by the port, helpless, do nothing except wait? This is not battle."

"No." Theo caught his friend's eye and held it. "But it is what we will do, nonetheless," he said quietly. "If the walls fall, we must be ready. The Arabs will give no quarter in their current mood."

They lingered a while, then they returned to their dromons to try for a few hours of restless sleep.

. . .

Sanyi had found him late at night, as men tossed beneath the dark, moonless sky, the new crescent long since sunk behind the earth. "I cannot shift Leontios's thinking," he said bluntly. He had gathered the kometes away from their dromons, which lay silent and waiting on the still water. They stood in the shadows by the ruins of the defensive wall on the west side of the harbour.

"Then what will you command?" Theo asked.

Sanyi glanced about him cautiously. "When the fighting begins, we will turn the dromons around in port. Order the two bow oarsmen and the *siphōnatores* on each to remain aboard, ready with the siphons facing the dock."

Theo nodded slowly. "It does mean that if an attack comes by sea, we cannot repel it with the fire siphons aimed onshore," he warned.

"That is true." Sanyi held his eyes. "But you and I both know there is no attack coming from the sea."

"What else do we know?" one of the kometes asked. There was a rumble of assent from those gathered, a few men spitting on the ground as they watched Sanyi for a response.

"We know Sebastopolis cannot hold if the walls fall," he said bluntly. "And we know there is dissent in the Slavic camp." He looked around at his men. "Should the walls fall, the Slavs may not long stand. That means that if the walls do fall, we are the only way out of this port. Every man, woman, and child will run to us hoping for escape. The dromons will be overwhelmed. We take what we are ordered to, no more."

"What about the women and children?" Theo nodded to where cloaked shapes lay against the walls, the villagers who were already guarding against the eventuality that they would be forced to evacuate.

"I know you have amongst them those who are dear to you." Sanyi looked at them with hard eyes. "But we are in the service of the emperor, and these dromons are for transport of his forces only. No women. No children. Nobody who does not take Justinian's coin boards these vessels. Do you understand? This is the clearest order I can give, and you will obey it. We will take as many of our men off these shores as we are able to safely carry – and not one soul that we cannot."

IT WAS the early hours of the morning when a light touch woke Theo from a restless sleep. He looked up to find Yosef standing over him. Yosef bent his head, and Theo followed his silent invitation out of the dromon and into the shadows around the docks.

When they were out of earshot, Yosef pushed Theo into a hidden alcove, not gently. "What deal have you made with Oppa?"

Theo broke free of Yosef's grip and glared at him. "Is that the reason for your absence? Spying on me?"

"Answer the question," said Yosef grimly. "He is here. He is not dead. There must be a reason."

"You have not killed him either."

Yosef did not smile. "I could have. I still can. I have not because there is something that you know and I do not." His eyes were hard. "I know you put your name to a parchment, Theo. I need to know why – and what you agreed to."

Weariness that had nothing to do with the tension of battle washed over Theo. "Spania is at war," he said quietly. "My father and brother are in rebellion against Egica. Oppa says Illiberis, too, seems unlikely to stay out of it."

"You knew this might happen." Yosef's expression had not changed. "Is it not much of the reason we set out on this journey from the start? We all knew it might come to this."

"But we did not know, then, what was coming for us. Not really." Theo gestured to the dark mountains beyond, in which lay the Arabic forces. "The Arabs were a distant threat, one we thought to deal with after we had shored up our own resources. Now, though… Yosef, you of all people have seen what power they wield, how fast they move."

Yosef frowned. "What point do you make, Theo?"

"You are right. I have spoken with Oppa. He, too, has seen the Arabic threat we face, knows Spania must adapt to face it. In this, I believe, we share a common goal."

"A common goal?" Yosef stared at him. "You think that Oppa wishes to shield Spania from the Arabs?"

"He is here, is he not?" Pricked by Yosef's hard expression, Theo ploughed on. "Oppa could have gone home many times. He has not. He fears for Spania just as we do. He knows his father does not understand the threat. I do not like Oppa, Yosef, any more than I ever have, but I do believe he wishes to find a way to protect Spania from the Arab forces as much as we do."

"Is that so?" Yosef stood back and folded his arms, his mouth a hard line. "And what is it that Oppa seeks from you, Theo, to help 'protect' Spania?"

"My family are condemned as traitors." There was a curious relief in speaking it aloud, even if Yosef's cold disdain made Theo sick inside. "But Aurariola is a strategic coastal holding. Oppa knows I have the skill to defend it and, with the dromons Laurentius has restored, the resources too. He will see to it that Aurariola remains in my family after the rebellion is done, regardless of my family's involvement."

"You say it like the rebellion is doomed to fail."

"Of course it is doomed to fail," said Theo harshly. "It always was. Oppa has had word from his father. Sunifred's forces are outmatched and outnumbered. They cannot prevail."

"I see." Yosef eyed him with an expression Theo could not read. "And what is it that Oppa would take, in exchange for allowing you to inherit your father's lands, Theudemir of Aurariola?" There was a sardonic accent to the way he said the title that made Theo flush.

"Egica is determined to have Illiberis," he said dully, forcing himself to meet Yosef's eyes.

Yosef nodded, as if Theo's answer was no more than what he had expected. "And let me guess," he said softly. "In exchange for giving it to him, Lælia will be spared and taken to the safety of Aurariola, where she will be married to you. Tell me, Theo – do you think Lælia will love you for giving away the land her people have belonged to since time beyond memory? Do you think she will rest quietly as lady of your lands, content for you to rule whilst she bears your children, embroidering cloth when you ride to battle?"

Every word thrust into Theo like a cold spear, stabbing through his confusion and uncertainty to the painful reality he knew to be truth. He spun away from Yosef's penetrating eyes and leaned against the wall, hearing the sound of his own pulse in his ears.

"Do you think I don't know that she will hate me for it?" he said, his voice rasping painfully. "But what am I to do, Yosef? Place my allegiance to Lælia, my love for her, above the future of the country our fathers fought to build? I do not like Oppa. I certainly do not trust him. But Spania itself is at stake, Yosef. If I return without his protection, I will be condemned as a traitor alongside my family, left with neither land, title, nor any means to play a part in Spania's defence against the Arabic threat we both know is coming. If I stay here in the Karabisianoi, I will be sent where the emperor chooses — and it is unlikely he will choose Spania's shores as worthy of defending. I must return, and when I do, I must be of use. I will not see Lælia sold at court to the highest bidder, even if she hates me for the rest of her days. Better she should hate me as my wife than love me as a whore at court."

The words were hot bile in his throat. He swallowed, reining in the turmoil that threatened to drown him. "Oppa is many things," he said grimly, "none of them honourable. But he wants power, and in Spania, he has the chance for it. That much I do believe."

Yosef regarded him with folded arms. "I believe that, also." Theo looked up in surprise. Yosef nodded. "That Oppa craves power, I do not doubt. Do you know why I do not doubt it, Theo?"

Theo watched him without answering.

"Because," said Yosef coldly, "Oppa has already made alliances to ensure his own survival should the Arabs take Spania." He met Theo's eyes steadily. "He has already considered that the Arabs might be victorious there — just as he has ensured they will be here, in Sebastopolis."

"Here?" Theo frowned. "What do you mean?"

"I mean that Oppa has made alliance with Mohammed bin Marwan." Yosef's words were hard as stones falling on the night. "He has been in contact with the Arab commander for months. I do not know the details of their alliance, but I do know that Marwan is certain of his victory here, and that Oppa's intelligence has been instrumental in making his plans. I know that Oppa has stolen coin from the taxes owed on both sides. Enough coin to make him a rich man and make each side doubt the other."

Yosef stepped closer to Theo and lowered his voice. "I do not know who amongst the emperor's forces Oppa has corrupted. But I, too, have sources in the Arab army. I know that Sebastopolis will fall tomorrow. And when it does, it will be to Oppa the Arabs owe their victory. In return, they will allow his escape through their ranks — along with the coin he has made here, and the dromons, men, and arms he has bought with it."

Theo stared at Yosef as he absorbed his words and what they meant. "He has played both sides this entire time." His voice sounded old to his ears. "His objective is not to defend Spania from the Arabs. It is to betray it for his own power and gain."

"And not only that," Yosef continued remorselessly. "If he gains both Illiberis and Aurariola, Oppa controls two of the most powerful and strategic locations in the south. It is no accident he made you sign that agreement, Theo. Oppa will have control of both a port where the Arabs can land and the most impenetrable fortress in Old Bætica."

"Tyr!" Theo gripped the stone wall, his head down between his hands. "I knew," he muttered hoarsely. "I knew what he was. And still I let myself believe him changed. I let myself be blinded by my own ambition, my own fears of losing my right to play a part in Spania's future." He shook his head, shame and anger curdling within him. "Leofric had the right of it," he said bitterly. "He said all that matters in battle is the men beside you. And I know Oppa enough to know I could never trust him at my side, with an army at my back."

"Athanais told me that you have been eyes for Apsimar," Yosef said quietly. "And I know you were not sure if I would return, nor if this mission of ours would ever amount to anything. I may not like the choice you made. But never think I don't understand it."

"Do not make excuses for me!" Theo pounded the stone with one hard fist.

"They are not excuses." Yosef put a hand on his shoulder and forced Theo to turn. "Do you think I have not doubted?" Yosef gave a short laugh. "In the years since we parted, I have found allies amongst enemies and myself a stranger to my own people. Do not think I judge you, Theo."

"But you no longer trust me," said Theo flatly. It was not a question. "Though you do Athanais."

"Athanais and I have business together that relates to the mission I left Spania to carry out. After we sail from here, I will share it with you. But before then, there is one thing I do know, and you must, also." He gripped Theo's shoulder. "Oppa has no allegiance to any but himself. He is more dangerous than the Arab army and more treasonous than any rebellion. We may not know where Spania's future lies, Theo, but we know this: it cannot be allowed to fall into Oppa's hands."

The sounds of night pressed in upon them, and the hour of war grew close.

"When this battle is over," said Theo roughly, "I must return to Spania, Yosef. I cannot stay away any longer."

Yosef nodded. "I know," he said quietly. "I know, Theo."

"He has my name on his parchment." Theo's voice cracked. "I gave him Illiberis, Yosef. That cannot be undone. And Lælia will never forgive it."

Yosef gripped his shoulder. "We will deal with it when we must," he said. "We will manage it together."

Theo shook his head. "I will not allow anyone else to suffer for my mistakes." He drew himself up and met Yosef's eyes. "When I return to Spania, I will go alone. You have no reason to land on those shores again. Go to Septem, to Ilyan, and manage your affairs from the safety of his court. Leave Spania, and Oppa, to me." He turned to face the horizon, where a dirty dawn glimmered.

"Where are you going?" Yosef asked.

"To the Slavic camp." Theo was already walking away. "I wronged a good man based on the whispers of a bad one. I do not deserve his forgiveness, but I hope he might heed my warning."

THEO APPROACHED the Slavic camp whilst dawn was still a distant thread. He handed a coin to the boy on watch and settled against the wall. He did not wait long.

"You are lucky I do not drink as my brudders do. They are not yet abed." Leofric shot Theo a bleary, resentful glance from an unshaven face. His swarthy features were tired and lined. "If you come for absolution, Spaniard, you waste your time."

"I do not come seeking forgiveness," said Theo quietly. "I come with a warning."

"Oh?" Leofric's eyes narrowed.

"Oppa has been negotiating with the Arabs," said Theo without preamble. "I do not know the nature of the deal he has made with them, but I do know he is the architect of the division between Neboulos and Leontios." He held Leofric's eyes steadily. "Oppa does not just believe Sebastopolis will fall," he said slowly. "He knows it will, which means he knows something we do not. I thought you should be aware of that, before you lead an army onto the field tomorrow behind his flag."

"Why would he ride onto a field he plans to lose?" Leofric was regarding him beneath lowered brows, his arms folded and expression forbidding.

"I do not know." Theo shook his head, frowning. "But ride he will, which should concern us all. I don't know what game he plays, only that he plays it. Now you know too." Theo turned to leave.

"Why tell me this?" Leofric said as Theo began to walk away. "Why not tell Neboulos?"

Theo paused but did not turn around. "Because," he said, the words painful in his throat, "it is you who once stood beside me. I know the man you are. I betrayed your trust once. I would not see you betrayed again." He began to walk away. "Tell Neboulos if you think it is right," he said over his shoulder. "You know better than I, Leofric, what should be done. I leave the choice with you."

"Where do you go now, Spaniard?" called Leofric after him.

"To a hell of my own making," said Theo quietly. He walked along the path that led to Oppa's tavern, unsure if Leofric had heard him or not.

46

OPPA

JULY, AD 692

Sebastopolis, Anatolia
Elauissa Sebaste, Cilicia, Turkey

The tavern was dark and shuttered against the growing dawn. Oppa sat in the gloom, pondering the day that was to come.

He had planned as well as he could, managed all that could be managed. He thought he knew how the day would go. But when it came to humans there were always unknowns, and in those grey areas, Oppa knew, plans could easily become unstuck.

Theo's face passed before his eyes, and Oppa tensed. Theo, he knew, was yet a grey area. The contract would bind him whether they remained allies or not. Should the truth of Oppa's role in Sebastopolis become known to Theo, however, Oppa knew the contract would be all that remained of their understanding. Time was short and the risk of discovery great. He thought once more of the dromons he had already sent on their way to Spania, and of the one that still waited for him to board – the one flying an Arabic flag in place of the Greek beside his own standard. Should Theo still be his ally at the end of today, he, too, would be aboard that dromon.

Oppa permitted himself a brief, tantalising vision of him and Theo sailing together toward Spania's shores. Such moments were a luxury he rarely afforded himself, for Oppa knew better than any the pain of dashed hope. But still the dream clung, a golden world he may yet, should today unfold as he hoped, inhabit. He had wished Theo might choose to leave earlier, before all the pieces Oppa had carefully manoeuvred came so close to touching. But he had known, somehow, that it would come to this, the pieces resting dangerously against one another, at any moment jeopardising the entire game. So much rested on this one day.

He was startled from his thoughts by a heavy pounding at the door. He let it go for a moment, but then, when it showed no sign of abating, he called Nicalo to see who it was. His old companion shot him a baleful look as he went to the door. Nicalo had wanted to be gone many months past. He did not trust Theo, and he feared Oppa's games. Nicalo was, Oppa knew, reaching the end of his usefulness. He had yet to decide just when that end would come. Then he heard the voice at the door, and Nicalo was forgotten.

"Fetch him." Theo's tone was curt, and a thrill of tension sang through Oppa's veins. "Now."

"You give orders freely, Aurariola, for a man who has sold his soul," sneered Nicalo. A moment later, Oppa heard the sound of Nicalo being flung hard against the tavern wall.

"Fetch him," snarled Theo. "Now."

"There is no need for brute force, Theo." Oppa stepped into the room, glad he had thought to dress in his finest robes. Theo released Nicalo and swung around, his eyes a hard, piercing green that held nothing of the clouded uncertainty Oppa had seen in their previous discussions.

"Nicalo," said Oppa smoothly. "Leave us." Nicalo, giving them both a resentful look, left.

"What deal have you made with Mohammed bin Marwan?" Theo demanded without preamble.

"Ah." Oppa's heart skipped, but his face, he was certain,

betrayed nothing of his disquiet. "The Persian's spies are better than I gave her credit for." He watched Theo carefully, but the hard green eyes gave nothing away, the scarred face grim and inscrutable as it had ever been. Oppa would have given a great deal to know how Theo had come by his information. There had been a whisper that the Jew, Yosef, had slipped through the Arab lines into Sebastopolis. If that whisper held truth, matters were complicated indeed. Theo, though, did not comment, and eventually Oppa continued. "But you misjudge me, Theo, just as you once did your Slavic friend. Again, you see only lines rather than the shades between them."

"The lines are clear." Theo's voice was flat and hard. "The Arabs are our enemy, whether here or in Spania. And you are dealing with them." He searched Oppa's face. "Why take the field against an enemy with whom you also trade?" he asked, and Oppa heard the genuine puzzlement behind the question. "What can you possibly hope to win by so doing?"

"Ah." Oppa kept his expression opaque. "Appearance is every-thing, Theo. And nothing is certain until it is won."

Theo made an impatient noise. "You speak in riddles. If you plan to betray the men at your back, then do not take the field at all."

It was time, Oppa realised reluctantly, to play his other hand. He raised his eyebrows politely. "I promised my father's standard would ride upon that field, and it will. But do you truly believe the Arabs to be our enemy, Theo?"

Theo glared at him. "Today I and my men will face an Arabic army who want to kill us in battle. If the Arabs win, they are one step closer to Spania's shores. You said yourself we cannot afford to allow them to gain another toehold. Yes, they are our enemy. What other truth is there?"

"Mohammed bin Marwan will take Sebastopolis," said Oppa flatly. "You know it, Theo, just as I do. Do not pretend that you face today with the hope of victory in your heart. Your mind is already planning how you will reach Spania."

The implacable features did not soften. "It is one thing to know

Sebastopolis cannot stand," said Theo. "It is quite another to actively plan its destruction with the same enemy you would have me believe we are allied against."

"We are allied for Spania, Theo." Oppa held his eyes, still feeling the tension of hope under his skin. "I told you once that you can never match me in the game of war. Since it became clear the treaty between emperor and caliph could not stand, I have had cause to reconsider who, or what, might best serve our homeland. The day may come, Theo, when being allied for Spania means reconsidering who our enemies are."

Theo's mouth curled contemptuously. "If that day comes," he said softly, "you will no longer be fighting for Spania, Oppa Egica-son. You will be fighting for power – as you have always done. As you do here, though I was too blind to see it." He moved closer to Oppa, his eyes glittering like shards of green ice. "I came for your copy of our contract," he said, fingering the sword at his hip. "Consider this conversation an end to our alliance."

"You are angry." Oppa regarded him evenly, not without effort. So much rested on this moment. "I understand your anger. I wish I could have confided in you regarding my conversations with our Arabic opponents, but it was not feasible. Surely you must see that?" He raised his eyebrows as if explaining a basic truth to a particularly slow student. "You are a man of honour, Theo. Men of honour need others to do the shadow work they themselves disdain. We do not need to like one another's methods, but I believe we might yet work together. If you had been party to the same information I was, you would have felt compelled to share it with your leadership; and that, I am afraid, would have served nothing."

"What information is that?" Theo ground out.

Oppa allowed a smile to play on his mouth. "If our alliance is at an end," he said softly, "I would be a fool to tell you. And besides – should you take that field, you will discover for yourself soon enough."

The first light crept through the window. "We do not have time for this," Theo growled. "Give me the contract and let us be done."

"You know I will not do that," said Oppa quietly. "You knew that before you came."

There was a pause, and a momentary shadow of something that might have been regret crossed the scarred face. "I had hoped," Theo said slowly, "that at least some of what you said was the truth. That you were not entirely lost to honour."

Seized by a sudden, visceral anger, Oppa moved with lethal swiftness, close enough to touch the gnarled runnels his whip had once carved into Theo's face. "I meant every word I said to you," Oppa said fiercely. "Soon Spania will face the Arabs. There is no man that I would rather have beside me when that day comes than you, Theo. Whether we receive them as friends and equals or face them on a battlefield, I would face them beside you." Despite his effort at control, Oppa heard the longing in his voice, and, tasting the acid burn of humiliation, cursed his weakness. He drew a deep breath and fought to keep what he felt from showing on his face.

Theo regarded him with a scrutiny that sliced brutally through his effort at concealment. "A wise friend," Theo said slowly, "once told me that all a man has, in war and in life, is the man at his side." His eyes bored into Oppa's. "I have lately come to learn the truth of those words. It is a lesson that has made me choose carefully those whom I stand beside. You are right," he went on. "I knew you would not relinquish the contract, though I hoped." His mouth twisted. "I truly did hope. But your refusal has made it easier to say now what I must." Theo leaned close to Oppa. "Spania may indeed soon face an Arab army. Perhaps it is even possible that one day the Arabs must be dealt with as allies, not enemies, for we have both seen enough of war to know such things are possible. But alliances are the result of negotiations made in the open, where all can see. They are not contrived in a sordid tavern, over the bodies of whores, with blackmail and stealth, by stealing from one and deceiving the other. I would never see the Spania I know traded as if it were no more than a plaything. The Spania I fight for is a country you have never known, for it exists only in the hearts of men who believe in it; and you, I know now, do not possess such a heart."

Anger gripped Oppa as Theo stepped back from him, the hard contempt on the other's face more cutting than any sword on his flesh could ever be. "I will never stand beside you, Oppa Egicason," said Theo coldly. "You may wave that parchment at whomever you choose. You may take my land and my title and throw your father's might at Illiberis. I will fight for both until my body can fight no more – just as I know Lælia will."

In the charged silence that followed his words, Oppa felt the air between them shift, taking with it the golden dream that had glimmered in his subconscious for years now, the alliance he had barely dared allow himself to believe in. The fragile threads of that alliance fell away cleanly as if a knife had sliced them through, and in the shearing away of the hope they had offered, Oppa felt a strange, almost welcome relief. The cut threads twisted and snarled into the tangled knot of enmity once more, one made more dangerous than their former hatred had ever been by the corrosion of failed hope.

Darkness deepened behind Oppa's eyes, and he saw its answering shadow on Theo's ravaged face.

"You will never leave these shores without my help," said Oppa coldly.

Theo's eyes gleamed. "You of all men should know I have a knack for escape. And you will not kill me. If you do," he said, "that contract you hold will be worth nothing. I am more valuable to you alive. So know this: where you go, you will find me. And enjoy the feel of that parchment in your hand whilst you still may. It will mean nothing at all when my sword slits your throat."

A queer thrill rippled through Oppa's body. "If you are so eager to see me dead," Oppa said, smiling silkily at him, "why not take your chance upon it now?"

Theo's mouth twisted. "You and I both know there are a dozen men listening to every word of this conversation who would never let me leave this room. I have been your prisoner once, Oppa Egica-son. I will never be so again." He smiled grimly. "Besides, I have men who depend upon me to lead them into battle today. Unlike you, I will not betray them."

Oppa's eyes narrowed. "You had best hope to die upon that battlefield, Aurariola. For should we both live to return to Spania, you know as well as I that such a betrayal will be the least of your concerns."

They looked at each other for a long moment. Then the door opened, and Theo was gone.

47

LÆLIA
JULY, AD 692

Illiberis, Spania
Granada, Spain

The men who had arrived with Theodefred had been camped in Illiberis for a quarter moon, and yet still Paulus did not ride north. "They came to fight," Lælia said abruptly one evening as they sat to meat. The heat of the day had been stifling. Even late into darkness the night felt close and hot. "Why do you wait here? For what?"

Paulus stabbed the meat before him and glared at her. "You do not lead the Illiberis thiufae yet, child." Acantha, who had taken to eating an occasional meal with them, suppressed a smile that served only to deepen Paulus's frown.

"No." Unmoved by his anger, Lælia ate calmly. "But you have taught me to ask when I don't understand. And I don't understand this delay. Messengers tell us daily that Sunifred does not have enough forces to hold Toletum. When Egica returns from his battles in the north, the rebellion will fail, and we will undoubtedly be condemned as traitors whether we fought at Sunifred's side or not. Why not fight, if we are to be damned anyway?"

Paulus came to his feet in an agitated push. Stalking away from the table, he stared out of the lattice window, through which floated the sounds of the encamped men, raucous with wine.

"The men grow restless," said Lælia quietly.

"Do you think I need your instruction on the perils of a thiufa with no war?" Paulus snarled with his back turned. A long silence ensued, during which Lælia looked at Acantha, and her grandmother gave an imperceptible shrug of her shoulders.

"I have written to Suinthila," said Paulus finally.

"Suinthila?" Lælia was taken aback. "I had thought him abed, close to death even." She remembered Suinthila as she had last seen him, white faced and devastated in the Toletum court as Alaric had walked away from his father, choosing to follow Sunifred's rebellion over Suinthila's diplomacy. "Why do you write to him now?"

"Suinthila commands more men than merely his own thiufae at Aurariola." Paulus spoke without looking at them. "He has spent his life training those who would serve under the Chrismon and peacock. Men from across the country send their sons to the headquarters in Emerita to learn the art of war from Suinthila. The thiufae he trained may serve Egica in theory, but their allegiance has long belonged to Suinthila – not only from respect for his training but for what he represents. Suinthila is named for his uncle and Liuvgoto's father, King Suintila, the man who united Spania. Suinthila's own father, Geila, was the greatest general Spania has ever known. There is magic in such memories. The names themselves evoke a time of miracles, when the Chrismon-and-peacock symbol became Spania's own and men proudly called themselves Spaniard in the knowledge that it meant something. All of this magic lies in Suinthila's name and in his hands. I am told that when Sunifred's force came to Emerita, the men followed Alaric without question. They followed the magic of that past." He turned back to face his wife and granddaughter. "I can lead men," he said harshly. "I know battle as well and better than any. But in the end, I am just another lord commanding men to ride away from the harvest lying on the fields and toward a war with a less-than-certain outcome. The men camped in my field are sullen. They do not know why they are here, except that Theodefred ordered them. They do not know for what they ride. The road between here and Toletum is long, with many opportunities for desertion. If I hope to march a decent force northward, I need men who believe in why they march. Suinthila's presence would inspire that belief, more than anything I might tell them."

Lælia stared at him. "Do they need more reason than the crimes Egica has committed?" Words she had not thought to speak rose inside her, anger she had disciplined herself to suppress. "Is it not enough that Egica took Theodefred's son by force? That his bastard son orchestrated an attack that killed dozens of Spania's own sons, then attempted to marry me against my will?" She held Paulus's eyes and willed her voice not to shake. "Is it not enough to tell them," she said, "that Egica was the architect of the attack that killed my parents?"

Paulus's eyes flared in surprise. "It was Giscila who –"

"Perhaps." Lælia cut him off curtly. "But I have met Giscila. Looked into his face. That he murdered my parents, there is no doubt. But I do not think he had either the ambition, the will, or the intelligence to execute such horrors alone. Egica, though – he is more than capable of doing so. Did he not return to court directly after the events? And do any of us doubt he was at least complicit in the attack upon the fleet in which Theo was almost killed?"

"Even if such accusations are true, they are hardly reasons I can give to the men camped on my ground." Paulus was staring at her, an odd expression on his face that looked almost, Lælia realised, like respect.

"Why not?" she countered. "There are men amongst those camped here who lost their own fathers, and brothers, in the same attack that killed my parents. There is a reason they call it the Summer of Blood, even now. Hundreds died that day. Men do not speak of it, but only because they were sworn not to. All know of it. They remember."

"Nothing can be gained from dragging up such events," muttered Paulus.

Lælia opened her mouth to argue. She was interrupted by the

clatter of a chair tumbling as Acantha, eyes flashing hard gold, came abruptly to her feet. She said nothing, merely stared at them both; then she turned and strode from the room.

By mutual assent, Lælia and Paulus followed her tall, stiff figure across the grass by the villa and passed the stables to the wide field where the men made their camp. At the centre of the hundreds who sat around cooking fires, drinking wine in the hot summer night, lay the wagons on which Theodefred had brought food for his men. Acantha leaped onto one and beat the side of it with the hilt of her knife until chatter ceased and men turned to her curiously.

"Tyr," muttered Paulus, but he folded his arms and stood still rather than interfere.

"Most of you know me," said Acantha. The fires lit her face, and she spoke in a low voice that carried clearly across the field. "For those of you who do not – I am Acantha, the Lady of Illiberis. This land has been that of my family since time before time, and it will belong to those of my blood" – she gestured to where Lælia stood – "long after these wars are done, and their kings with them."

There was a low, superstitious murmur at this. Men crossed themselves. They had all heard the tales of the horse herders of Illiberis and their mane magic. Southern they might have been, but the men gathered attended church and prayed to the God they found there. They eyed Acantha suspiciously. Some spat to one side.

"You may fear my kind," Acantha said, "and curse me as witch. But know this: it is not my belief in different gods that prevents me from taking my place at my husband's side in Illiberis. There are those here who remember the years when I did stand beside him. Perhaps I would still – had it not been for the time you know as the Summer of Blood."

A hush fell across the field. The men stared at her, fully attentive now.

"*Ja.*" Acantha watched them with some satisfaction. "You all know those words. If you were not alive, you have heard the tale. Fever, people said. It was the summer of fever. Barbarians from across the sea took advantage of the illness and attacked the lands of my daughter and her husband. Many are the tales told of that day. But I know, as do you, that none of them are true."

A murmur rose amongst the watching men.

"More recently," Acantha went on, raising her voice to speak over them, "there was another attack, this time at sea. Many were lost, including the man destined to marry my granddaughter. Another attack on Illiberis. Again, we were told it was unfortunate. A storm, bandits looking for fortune. Another tale."

Now the murmuring rose louder, and men began to fold their arms and nod in agreement.

"Do any of us believe these tales?" Acantha gripped the side of the wagon and stared a challenge out at the watching men. "Do any of you believe these attacks were accidents, misfortune given by God to the house of Illiberis?"

"No!" called one of the watching men, and others took up the cry.

"No," repeated Acantha, looking at them. "No, they were not. Just as the king sending his bastard son Oppa to Illiberis four years ago was not by chance. Oppa's rape and torture of an innocent girl during his visit was not an accident, and nor was his blaming a Jewish boy from Garnata, Yosef ben Arun, for that same crime. Nothing done by this king and his family is done by chance." At this, there was a swell of indignation from the local men in the crowd, many of whom had witnessed the sadism of Oppa's actions when he had come to Illiberis four years earlier.

"I have stayed silent long enough." Acantha had the crowd captive now. "I have retreated to the mountains and raised our horses, far from the men who committed these acts and those who would hide them. But now we have an opportunity to overturn those who have visited such pain upon my family. To honour the Chrismon and peacock that my family fought and died for, instead of the corruption of those who seek to suck Mater Spania dry."

Men roared at that, banging their swords against their shields.

"They are listening to her." Paulus stared at his wife with narrowed eyes, a strange light stirring in their grim depths. "She has them, by God."

"My husband" – Acantha gestured at Paulus – "will not invoke such old revenge in his bid to lead you north, to war. He is a man of honour and not given to such tactics. But I… I am a woman

who has lost her last child and who cares no longer for the opinions of men or priests. I have defended Illiberis before. I will do so
again. I am not afraid to die for the land I love. My granddaughter
and I will hold it with our last breath – and defend your women
and children with it, for we are women of Illiberis, and this is our
right." She drew herself up proudly at their cheers and faced
them, eyes flashing in the light of the fires burning around the
camp. "In the next days," she cried, "you will ride behind my
husband to war. Not a war for coin, or one between lords for
reasons you do not understand. This war is vengeance. It is
retribution for the lies we were told and the wrongs we have swallowed. It is for the land we stand upon, land this king has
conspired again and again to take from us. I will die before I relinquish Illiberis, and in the days to come, we might all have to make
that choice!"

They were cheering her now, a roar that swept over the grounds,
men clashing their swords against anything they could find, crying
out their battle rage and anger. From the mountains above came the
thunder of the horse herders' drums and the savage cries of those
who had called Illiberis home long before Roman, Goth, or Greek.
Acantha stared over the crowd to Paulus, her chest rising and falling
as she heard their cheers. She thrust her own knife savagely to the
sky in defiance.

Striding across the ground, Paulus climbed onto the wagon
beside her. "I have a message," he said, his normally rough voice
hard and clear, the commander who had led men onto a hundred
fields in his youth. "You!" he pointed at one. "You will take four
others, along with our fleetest horses. Ride for Aurariola. Tell Count
Suinthila that Illiberis will bow no longer to those who killed our
children." They roared their approbation, and he turned to Acantha. The firelight lit her eyes a blazing red as she stared at him,
something wild and beautiful in her face Lælia had never seen. "Tell
him," he said, and though he spoke to the crowd, the small smile on
his face was for Acantha alone, "that we ride north, for Egica and
for blood."

As the men cheered, for Illiberis and for war, Paulus turned to
Lælia. "And you," he said, in a voice meant only for her, "will send

word to your desert witch. Tell her it is time she made good on her promise."

"But we are not yet under attack," said Lælia, her heart tripping unsteadily.

"No." Paulus's mouth stretched in a grim smile. "But after this, child, we will be. Mark my words."

48

THEO

JULY, AD 692

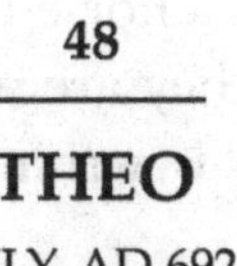

Battle of Sebastopolis

The battle for Sebastopolis began at mid-morning, when a white sun turned the harbour to shimmering glass. Theo stood on the dock, eyeing the dromons critically, turning constantly to the hilltop beyond the agora, his mind on the serried ranks beyond the walls. He had sent a messenger to Leontios but received no response, which had not surprised him. Theo was unsure what warning he could have given anyway. He knew only that Oppa had contrived to betray them, not the means by which that betrayal would occur. And Leontios, he knew, was not the man to heed a vague warning. The battle was upon them, and they must fight it as it came, however it came.

From the docks Theo could see nothing beyond the walls, and for a time he heard only the dull thud of horses' hooves, the faint jangle of steel as men gathered in preparation, but nothing of the violent screams of blood.

Then Pelagia tumbled down the hillside. Theo caught the child as she came to a stop. "The Arabs," she panted. "They have ridden to their lines. And they carry a sea of parchment with them."

Theo frowned. "Parchment? What do you mean?"

"Every man mounted on a horse has one," said Pelagia. "Pinned to the tips of their lances. They are waving them, in place of flags. One of the men said there is writing on them, that they are the pages of the tree– the tret–"

"Treaty?" Theo's eyes widened. "The treaty between the emperor and the caliph? They've ridden to war flying pages of the treaty that Leontios betrayed – on their lance-tips?"

Pelagia nodded eagerly. "And when Leontios tried to speak, they waved their lances in the air and burned the parchments."

"I knew it," Theo said grimly, glancing sideways at Silas. "The time for talking is done. The Arabs will not negotiate." Pelagia turned to go, and Theo took her arm. "Here! You stay with us. If the walls fall, it is not safe for you, do you understand? You need to be close."

Pelagia stared back at him. "Why?" she asked bluntly. "I heard what Sanyi said. You cannot take us if the walls fall. We are to be left behind."

Theo's face tightened. "We are trying to find another option. There are merchants' ships still here."

Pelagia rolled her eyes. "Merchants need money. We do not have enough. And besides, who else will warn you if the walls are falling?"

"I rather think we will know immediately if the walls fall," said Theo drily.

"Pelagia." Silas stepped forward. "The Slavs," he said, frowning. "Where are they? Do they stand?"

Pelagia's eyes slid away from his face. "Yes," she said quietly.

"Pelagia," Theo said, taking her arm again. "What is it?"

She looked between them, her face troubled. "I have heard the Slavs talking," she said. "In the tavern where Elpis is now."

"And?"

"They are not happy," she said quietly. "Not after Neboulos was whipped. They are saying bad things about Leontios." She looked at Theo. "And about the man with the whip." Glancing at the walls,

Pelagia backed away. "If the walls come down, I will be here," she said, then scampered off up the hill.

Silas watched the little figure go, his face troubled. "Will the Slavs stand? That is the question." He shook his head. "I do not like this."

Theo squinted into the hard sunlight, his jaw set and hard. The villagers had gathered atop the walls. From a distance they looked like a swarm of insects, tiny black dots clinging to the faded ochre, watching the coming carnage. *They will all die*, Theo thought. *They have nowhere to go but into the water — or beneath an Arab sword. They are Maronites, Christian rebels not only against Islam but against Marwan himself. They will be shown no quarter.*

"What did the merchants say about taking Elpis and the other girls?" he asked aloud. Silas shook his head silently. "There must be someone!" Theo ground out the words, trying to think. "We cannot leave them here, Silas. I will not."

As he spoke, a roar broke the morning air, and the very light seemed to ripple about them. A hollow rumble travelled over the ground, echoing up into their own feet. Theo was still, fists clenched at his sides. Behind him the crews of the dromons stood quivering to attention in the ships, every man straining toward the sound of battle over the hill, trying to envisage the movements beyond.

"Cataphracts," murmured Silas. They felt rather than heard the clash as the cataphracts broke against the Arabic forces. Theo could imagine that first rush, the heavily armoured horsemen charging to meet their Arabic counterparts. A flood of arrows from the rear, then the lances, thrown as they came closer, effective against the lightly armoured Arabic horses. Then, finally, wicked maces drawn and whirled to a frenzy, the momentum of horse and arm driving deadly iron spikes right through a man's body. Theo had seen men die from the mace even beneath steel helmet, the sheer weight of the blow breaking their necks. His own body quivered, part of him on the battlefield living every moment as the thundering hooves broke into a melee of clamour and steel. Above it all came the high-pitched screams of the Arabs, a chilling sound that hung over the port and drowned out the guttural, hoarse cries of the emperor's forces. The sound grew louder, became triumphant, and as it did they heard a fast, drumming sound accompanied by a strange whistle on the wind.

"Cavalry with bows," said Silas grimly.

Theo's mouth tightened with cold fury as he thought of Oppa riding beneath the Chrismon-and-peacock insignia beneath which Theo's ancestors had fought and died, the Slavic forces blindly following his lead, probably to their deaths. Then he frowned. *I cannot imagine him there,* he thought suddenly. *Oppa, in danger? At the head of an attack?* He recalled Oppa's words with a terrible, bitter sense of misgiving: *Appearance is everything.*

"Ergan!" He called one of Pelagia's young friends over from where he had been huddling with his mother against the wall. Many of the villagers had taken refuge by the port, hoping to beg passage on the dromons if it came to that. The boy approached, and Theo pressed a coin into his hand. "Run to the walls," he said curtly. "You know the Spanish bastard, the one with the whip?" The boy paled and nodded. "Tell me if it is he who rides with the cavalry. Go." The boy ran swiftly. Theo turned to Silas. "I have known Oppa many years," he said. "And I have never known him to directly endanger himself."

Silas frowned. "You said he planned to take the field."

"I was wrong." Theo's mouth was tight. "Oppa said that 'his father's standard' would take the field – not that he himself would. I did not see him mount up this morning. Nor lead his horsemen to battle."

Silas stared at him as the words sank in. "If he is not on the battlefield," said Silas slowly, "then where is he?" He looked up at the hilltop, fingering the curved swords at his side. The roar became louder and, atop the walls, the black dots began to move, swarming down the hillside in a trickle that became a torrent, racing toward the port. The movement broke the deathly silence on the docks.

"Fetch Athanais and her girls," Theo ordered the messenger who had been standing by.

Silas raised his eyebrows. "Why?" he asked bluntly. "We can do nothing for them, *wenkai.* You know this."

"There will be fighting in the streets soon," said Theo grimly. "I would at least protect them as long as we are able."

The messenger had barely moved on his errand when Yosef appeared, leading a string of girls from Athanais's tavern, all carrying their goods wrapped in bundles on their backs. Theo felt a sudden, deep sense of relief. He had not dared ask Yosef his plans. It was only as he looked at his friend's face now that Theo realised how much he had dreaded knowing the answer.

"Theo," Yosef said lightly. He was as immaculate as ever, seemingly entirely undaunted by the increasing chaos around them, but a faintly guarded expression cloaked the eyes that met Theo's, and he waited for a moment as if to gauge both Theo's actions and his own reception.

Theo gripped his arm, his touch saying what he did not trust his voice to. "We cannot take them," he said instead, his tone rough. "I have asked every merchant on the docks – even offered them coin, though we have little between us – but they have all been bought."

"I have bought the services of that dromon." Yosef nodded at the largest of the merchant ships, a wide, flat-bottomed vessel. "And loaded it with cargo. What space is left will go first to Athanais's girls and then to any others we can fit aboard." His eyes met Theo's. "But it will leave now, not after the battle."

Theo stared at him, questions swirling in his mind with no time to have them answered. "Where is Athanais? Elpis?"

"Elpis I have not seen. Athanais, though, will not be joining us." As Theo barked brief orders to his men to load as many as they could onto the dromon, Yosef took him aside, out of earshot. "She left last night, by an overland route, under protection of those loyal to Apsimar. She must travel to Constantinople, on business I can trust to no other and that cannot wait. She asked me to bid you farewell and said that she will see you again – in time. She entrusted the care of her girls to me – to us."

Theo looked at him. "Us? Then you will sail with me when this is done?"

"If we do not board that dromon now, Theo, we may not sail at all."

When Theo did not answer, Yosef gave him the ghost of a smile. "If we live," he said, "then, yes, Theo, we will return together."

"Return?" Silas shifted dark eyes to Theo. "What is it that you plan now, *wenkai*?"

"You need worry only for what I plan today," Theo said. "If we survive that, where I go will no longer be your concern."

Silas's eyes narrowed as he looked between Theo and Yosef. "To Spania, is it, that we sail now?"

"Not you," Theo said bluntly. "You were right, Silas, just as Leofric was. It was Oppa behind the missing coin. The price of my mistake is one I will pay for the rest of my life – but I will not allow any other to pay it with me. After this day is done, I must find a way back to Spania, for if Oppa is not on that field, then even now he sails for home." He held Silas's eyes. "This is not your fight," he said quietly. "You will not travel at my side."

Silas stood with his arms folded silently for a long moment, then he made a rough noise. "Ho!" He gave a low cough of laughter, gripping his sword hilt. "And is it your place, now, to tell a man which fight to choose?" He clapped Theo roughly on his shoulder, his eyes saying what his words did not. His eyes rested doubtfully on Yosef, taking in the rich merchant's robes and urbane appearance. "You, however, should perhaps reconsider your decision." He tilted his head at Theo. "Where this one leads, trouble usually follows."

"If you do not cease talking," said Yosef dryly, "trouble will already be here."

"Theo!" Sanyi's shout returned Theo to the chaos around them. The docks were a swarm of panicked townspeople rushing from dromon to dromon, begging for help to escape the city. Theo's men, grim faced, were boarding all they could onto the merchant dromon, holding others off their own dromons with lance and spear. The crowds pushed at them dangerously. "Take ten good men and ride to the walls," Sanyi called to Theo. "No messenger has returned. We cannot hold them off much longer. I do not know if we are making ready to sail or staying to fight. Go."

Theo was turning for his horse when a long wail rose from somewhere in the city and Ergan tumbled to a stop beside them, breathing heavily. Theo grasped his arms and the boy looked up at him, his face pale. "The Spanish bastard is not there," he said. "I saw a man wearing his armour, riding under the Spanish standard, but he fell and his helmet came off, and it was not the bastard. It was an Arab." Theo felt the blood drain from his face. Behind him Silas swore quietly. "But that is not important, not now!" Ergan went on, fear in his voice. "The Slavs," he said. "They have turned. They have betrayed us. They have joined the Arabs."

As he finished speaking, from the western end of the wall came the sound of hoofbeats. A small contingent of Slavs swept around the corner, Neboulos at their head. He was covered in blood, his horse blown and enraged. Ergan scurried away as Sanyi and Theo's men drew their swords, grim faced.

"Hold." Theo's voice was steady. "If they come here, it is not Neboulos who betrays us." He faced Neboulos's approach with a wide-legged stance, his hands clearly free of weapons. Theo's heart jolted as he recognised Leofric's swarthy, blood-covered figure at the commander's side.

Neboulos rode directly to them, reining abruptly in front of Theo. "I did all I could," he said thickly, leaning from his horse. "But I was too late. I've lost them. My army have joined the Arabs. They ride for the walls now, slaughtering everything in their path. Every man, woman, and child who remains in the city is as good as dead."

"You knew!" said Sanyi angrily. "You knew they planned this, and still you did nothing to prevent it!"

Leofric spun his horse and swept the *tourmarchai* aside with one heavy, brutal blow. "Neboulos did everything to prevent this!" He leaped to the ground, glaring at Sanyi. "My brudders would have turned months ago, or weeks, at least, if not for Neboulos. But he held them, and he might have prevailed still." He shook his head. "Your warning was welcome, *schnecke*," he said, meeting Theo's eyes. "It just came too late."

Neboulos turned to Theo, his face black with rage and his accent thickening. "Oppa, that bastard son of whore, never even took the field. He sent imposters to ride on his Spanish horses under his own banner. And it seems he'd already bought half of my army. It did not take much after they turned for the rest to either betray us or run. I'd lost them before we ever set foot on the field this morning." He glanced darkly around. "There are those who are still unaccounted for. Some at least will be coming for your dromons, Theo. They, too, seek to escape this damned port."

But Theo was not listening. "Where is he?" he demanded. "Where is Oppa?"

"Does it matter?" Neboulos looked around at the milling chaos on the docks. "It is lost."

A small hand tugged at Theo's sleeve. He frowned when he saw Ergan, pale and trembling. "What are you doing here? You should be aboard, preparing to leave."

"It's Pelagia." Ergan's eyes were wide. "The bastard's men have taken her, and they say he has her sister too."

Theo thought of Pelagia's impish smile, then of Oppa fingering his whip. He felt something cold grip his heart.

"Theo!" Sanyi was already moving away. "We have no time for this. Ready your men. We sail now." He nodded at Neboulos. "I wish you well," he muttered, but he did not offer to board the Slavs.

Neboulos's face tightened, but he did not look surprised. He glanced briefly at Leofric's burly figure. "Mount up. We ride." He nodded to Theo as he turned his horse. "I wish you well," he said.

"Go," said Theo curtly to his men as he returned Neboulos's nod. "Follow Sanyi's orders."

"What of you?" asked one of them, frowning at him.

"Board as many as you can," said Theo, ignoring the question. He glared at the man. "Go! And do not wait for me, or any man who rides with me." He turned to find Leofric still standing there, looking after Neboulos's retreating figure. "You should go," Theo said curtly. "You might still make it to safety."

Leofric eyed him. "You owe me a wine flask," he said gruffly.

"A new one would serve you better." Theo threw him the flask. "Go with Neboulos, Leofric."

"Ah." Leofric shrugged. "A man gets used to his wine a certain way."

"I do not sail with the fleet."

"I know that." Leofric wiped the blood from his sword and thrust it through his belt. "You told me it was my choice," he said quietly. "This is me making it, *schnecke*."

Theo's mouth tightened. He turned to the boy at his side.

"Ergan," he said roughly. "Where have Pelagia and her sister been taken?"

"The people who ran from the walls told me they saw the men carrying Pelagia toward the old ruins." Ergan glanced fearfully at the crowd swarming down the hill.

"Good lad." Theo released him. "Run for the dromon," he said. "Go, now." He reached for his horse, glancing at Yosef. "I know where he will be," he said.

"No, *wenkaï*!" Silas grasped Theo's arm, his face dark. "Oppa does this knowing you will come. He plays you like a balladeer plays the strings! Every time he whistles, you run precisely where he wishes you to be. Leave the girls, Theo, no matter how hard it might be."

Theo met Silas's eyes. "No," he said simply. He glanced at Yosef, who nodded and mounted up as Theo did.

"You!" Leofric said, glaring at Silas. "I leave the *schnecke* in your charge, African, and this is what you do? Have you not learned that Jew brings trouble wherever he goes?"

Silas gave him a sideways glance. "But then, he brings dromons and coin too, and that is more than you ever have, Slav."

Leofric snorted.

Silas looked at Theo. "We must hurry. The walls will soon fall."

"Is typical," said Leofric resignedly, swinging himself onto his horse. "The women sail away whilst we ride toward a battle we cannot win."

Still Theo hesitated. "When today is done," he said, "Yosef and I return to Spania. If you both leave now you may still remain with the fleet."

Leofric snorted again and rolled his eyes at Silas. "And now he thinks he can fight without us? It seems he is even more stupid than when I left." Without waiting for an answer, he spurred forward, and despite the chaos around him, Theo knew a moment of fierce, painful joy in the Slav's rough presence at his side once more.

They forced their horses against the panicked tide of humanity that poured down the hill and past the agora where people ransacked the market stalls, taking what they could carry. Theo saw a group of villagers leaving the church, carrying the tabernacle between them. Theo and his men rode hard through the streets, occasionally knocking people out of the way. They turned past the old theatre and up to where the abandoned walls stood.

"Run!" a wild-eyed woman called to them as they rode past her. "They are coming! The Arabs are coming!"

Theo leaped from his horse and flung the reins to one of his men. He, Silas, and Leofric scrambled to the top of the defence. The scene below them was one of carnage.

Barely a thousand men of the emperor's force remained standing before the walls. They fought in a narrowing circle, the Arabs closing in around them, the Slavs fighting those who would have approached from the wings. Leontios himself had turned in an attempt to flee. Surrounded by his closest guard, he was hacking a pathway through the Slavs to the narrow trail leading down to the harbour. As Theo watched, he cut through the last of them, disappearing from sight.

"Cowardly bastard." Leofric spat into the dirt contemptuously. But Theo was no longer focused on the strategos. He was looking uphill, beyond the battle, to the ruins high above.

"*Wenkai.*" Silas tugged Theo's arm. He looked back over his shoulder to see the merchant's dromon sailing out of the harbour, surrounded by dromons of the fleet that belched fire onto the docks where Slavic soldiers hacked their way through the crowds, trying to board those left. "The Slavs who did not betray us, trying to escape," said Silas sadly, watching them. "They are as dead as any other now." Even as they watched, the Slavs fell, screaming, beneath fire from the dromons. They stared in silence for a moment, watching as the fleet slowly pulled clear of the shore.

"Come," said Theo, turning back to the battle and casting a wary eye on the approaching forces below. "We have to ride before the battle enters the city proper."

They rode clear of the walls and up the rugged tracks that led away from the port. "Oppa will have men," Theo said, reining in when they were clear. "Many of them. We cannot simply attack the place where he holds them. He will be prepared for that."

"I have some men who can help us," said Yosef. "I can fetch them, but you will need to buy me some time."

Theo saw Leofric and Silas exchange a glance. "This is no place for merchants," said Leofric finally, glaring at Yosef. "If coin and dromon you have, Jew, you should leave."

"Oppa has taken more from me than you could ever imagine. I will not ride away." Yosef's grim expression softened marginally. "Though, of course, my merchants and I shall rely upon you to do the fighting, my estimable Slavic friend."

Leofric gave Yosef his most savage glare. When the other regarded him with little more than faint amusement, he rolled his eyes. "All I ask," he said resignedly, "is that you do not get in the way of my sword."

Yosef nodded politely. "I shall endeavour to be no hindrance."

"I will give you as much time as I may," Theo said. "And wait for my signal before you attack, Yosef. Oppa will have men hidden, I know it."

"Then you will need decoys, also," came Silas's calm voice. "He will not believe you attack alone."

"And I suppose," said Leofric resignedly, "that this is the part you plan for us, African."

THEO CREPT TOWARD THE LOW, arched wall that guarded the ruins atop the hill. He heard the sound of voices and crouched low, listening.

"We will wait." He heard Oppa's voice, clipped and tense. "He will come, for me if not for the girls. If he wishes to have a life to return to, he cannot afford either to reach Spanish shores."

"And we cannot afford to wait. We must leave now. There are many who wish us dead – not least Aurariola." Theo recognised the voice as belonging to Nicalo, the surly-faced Spanish nobleman who had once held Lælia captive in the woods. Theo's hand tightened on his sword hilt. "If he comes, it will be to kill you, not talk. You know it as well as I."

"Perhaps." Oppa's voice was cold. "But he is also desperate to return to Spania, and he no longer has dromons in which to sail."

"We must hope that we still do. Your dealings with the Slavs have made us dependent on the Arabs now. If they let us down –"

Oppa gave a hard laugh. "The Arabs owe me much." Theo heard the snap of Oppa's whip. It was, he thought, a sound he would know anywhere, a reminder of past humiliation that turned his tension to a cold, hard resolve. "I have delivered the Slavs to Marwan," Oppa went on. "Given him an undefended port, the most strategic in all of Anatolia. My dromons are guarded by Marwan's own men. We will be gone before sunup tomorrow, and I will return to Spania with a parchment in Aurariola's own hand, and chests of both Arabic and Greek gold. Enough to buy what is needed if it cannot be won."

"If Aurariola should return to Spania alive, and as an enemy, we are doomed, you and I." Nicalo's voice was fearful.

"As you have repeatedly reminded me. You become tedious, Nicalo," Oppa said contemptuously. "Aurariola will return to Spania in my company. He will return as my guest, or as my captive – or as an unfortunate corpse."

Theo smiled grimly and crept over the crumbling stone, flattening himself against the wall and peering into the room.

Pelagia and Elpis were tied to chairs. Oppa stood staring at Pelagia, fingering his whip, his back to Theo. He saw the hard set of Oppa's shoulders and felt an answering tension. He had seen that stance before. Oppa was dangerous in this mood.

Where are the rest of his men? Theo thought. *How many are in the villa?* Theo could see only Nicalo and Oppa, but he was certain Oppa would not endanger himself by luring him here without backup. Silas and Leofric would take care of the guards placed strategically around the hilltop, but they were some way distant, and Theo had seen no others on his way in. That, though, Theo knew, meant nothing. He eased back from the wall and slid through the ruins and rocks, feet soundless on the broken stone. Far below, the battle raged, screams echoing up the hillside. The villagers were dying, and he could smell the port burning.

He found only two horses, tied beyond the ruins. *It feels wrong*, he thought. *There are others here; there must be.* Then Pelagia screamed, a high, thin sound, and he knew that no matter what danger he walked into, he could no longer hesitate.

Theo heard the whip before he reached the door, the crude hum of the ropes as they cut the air. The sound roiled his gut.

Pelagia's eyes widened when she saw Theo move into the room. Then he saw alarm creep into them and knew he had been right – there was something he had missed. Then Nicalo was coming for him, and he had no time to consider what it might be.

He met the burly man with a cold, hard rage, the memory of Nicalo's crimes making his arm fast, ruthless, and lethal. It was not a pretty killing. Theo's knife flashed across his neck and blood sprayed over the broken tile, then the heavy body slumped unceremoniously to the floor, where it twitched a few times before lying still. Theo stood over the body, staring at Oppa with hard eyes. "You should take better care of your friends."

Oppa smiled at him, fingering the whip. "On the contrary," said Oppa lightly. "You did me a service. Nicalo had served his purpose. In Spania, he would have been a liability."

Theo eyed him contemptuously. "He knew too much."

"Just so." Oppa's tone was careless, but there was a dark light of anticipation in his eyes. Theo was aware of every inch of the room. It was empty, but something was wrong, and he could not fathom what it was. Elpis and Pelagia, both bound and gagged, stared at him from their chairs with pleading eyes. Pelagia's darted about wildly, as if trying to speak to him, but Theo could not make out her meaning.

"Let them go," he said. "It's me you want, and I came. There's no need to hurt them."

"But that is where you are wrong." Oppa's eyes were cold. "I have not got what I want. I had time to think after you left me last night. I had intended to sail without seeing you again. Another part of me would like nothing better than to see you bleed on this floor. But upon consideration, Theudemir, I have decided it will serve me infinitely better if you reconsider your position and return as my ally."

"I have already made my position clear. I will never be your ally."

Something flashed in the dark eyes. "Ally, captive – there is so little distance between the two, would you not agree? You, I think, no longer have the options you did when last we spoke. And despite all your time at war, you neglect its first rule, Theudemir."

"And what is that?" Theo's eyes roamed the room, assessing the risks, deciding his strategy.

"Know your enemy." Oppa smiled coldly. "You may not wish to ally with me. But returning home – that is something you do want, very much. And you no longer have dromons of your own in which to sail. I feel that alters the terms of our friendship. Perhaps I might remind you of what happens to your betrothed should I reach her before you do." He lifted his whip, and Pelagia screamed hoarsely behind her gag as he brought it down toward her. Theo lunged forward, putting himself between Pelagia and Oppa. He swept his knife arm so that it deflected the stroke, though the ends of the whip licked the flesh of his neck in a touch so familiar it sickened him.

"Ah," said Oppa lightly. "You remember the touch of it, *ne?* We all do. Once felt, the whip is not something the body forgets. It remains in your blood, in your flesh."

Theo swept his knife again, but this time the whip was too fast, coiling about his wrist, then wrenching the knife from his hand, flinging the steel to clatter on the floor and leaving crimson stripes across the fingers, below his vambraces.

"When you allow yourself to imagine my whip on your betrothed's flesh" – Oppa flicked the whip suddenly and fresh blood slipped from Theo's neck, the heat of the lash coming after it – "perhaps you might find yourself more willing to be ally than captive. It would, at least, make for a more pleasant return journey for us both."

But Theo had already read the motion of the strands and seen his opening. He ducked beneath their reach and spun behind Oppa, his spatha coming up in his hand, poised to take the other man from behind, straight through the kidneys. He was aware of a strange noise as he did so – like the creaking of a door – but there was no wooden door to the ruins, he thought, as he spun. He realised too late what it was.

There is a cellar, he thought, even as he felt iron arms catch him before the sword entered Oppa. *They are hidden in the old wine cellar where Kyros once brewed his arak, and Oppa has cornered me where they will enter.*

He took the first few men who emerged with his sword, another with a brutal blow to the head, several more with blade and fist. Then they were too many, and he went down beneath a rush of mail and steel, fighting until he hung uselessly between the men.

"Ah well." The smile was gone from Oppa's face. "You will have some months to reconsider your position. Tie him tightly," he ordered. "He will sail with us." He gave the order with cold precision. "But be careful. There will be others hidden somewhere."

"We found them already," said one of the men. "The big black one killed most of the men you set as guards. But he is ours now."

"Good," Oppa said. "Make sure he is dead before we leave." He turned to Elpis and smiled silkily. "Come, my sweetling. I would ensure you are safe aboard when we sail."

Elpis rose from the chair, revealing the ties as no more than loose loops. Turning very deliberately toward Theo, she smiled coldly, then she reached up and touched Oppa's face in a gesture of intimacy that made Theo wince. Oppa caught her hand and kissed it, a small smile playing on his mouth. "The first rule of whores," he said lightly, "is to always ensure it is you who pays them."

Theo spat blood onto the floor. "I am sorry," he said thickly, meeting her eyes. "For what I did to you – and for what you will face still at his side. He is not your friend, Elpis."

Elpis made a hard noise. "A whore does not need friends," she said. "She needs coin, and a master to protect her. If you had taken me that first day in Gortyn, I never would have taken his coin. I loved you at first, Theo. And still you cast me aside as if I were no more than rubbish to be left behind. All that I have become is because of you."

"I suspect," said Oppa, watching Theo's face with a small smile, "that Elpis will enjoy making the acquaintance of your betrothed, Theo. They will, I should imagine, have much to speak of."

"May I take Pelagia?" Elpis asked, casting her eyes flirtatiously at Oppa from the door. "You promised that she could come with us."

"I will not," said Pelagia, glaring at Oppa. "I'm not going anywhere with him."

"Pelagia," said Elpis, her smile slightly strained. "Come now, hurry –"

"Go to the dromon," Oppa commanded Elpis, all trace of softness gone. "I told you the little one would come with us. We will join you soon."

Elpis, seeing the hard light in his eyes, turned reluctantly and left. The hilltop was oddly silent but for the pounding of Theo's heart and the soft hitch of Pelagia's breath.

The whip flashed out and this time it was no mere scratch; the blood flowed freely from Theo's neck, warm and unwelcome as it ran down his chest. He must hold on, he told himself. He had to hold on until Yosef came, and until he was sure no other surprises waited in the shadows.

"This one" – Oppa turned to Pelagia and stood behind her, one hand stroking her cheek gently – "do you know why I kept her here, Theo?" He stroked the handle of the whip down her face, and the girl's eyes widened in fear and revulsion. "Because she reminds me of the heiress from Illiberis," said Oppa, dark eyes flashing. "She reminds me of Lælia. And before you board my dromon, I wish you to remember what I will do to Lælia if she does not relinquish Illiberis peacefully."

His whip whistled through the air without warning, opening Pelagia's flesh from shoulder to shoulder. Theo roared and Oppa spun, bringing the lash across the old wounds on his face. The world faded for a moment and Theo did not know if it was pain or fury that made his vision swim, but for a moment he feared he would lose consciousness, and he knew he could not, he must not. He must find a way to free himself from the cords and at the very least loose Pelagia so that she might escape before the whip rendered her unrecognisable. Oppa twisted between the two, his whip falling first on Theo, then on the child, who stared at him in mute anger, biting her lip to prevent herself from crying out. Theo felt the knots begin to give, the corded muscle of his arms beneath the rope manipulating the fibres and working them loose. He forced his eyes to remain on Oppa's as the whip continued to hiss through the air, trying to remain alert to any other sounds before he called for help.

And then there was the sound of men and sword from beyond the ruins, and Oppa swung around, his face a picture of alarm.

A figure leaped into the room, spinning so fast Theo could barely discern who it was. With a flash of the newcomer's knife, Pelagia was free, and at a murmured order she was racing from the ruins, clutching the shreds of her dress about her. Theo's bindings were cut and he slumped to the floor, temporarily incapacitated as the blood raced back to his fingers. He raised his head to find Yosef facing Oppa, twirling a long, lethal sword, a small smile on his face.

"I know you told us to wait, Theo," he said softly. "But the situation seemed to be growing rather urgent."

"You." Oppa stared at Yosef. "The Jew."

A slow smile curled Yosef's mouth.

"Yes," he said softly. "I am a Jew." Without warning, Yosef spun and vaulted into the air. When he landed, the whip was gone from Oppa's hand, its coils wrapped around Yosef's, the heavy handle dangling toward the floor. "Do you know," said Yosef softly, staring at Oppa, "what Seneca said about the whip?" He spun and crashed the whip handle across Oppa's face, a heavy blow that knocked him sideways. Yosef's foot caught Oppa in his throat, knocking the air from him. Yosef pushed him up against the wall, the handle across Oppa's throat holding the other man easily as he struggled against it. "You would not know of Seneca," said Yosef, pushing the handle steadily harder so that Oppa's eyes began to cloud with blood. "Because you, just as your father before you, know nothing of the wisdom before your own time. Know nothing of learning, or knowledge, or beauty; value nothing more than the petty strength of your own arm."

"Yosef," rasped Theo, suddenly aware that the sounds of men and steel outside were coming closer. "We must hurry."

"Seneca said," went on Yosef, in the same calm, unhurried voice, "that there is no person so severely punished as those who subject themselves to the whip of their own remorse." He pushed his face close to Oppa's. "But you," he hissed, "you have no remorse, do you, Oppa Egicason? You do not know what remorse is." He pushed the whip handle hard against Oppa's neck, then let it fall away. Oppa fell to the ground, panting, fingers clawing at the skin where the handle had been.

Theo had pulled on his clothes, wincing as the material brushed the raw meat where the whip had struck. He watched Yosef from the corner of his eye, seeing him raise his arm to deliver the death blow.

Then the door opened and men crashed through it in a haze of weapons and blood, Silas struggling in their midst. The room was suddenly full of steel and flesh, the deathly whirl of battle. Theo saw the welcome figure of Leofric lunge through another wall and cut Silas free from their grasp. "Theo!" Silas yelled. "Come! We must hurry!" Theo tried to cut his way through the crowd, but man after man poured into the small space in a steady stream: Slavs he knew from the camp, making a wall before Oppa and another behind Theo, preventing escape. Then there was nothing but the grim work of death and cutting. Yosef fought at his side with Silas and Leofric, the four of them grappling sword, iron, and mace, Theo's blood and pain forgotten as he cut down man after man. It was terrible fighting, close and bloody, and for long moments there was nothing but grunts and bitter survival, but finally Theo saw the Slavic expressions turn from fight to fear, and they began to fall back.

But just as he pressed his victory, Theo staggered on a fallen body, and when he came up he realised it was not him the Slavs had run from, but whatever it was behind him. The Slavs looked over their shoulders, pointing and shouting as they ran down the hill. With sudden dread, Theo turned – and found himself facing a wall of spears and a sea of unfamiliar, Arabic faces.

One man stepped forward. Jerking their hands behind their backs, he clasped manacles about their wrists. "Oppa," snarled Theo, lunging against the iron, bloodlust still coursing through his veins, watching in frustration as the Slavs pointed up at them from far below, clearly gloating over their capture. "Where has he gone?"

"Be still," came Yosef's voice, oddly calm, behind him. "Oppa did what he always does when he faces a fight he cannot win. He ran, Theo."

Theo struggled impotently, staring out over the water far below as Oppa and his dromon pulled out, bound, Theo knew with dull certainty, for Spania and Lælia, safe in the knowledge that Theo would soon be tied to an Arabic oar and powerless to stop him telling whatever lies he chose.

Theo felt the cold weight of iron on his wrists, and dark despair grew within him.

The Arabic fulk bobbed up and down, Sebastopolis smoking and receding before Theo's eyes as the harbour gave way to the sea. In a grim reprieve Theo did not yet understand, he and his three companions were the only prisoners not attached to oars. The other slaves, captives from lands unknown to any of them, stared at them in dumb incomprehension, not understanding their words. *At least,* Theo thought bitterly, *it is not Oppa's dromon.* Their captors were Arabic, not Oppa's paid mercenaries. The knowledge did little to appease him.

"Every time," said Leofric bitterly, "that I follow you, Spaniard, I find myself in chains." Silas's heavy shoulders shook, and for a strange moment Theo thought the big man was crying; then he realised, with something of a shock, that Silas was shaking with suppressed laughter.

"You laugh!" Leofric spat into the ground, glaring at Silas and then at their Arabic captors. "You have a strange humour, African! Our dromons, they left. Dromons bound for Constantinople, to wine and women. We could have sailed, but, oh no. Instead we ride to find yet another enemy, and to the rescue of whores who do not wish to be rescued. And after all that, we do not kill the bastard and his whip. Oppa is gone. The child is gone." His face darkened. "And this child," he said roughly, "I like." He spat to cover his emotion. "Theo is covered in whip marks. And you and I, African, once more, we are in chains." Leofric lowered his head and shook it in sheer frustration. "It is done! I am done! The next time we fight, I leave you fools to die. How many times must a man tolerate chains? And now we have a Jew to add to our troubles." He shot Yosef a faintly apologetic glance. "And I am having nothing to argue with Jews, you understand, but they are not easy travelling companions, *ne?* People, they are not liking so much Jews in many places – so now we have another reason to be killed. As if we need any more. *Yehbach!*"

"Why are we not rowing?" Silas said, looking around them. "This is something new for us, *wenkai*, no?"

But Theo did not answer. He was watching Yosef, who sat silently, a small smile on his face.

One of their captors moved from the prow of the fulk down to where they huddled around the thin mast, followed by another of his companions. Their features were broader than those of the Arabic captain, and when they reached Yosef, a smile broke out on their faces. Turning to check the sea behind them was clear of watching eyes, the first man reached down and removed Yosef's manacles. "It was as you said it would be, Jew," he said, grinning. "They saw what you wished them to see. Though I am sorry we lost your Spanish friend. He is a slippery one."

Yosef gripped his arms, smiling. "You did all you promised, and more besides. Had you not come when you did, we would be dead. As it is, Oppa will certainly believe us to be, and that can only be an advantage." He pulled a canvas away from some crates, and Pelagia scrambled from beneath it, hurling herself into Theo's arms. Over her head, Yosef met Theo's astonished smile with his own. "Oppa is not the only one to have made alliances in the Arabic camp," he said. "But my allies have as much wish to return to their homeland as we do to ours – and allegiances that far outweigh Oppa's coin." He reached out to draw two men forward. "My friends have most recently been swords for Mohammed bin Marwan. In their homeland, however, they are known to all as sons of Dahiya, Queen of the Jerawa – and to me as my brothers. Their names are Bagay and Khanchla, and they have offered to facilitate our passage west to Septem and, from there, on to Spania."

49

LAURENTIUS

JULY, AD 692

Hispalis, Spania
Seville, Spain

"Given that every available man has already ridden north, leaving their crops to die in the fields and us all likely to starve come this winter, would you like to join me at meat tonight?" Laurentius's tone was light, but his grey eyes were shadowed. Shukra was plaiting rope, his head bowed. The dromons lay slack in the river, their sails rolled in hemp sacking and safely stored. The young men they had worked so hard to train were gone, conscripted on one side of the war or the other.

None could stay out of it now. As the long days brought summer closer, the war had become a line dividing families, estates, and provinces.

"Are we to pretend at friendship, then, *aziz-am*?" Shukra spoke without looking up, and though his tone was mild, Laurentius heard the tension beneath it. "We have managed many months of strained silence. I do not like it. But I prefer it to eating good meat in bad company."

"I do not forgive you for making Athanagild your spy, Shukra." Laurentius's tone was grim. "But this has gone on long enough. We can no longer afford petty quarrels to lie between us."

Shukra snorted softly, not looking at him. "And so it is eating meat and sampling your finest vintages we will be – as everyone we know risks their lives?"

Laurentius stared at him. "You would censure me? On what grounds?"

Shukra flung down the rope and faced him. "What are you thinking will happen when this is over? Are you thinking that Theo will come back to Spania? That Yosef will? That Athanagild will find himself in a church untouched by corruption? That Alaric might somehow survive and live to actually command this fleet that we both know was only ever a cover for your presence here?" He flung a hand in the air, eyes flashing, his face uncharacteristically dark. "You and I both know war. Most of those we trained will never return to us, *aziz-am*. Even if they do, they will be different to the boys they were when it began."

"What of the mission we sent Yosef and Theo upon? What of Garnata, and Ilyan, the alliances we have laboured to put in place?" Laurentius looked at his friend, his face gaunt and pale. "Do you think those, too, doomed? What is it you expect me to do – ride to war myself, when it is you who have counselled discretion these four years past and more? If I declare now, I lose any hope left to me of helping them all. I will no longer be neutral, will be named traitor and imprisoned, at best." His mouth tightened grimly as he stared unseeing at the dromons on the water, silent and still. "If I join this fight, who will they have to fight for them when this is done? If I ride to war, who will ensure their sacrifices are not in vain?"

"Ah!" Shukra paced agitatedly. Then he slowed, and his face softened as he looked at the tall, strong shoulders upon which so much rested that could not be shared. "*Aziz-am*," he said gently. "I am not thinking good, nor speaking, nor doing. Forgive me."

Laurentius turned, his face tired and resigned. "But you are right," he said bleakly. "I cannot stay out of this any longer. I cannot bear to."

"And yet you must."

Laurentius raised his eyebrows. "Were you not just saying that I should –"

Shukra waved an impatient hand. "Are you not knowing by now that you should be ignoring what I am saying? Surely after all these years you are knowing I speak without thinking?"

"What is it, Shukra?" Laurentius frowned at his friend. "Even your silence – which, I should tell you, is not so inscrutable as you like to believe – has been like a stirred wasp nest since you returned from Toletum." His face coloured faintly, and he cleared his throat behind his hand, trying to keep his voice steady. "Is it Athanagild?"

Shukra eyed him narrowly. "The last time I am speaking of Athanagild you told me you could not look upon my face, and here we are, months later, still arguing. Do not blame a man for caution, *aziz-am*."

"I know he continues to work for you." Laurentius's mouth tightened in a thin line. "I do not like it, but I know it. I know you saw him," he said roughly. "And though I might despise the fact of it, I can bear even less not knowing what danger he is in."

"There are things I do not say, with good reason. On your orders, I might add." Shukra gave him a grim look. "This is being one of those things you do not want to hear."

Laurentius took an uneven step forward. He gripped Shukra's arm. "Is he… is Athanagild…" He swallowed, eyes searching Shukra's face; then he released his grip and stepped back, fighting to regain control.

"If you are asking me," said Shukra flatly, "how Athanagild is, I can tell you this: the young man – he is not a boy, Laurentius, and he has not been one for a long time, so do not be looking like this to me – the young man is in perfect health. He is a fine priest and an intelligent scholar." He looked at Laurentius shrewdly. "He is also the most lonely, and alone, person I know. Except, perhaps, for you."

Laurentius stared at him, colour chasing over his face, white to flushed and back to white again.

"You are asking me," Shukra said quietly, "what I am thinking you should do in this ridiculous war. You and I are both knowing Sunifred's cause is lost, was lost before it was ever starting. All of the south is knowing this, though they are having no choices but to fight. But this fight, you are right in knowing, is not being your fight. You have no lands, command no men. You need not declare at all; you may sit here, in Hispalis, and pretend to ponder your books and train your fleet, and no man can ever prove you do otherwise. This is being the smart thing. The safe thing. The right thing for all the reasons you are saying.

"But in Toletum, a young man is risking his life every day. He is having nobody to speak with, nobody to counsel him in what is right. On his shoulders he carries more weight than any other man in this kingdom, perhaps, at this time is carrying. And he is making decisions any grown man would drink himself to death attempting to fathom, whilst you hold yourself aloof, out of some misguided sense of honour."

"But –"

Shukra held up a hand. "Do not," he said bleakly, "be explaining to me. You are as my brother and are the only family I am having since we were both boys. We do not speak of your nature, not because I am repulsed by it but because you worry I will be. No, *aziz-am* – you will not wave me away. I have long known what you are. Do you think I would stand at your side if it concerned me? Did I not say as much, many years ago? I take my women in taverns, Laurentius, and more of them than many men would think rational. If you take your pleasure from a different tavern, who am I to care, or judge? But you do not even do this since your return to Spania. At first, I am thinking it is because your Church here is so stern and your people so grim. But it has been long now since I have known the true reason. I stayed silent only because I am respecting your wishes. But I can no longer be silent, *aziz-am*. I will no longer be silent."

Laurentius frowned but did not speak.

"I will not listen anymore," said Shukra, "to your reasons for this distance from Athanagild. I cannot hear the excuses you are telling yourself. I am not pretending to know what may lie in your heart, for no man can know the truth of another's. I am knowing only this: that whatever comfort you both seek does not lie in my power to give, and that it is long past time you spoke to one another rather than through me. There is but one battle at this time that you must enter, *aziz-am*," he said softly. "Only one battle that requires your honour, and only one warrior who needs your strength. And whilst we both must live with the decision to stand aside from a war we both know lost, I do not wish you to stand aside from the one battle that may still be won. And now I am saying all I must." Shukra gripped his shoulder briefly then walked to the door. "Come, old friend. You can show me how your poor Spanish cook has murdered the meat this time."

But he spoke to the air, for Laurentius had already gone. Shukra smiled to himself. "Go, *aziz-am*," he murmured. "Go, and may Ahura Mazda bring peace to your heart."

LAURENTIUS RODE hard through the night, his blood racing with a curious mixture of euphoria and dread. The air was hot and foetid, stars dim behind dust haze. War seemed to have trodden the very sky into sullen waiting, as if all the world hung on what was coming.

It was strange to ride from Hispalis to Toletum barely seeing any evidence of the war itself. In the north, he knew, battles were raging, coming ever closer to the capital. But south of the great plains, what men were left gathered their crops and tended their herds, raking the ground beneath the olive trees in preparation for the coming season.

He tried not to think of what he would do once he reached the capital. He must enter it officially, but clearly as no more than a visitor, a man who owned one of the greatest libraries in Toletum and had a right to be there. To appear otherwise would mean destroying his carefully guarded position of neutrality, and this he could not afford to do, no matter how much it chafed to be thought an idle aristocrat in a time of war.

He slept beneath a bush by the roadside as the sun rose, wrapped in his cloak, and rode as the shadows grew long, and under cover of darkness. He crossed the Tagus at the old Roman bridge on the eastern approach, the guards in the fortress accepting the scrolls he offered without question since they bore Sunifred's own seal. Contemptuous of Laurentius's neutrality Sunifred might be, but he was astute enough to know the value of the Severianus name on his council and had already asked that Laurentius advise him when peace came. Privately certain the day would never come when Sunifred would reign over peace, Laurentius nonetheless maintained good faith. *Diplomacy, after all,* he thought bitterly as he rode the steep road up to the *domus* he had long left unattended, *is what I do best now.*

He stabled his horse at the rear and entered the silent house quietly. He had sent no word of his arrival. His servants were all in his family villa, beyond Toletum's walls. He had come here desiring few to know of his presence. He was relieved to find the place empty. He found wine in the cellar and ate the cheese and bread he carried, washing in water from his flask. He slept fitfully for the remainder of the night, wrapped in his cloak on a lectus, and made his way to the monastery in the still predawn. The priests were leaving the church after lauds, shuffling quietly back to the monastery to break their fast.

Laurentius spotted Athanagild immediately. *Shukra is right,* he thought, shrinking against the wall near the church as he watched from a distance. Athanagild was no longer a boy – though, in truth, Laurentius knew Athanagild had not been a boy for many years, perhaps not since they had met. It was a fiction Laurentius had told himself, a wall his conscience had built to shield his heart from what it had known from the first time he had looked into Athanagild's perceptive hazel eyes.

The young man in front of him was tall and lean, and he walked with an assurance that belonged to one much older. He bent his head to listen to a senior priest, his face alert and intelligent. Perhaps because of Shukra's words, Laurentius saw in Athanagild's expression a certain watchfulness he had not before noticed. Guilt and affection seized his heart like a physical pain.

A young boy was collecting water at the pump in the square. Laurentius beckoned him over and handed him a coin. The boy raced off, and when Athanagild held the door open for the older priest, the boy tugged his robes and the tall figure bent down to listen. Laurentius saw something in his face flare, a sudden rush of emotion; then the pale mask was back, and Athanagild nodded and held his hand on the boy's head as if the child had done nothing more than ask a blessing.

Laurentius moved away, his heart thudding, and made for the bathhouse by the river.

"You should not be here."

Athanagild moved into the dim light and closed the door behind him. His face was guarded, and he eyed Laurentius with a wariness that hurt the older man somewhere deep inside. *I have done this,* he thought despairingly. *It is I who taught him that caution.*

"This is a fine greeting," said Laurentius, attempting a smile. Athanagild didn't return it.

"Why did you come?"

Laurentius found himself uncharacteristically disconcerted. He waved a hand aimlessly. "Shukra —"

"He told you." Athanagild's composure broke, and he spun, knocking the brazier to the floor in an angry clatter. "I knew he would," he muttered. "Can nobody be trusted?"

Something warned Laurentius to remain quiet. "He meant it for the best," he said, feeling his way carefully. "Shukra worries for you a great deal, Athanagild."

"It was not his fault." Athanagild looked at him, shame and defiance warring in his eyes. "I gave him little choice in the matter. But the ruse worked. Liuvgoto and her daughter fell ill, but the poison failed. They live because of our interference. And Sunifred will not readily make the same attempt twice. Sisebut himself is terrified at how close he came to accusation. The abbess asked some very probing questions during the time Liuvgoto and her daughter lay ill."

Laurentius stared at him. "Poison," he said blankly. "You gave Cixilo — the *queen* — and her mother poison?"

The colour drained from Athanagild's face. "Shukra did not tell you," he said.

Laurentius shook his head. "No," he said slowly. "Not this." There was a moment's silence in which they stared at each other; then Laurentius exploded. "If they had died," he said furiously, "what then? The south would have erupted into open war amongst themselves. Not only would this doomed rebellion have failed, but the very men who now at least find amity in their hatred of Egica would have turned on one another. Such an act is not only folly, Athanagild. It is vicious, the act of a madman or a fool."

"Precisely." Athanagild's tone was cold. His eyes glittered dangerously. "Which is exactly why I sought Shukra's help to neutralise the poison and render it harmless. And despite his own bitter opposition Shukra did so, knowing it was the best choice available."

"The best choice?" Laurentius gaped at him. "As decided by whom? You, Athanagild?" His hand struck the wall so hard the sconce trembled. "How does it come to be that a boy who has barely taken orders is taking decisions a grown man would blanch at? Are you so seduced by the world of whispers you think yourself immune to the judgement of God?"

"The judgement of God?" Athanagild laughed derisively. "Listen to your own words! Since when have you cared for the judgement of God? And do you share your own plans with any? Plans that I know go far beyond the careless attitude you adopt at court or the fleet that conceals the mission upon which you sent my brother. You seem free in your condemnation of others whilst disdaining ever to lay your own agenda open for scrutiny. Yet you dare stand here and question my actions?" Athanagild shook his head impatiently. "You dare," he said softly, holding Laurentius's eye, "to deny who you are – *what* you are?"

Laurentius met the hard, glittering challenge in the hazel eyes, tasted the danger in the air. The words hung between them, living coals making the air spark. Laurentius felt the iron control he had clung to in the long, lonely years since his return to Spania falter, then finally fall.

"Damn it," he muttered roughly. "I have tried, Athanagild. Xristus knows, I have tried to stay away."

"Then don't," whispered Athanagild. "Please – don't."

Then Laurentius had the pale face between his hands, Athanagild's lithe form against his own, and his mouth was hard and bruising on the other as he thrust him backward against the wall. For a moment Athanagild was frozen beneath his touch. Then he surged against Laurentius, taking as fiercely as Laurentius gave, the sparks in the air becoming a roaring blaze so the blood pumped in Laurentius's ears and there was nothing but the pounding of his heart and the lean, hard body in his arms. He lost himself in the savage passion that had burned for years now until it melted, slowly, into something else, something deeper that made him groan in the back of his throat and finally push himself away so they stood staring at each other, breathing hard.

"Not here," said Laurentius hoarsely, looking around at the bathhouse. "We need to talk. We need privacy."

"No." Athanagild's hand came up and touched Laurentius's cheek, then fell away. "No talking. Not now. Not with all this." His waving hand indicated the world beyond the bathhouse: the war, the Church, his family. "We cannot stay here," he said roughly. "This place is watched. And if I leave with you, if we are found together, Sisebut will kill us both. For now – at least – you must leave by the front entrance, perhaps take a whore with you. For now, this cannot be."

Laurentius nodded slowly, his blood racing with a strange, reckless euphoria he had never thought to feel again, like a lick of freedom amidst the cold, grey control he exerted on every other aspect of his life. He reached out to touch the pale face. Athanagild bent his head, leaning into the hand calloused by sword and war, his hazel eyes fierce in the dim light. Laurentius felt the mad heat of lust simmering beneath his skin. Searching for distraction, he cleared his throat. "Tell me though," he said. "Liuvgoto and her daughter Cixilo. Are they still in danger?"

Athanagild nodded, and Laurentius felt the frantic tension of his jaw against his hand. "I cannot risk visiting them too often." He looked at Laurentius, his eyes heavy with hidden knowledge.

"Everything is watched, you understand," he said in a low voice. "Every visit, every word. To slip is to die."

Laurentius shook his head. "My God," he said softly. "All this you have lived alone."

Athanagild's hand came up and covered his own. "But not anymore," he whispered.

"No." Laurentius's eyes searched his face, and a quiet joy spread through his chest. "No, Athanagild. Not anymore."

50

ALARIC

SEPTEMBER, AD 692

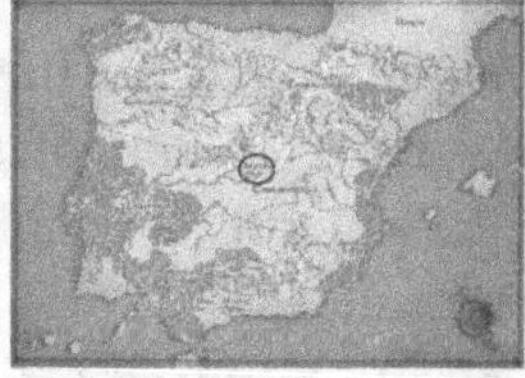

Toletum, Spania
Toledo, Spain

"My lord, the die cutter is here to discuss your coins."

Sunifred's face lit up. "Send him in, send him in!"

Alaric and Teudolfo exchanged a glance. "My lord," said Alaric carefully, "we need to discuss strategy in the north. Favila has been captured, and Egica is riding for Vallisoletum. It is less than three hundred miles from here. We do not have a lot of time."

Sunifred's face darkened. He drank deeply from his wine cup. "I have already sent messengers to the lords on the plains between here and there, ordering them to lay down arms. When my coins are struck, they will become the new currency. Anyone trading in Egica's coin will be known as a traitor." He sat back and looked at them with a smug smile. "See how long they remain in rebellion once Egica's coin cannot buy so much as a goat for meat."

Alaric stared at him. "My lord —" he began tentatively.

Sunifred waved him aside. "Wars are no longer won," he said

loftily, "with the sword alone. They are won primarily with coin, and persuasion. It is time for the harvest. Men's thoughts turn to the coming winter and how they will feed their families."

He beckoned Cato, the die cutter, forward. The man wore rich robes and eyed Sunifred disdainfully. His, Alaric knew, was a private trade, handed down from father to son, jealously guarded. Sunifred had sent Alaric to search the man out, and it had taken considerable amounts of both ale and coin before Cato had condescended to attend Sunifred's court. He did not choose who sat on the throne, Cato had sniffed to Alaric, and must cut the dies he was ordered – but since his family were the sole owners of the secrets of punching the planchets into shape, he did not demean himself to those whose images graced his finished product.

Now he handed the dies to Sunifred for examination. "My lord has not granted enough time for sophisticated work," he said.

Sunifred waved his hand dismissively. "Read it to me."

"Sunifred," intoned the cutter, tracing the letters. "Victor of Toletum." He glanced at Alaric, who nodded for him to continue. His lips pursed. "My son has made the same for the city of Emerita, as you decreed."

"Good." Sunifred nodded at the die. "And the bust – it is as I ordered: of myself, not of Christ?" Behind him, Sisebut's mouth tightened.

The die cutter cast the archbishop a wary glance, then nodded to Sunifred. "I have removed the three-pointed cross, my lord."

"*Gut*." Sunifred nodded in satisfaction and dismissed Cato with a wave. The cutter pursed his lips and cast a resentful glance at the throne as he gathered his dies. The planchets, he had informed Alaric haughtily, would be of the crudest alloy – and he would make certain no mark was left to designate such barbaric coin as his own work.

Sunifred watched the man go, a satisfied smile on his face. "Sisebut," he said. The archbishop moved to stand behind him. "Do you have the list of names I asked you to prepare?"

"I do, Fráuja." Sisebut nodded to a young deacon, who scurried out of the hall. "We can review them immediately."

"Fráuja." When there was no response, Alaric took a deep

breath. "Sunifred." The king gave him a look that would have dissuaded most men. Alaric coloured but met it, his face grim. "This is no time for coins and priests," he said bluntly. "If we do not devise the proper defences, Egica will be in the city within weeks. I ask that you allow me to lead the men of Emerita north, win us at least some time to send south for aid. We have not the men to hold Toletum nor the forces to face them on the plains. The lords to whom you have sent word have not replied. We must assume they are, for now, loyal to Egica, whether out of fear or allegiance. If I go in person, we may sway them. But if we do nothing, Toletum is as good as lost."

Sunifred stood abruptly, his fists clenched, and had opened his mouth to make reply when another voice cut in.

"He is right."

Alaric swung around, his heart skipping unsteadily. His father stood in the doorway, surrounded by his *gardingi*. Suinthila strode into the high, airy palace forum, waving away Sunifred's guard with an impatient hand. Despite the pale face and gaunt figure that betrayed his long years of illness, it was a measure of his authority that none dared challenge him.

Alaric willed his rush of passionate relief not to show on his face. It was all he could do to quell a childish impulse to rush at his father, seeking his rough embrace as he had not done since infancy.

Sunifred's fists clenched. "Were you here when we took Toletum?" he growled, offering no formal greeting. "When we fought our way from Hispalis to the Tagus? Where were you then, Suinthila?"

"I was minding my own lands, hoping you would discover the sense to desist from this folly of a rebellion." Unmoved by Sunifred's glowering rage, Suinthila faced him calmly. "Sadly my hopes were in vain. Now, here we are. But unless you cease this ridiculous posturing, Sunifred, Toletum will be besieged and the crops from here to Vallisoletum razed to the ground. Even if by some miracle we retain the city, we will starve come the winter."

"We hold the south!" Sunifred was red faced and choleric, his eyes shifting uneasily beneath Suinthila's steady gaze.

Suinthila made a dismissive gesture. "The war is in the north. If there is a south to be held at this time, then it is Paulus who holds it." Suinthila shook his head. "And he holds it by the grace of Theodefred, who risks everything to allow his men to fight beneath your banner."

"As he should!"

"No," said Suinthila wearily, shaking his head. "He shouldn't. You have forced Theodefred to show his hand when it would have been better for us all if he could have remained neutral. Now he must play a dangerous game, riding at Egica's side and pretending loyalty to the king even as his own thiufae gather in opposition. This foolhardy rebellion of yours has left coastal fortresses unguarded, a harvest to bring in, and men far from their homes fighting a war few understand. Your actions left neither Paulus nor Theodefred a choice. The south must fight or die. The men from Theodefred's lands north of Corduba ride beside him and Egica. Those from his southern estates gather under Paulus, and ostensibly against their own lord. Their faith is tenuous, their resources even more frail. Every one of them has left women and children alone, with barely any protection should your forces fall."

"And have I not left my own daughter and wife thus?" Sunifred demanded in a tone of wounded injury.

Alaric stepped forward. "I have asked before," he said, emboldened by his father's presence, "that you allow me to send men to escort Rekiberga and your wife south to Illiberis." He did not look at Suinthila, but he felt the warmth of his father's eyes and drew strength from his calm authority.

Sunifred waved his arm in dismissal of Alaric's words. "Send my own blood to be protected by Paulus, who, like your father, did not deign to raise a finger in support of our cause when help was needed? Who sits in judgement upon me whilst he trains his own granddaughter to be thiufadis if he should fall? Tyr! What man delegates war to a girl? That grandchild of his is little better than a savage, by all accounts. I would not allow Rekiberga a hundred miles near Illiberis."

"This achieves nothing." Suinthila stepped forward, his jaw working in frustration. Men looked at each other warily, hands drifting toward sword hilts. The tension was broken when the heavy doors opened and Paulus strode through them.

"*Háuheins Gud*," muttered Alaric, his hand relaxing. Praise God.

Paulus approached the throne without asking permission, looking neither right nor left. "Egica's men have ridden for Vallisoletum," he said bluntly. "Why do your forces remain here?"

Sunifred glared at him. "This is how you address your king?"

Paulus gave him a look of withering contempt. "When Egica's sword rests in your hand and your men hold every fortress currently flying that ridiculous eagle standard he affects, I may call you king. Until then, I would suggest your time is better spent in determining how you intend to bring that end about rather than dallying with that damned coin cutter I saw leaving on my way in."

Alaric felt his heart begin to thud with a savage excitement. He caught Teudolfo's eye and saw the same exultation and passionate relief. The combination of Suinthila and Paulus in the same room changed the atmosphere, gave a sense of purpose and focus. Alaric no longer felt alone.

Sunifred's face had reddened, his mouth working uncomfortably. Paulus gave him a scathing glare and turned to Suinthila. "What is our strategy?"

Suinthila, stifling a smile, said: "We were just discussing that."

Paulus looked at Sunifred. "Well?"

"I have sent messages to the lords between here and Vallisoletum," said Sunifred resentfully. "There are those amongst them who have indicated they will provide a defence, should it come to it."

"It has already come to it." Paulus stared darkly at Sunifred. "Do you mean to tell me," he said softly, "that you have no forces arrayed between here and Vallisoletum? That you have left those lords to make their own defence?"

"We must hold Toletum," said Sunifred, attempting to regain the ascendancy. "It is vital the capital stands."

"Three moons from now," said Paulus brutally, "Toletum will starve. We cannot hold the city from every direction, and even if we could, we do not have the men to hold a supply line open for grain to be delivered. The south cannot feed you if they cannot reach you."

Sunifred coloured and looked away. He lowered his voice. "The men from Hispalis are not eager to move into the northern provinces," he said tightly.

Paulus made an impatient gesture. "Of course they are not," he said. "They are sworn to protect the south, their homes and families. But there are northern lords in your alliance; send them."

"And do what?" said Sunifred angrily.

"Withdraw to the south." Paulus stepped forward and looked at Sunifred intently. "Move our forces back behind the mountain lines into Old Bætica where we know every pass and have the loyalty of every household. The north is lost. Toletum is a figurehead, a symbol of kingship that means nothing unless the king who sits on the throne here controls every lord in the country. And you, Sunifred, do not."

"I will not relinquish it!" Sunifred stood and paced agitatedly across the broad marble floor, his hand on one of the wide columns, stroking it as if to reassure himself it was real. "No king has ruled Spania in a hundred years or more who has not held Toletum. Sisebut is archbishop here, prime amongst all the bishops in Spain. He alone can anoint a man king."

"Then take Sisebut with you and make Hispalis the primary archdiocese!" Paulus waved his hand dismissively. "Have yourself crowned there, surrounded by lords who will cheer you as their saviour, if you choose. Not here, amongst a resentful populace terrified of starvation and men who wish only to return to their homes."

"We won Toletum!" Sunifred was red faced, his finger stabbing the carved wood of his throne. Alaric looked away, uncomfortable at such a loss of control. Suddenly Sunifred seemed no older than the men Alaric himself commanded. His face had a petulant cast, an uncertainty, and Alaric felt himself withdraw from the weakness he saw there. He thought of Teudolfo's long-ago words: *You cannot split the heart of a man from his cause.* How right, he thought, his friend had been.

Paulus snorted in contempt. "You did not win Toletum," he said to Sunifred. "Egica allowed you to take it. And if you remain here now, if you spread our forces so thinly, he will have achieved the very outcome he foresaw when he rode north. Toletum will fall, and our forces will scatter." He gripped Sunifred's arm hard. "Ride south," he said. "Mount your defence from behind the mountains, and I guarantee that every lord from Malaca to Emerita will stand fast behind you."

Sunifred stared at him resentfully. "But not unless you command them to do so. Is that what you imply, Fráuja Paulus?"

Alaric tensed. He had seen Sunifred in this mood before. Paulus was backing him into a corner, and once there, Sunifred would become an immovable rock of stubborn pride. Alaric stepped forward. "I have already offered to lead our forces north," he said, not looking at his father. "The men from Emerita, and others, will ride with me."

Paulus glared at him. "Then withdraw your offer," he said bluntly.

Sunifred moved beside Alaric, placing a proprietary hand on his shoulder, eyeing Paulus and Suinthila with satisfaction. Alaric forced himself not to flinch at Sunifred's touch. "No. I have heard you all, and now the decision is mine." There was an unsavoury note of triumph in Sunifred's voice. "Alaric, we have the reinforcements you wished for. Now you will ready the men and ride north in the morning." He turned calculating eyes to Suinthila. "It would seem men of the south will follow more than only you, Fráuja."

A muscle worked in his jaw, but Suinthila maintained his composure. Alaric wanted nothing more than to step forward, to lay his sword and responsibility at his father's door. But it was already too late for that, and as he watched concern and anger war on Suinthila's face, he realised his father, too, knew it. "If you are thus resolved," said Suinthila grimly, turning to his son, "then you must go without delay. What is your plan?"

Alaric shot an embarrassed glance at Sunifred.

"We were discussing that," said Sunifred coldly, "when you entered, my lords."

"Good." Ignoring the rebuke, Suinthila looked at Paulus and called forward his *gardingi*. "Then we have work to do."

. . .

"THEODEFRED'S MEN ARE UNEASY." It was late at night and they ate by firelight, the sound of men and iron in the air. Paulus's men had joined those of Alaric and Suinthila in the old Roman circus, which had become barracks and fortress. Paulus speared his meat and glared at the flames, speaking in a low voice. "They rode to fight for the south. They will desert if Sunifred asks them to ride north." He speared more meat, his actions sharp and aggressive. "They may desert anyway. They will not wish to be caught on this side of the mountain passes when the snows come, leaving their lands and families unprotected."

"How did you come to lead them?" Suinthila asked. "I thought all of Theodefred's men had ridden under Egica's command?"

"They are his own household force," said Paulus. "And others who would normally protect the walls of Corduba, or the towns to the south. Men who would not fight beyond their own lands unless they have good cause."

Suinthila looked at him curiously. "And do they?"

"*Ja.*" Paulus sat back on the bench and washed his meat down with wine, his face lined and dark. "They do." His eyes travelled to Alaric, then slid away. "Lælia," he said, "met with Giscila during her time across the seas."

Alaric tensed. He glanced at his father. Suinthila had paled, his face tight and closed, as it always was when mention was made of Alaric's mother. "*Ja?*" he said roughly. "What of it?"

"Giscila admitted it was he who launched the attack that killed our children." Paulus spoke bluntly, but he could not quite disguise the rough edge to his voice. "The men who ride behind me know the truth of those days. They know, too, that it was Oppa who orchestrated the attack that nearly killed Theo."

"And this was enough to convince men to ride with you?" Suinthila's tone was hard and sceptical. "Uncommonly altruistic for fighting men, is it not?"

"The southern lords all recall the Summer of Blood." Paulus's face was grim. "And they all lost sons in the doomed fleet that Oppa attacked. You know as well as I that the south has never truly bowed to rule from Toletum. They needed little other encouragement." He gave a half smile. "Besides – it was Acantha who persuaded them,

not I." He waved aside Suinthila's raised eyebrows. "It is not important. You know as well as I the nature of Illiberis women. They are
not easy to gainsay." He leaned forward with his hands clasped
between his knees, grim once more. "But the men will not ride
north, Suinthila. They will not give a single life to see Sunifred's
purse increased, nor the wealth of the northern lords protected.
They will fight for Toletum, and to protect the mountain passes to
the south, but that is all. If Alaric does not turn Egica's force, it will
be a desperate stand. One we are unlikely to win."

"It was never likely," said Suinthila quietly, "that we would win."

Paulus stared at him for a moment. Then he passed a weary
hand over his face and sat back. "*Ja*," he said. "It is true."

Suinthila looked at Alaric. "We will do what we can to prepare
Toletum for what is to come," he said, "and we will ensure you have
men to ride with you. I will not send you across those plains with no
more than a single thiufa and the cheers of a fool."

Alaric looked at Paulus, who nodded. "*Ja*." The older man
gripped his arm. "We will stand behind you, *magula*."

"He is no longer *magula*. He is not a boy." All three turned to
look at Teudolfo. "Alaric is the only reason Sunifred has a force at
all," said Teudolfo quietly. "And he has proven his worth a hundred
times over these months past. He may be many things – but he is no
longer *magula*. He is a man."

Alaric felt the warm strength of his father's hand on his shoulder
and was grateful for the shadows that hid his face.

There was a movement next to them, and they turned as one to
see Laurentius emerge from the darkness. "May I join you?" He sat
without waiting for permission. He looked oddly lighter, Alaric
thought, as if an invisible weight had lifted. There was something
animated in his face, as if he had found hope in the darkness.

"Why are you here?" Paulus asked him. "Hispalis is the wiser
place for you, my friend." But a slight smile touched the edge of his
mouth, and his tone was humorous rather than stern.

"Ah," said Laurentius lightly, "but Hispalis offers none of the
entertainment of Toletum in this season, wouldn't you agree?"

Paulus, Alaric thought, held true affection for few men – but
Laurentius seemed to be one of them. Severianus the Elder and

Paulus, he knew, had been good friends, allies for thirty years. Paulus's regard for the father had passed to the son. Seeing the effect of Laurentius's company on Paulus's grim countenance was like watching a balmy tide washing over a storm-ravaged coast.

Paulus grinned. "And what entertainment is it that amuses you in our royal capital, then? I do hear your Persian friend has a certain appetite for whores, and war has certainly seen an increase in their numbers."

"Shukra," said Laurentius, "could find a whore amidst a sandstorm in Africa. But no," he went on, as the other men laughed, "that is not why I am here. Felix," he said, leaning forward, "the bishop of Hispalis, is concerned that the precious books in my father's library escape the current conflict unscathed. We have not the time to move them to Hispalis, so I am removing them, for safekeeping, to a monastery just outside Toletum." Paulus raised his eyebrows. "By a happy accident," said Laurentius, his own mouth curling, "it is the same monastery that harbours the honoured dowager, Liuvgoto, and her daughter, Cixilo."

Paulus nodded his approval. "And Shukra?" he said dryly. "What mischief is that little Persian devil making as we speak?"

"Shukra," said Laurentius, "is turning his attention from whores to bishops." His tone might have been light, but Alaric, who had become attuned to his moods in the long months of training, heard the ruthless note beneath the urbanity as he went on, "Shukra has always maintained, however, that there is often little to choose between the two."

The others laughed and turned away, but Alaric, seeing the deadly glint of steel in the grey eyes, thought that he did not envy the unfortunate bishop who found himself the object of Shukra and Laurentius's combined wrath.

51

BISHOP FELIX
SEPTEMBER, AD 692

Hispalis, Spania
Seville, Spain

Bishop Felix of Hispalis prided himself on moderation. He took seriously the strictures of office and, as befitted an acolyte of Julian, prized humility and learning over ambition and politics.

But even the most humble man, he reflected as he passed through the corridors of the monastery in Hispalis, could not help but find himself excited by the heady contents of the letter he had recently received.

The parchment bearing Athanagild's mark lay against his chest. He did not dare leave it anywhere it may be found but nor could he bring himself to destroy it. The contents in it were too sensational – and, frankly, too dangerous – to risk discovery. He had found them so controversial he had sent a monk of his own to discern what he might. What little the man had discovered had amply verified Athanagild's claims, and more. So disturbing were the discoveries that Felix had carried the letter close to his chest like a hair shirt, the familiar edges pricking his skin. He found himself touching his robes occasionally, feeling the shape of the letter beneath, reminding himself that what he read there truly existed.

He knew he should not covet power, nor worship at the altar of ambition. Felix had seen good men undone by their desire to wield power in the Church. Julian had groomed him to be a better man than such opportunists, to be one who served the Church, and God, rather than seeking to put either at his own service.

And yet.

His hand touched the parchment.

When God himself presented such an opportunity, should it be denied? When such corruption was exposed to his eye, was there not a duty to correct it, to restore honour and integrity to the office Julian had worked so hard to elevate?

I have witnessed depravities of such vile corruption I cannot speak of them...

Felix had read Athanagild's parchment so many times the words played in his mind like an oft-sung ballad. The queen herself and her mother the victims of a poisoning thwarted only by careful planning. The Church made vulnerable by a plot that, if widely known, would threaten forever its credibility and honour.

Felix halted in the corridor, sick and breathless with what the words meant. "Sisebut must be removed," he said aloud; then he glanced around, colouring, his heartbeat calming only when he knew he was alone.

There is no other way, he thought. Athanagild's delicate phrasing had not deceived Felix. He had not lived his whole life in the Church without knowing the sins of which its adherents were capable. He had easily read between the pained lines. That Athanagild did not state his plight openly spoke only of the poor child's own honour, his desperate and lonely attempt to ask for help without condemning his superior beyond redemption. But Felix was not fooled.

He was furious.

If, as Athanagild intimated in his letter, Sunifred himself suspected his archbishop's depravities, sought even to exploit them, then Sisebut must be exposed, condemned, and made a symbol of what the Church would not tolerate within its ranks. If any should know of this conspiracy of priests and sodomites, kings and poison, the Church would be lost, undone forever, its rule destroyed and its authority forever tainted.

The responsibility for the plot against Liuvgoto and her daughter must live and die with Sisebut and Sunifred, Felix thought, *associated with the ambition of corrupt men and decisively condemned by the Church and all within it.*

So absorbed was he in the thoughts that had whirled in his mind since the letter had been slipped into his hand that Felix did not notice the shadow that did not belong in the corridor, nor sense the presence of another until an arm whipped about his throat, pulling him beneath the cover of an archway and into blackness. He struggled briefly, but the embrace held him like a vice.

"The letter you hold," came a voice in his ear. "From whom was it sent?" Felix felt a cold terror grip his throat; he knew only that he must not betray Athanagild at any cost.

"I do not know what you speak of," he said, his voice quavering but clear.

"Yes, you do." One hand touched Felix's chest, covering the outline of the parchment beneath. "You touch it so many times a day you have worn a stain in your robes. Is it a letter of romance you so treasure? Do you, like your brother in Toletum, lust after young men in the service of the Church?"

"No!" Felix gasped, his horror genuine this time. "I have never... such atrocities defile the word of God –"

"But you tolerate them," went on the voice in his ear. "You allow others to pursue their desires, to make victims of innocents. All this horror you allow, to protect your Church and your God."

"What do you want?" Felix squirmed against the iron grip, but he was held as easily as a worm on a hook, unable to turn to face his captor. "Why do you come here?"

"Because I know the words of the letter you hold," went on the voice, its chilling clarity striking terror deep into Felix's blood. "I know who it condemns, and for what. My question to you is this: who will you see suffer for its contents? Who does the Church intend to see publicly exposed?"

"I do not know of what you speak," said Felix, and now he

found an ice-cold resolve within. *Even if I die,* he thought fiercely, *I will see that Athanagild, who has risked all, will suffer no more. I will not allow such sacrifice.* Athanagild's gaunt hazel eyes crossed his mind, and he felt again the mingled shame and rage that such a child, a noble child offered to God, should have been used in such manner.

"Do you believe me," hissed the voice, "when I am saying that should you so much as whisper of doing harm to the author of those words that I will be seeing you dead and the Church you love so dearly exposed to the world?"

Felix frowned. He had heard that odd lilt before, yet he could not precisely place where. "I told you," said Felix resolutely. "I know nothing of any letter, nor your purpose here."

A soft chuckle moved the hair by his ear, and Felix flinched. "I am thinking," came the voice again, "that you were the right choice, *aziz-am.* I had not thought to find an honourable man in your number. It seems that, for once, I was wrong." Felix felt a fierce rush of relief, which disappeared when the grip on his neck tightened. "But you will be remembering," came the voice again, and this time the deadly note in it had returned, "that I am watching you. I am protecting the hand that wielded that pen. Should you be thinking that perhaps your loyalty is misplaced, I will be there, my friend, to remind you. Do you understand?"

Felix did not speak, though his head moved briefly in a curt nod of agreement.

The soft chuckle came again, and the grip on his neck loosened. A moment later, Felix spun wildly on the spot, his eyes searching the empty corridor. But the shadow was gone, and there was nothing but the still, dark silence of the house of God. Felix stood for a moment, his heart thudding sickly. *What would cause a man to risk his very soul by attacking a priest in the house of God?* he thought. *And that accent – where have I heard it before?*

An image of Laurentius Severianus crossed his mind. He shook his head. It was not the scholar, he would swear it. He knew Laurentius well, had sat whilst Severianus's son and Julian discussed books until late in the night. The man was many things, and Felix would gamble his career – and more – that Laurentius's sword had tasted blood more than any priest might wish to know of, but he was not a shadow who skulked in corners, of that he was certain.

Then why do I think of him when I hear that voice?

He frowned, searching his memory until he remembered standing outside Laurentius's study in Hispalis, long ago, by a half-opened door. *I forbid you to approach Athanagild again, Shukra,* Laurentius had said. *I do not know what games or whispers have brought you to his door, but you will desist ... And for the time, at least, remove yourself from my house and from my sight. I cannot look at you any more than I can look at myself.*

Shukra.

That is his name, Felix thought. *The shadowy Persian who trains Laurentius's fleet, who has unfettered access to all those young men. The man my monk suspected of meeting Athanagild in a house of sin in Toletum.*

Laurentius's words came to him again: *I do not know what games or whispers have brought you to his door, but you will desist...*

He remembered the white face and stricken eyes of the Persian when Shukra had pushed past him in Laurentius's house that day long ago. So intent upon his own business had Felix been that he had not given much thought to a private quarrel. Besides, training young men in the art of war was, he had imagined, a volatile exercise.

But now the exchange played through his mind again, and he sifted through the information he knew about the foreigner. *He has made it known that he frequents brothels,* Felix thought. *Has paraded it, in fact. I know barely anything of the man, but I know that. His antics with women are the stuff of legend in Hispalis.*

And what better way to disguise his true proclivities?

Felix clenched his hands in anger. He thought of Laurentius Severianus, a man of unimpeachable honour, probably dependent on Shukra's alliance with Count Ilyan and the coin sent from across the seas. What injustice, for a man of Laurentius's calibre to be forced to endure the company of a depraved sodomite and yet unable to condemn him out of duty to Spania! Felix bowed his head sorrowfully at the thought of Laurentius's nobility and sacrifice.

And now this Persian, the descendant of sorcerers and heretics who practised arcane arts and defiled the name of God, came out of the shadows and threatened one of God's own – all because he wished himself to pursue the innocent young man he purported to defend.

He desires Athanagild for himself, thought Felix in disgust. *And he wishes to ensure the boy is protected, all the better for him to take what is left when Sisebut is condemned.*

Athanagild's letter had not stated so blatantly his relationship with Sisebut. But Felix could tell the enormous pressure the boy was under, the impossible position in which he had been placed. *And now,* he thought bitterly, *when finally he reaches out for help from those who should have protected him, another waits in the wings, already planning his insidious approach.*

"Well, I will not allow it!" Felix's own voice startled him. He looked around guiltily, but none had heard him. "I will see both of them condemned for this horror," he whispered, picturing Sisebut's plump, lascivious face and the dark-eyed, slender little Persian, who now, in his mind, appeared the very essence of stealth and deception.

"I will see both held accountable for their horrors to God and man. I will give that brave child the satisfaction of the Church's justice. I will see he is rewarded for his extraordinary loyalty to the institution sworn to protect him – and which yet betrayed him in the foulest way imaginable."

He began walking again, his heart beating steadily now with the intensity of his purpose. *I will do what must be done,* he thought resolutely. *I will honour Athanagild's confidence by bringing to public justice those who would threaten him.*

And content in the knowledge that he trod a moral path that would deliver a justice others could never appreciate, Felix, bishop of Hispalis and soon to be prelate over all Hispania, returned to his bedchamber – and to the untroubled sleep of a man assured of his righteousness.

52

OPPA

NOVEMBER, AD 692

Carthage, Mauretania
Carthage, Tunisia

The port of Carthage, Oppa thought, seemed an oasis after the cesspool of Sebastopolis. As busy and hurried as the docks were, still men paid him barely a passing glance as he disembarked. He was no more than another wealthy merchant in a port full of them. A few cursory enquiries led him to a tavern on the outskirts of the city. It was barely sundown, but Giscila had clearly been there for some time.

"Uncle." Oppa looked about him in distaste. "Surely my coin buys better surroundings?"

"In Carthage," said Giscila, spitting to one side and looking about blearily, "it is often better to remain in the shadows. It is not a city for ostentation."

"There is a fine line between the shadows and the gutter." Oppa wrinkled his nose. "This establishment crossed that line long ago."

"I am certain we have better things to discuss than the quality of the tavern." Giscila gestured for wine as Oppa took a stool opposite him. "I will confess, I am glad to see you. I had heard ominous rumblings from the Arab merchants arriving here."

"Sebastopolis fell to the caliph's forces," said Oppa bluntly. "It was a rout."

"And yet you escaped?"

"Of course." Oppa shrugged. "I made alliance with the winning side long before it came to war."

"And Theudemir of Aurariola?"

It was only long-established habit that kept the emotion Oppa felt from showing on his face. It had taken most of the voyage from Sebastopolis, and the frenzied whipping of several unfortunate slaves, before he had managed to get his rage under control.

"If Aurariola is not dead, he is a slave of the Arabs." Something of what he felt must yet have been discernible in his eyes, for Giscila recoiled slightly. Oppa felt a flash of savage satisfaction. It did not hurt, he thought, for men to suspect something of the darkness within.

"I had thought," Giscila said carefully, "that you meant to find common ground with him."

"I found it for long enough to catch him in a trap that will make him mine should he dare return to Spania." He gave Giscila a hard look that forbade any further enquiry. Oppa was not a man who liked loose ends. Theudemir of Aurariola was a dangerous loose end, one Oppa would have preferred tied neatly in a knot of his own devising before landing on Spania's shores.

"The heiress from Illiberis," Oppa said. "I heard you found her?" He saw surprise flare in Giscila's eyes. In fact, Oppa had heard no such thing, had not known it until he saw his relative's reaction. But there was no reason for Giscila to know that.

"You have good sources," said Giscila, eyeing him warily. When it became clear Oppa would give no answer, Giscila continued: "I found her, yes."

"And?" Oppa turned the cup slowly in his hand, feeling no satisfaction at the wariness he saw in Giscila's eyes.

"I assured her of my support should she ever wish to call upon it." When Oppa continued to look at him, Giscila sighed. "She did not welcome my offer. But I believe I sowed doubt enough to make her question what she did not before – Theudemir's loyalty."

"Good." Oppa sat back, stroking his wine cup meditatively. Lælia's uncertainty, combined with the presence of the whore Elpis and the parchment Oppa never let out of his tunic, were tools enough to destroy Theudemir should he make another miraculous reappearance. "This gives us something, at least, to work with."

"How?" Giscila leaned forward. "There is a great distance between sowing doubt and alliance. Lælia of Illiberis is not like to trust me simply because she no longer knows if her betrothed is loyal to her."

"Not knowing whom to trust may not be the basis for alliance. But it does provide fertile ground upon which a successful attack might be launched." He met Giscila's eyes. "What word from Spania?"

"Toletum has fallen to Sunifred, Duke of Hispalis."

Oppa's hand clenched hard on the wine cup. He felt cold dread squeeze his chest. "Fallen," he repeated, endeavouring to keep his voice even. "And my father?"

"Egica lives." Oppa was aware of Giscila watching him closely. "He is not yet beaten. Only a matter of days ago I came across a Spaniard who recently fled our beloved homeland. Now that his enemies have shown themselves, Egica turns south, razing everything between the northern border and Toletum. He rides to take back the capital, and he shows no mercy to those who betrayed him. The man I met had lent his support to Sunifred. He was forced to flee with no more than his wife, his children, and what he could carry." He met Oppa's eyes. "He believes Egica allowed Toletum to fall deliberately."

Oppa felt satisfaction curl in his stomach. "Yes," he mused. "That was always my father's plan, to lure our enemies into the open."

"And what do you plan?" Giscila looked at him. "Will you return?"

"I think I must."

"What will you do?"

"First," said Oppa, smiling faintly, "I will ride to Illiberis. I have men enough, I think, to take it, and I can buy more whilst here. Sebastopolis proved more lucrative than even I had imagined. After I exchange the Arabic coin I hold here in Carthage, I will have resources to rival those of my own father." He smiled at Giscila's shock. "And you, Uncle? Will you stay and drink in Carthage – or join me on my return?"

Giscila spat to one side and looked at Oppa with narrowed eyes, all trace of drunkenness gone. "I think, nephew," he said, "that it is time I went home."

Oppa nodded slowly, feeling excitement unfurl inside him. At last, he would return. He would take both Illiberis and Aurariola and, if Theudemir lived still, he held a parchment that would do it for him whilst also driving a sword between Theudemir and Lælia that could never be truly removed. If Theudemir of Aurariola dared return, he would live only by his, Oppa's, mercy and absolutely under his control. And control, Oppa would have.

Oppa was no longer dependent on his father's coin or goodwill. He had no need to bow to the Church unless it served his purpose. And if the Arabs came, he would be the man with whom they dealt.

I need never, Oppa thought with a savage satisfaction, *bow to anyone again.* He thought of Lælia's golden stare, her defiance in court. *We shall see,* he thought exultantly, *how defiant you are when your grandfather is dead, Theudemir is gone or condemned as traitor, and you face the might my coin can buy.* His mind was already busy plotting his conquest. Illiberis would have sent men to fight alongside Sunifred. Its defences would be weak and focused on the northern approaches.

They will not expect attack from the south or east, he thought, *and I will ensure none know we come until it is too late. If it must be taken by force, take it I can.*

He raised his cup, and Giscila met it with his own. "To Mater Spania," Giscila said.

"*Ja.*" Oppa smiled. "To going home."

53

ALARIC

JANUARY, AD 693

Toletum, Spania
Toledo, Spain

The plains were bitterly cold. Alaric and his men rode with hard rain in their faces and no sound but the dull thud of hooves and despair. They were too tired to talk, and too filled with what they had seen to wish to share it. Of the five thousand men Alaric had led north, barely five hundred remained. Of those, most were on foot and scattered now across the country, trying to find a way back to their own lands unmolested after their cause had been lost.

"They all knew you would have to ride hard in retreat if it came to it," Teudolfo said, riding close to him. "You cannot fear for them now, Alaric. We can only return to Toletum and hope to hold it."

"We cannot hold it," said Alaric bitterly. "Just as we couldn't hold Egica."

"Six battles in as many weeks!" said Teudolfo. "You held him longer than any could have expected – and the men love you for it, Alaric."

But Alaric couldn't talk. He didn't want to. He spurred his horse forward, his mind dull and blank, the faces of those he had lost running through his head. He thought of Rekiberga with the fierce bolt of longing that had both haunted and comforted him through the cold nights in the mud, the hard days of sword and tension. The memory of her blue eyes and auburn hair, the soft feel of her body and touch, ran through him like a lick of flame amidst the freezing dark of winter.

I must get her to safety, he thought. *I must go to her as soon as I can.* But then he thought of Toletum and of his father waiting for him, trying to hold the weakened capital with a force both unwilling and incapable of doing so. He turned to Teudolfo.

"As soon as we arrive," he said, "I want five of our most trusted men mounted on the best horseflesh we can find to ride for Hispalis. They must take Rekiberga south."

"We can ride ourselves," said Teudolfo, glancing sideways at him. "Are you sure this is a task you can entrust to another?"

"There is Toletum first," said Alaric grimly. "And then Illiberis. I cannot be in all three places. Two of them I am sworn to defend. One to my king, and the other to my brother."

"Lælia," Teudolfo guessed. Alaric nodded. "She defends Illiberis alone," he said. "And if – when – Toletum falls, holding Illiberis is our only chance if we are to escape to Septem. We knew it might come to this. I will not wait for it to be too late."

Toletum came into view through the grey cloud of rain, and they clattered beneath the horseshoe entrance, up the winding street to the palace on top of the hill. The wide, bronze-studded doors were thrown open and Alaric strode inside, trembling and weak legged.

Sunifred was there, his *gardingi* standing by him, their faces grim.

"Egica is coming," said Alaric without preamble. "We have no more than days."

THE CIRCUS HAD BEEN FORTIFIED to the fullest extent Suinthila and Paulus's combined efforts could make it so, the men guarding it organised into effective units. "But nothing can disguise the fact that we have four thousand men at best," Paulus told Sunifred grimly. The once mighty Duke of Hispalis was a shadow of the man Alaric had followed to war months earlier. His face was pinched and florid, his eyes restless, darting around the room uneasily.

"If you had not permitted men to ride south," Sunifred said fretfully, glaring at Paulus, "we might have had thousands more."

"I had to give them the choice. Those who left would have been more hindrance than help." Paulus dismissed Sunifred's protestations with a contempt that showed Alaric it was a conversation that had been had many times. "They would have run at the first chance they were given. Their lands and wives are in danger."

"All the more reason for them to stay here and fight in a united front!"

"When the war moves south," said Paulus coldly, "they will join us again."

"When!" Sunifred glared at him. "Is it any wonder they left, if their own thiufadi believe the battle lost already?" He turned to Alaric. "Tell me again the size of Egica's forces."

"His cavalry alone number over four thousand," Alaric said flatly. He did not attempt to hide his impatience. His diplomatic skills had fallen with a thousand good men into the dank mud on a rainy day near Vallisoletum, when he had watched them die in a single rush of Egica's mounted force. "Spear and sword are hard to guess at, but we faced five entire thiufae on the field at Vallisoletum, and that was not the entirety of his force."

"Were the thiufae at full strength?" asked Paulus.

Alaric nodded. "Every thiufa was the full thousand, trained and armed. Egica's force is no hurriedly arrayed militia. They have experience fighting on the northern borders against the Franks and the insurgents in the mountains. They are tough and skilled." An image passed in front of his mind of the southern forces, exhausted and starving, armed with the dull blades and crude weapons they had carried from home, cold and miserable in the freezing mud. "Our men didn't stand a chance," he muttered bitterly. His father put a warning hand on his shoulder. Alaric shook it off. "Your daughter," he said, staring hard at Sunifred. "What precautions have you taken for her safety?"

"I have good men holding Hispalis," Sunifred blustered. "Some of my best. It will not fall."

"Yes," said Alaric simply, holding his eyes, "it will."

"Then we will send more men!" Sunifred's eyes darted restlessly around the room. "We cannot lose Hispalis. My wife is there. My daughter."

"Your daughter will not be much longer there," said Alaric brutally. "I am sending my best men to Hispalis. They will take Rekiberga to Illiberis."

"You would make such decisions without consulting me!" Sunifred leaped to his feet, eyes flashing. "Do you forget who sits on the throne, boy?"

"Sitting on a throne," said Alaric evenly, "is not the same as ruling from one." A tense silence fell across the room. Alaric's hand hovered at his side, and he saw Sunifred's eyes slide to it. *He is scared,* he realised with contempt. *He speaks of men dying as if it is nothing – and yet he is scared.* He stared at Sunifred, then he turned away, looking at his father. "Abba," he said quietly. "Perhaps you might tell me news of our family."

He left the council with Paulus and Suinthila in a grim silence, feeling Sunifred's eyes at his back. They rode toward the circus where their men were encamped.

"Where are Elsuith and Egilona?" he asked his father, referring to his stepmother and sister.

Suinthila's mouth tightened. "Egica took Egilona. She is in Tuy, where Egica has his own son, Wittiza, along with Theodefred's son, Roderic, and Pelayo, the son of Favila. He leaves nothing to chance." His mouth tightened. "Elsuith is with child." Alaric started, but his father's face was grim enough to preclude any comment he might make. "It is too close to her time for Elsuith to leave Aurariola. And besides, she still hopes Egilona might be returned to her. I have left instructions that she leave by dromon should it come to it." The tired light in his eyes said all his brief words did not.

"I fear it will come to it," said Alaric heavily. "Egica was waiting for this moment. He has gathered men from the north and paid mercenaries from Frankia. He will not lose." He smiled a tired greeting at Laurentius, who rode in as they dismounted.

"Alaric." Laurentius's face was as grave as the rest. "Shukra and five men rode to Sunifred's villa half a moon hence. Shukra saw Rekiberga safely south before he returned here."

Alaric felt a wave of profound gratitude sweep over him. "I was about to send men of my own," he said, almost swaying with relief.

"It is not me you should thank, but your brother." Laurentius's face stretched into a grave smile. "He was most insistent that we make her safe," he said quietly. Alaric found, for a moment, that he had difficulty speaking.

"Is Athanagild safe?" he managed finally.

Laurentius's smile faded. "He remains with Sisebut," he said stiffly. "Who is increasingly worried he may have to stand beside Sunifred and answer to Egica."

Alaric frowned and glanced at his father. "If Toletum falls and Athanagild is found in the palace," he said, "he will be condemned as a traitor with Sisebut. He should ride now." He looked at Laurentius. "You both should," he said, slightly awkwardly.

Laurentius met his eyes evenly. "Liuvgoto and Cixilo remain at the monastery north of Toletum. So far, no less than three attempts have been made on their lives. They were not all done by Sunifred and the Church, which means Egica, too, would rather see her dead. I have mounted a permanent guard on their room. Athanagild brings news when he can. If it comes to it, we will both go to the monastery. We will not allow them to fall into Egica's hands, even if it means a fight."

"I thought you were set on maintaining neutrality?"

Laurentius smiled wryly. "I was." He saw the exhaustion in Alaric's face and put a hand on his shoulder. "You did all you could, Alaric. More. As much as any man could have done."

"It wasn't enough," said Alaric dully. "All those men – good men, men with families and homes – they followed me out of loyalty. To my father, to the memory of Geila. And I led them to a dismal death, and defeat." He shook his head. "You were right," he said, looking around at Paulus's and Suinthila's grim faces, "all of you. If I had listened to you from the beginning, Sunifred might never have ridden to war. Those men would live still. I was a fool," he said bitterly, staring at the hard ground. "An arrogant, ignorant fool who thought my voice could make a difference to a man who will listen to none but his own. That arrogance has cost lives. Lives I had no right to take."

"Alaric." Suinthila gripped his son by the upper arms. "Look at me," he commanded.

Alaric raised his eyes knowing that he must at last face his shame, accept responsibility for what his hubris had wrought. To his surprise, however, he found no censure in his father's face. Suinthila's expression was grim and worn, but his eyes were soft with an understanding that hurt Alaric's heart. "You followed a cause you believed in, and no man will ever fault you for that. It is Sunifred who is the fool, not you. And when such fools play politics," said Suinthila roughly, "good men die. Men who fight not for what they might gain, but for what is right. You were right, Alaric, in believing your brother alive and in suspecting Oppa's murderous intent. You, Athanagild, Lælia – you suspected the truth of it from the beginning." He glanced at Paulus. "You had faith where we faltered. Had we listened, acted earlier, we might perhaps have undone Egica's rule without any blood being spilt. Your cause was right." He met his son's eyes. "It is not your fault you did not have a better man to lead it." He lowered his head. Suinthila, Alaric realised with a shock, was ashamed of himself.

When Alaric would have spoken, his father gripped his arms with renewed force and shook his head. "You did not create this war, Alaric. It was made by men of my age, who forgot that a nation lives only so long as the men who walk its earth believe in it. I will die in this war, yes, and Paulus too. No – do not look at me like that; I have wielded my sword on too many fields not to know a killing ground when I see one. Ours will be a battle men will sing of down the ages, but it will be lost still, and all here know it." Alaric looked around at the gathered faces, saw Paulus nodding in grim agreement and Laurentius's face, grave and dark. None argued.

Alaric stared at his father, unable to speak. Suinthila released him. "You will ride from here long before Egica reaches the gates." Alaric would have objected, but there was that in his father's voice that forbade argument. "Ride for Illiberis," said Suinthila. "Hold it if you can. We will give you as much time as we can. With enough men and careful planning, it can perhaps be held, and the southern ports with it. If not, Alaric, go to Septem with Lælia. Find Theo again. But you must not die," said Suinthila roughly. "And I will not allow you to sacrifice yourself for an idea that I taught you to believe in, for a duty that was never yours, or your brothers', to uphold. You, Athanagild, Lælia – you can and will endure beyond this disaster. Live to see Theo once more. And when you do" – his voice cracked slightly and he gathered himself, going on – "tell him that I never lost faith in him. That I know him to be the best of men, as are all my sons. All of them." He glanced at Laurentius on the last words and the other man nodded.

"Either way, Alaric, the only thing I can truly ask of you all now is that you live, my son, according to your own moral ground, for it is a strong and unerring one. Leave the dream of Spania, and this farce of a war, to the old men who created it." His face tightened, a note of steel entering his voice. "If he must do it with my sword at his back, I will ensure that it is Sunifred who leads those he has condemned to death onto the field." He turned to look over the ground, the killer Alaric had never seen written in hard and unforgiving lines on his face. "And if God knows anything of justice," he murmured, "he will ensure Sunifred lives to watch every one of us die, and to suffer Egica's punishment."

54

OPPA

JANUARY, AD 693

Aurariola, Spania
Orihuela, Spain

"But I wish to see Spania."

Elpis's expression was petulant. Oppa's hand stroked his whip handle longingly. He regretted, not for the first time since sailing from Sebastopolis, the need to keep Elpis in perfect condition. Never had he longed to whip a whore more.

"And you will, my pet, I promise you. In time, you will not only see Spania. You will walk the corridors of its palace, in the finest gowns coin can buy." The gleam in Oppa's eye had nothing to do with the vision his words invoked and everything to do with the savage delight he would take in parading Theudemir's whore before the cowed figure of Lælia of Illiberis. "But, for now, you must stay aboard the dromon and out of sight. Once I know the villa ashore is safe, you may remain there until I return for you."

"Will you return?" Elpis clung to his arm, her expression suddenly fearful. "You will not abandon me as you did Pel–" She swallowed the rest of her sister's name, dropping her eyes from his suddenly hard face.

"We have had this discussion too many times." Oppa's voice was cold and clipped. "Your sister was killed in an attack I could not possibly have foreseen. It was an accident, no more." Tired of talking, he turned to look up at the steep cliffs that were the welcome to any arriving at the lands around Aurariola. "Stay hidden," he ordered as the cliffs came nearer. "I will send men for you when I know it is safe."

"This is hard country." Giscila eyed the cliffs with distaste. "A good place for an ambush." Thus far, Oppa thought, Giscila had proven himself a rather better travelling companion than expected. He asked few questions, showed little interest in anything other than coin, and did not blanch from even the most delicate of tasks.

"There will be no ambush." Oppa leaned his elbow on the bow and scrutinised the cliffs. "There will be none left here but old men collecting what harvest they can."

"You seem very certain."

"The scouts we sent tell me there is no force of significance." Oppa clapped Giscila's shoulder. "Although I do expect that those we sent further inland will bring different news. Here, though, we come for something rather more important than battle." He did not elaborate but turned to give commands to his men. They landed the horses and rode up over the cliffs, meeting no opposition. The barley grew tall in the fields, rippling beneath the sun.

"Rich, no?" Oppa saw Giscila's eyes widen as they passed through the endless fields of grain.

"These lands are unfamiliar to me," said Giscila, frowning. "Who holds them, and where is he?" No Goth was yet born who didn't covet his own crops, no matter his years an exile at sea.

Oppa's mouth smiled in a hard line. "These are the lands of Suinthila, Count of Aurariola."

Understanding dawned on Giscila's face. He spat to one side. "It seems the father does not possess his son's talent for survival. He is foolish to leave his coast so vulnerable."

"I think we may assume Suinthila has joined the rebellion against my father. He would think his lands safe from attack by sea." Oppa looked around with an assessing eye. "His treachery will mean this land is already forfeit to the Crown. I wish to discover if the women of his family are equally vulnerable. Suinthila, if I recall, has a daughter." He glanced at Giscila. "It is better to marry land than to take it, or to wait for a king's gift. Marriages are always more… final."

"Marriage?" Giscila could not hide his surprise.

"Oh, not mine." Oppa waved a careless hand. "I have other ambitions." He looked over the barley, then back at Giscila. "But you, Uncle – how would you like to plough fields such as these?"

Giscila didn't respond, but his eyes narrowed in calculation as they rode, widening as they approached the villa, set high on a hill overlooking the harbour, surrounded by thick walls. "It is grand, *ne?*" Oppa reined in his horse and frowned at the walls. "Shall we see what lies within?"

They rode between the tall, stone gate piles. The gates themselves were propped open in invitation. The trees along the approach were neatly kept, their fruit harvested, yet Oppa and his men rode into the courtyard without opposition. The villa stood silent and dark, and none responded to Oppa's calls.

Then an old man shuffled around the corner and stood on the portico, eyeing them warily. "*Swrs Reiks,*" he greeted them formally. Honoured King. It was an old term, one rarely heard in these times.

"Abba," replied Oppa respectfully. "I am Oppa, son of the king, and I require you to fetch your mistress."

The man bowed his head. "There are none such here," he said. "You may check for yourselves. The men of Aurariola have ridden to war, and their women have been taken to safety."

"Then these lands are forfeit to the Crown," said Oppa brusquely, "since I assume the men have not ridden to support my father in putting down this rebellion." The man bent his head in acquiescence but did not reply, staring stolidly at the ground. "Search it," Oppa ordered, and his men dismounted, weapons ready, and began to comb the villa's grounds. "Tell me," said Oppa conversationally. "Do all of Suinthila's sons ride to war at his side?"

"Alaric, the eldest, leads his father's men," replied the old man. "Athanagild, the younger, is a priest in Toletum."

"I thought," said Oppa, "that there were three sons?"

"Once, perhaps," said the old man. "But Theudemir went to sea in the emperor's fleet, and we have had no news of him these many years now."

"Ah." Oppa bowed his head. "That is sad indeed." He looked out over the fields, frowning as if in memory. "There was a daughter too, was there not?"

The man's face tightened. "Egilona," he said quietly.

"You are fond of her," said Oppa, watching him.

"I have known the child since her birth. Yes, I am fond of her."

Oppa swung down from his horse and approached him. He leaned in close, studying the old man's face. "Fond enough to protect her?" he asked softly. "To hide her, perhaps?"

The old man's face darkened. "Egica, the king, has taken Egilona to Tuy as companion to his only son."

Oppa's mouth tightened in annoyance. "My father is ever attentive to detail," he said lightly, but anger curdled his stomach. He did not like having his plans thwarted. "And the lady Elsuith?"

The rheumy eyes were surprisingly clear, a faint smile lurking on his mouth when the man answered. "Fráuja Suinthila wondered if perhaps someone may come asking such questions," he said. "He instructed me to tell you this: his wife is safe, in a place none can reach her."

Oppa stared at him. "Brave words," he said softly. "For a dead man."

"I was dead long before you sailed here, Oppa Egicason." The old man's eyes narrowed as Oppa called one of his men over and said something in his ear. The man mounted his horse and rode toward the coastline cliffs from where they had recently come, gesturing for a small party to follow him. "But that is where I have the advantage over you."

"Oh?" Oppa's mouth curled. "And why is that?"

"Because you, also, are a dead man." The old man smiled at him. "You just don't know it yet. You may take Aurariola. Its crops and oil belong to him who reaps them. But the land — the land belongs to the blood of Suintila, and whilst that blood lives still, Aurariola will never truly be yours."

Oppa's knife flashed in the sunlight. Blood sprayed through the air in a fine arc, and the old man fell to the stones, the last of his life leaching into the pale earth. Oppa stood in the hard sunlight, thinking.

"That may not have been wise." Giscila spat to one side. "How are we to find the woman if our only source of information is dead?"

"In Sebastopolis," said Oppa slowly, "I met many men who had fought alongside Theudemir of Aurariola. I paid for their wine, and I listened to them talk. There was one story they told, more often than any other. Do you know what that story was, Uncle?" Kneeling, he wiped his knife carefully on the grass.

"Of course I do not know it," said Giscila impatiently. "Enough of your games, nephew. Spit out what you mean to say."

"You lack subtlety, Uncle." Oppa's tone was mildly reproving. "But no matter. The story goes that Theudemir of Aurariola gained the attention of the mighty commander Apsimar very early in his training during a drill on the coast. Theudemir, it seemed, correctly predicted the location of the mock enemy force by identifying bat droppings amongst the rocks on the coastal cliff. He said, when asked, that in the cliffs where he played as a boy, such a large quantity of bat droppings signified a cave big enough to shelter many men." His eyes searched the barley fields restlessly. "Apsimar was so impressed by his powers of discernment that he promoted him soon after. Such stories become the stuff of legend. I heard the tale so many times I tired of it."

The men sent to search the villa came out, shaking their heads. "The woman isn't here," said Giscila, eyeing Oppa impatiently. "We can leave a handful of men to hold it if you will, but we should ride before news travels of our arrival. You can tell me these stories of yours as we ride."

"You miss the point, Uncle." A figure appeared in the distance, then another. As they gradually came closer, Oppa allowed himself a grim smile. "Those stories you so disdain are the key that unlocked the treasure I sought." Giscila swung around, his mouth slack with shock as he saw the woman held captive in front of the riders, red-haired with wide hazel eyes and a tearstained face. Her swollen belly rode before her.

"You found her," said Giscila, looking at Oppa with reluctant admiration.

"Of course I found her." Oppa's face was cold once more. "She was hiding in cliffs on the coast. I knew it as soon as the old man said she was safe somewhere we would never find her." He glanced at Giscila. "Know your enemy well," he said. "It is a lesson learned from my father."

"And now?" Giscila looked at the woman as she came closer. "What will you do with her?"

"I had intended to use mother and daughter as pieces in the game." Oppa eyed Elsuith's swollen belly. "Another son to Suinthila, though – that is one piece too many, I fear, for the game I have planned."

His sword flashed in the sun, the fine edge of steel lethal and sharp. Elsuith's eyes widened as it neared her. "Better, I think," said Oppa softly, "that both pieces are taken from the board." The steel slid across Elsuith's throat. Her eyes flared in shock, then faded as if part of her had known all along that there was only one outcome. Her hands covered her belly protectively, but as she slipped from the horse, Oppa's blade pierced the gap between her fingers, straight through the mound of her belly in an act of finality that made even his own men blanch.

"I do not like surprises," Oppa said, as her lifeless body fell atop that of the old man. "And I have my own plans for the lands around Aurariola." He nodded at the man who had recently captured Elsuith. "Secure the perimeter of these lands and bring the whore, Elpis, ashore. You will remain with her here until I send for you." He fixed the man with a hard gaze. "I expect to find her as untouched as I leave her. I do not care if she strips before you and begs to be taken – you will not do so. You will treat her as the most precious of your treasures. Should she be harmed, you will answer with your life." He looked around narrowly. "I will leave enough men to hold the lands should it be necessary, though I do not think it will. The men from here ride at their lord's side, against my father."

"I am surprised that you did not send Suinthila's woman to your father as a gift." Giscila eyed him curiously.

"Are you?" Oppa's eyes were flat and hard. "I am not entirely certain what I might find in Toletum. It is best, I think, that we hold some of the most valuable pieces and play them our own way, would you not agree, Uncle?"

Giscila eyed him with wary respect. "You play a hard game, nephew."

"Hard games," said Oppa, "are the only ones worth winning." On the horizon, a man was riding fast toward them, his horse lathered and weary. "Ah! One of our messengers returns already." Oppa frowned. "I wonder what he might know so soon?"

The man reined his horse in a cloud of dust. "Fráuja," he said, his face excited beneath the exhaustion, "I came upon some news and thought it best to bring it to you directly rather than continue."

"Well? What is it?"

"Egica rides south for Toletum. They say he is so certain it will fall that he sends men already to take Hispalis after it does," said the man. "But the man I met told me that Sunifred's daughter has made her escape from the city in the company of no more than a handful of men. Even now she rides south – for Illiberis."

Oppa felt a surge of excitement. "Take a party of twenty men who know the land between here and there," he ordered. "Ride hard. Make certain she does not arrive in Illiberis." He met Giscila's eyes. "It seems another valuable piece has been put into play."

Giscila smiled grimly. "It is a land of riches, this Spania." He spat.

"Indeed." Oppa turned his horse back toward the coast. "But more than that, Uncle. Do you know who is betrothed to marry Sunifred's daughter? No, of course you would not. It is another son of Aurariola. The heir, this time. It seems God has seen fit to put in our way the means not only to distract the man who would oppose my father but to torture him also. Our net may yet scoop up more than one fish when we arrive at Illiberis."

"And when will that be?" Giscila asked.

"For you, sooner than for me. You will head my force of men south and west, ahead of my father's army. You need take only the fortresses closest to Illiberis, and they are lightly defended, if our sources are true, and we have no reason to believe they are not. You will send word when you are ready to attack Illiberis itself."

"Send word where?" Giscila looked slightly confused.

Oppa's smile grew. "To your own dromons, Uncle. Mine will remain here, where it will be said I landed with them. I will take your rather less ostentatious force south to lie off the coast, just as you promised the young heiress to Illiberis you would. I shall await word from you both. When I receive yours, I shall send word to Lælia of Illiberis, if she has not seen fit to send for me first."

"Why would you do this?"

Oppa's smile faded, the hard light in his eye growing. "Because I would know what forces come to Illiberis's aid from the south. I would know what enemies we might face when this is done. And because Illiberis has never been taken from the north and, no matter what strength we have with us, never will be."

"Then why send me to do so?"

"You need only attack, Uncle. Not win. Hold them from the north, have them expend their defences in repelling you. I shall come from the south and do the rest. But" – he fixed Giscila with a stern eye – "they must know it is you who attack them. Everything rests on that. Ride at the forefront of your attack and be certain they see you." His face darkened. "Betrayal," he said softly, "is the greatest lure any trap can hold. Not only will Lælia of Illiberis face the man who murdered her parents; she will also face the man a part of her has begun to trust – one she will now understand was, all this time, allied with me and my family. And even if she somehow resists such heady bait, the men around her will not. Trust me, Uncle – if the men of Illiberis believe it is you who ride to take their lands, no force on earth will stop them throwing their might at your army, and certainly no young girl untried in battle."

"And this is good?"

"It is good, Uncle." Oppa could not stop the smile spreading across his face. "It is good, indeed."

55

ATHANAGILD

FEBRUARY, AD 693

Toletum, Spania
Toledo, Spain

From atop the city walls, Athanagild watched Egica's forces approach through the olive groves surrounding Toletum, their armour amongst the trees like a gleaming silver sea. "We are lost," he said bleakly.

Sisebut gripped his arm. "No. Toletum will fall, it is true." His eyes darted about like a trapped animal. "But I have made plans to ensure our safety." His body next to Athanagild's radiated a sick heat.

"We should be careful." Athanagild glanced around to hide his revulsion. "There are many eyes watching. Sunifred trusts no one, especially you, and especially now. He fears what will happen when Egica rides through those gates. He will not hesitate to condemn you to save himself."

"We will not be here when he comes." Sisebut's breath was sour with wine. "There are horses waiting for us below the city walls, by the river. I have found men who will guard us as far as the coast, where a dromon waits to take us to Rome. We can leave, Athanagild, with enough gold to begin another life. None will question two men of God fleeing a civil war."

"And leave our brothers in Christ to face Egica's retribution, alone?" Athanagild tried to hide his disgust. "Leave my own brother Alaric to die a traitor, alone?"

"There is nothing we can do now!" The colour had fled Sisebut's face. His fingers were like pincers in Athanagild's skin. "They are dead men, Athanagild. As we will be if we stay. No matter your uncle's influence. All know you are my clerk and part of Sunifred's council. You cannot escape their fate if you remain." He stepped closer, his eyes flat and hard, the hands on Athanagild's shoulders possessive now. "You are mine," he said, his voice soft and insidious. "We are bound by secrets that would destroy you if any knew them. Come with me, and I will ensure you want for nothing. In Rome we may live as we wish. Apart from the Church, maintaining a household of our own."

Below them came the sound of men and steel. Athanagild met Sisebut's eyes, forcing his own to give nothing away. "I will wait until the outcome is certain," he said. "When it is known, only then will I come. But we cannot be seen together. Do you know the pleasure house on the way from the city, the one by the river?"

Sisebut smiled coldly. "The one where you met the Persian?" His mouth twisted at Athanagild's face. "Of course I know it," he said contemptuously. "What do I care if you dally with the little heretic? I have always known you are mine, Athanagild. Now it will always be so." His hand cupped Athanagild's chin, not gently. "Do not cross me," he whispered. "If you betray me, you will be dead before the dawn. Do not think I cannot do this." His hand dropped away and his tone became soft once more. "I will meet you in the brothel by the river as soon as the city is known to be lost – and lost it will be. But be warned, Athanagild – your treachery will also be your death."

He spun away and disappeared into the night, leaving Athanagild gulping air, his heart racing with anger and tension. *I could have killed him,* he thought, his hand closing on the knife he had placed inside his robes. *Why did I not kill him?* Yet he knew, even as he asked the question, that he did not truly regret leaving Sisebut alive. *What does my faith mean if I take the life of a man of God?* He shook his head. "I cannot kill him," he muttered bitterly. "I cannot."

He heard a faint movement and spun around, his hand relaxing on the hilt when he saw who it was.

"No, Athanagild." Shukra's face was weary, tired in a way Athanagild could not recall seeing before. "You cannot kill, and I would not wish for you to do so. It is not good deeds for you, this."

Athanagild looked down at the men gathering beneath him and thought of his father's instructions to leave Toletum, and the battle, behind. "Nor can I leave my father to die alone."

"But you will, Athanagild. Laurentius thought you might feel this way. He sent me to ensure you do not die, against your father's wishes."

Athanagild stared down at the gathering battle. "I can't bear to think of him facing it alone."

"It is your father's choice. Just as it was yours to let Sisebut live."

"I should have killed him," Athanagild said bitterly.

"No. Sisebut you will be leaving to his own fate."

Athanagild, hearing the cold note in Shukra's voice, frowned. "Sisebut is a dangerous man."

"Danger!" Shukra curled his mouth. After a short pause, he spoke again. "The only danger I am in is of dying of boredom. Pah! For such a battle to be coming, and unable to do anything but watch it." As he spoke, a great crash echoed across the rock by the River Tagus, and the immense oaken doors of the fortress gate at the bridge splintered open beneath Egica's battering ram. "And now it begins," murmured Shukra, his face dark.

Paulus's men were readying their horses at the northern end of the circus. Suinthila held the southern end with those on foot.

Egica's bowmen thundered over the bridge, bows raised, splitting into wide lines that rode down upon the fragile defences of the circus. Their arrows flew at the men who stood on the flimsy scaffold on the circus walls, cutting them down with horrible precision. By the time the third line had fired their hand, those who remained on the scaffold were already reaching for sword and spear, anticipating the rush of horse at the walls. The cavalry rode for the weak opening at the southern end, where men had worked tirelessly for weeks shoring up the great gaps in the walls with earthworks and timber reinforcements. They barely held against the first wave of horse and began to crumble at the second.

Athanagild watched his father lead a charge over the wall and onto the field, sword held high, face hidden by an iron mask. Even from here, Athanagild could hear the roar of his battle rage, see the blind fury with which he faced the horde that rode against them.

Then the Illiberis horsemen came from the rear of the circus in a diamond-shaped arrowhead of retribution, Paulus riding at their fore. They crashed over the wooden stake barriers and into the oncoming cavalry, taking down horse and man in a deadly crush. From the walls of Toletum, bowmen rose and took aim, showering Egica's oncoming foot soldiers with an incessant rain of arrows that kept them from closing in on the circus itself.

Paulus's men had cut through the lines of horse and were now pincered between the oncoming foot soldiers and Egica's horsemen, meaning the bowmen on the Toletum ramparts could no longer fire at will. "Are we to simply stand here," said Athanagild tightly, "and watch them die?"

"There is still a chance," said Shukra, "if Sunifred can take Egica's horsemen."

The bulk of Egica's attacking cavalry fell between the volley of spears and arrows from the circus and walls and repeated attacks by Paulus's horsemen, who wheeled and regrouped with a lightning swiftness. They were Illiberis men, raised on horse, and moved with a dexterity that both confused and destabilised the attackers. They moved through the milling horsemen, cutting them down with ruthless speed, but they were hopelessly outnumbered, and even as Athanagild watched, the sheer bulk of Egica's forces began to overpower them. "He must hurry," murmured Shukra, gripping the wall as he looked at Sunifred's men huddling behind the circus wall. "He sends them in now or it is lost."

But despite Suinthila roaring for reinforcements as he hacked about him, Sunifred did not come. Athanagild saw him reach out and forcibly pull one of his thiufadi down beside him, gesturing for his men to maintain a defensive position. Finally, realising reinforcements would not come, Suinthila bellowed a command to retreat. Paulus's Illiberis horsemen covered the men as they scrambled behind the walls, many of their number falling as they held the defence. They fought until the last of Sunthila's men had retreated before racing behind them to take position on the crude walls. Egica's men approached warily, picking their way through the bodies littering the ground. Despite their number of fallen, they kept coming in an endless flow, until the sheer weight of their numbers became a river, then a torrent, against which the earthen circus walls had no chance of standing.

Athanagild watched the terrible sight until he saw the defences crumble and his father and Paulus fall beneath the dreadful rush of men. Shukra turned to Athanagild, his face dark. "Now," he said, "you must ride for the monastery and Laurentius. You can no longer be here."

Athanagild looked down at the blazing field, where the hordes of Egica's men now poured across the bridge. From the walls of the city, the southern forces were no longer even discernible amongst the might of Egica's numbers.

Athanagild turned away, dead inside.

"Ride." Shukra's cloak hid his face. "I will meet you there. But you must go, now."

"Yes." Athanagild's voice seemed to come from far away. "I will go."

He left the city by the lone northern road, his horse picking its way through olive groves littered with bodies. Night had fallen as battle raged. A dull moon showed blood in dark patterns on the olive leaves, but with the fighting having long moved south, the fields were strangely peaceful, so at odds with the destruction behind him it felt unnatural. Grief and guilt sat on Athanagild's heart, heavy as the low mist that covered the dead. He wondered why he should ride at all. He should have been on the field at his father's side, no matter the old warrior's instructions. He did not know where Alaric was, but he could not imagine any surviving that slaughter. He could not bear to think of it, nor of his own terrible failure to do anything of material help.

The olive trees had given way to holm oak, and he had turned toward the monastery, sick at heart, when horsemen barred his way. "I am a priest," Athanagild said dully, caring little if they killed him. "I have nothing of value for you."

"Except," said a familiar voice, muffled by a helmet, "a farewell, perhaps."

"Alaric!"

Athanagild tumbled from his horse and met his brother in a hard embrace, the ground soft beneath their feet as holm oak dripped overhead.

"I hoped to find you," said Alaric, his eyes searching his brother's face. "You are safe, then. Thank God you did as Father ordered – I was not sure you would. And Laurentius? Shukra?"

Athanagild nodded. "All safe. Laurentius is at the monastery with Liuvgoto, Shukra close behind me. We did as you ordered – as Father ordered." His mouth worked. "Though nothing has ever cost me so dear as to stand aside and watch it," he said roughly. "Nor left me more shamed."

Alaric gripped his shoulders. "We must honour their wishes, Athanagild, no matter the cost. It is the right thing," he said, his voice hoarse with pain. "You know it as well as I. This battle could never be won. Father knew it, as did Paulus. That is why they ordered us both to leave."

Athanagild swallowed, nodding. "And you?" he asked. "Where do you ride now, Alaric?"

"To Illiberis, for Rekiberga and Lælia. On Father's orders."

"He lives then?" Athanagild searched his brother's face, hungrily.

"He lived an hour ago. Now – I do not know." Alaric met his eyes. "I do not think it likely, Athanagild," he said quietly. Alaric glanced at the men behind him, then drew Athanagild aside. "I must trust Shukra's men got Rekiberga out of Hispalis," he said grimly, "for there is no time to ride there. Egica will not wait long after Toletum falls. He is hungry for vengeance and will give the south no time to rally. I must ride for Illiberis."

Athanagild gripped his brother's arm. "Lælia."

"I know," said Alaric harshly. "I remember our promise to Theo. I will see her safe."

Athanagild nodded. They embraced, hard and briefly, and mounted their horses.

"I will pray for you," said Athanagild.

Alaric turned to his horse. "Don't." His smile was ironic as he mounted. "I'm far beyond salvation, Athanagild, as well you know."

"Keep Lælia safe," said Athanagild again.

Alaric's mouth twisted. "What are brothers for?" For a moment they looked at one another, their eyes full of memories and of what could not be said. And then the brothers parted ways, riding in opposite directions.

Neither looked back, for there was nothing left to say.

56

LÆLIA

FEBRUARY, AD 693

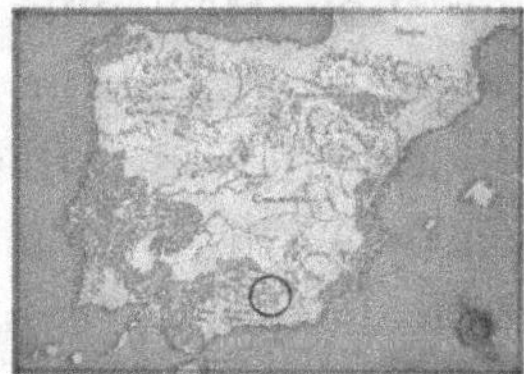

Illiberis, Spania
Granada, Spain

The Riders had landed at six different points on the coast, under cover of darkness and wearing the red tunics of the Karabisianoi. They were met by tribesmen who had spent the past months training Illiberis horse on the plains near Sexi, waiting for this moment. The Riders bundled the red tunics into their sleeping blankets, changed into their robes, and travelled through the night on mountain paths known only to the tribes, staying away from the eyes of those who would notice such things. They arrived at the villa three days later.

Lælia greeted the first detachment on a winter dawn, and her face broke into a smile. "Zdan," she said, greeting one of Dahiya's oldest and most trusted lieutenants. "I did not think Dahiya would spare so valuable a man to my cause."

Jadis gambolled happily about his feet. The scarred old warrior bent his head courteously, but there was a glimmer of humour in his eyes as he patted the cat's head and said, "With two hundred head of horse at stake, do you think she would entrust her Riders to anyone else?"

The men behind him chortled with laughter, and then they were crowding around Lælia, greeting her with the gleaming eyes and open smiles she had not realised she missed until she felt their warmth again. Zdan, she noticed, greeted Acantha with unfeigned affection, hand over his heart.

"We rode together," Acantha said by way of explanation when they had finished their greeting. Her smile, rarely seen, was wide and unaffected. "It is good to see a face from those times."

"Gratimo," Lælia said. Illiberis's aged thiufadis stepped forward, eyeing the newcomers warily. "This is Zdan." She introduced the Amazigh man. "Dahiya of the Jerawa considers him one of her finest Riders."

The two men, both hard and marked by war, eyed each other for a moment. "You and your men are welcome," said Gratimo stolidly, with barely an ounce of warmth.

"We are grateful," said Zdan, with a similar lack of enthusiasm.

Lælia exchanged glances with Tosius. The little tribesman rolled his eyes, and Lælia stifled a most undignified laugh. She suspected that half her battle might be won just in coercing the two old warriors to fight a common enemy rather than one another.

"And so it is not yet battle," said Zdan later that day as they rode out toward the hilltop fortress on their boundary. Jadis ran silently ahead, sniffing the air. Lælia had settled the Riders into the round huts of the tribesmen in the mountains around Illiberis. Such quarters would conceal their presence from casual visitors, but Lælia also suspected the Riders themselves would find more familiarity amongst the warm smiles and easy manners of the tribes than amidst the suspicious glances and superstition of the Illiberis men. Of the south the Illiberis men might be, but the sight of the dark-skinned Imazighen, faces swathed in cloth and speaking a foreign tongue, had turned most of them sullen and quiet. Placing the defence of the country they loved into the hands of those they had been raised to fear as pirates and barbarians went against their every instinct, no matter Lælia and Acantha's assurances that the men came to help.

"It is not yet battle, no." Lælia glanced sideways. "But we expect it to come any day now."

"Do you have messengers posted?"

Gratimo, on her other side, made a gruff sound. "Of course we do." He glared across Lælia. "If so much as a flag should raise between here and Toletum, we will know of it."

Zdan cleared his throat in a sound that managed to convey both acceptance and scepticism at the same time.

"On our voyage here," said Zdan, ignoring Gratimo's glowering expression, "we saw a dromon pulling south, from the east, close to the coast. I have seen this vessel before, many times, at port in Septem and drawn ashore near Carthage." He glanced at Lælia. "It belongs to the man who once called himself brother to a king."

"Giscila." Lælia nodded. "We met on my return journey from Septem. He offered me his help."

Both Zdan and Gratimo looked at her sharply.

"Sheath your steel," said Lælia genially. "It is not help I intend to take."

"I do not like such a man close to our shores." Gratimo spat to one side, his face dark, and touched the place where his eye had been lost during Giscila's long-ago attack on Illiberis. "Nor do I like that he came so close to you."

"He came aboard my vessel at my invitation," Lælia said. "I wished to discover what manner of game he would play."

"And did you make this discovery?" asked Zdan in his grave, quiet way.

"In part." Lælia frowned. "He wished me to believe he would protect Illiberis against Oppa's greed. From which I understood that he expects Oppa's return." She did not mention what Giscila had said of Theo fighting at Oppa's side. She did not yet know what truth was in it, and she was loath to plant so much as the seed of doubt in the minds of men who already had much to fear. "Then not a week ago," she went on, "Gratimo received word that a large force had landed to the north east – close to Aurariola."

"The messenger said the force landed and rode south without meeting any real resistance," said Gratimo grimly. "Suinthila has taken his men to Toletum, and there is no other lord along that coast with men enough to mount a significant defence."

Zdan frowned. "Where is this force now?"

"Riding south," said Lælia. "But so far they have not attacked any of the fortress holdings along the way, nor called upon the hospitality of the lords upon the road for shelter. They fly no standard, and if they come to fight for Egica, they do not ride north to join his forces." She looked at Zdan. "Do you think Giscila recognised you and your men as Riders when he passed you at sea?"

"We travelled with the Karabisianoi. Their dromons are a common sight in those waters, and my men wore rough red tunics that would pass from that distance. We did nothing to rouse suspicion, and Giscila's dromon showed no interest in our passing. I asked the rest of my men, but no other encountered him on their passage. I think he saw only us."

"We must hope so," said Lælia grimly. "Everything we do now relies on Egica, and Oppa if he comes, believing we are poorly defended." They came to the bridge, and she drew rein. "This," she said to Zdan, "is our last line of defence. If all else falls, it must be held if Illiberis is to stand."

Zdan nodded, studying the terrain around it through narrowed eyes. "It is not a terrible place to stand," he said.

Gratimo snorted derisively, then he caught Lælia's warning glance and held his tongue.

They rode on, up the steep track, to the fortress atop the hill. Zdan took in the tall wooden gates and the men busying themselves on the ramparts without comment. Gratimo's mouth twitched in a satisfied smile he did not quite succeed in hiding. They rode up the winding path to the fortress, and Zdan stared down the steep shale drop to the wide plain below. "This," he said, with open satisfaction, "can be held."

Gratimo sniffed. "I had thought to do more than simply hold it."

Zdan turned raised eyebrows to him. "If your men can hold it, old man," he said disdainfully, "mine will ride onto the plains and kill whatever enemies dare come at us."

Lælia interrupted before Gratimo could deliver the scathing rejoinder he was clearly preparing.

"I have no doubt," she said, "that between you, Illiberis will be well served. Tonight we will sit to meat and you will present to me your plans for defending the fortress. Now I will meet with Tosius and the tribes and discuss how best to defend the walls of Garnata. When we talk later, we will share our plans and decide the best course of action. Are we agreed?"

The two men gave reluctant nods, both as rigid as the granite walls surrounding them.

Smiling to herself, Lælia left them to bicker amongst themselves and rode down the slope, Tosius chuckling quietly at her side as they went.

Later that night, after a quiet meal eaten in the intimacy of the Illiberis kitchens rather than the grander surrounds of the œca, Lælia leaned forward and stared into the glowing coals of the fire in her grandfather's study. Zdan and Gratimo, their mutual animosity temporarily suspended in the afterglow of good meat, wine, and a day during which both had established to their satisfaction that the other was not entirely imbecilic, sat quietly at her side, whilst Acantha and Tosius sat at a short distance.

"Tosius," Lælia said to the little tribesman. "Tell the others what your friends in Sexi told you of the dromon Zdan saw."

Tosius bent his head. "The dromon at Sexi does not carry Giscila, brother to a king," he said, in the chirruping accents of the tribes. "It holds Oppa, bastard son of a king, and a thiufa of his men."

Zdan and Gratimo exchanged a startled glance. "How did you discover this so quickly?" Gratimo asked, frowning at Tosius, but it was Lælia who answered.

"My tribesmen have spent a year paying for eyes in every port on our part of the coast," she said. "When I sent men to meet Zdan, I also sent messengers to those ports. It did not take long to find the eyes that had seen Giscila's dromon resupply at a small port near Sexi, nor to discover that the man who had paid for the supplies was not Giscila, who is well enough known on those waters. What I did not know, until you told me where you saw the dromon, Zdan, is what game Oppa played."

"But now you do," said Gratimo, eyeing her with something akin to respect.

"Almost." Lælia's lips pursed. "I know he sent Giscila to offer me help. I know that he is now in Giscila's dromon, purporting to be him, by all accounts. I know that a large force has landed to the north east. And today, thanks to Zdan, I learned that Oppa sailed to the south from a north-easterly direction. Between those facts, I believe, it is easy enough to deduce that Oppa has sent a force, presumably under Giscila, to distract us with an attack from the north whilst waiting for the moment to attack us from the south."

"What do you suggest we do?" It was Acantha who asked the question.

Lælia looked at the expectant faces and smiled grimly. "I intend to do exactly what Giscila asked. I will send for help."

"And then ambush his forces on the road." Zdan nodded. "That is a good plan, *lalla.*"

"No," said Lælia. "I am going to let him come all the way to Illiberis." She stared into the fire, feeling its heat upon her face.

Gratimo stared at her in bewilderment. Zdan's eyes narrowed. When Acantha spoke, it was with exaggerated patience. "Might you then share with us what it is that you do plan, child?"

Lælia pushed her boot into the fire, sending a spray of sparks up into the chimney. "I will let Oppa commit every resource he has to capturing Illiberis," she said grimly. "And I will ensure he believes he has won. Only then will I defeat his army and take him captive."

"You do not intend to kill him," said Acantha, watching her.

"No." Lælia met her grandmother's eyes. "The Crown has played with Illiberis for long enough. It is time we took back their most valuable piece – and made the game our own."

57

SHUKRA

FEBRUARY, AD 693

Toletum, Spania
Toledo, Spain

The bathhouse was deserted, the whores gone to ground in places of their own hiding. With no candle to light it, the room was blacker than the darkest night. The air smelled dank and still, the warm perfume turned now to rot. Shukra waited, silently working the razor-sharp edge of the blade with his thumb. Never could he recall longing to use it more.

The sound of battle continued beyond the city. Egica's forces had not yet breached the walls, but Shukra had seen enough to know it would not be long now. He had waited until the outcome was certain, and desperate men would seize any chance they saw.

And Sisebut, as Toletum fell, was as desperate as any man could be. Shukra thumbed his blade, listening and waiting. The roar of battle had edged closer when he heard the more immediate sound of humanity in the room beyond. He tensed, taking his position at the rear of the bathhouse.

The door creaked open. "Athanagild," Sisebut whispered, his cowled figure peering blindly through the opening. "I am here. Where are you?"

Shukra moved forward, the hood hiding his face, no more than a dim shape in the blackness.

"Athanagild!" Sisebut did not attempt to hide his relief. He stepped forward, hands out eagerly. "We must run, and quickly. They breach the walls – soon there will be no escape." He squinted in the darkness, his plump figure quivering with uncertainty. "Athanagild?"

Shukra stepped out of the inky blackness and slipped the cowl from his head, dark eyes glowing like coals in his face. "Athanagild," he said in a lethal undertone, "will not be coming. He is busy protecting the two women you attempted to poison. I am afraid it is me you are fortunate to be meeting, my dear father in God." The silken caress of his words did nothing to hide the death in them. Sisebut shrank from the figure before him, turning blindly for the doorway, but Shukra was already there, his lithe figure closing the door, plunging them into pitch blackness. "You thought," he went on in the same low tone, "that you are owning the soul of the young man you corrupted. In your hubris, the unholy pride and arrogance sanctioned by that frock you hide behind, you are thinking Athanagild no more than a plaything, there for your own convenience – is it not so, Archbishop?"

He moved quickly, the blade silent and sharp through the blackness, drawing a searing line of fire across Sisebut's neck. The archbishop let out a shrill scream, clutching at a thin scratch that leaked small droplets of blood onto his fingers.

"Ah," said Shukra mockingly. "You fear the touch of my knife, is it so? I can understand. There is nothing more terrifying – no? – than that which comes at you in the darkness, when you cannot see nor protect yourself." Again the knife sliced the air. This time, droplets sprayed from Sisebut's face, and he whimpered, turning this way and that in an attempt to see where Shukra was. "And yet this is what you did," went on Shukra's low, merciless tone in the darkness. "You stalked an innocent through the darkest nights, causing his life

458

to be a nightmare of fear. You thought to implicate him in your foul schemes, asking him to be crutch and conspirator, lover and slave – whilst never once asking what you took from him." The knife came close to Sisebut's face, a threat, no more, and the archbishop threw up his hands in a blind defence, crying out.

"No!" said Sisebut shrilly. "Athanagild was never my slave, never forced! He loves me; he always has. He could have left me a thousand times and yet he never did. I forced nothing from the boy he did not want to give. You accuse me falsely, no doubt from your own jealousy!"

"My own jealousy?" Caught by surprise, Shukra paused, his knife held high. "You think," he said slowly, "that I come here to kill you because I am wanting Athanagild for myself?" The door cracked slightly open, and in the dim light he saw the mingled hatred and fear on Sisebut's face.

"I have seen the way you look at him!" Sisebut flung the words at him in the darkness with all the petulant fury of a thwarted lover. "He believes you friend, but I have seen it in you. I have seen the way you covet him, the elaborate lies you weave to win his confidence, the whoring and pretence. But God sees you, Persian or not, damned heretic that you are. God sees your corruption and your lies. He is not fooled – and nor am I." Sisebut stepped forward, mistaking the blank shock on Shukra's face for something else, shame, perhaps. He advanced upon Shukra with a finger pointed accusingly, his tone quavering and self-righteous. "You would bring me here by lies and scheming. Judge me, take my very life, no less, all so you can take Athanagild for yourself, take the body I have loved and protected, that even now I risk my own life to save. But I swear to you I will not allow it. Athanagild belongs to God, and to me. Those are bonds not easily broken by any normal man – and particularly not by a pagan heretic, corrupted by his own sick desires."

Shukra's expression had altered from one of shock to an uncharacteristic blind, unadulterated fury. All trace of the mercurial trickster was gone, replaced by the cold killer who had been torn as a child from a temple in Persia and forced to watch whilst the last great magus of his temple was burned in the same fires he had been raised to tend. The boy who had been tortured by those who would force adherence to a God of their own choosing loomed over Sisebut, his face as hard and terrifying as any avenging angel. "I was raised to do nothing to transgress the will of Ahura Mazda," he said coldly. "But I believe, in this instance, I am forced to be making an exception." For a moment they were face to face, the hatred between them as raw as lust.

Then the door behind him opened, and a lantern spilled light into the darkness. "The two of you will not add to your vile natures the sin of murder," came a cold, austere voice. "You will, however, face a council of your peers, Sisebut of Toletum – and the judgement of God Himself." Felix of Hispalis stepped into the room, his features dripping contempt as he eyed the two men before him. "I have seen many things in my life to cause me to question the morality of man," he said icily. "But never have I witnessed anything more despicable than two grown men squabbling between themselves for the right to defile the body of an innocent young man consigned to their care.

"One" – he glared at Sisebut – "entrusted with the transmission of God's own light to young minds, charged with the safekeeping and guidance of innocent souls. And the other" – he turned hard eyes to Shukra – "with the training of young men given by the best families in the land for the defence of her borders. And how do you both repay this trust?" Felix beckoned to the street beyond, and a string of armed men entered, brutally shackling Shukra and Sisebut so they were bound to each other, ankle and wrist. "You repay it by nigh on destroying a young man who has shown more bravery, integrity, and moral strength in his short life than either of you in your finest hours have dreamed of. And I" – Felix spat the last words with an icy fury – "intend to ensure you both hang for it."

He stared between them for a long moment.

"Well?" he ground out finally. "Do neither of you have anything to say?"

Sisebut hung limp on his shackles, his face down, defeat written in every inch of his slack frame. But Shukra met Felix's eyes. His own were full of a pain that made even Felix pause, and his mouth curled in an odd, twisted smile when he spoke.

"No, *aziz-am*," said Shukra quietly. "I have nothing to say in my defence – for every word you say is correct. I accept your punishment, and that of Ahura Mazda, the One who sees all and knows the truth that lies in the hearts of men – even when we, in our hubris, think ourselves above it."

58

YOSEF

FEBRUARY, AD 693

Septem, Mauretania
Ceuta, Morocco

The doors of Ilyan's Septem palace flew open, and Dahiya strode through. "Ilyan," she said.

"Let me guess," said Ilyan drily. "We must talk?"

She tilted her head to one side, a small smile playing around her mouth. "In fact," she said, "this time it is not I." She stood to one side and gestured behind her.

"Yosef!" Ilyan leaped to his feet, his customary detachment temporarily abandoned. His eyes shone as he took the steps down from his dais in three easy paces and came forward, his hands outstretched in unfeigned delight. "I had not thought to see you so soon. I did not... but never mind that now." He grasped the younger man's hands, his eyes roaming over Yosef's face. "You live. And you are here."

Yosef bowed his head. It was a strange thing, to be back in Septem, a reminder of a place and time that seemed so far removed he could barely remember the days he had lived here, nor the person he had been when he lived them.

"We have much to speak of." Ilyan waved him to cushions nearby. "Will you sit and take wine?"

"I will, Ilyan, but briefly, I fear. I confess I come only to bring you information. I sail, today, for Spania."

"Spania?" Ilyan sat back with a quizzical expression. "I might advise you to wait, my friend. For wine and a meal at the very least. Spania's fortunes are, at present, somewhat in the wind."

"I will leave you to talk," said Dahiya. "I have much to arrange, for young men, it seems, lack both patience and sense, and I must also stop in the market." The smile she exchanged with Ilyan was brief, but it seemed full of something Yosef could not quite read. "I will return shortly, Yosef."

"Wait." Dahiya paused but did not turn around. "The young men who are so impatient," Ilyan said mildly. "Do they have names?"

This time her smile was wide, the amber eyes dancing with a rare light. "They do," she said. "Two of them, in fact, bear my own name, are of my own blood. And the other is a name we both feared might never be heard again: Theudemir of Aurariola." Waiting just long enough to see wonder light his eyes, she left the room, the smile still curving her mouth.

"Clearly," Ilyan repeated as she left, "there is much I do not know." His customary insouciance was betrayed by a smile he could not hide, an almost savage excitement in his face. "But you return, Yosef ben Arun. A man grown. One with tales to tell, I have no doubt. The things you must have seen!" He shook his head, eyes gleaming, and for a moment Yosef glimpsed the man within the urbane shell of the diplomat. Ilyan, he suspected, dreamed of shores far from the complex ones he governed. "But tell me," Ilyan went on. "Did you achieve what you set out to do? Did you make it to Serica and discover the workings of silk?"

"I did." Yosef leaned forward. "The secrets of silk are nothing as we had thought," he said.

"Then you could not bring back the seeds of the tree?" Ilyan could not hide his disappointment.

"The tree itself is of small import, and easily managed." Yosef smiled faintly. "It is the worms that feed upon the trees themselves that are our business, Ilyan."

"Worms!" Ilyan shook his head in wonder. "But how?" He looked around. "And where are they? Do you carry them with you?"

"They are a delicate species," said Yosef, "and could not bear such a voyage. I had to decide between remaining with them in a climate where they could hatch and returning to Spania."

"And you chose to return?" Ilyan frowned. "I would have thought such a valuable resource one worth the sacrifice of time."

Yosef smiled. "I did not sacrifice them," he said. "The worms are best carried by a woman, close to her body. They require very specific care. It took me some time to find the right woman and a solution that would keep them safe."

"But you found such a solution," said Ilyan, looking at him curiously.

Yosef nodded. "I did." He gave Ilyan a small smile. "I believe you might be acquainted with the woman, Athanais?"

Ilyan's eyebrows lifted so high they almost disappeared into the wild shock of white hair. "The Persian! Of course I remember her. Quite the most outstanding of whisperers I have met, save Shukra, of course. This is a day of wonders indeed! But you do not mean to tell me you left the worms with Athanais?"

"I bought her safe passage on a dromon to Constantinople, where people already know her as a whore keeper, and where she will be one once more, for a year at least. There she will join the Jewish partners my father once traded with, experts themselves in cloth. There are those amongst them who know some, but not all, of the secrets of the silk tree, for the emperor himself has rooms beneath the palace where the fibre is produced in secret. The means of doing so is carefully guarded. Until now, there has been no other source of the fibre, no knowledge of the full process, and thus no way of weaving the cloth."

"But this will change that." Ilyan's eyes gleamed.

"Yes." Yosef smiled. "It will. When the season turns again, Athanais will sail west, bringing our precious cargo with her.

Mishaps notwithstanding, we will have our industry in the turn of a year."

"Silk," breathed Ilyan. "With the means to weave the cloth, we will have secured our future, Yosef, and that of your people. They need never live in fear again." His eyes darkened suddenly. "Nothing must happen to endanger this," he said. "I will send men to Athanais to ensure her safety." He was restless, already making mental plans.

"No," said Yosef. He stood up, placing the wine cup, barely touched, back on the table. "Athanais knows that the best way to move undetected from one place to the next is to be the wind, Ilyan, no more. When we set sail, the wind is caught. Let Athanais come to you. She will take what disguise she must, become who she must, in order to avoid detection."

Ilyan nodded slowly. His eyes on Yosef were curious as he stood up. "You are much changed, my young friend," he said. "And now you would return to Spania. I confess, I had not thought you would ever wish to land again upon those shores whilst Egica remained king." He shrugged. "Which, I suppose, he may not still be."

"It is not for myself that I sail," said Yosef. "There is nothing left for me in Spania. I know that. I will return to Septem before the turn of a moon, I imagine."

"Then why?"

"We stopped at Carthage on the way here." Yosef's face tightened. "It appears we missed the pleasure of Giscila's company by barely a day. He had just sailed – and with him, Oppa."

Ilyan's smile vanished. "That is not possible. Nobody passes my port without my knowledge."

"I believe they may not have passed it but landed on Spania's eastern coast instead." Yosef turned for the doors. "Which is why we sail, with the horses and men Dahiya has so kindly offered to provide, on the outgoing tide."

"I would not delay any help they may offer Illiberis," said Ilyan, "though I am sorry I do not welcome Theudemir of Aurariola to my court. I have heard much of him." Seeing that Yosef was preparing to leave, he put out a hand. "Since it appears your time here is short," he said, "might I suggest that you use it wisely? You may be right in believing that little awaits you in Spania. But a great deal has awaited your return to Septem."

He gave Yosef a small smile. "Some," he said, "you will learn of soon enough and, I hope, be glad to know. But there is other news that you should know of before you sail." He leaned forward. "The Jews of Garnata have been fleeing Spania in increasing numbers," he said. "However, they are not content to flee to peaceful exile." He smiled grimly. "It seems that Spania's Jews have decided that the time is ripe for them to fight for their rightful place in Spania."

Yosef felt his heart stutter, then begin to beat again, harder this time. "They mean to launch another rebellion," he breathed, barely daring to say the word.

Ilyan nodded slowly. "They are not yet ready," he said quietly. "And there is much that needs to happen before they will be. The current war in Spania will be done before they are ready. Most of all, they need a leader." He met Yosef's eyes. "One who knows both the threat they face on these shores and the enemies they face on Spania's. One whom they trust to lead them."

Yosef stared at him. "You cannot mean me," he said flatly. "I am no warrior, Ilyan."

Ilyan sat back and raised his eyebrows. "Are you not?" He shrugged. "This is not what I hear of you, Yosef. And at any rate, not all wars are won by warriors. Men with swords are easy to buy. It is the sense to lead them wisely that is the true commodity. And though I may know little of you, Yosef, this I do believe: you have sense enough both to lead an army and to manage whatever outcome it may face. Before you sail to Spania on this rescue mission of yours, I would have you know your life must yet serve another purpose." He smiled wryly. "So you do not too lightly throw it away."

Yosef turned the wine cup in his hand. "Once, I would have thrilled at the thought of my own people rising up against the Goths."

Ilyan looked at him closely. "But now you do not?"

"I have seen what war can do. And how easily it can be lost."

"Sometimes war is necessary."

"No, Ilyan." Yosef's voice was calm and clear. "War is never necessary. And I will not be the man who leads others into it."

"Spania cannot continue as it is, Yosef. Change must come."

"I am no longer certain," Yosef said quietly, "that my future lies in Spania."

"Ah." Ilyan leaned back, toying with his cup. "Well, perhaps this may change your mind."

Yosef frowned. "Time is short," he began, but as he spoke, the great doors swung open to admit Dahiya once more. Her face wore the same odd smile it had earlier. "There is someone," said Ilyan gently, "who has waited a long time for your return. And someone else who has been waiting to meet you."

Dahiya stepped aside, and Yosef felt his heart stop. Standing behind her, a tremulous smile hovering on her mouth and deep-brown eyes looking at him hesitantly, was a woman with a heart-shaped face and thick chestnut hair that hung just as he had seen in his dreams. Holding fast to her hand was a small, dark-haired boy, no more than four years old.

Ilyan rose from the cushions. "Sarah, my dear," he said, brushing her cheek with a light touch as he passed. Extending a hand to the child, he said gravely, "Arun, I believe I have not yet shown you my gardens. Would you like to walk with me?" Capturing the boy's hand in his own, Ilyan quietly closed the doors behind him.

"You have a child." Yosef's heart beat in a slow, thick pulse. He found his mouth was quite dry. His voice seemed to come from far away. "And after all you suffered, you gave him my father's name." The words seemed caught in his throat. "A letter came. I thought it was madness. But is it possible? Does my father...?" He stopped, unable to finish the sentence.

Sarah stepped hesitantly forward. "No man could survive such injuries," she said quietly. "But I was with your father when he died. He gave me the silk cloth and dictated a letter. He told me to bring them here, to Ilyan, who would ensure both letter and cloth reached you." She lowered her eyes. "After... what had happened, he worried you might never return if he did not send word."

"I thought I had nothing to return for." Yosef heard the question in his own voice but could do nothing to stop it.

Sarah nodded and looked away briefly, drawing a deep breath. "I told your father what happened to me at the hands of Oppa's men," she said, and now there was a note of strength in her voice. "That I knew myself to be carrying a child my parents would never accept. Your father told me that Yahweh would never shun a child born of such sin, nor the woman who carried it. But he suggested that it might be easier for both across the seas, where we were unknown." Her face softened. "It was he who gave me the coin to come to Septem, and the words to tell Ilyan."

"All this," said Yosef hoarsely, "you bore alone."

"Not alone, Yosef." She stepped forward as he stepped down from the dais, and then she was before him, so close he could smell the faint citron scent of her, so sweet and achingly familiar it twisted his heart so he could barely breathe. "You," she whispered. "You were there, through it all. I saw you in my dreams. The night Arun was born, it was you who held my hand. You have been there every day of my life since you left."

Yosef reached out a hand to her. Then he remembered Fei Hong, and the many forgotten faces along the miles he had travelled. He stepped away, the cloak of anonymity he had practised so long falling about him. "I am not the man you knew," he said quietly. "I am not Yosef anymore, Sarah. I have seen things, been things, you cannot imagine."

"And I?" She stepped closer, the defiant look back in her eyes, breaching the space he had placed between them. "My parents cast me from their house. I bore a child of rape, Yosef. I moved to a foreign land and made a life beyond everything I knew. Do you not think I, too, am changed?"

"I took a woman." Yosef forced himself to say the words. "More than one, Sarah."

"Do you think I care about that?" Reaching out, she touched his face. "I know my child is not yours," she whispered, "and that I am not the girl you left, nor perhaps as beautiful as the women you may have loved since. I do not expect you to feel for me what you once did, Yosef –"

But she did not get a chance to finish her sentence, for Yosef closed the last space between them and took her face in his hands. "I love you," he said fiercely. "I've loved you from the day I saw you and every day I have walked since. I loved you through countries where I forgot my God, and wars when I thought I would die. Through it all, Sarah." He stroked her face. "I do not care who fathered Arun," he said roughly. "He is mine, as are you, Sarah — and I will never let you go. Not ever again."

It was a long time later when Sarah stepped back from him, her eyes misty. "Yosef," she said. "I know you will come back to me. But now you must go with Theo. To Garnata."

"No." Yosef drew her close to him. "Theo will understand. I will not go, Sarah. Not now."

"Yes, Yosef." Her face was quietly determined. "You must. Not only for Theo and Lælia." Her hands closed on his shoulders. "Our people are waiting for you," she said softly. "They are ready, Yosef. As are the Jews of Septem. You will go not only to help the defence of Illiberis. Go to tell them that Ilyan will help them rise up."

Yosef felt his stomach tighten. "What do you mean, rise up?"

Sarah's eyes were intent and serious on his. "The time has come, Yosef. Our people will not suffer Egica's oppression any longer. We have swords, and the money to buy more. Garnata was ours long before the Goths came to Spania. It is time for us to take it back. We are ready, Yosef, and Spania is weak." Her face became animated, lit by an inner fire that Yosef had seen before in the faces of men who fought for a cause. Yosef had watched those men fight. He had watched them die.

"Sarah," he began.

"No, Yosef." She put a finger over his lips. "You think you are not ready to lead us, but you do not know what you mean to our people, what you represent. I have waited for you. We all have." Her face came up to his and her lips touched his own so Yosef groaned against her, wanting only to hold her close, to lose himself in the sweet comfort of her presence. She pulled away from him and held his face in her hands. "You are hope, Yosef," she said softly. "You are the hope we have held on to, and the leader we need."

Yosef felt the conviction in her eyes turn to dread in his soul. "Sarah," he began again, and again she cut him off.

"Do not say no yet," she whispered, her hands entwined about his neck. "Go with Theo. Meet with our people in Garnata. Let them see you. Then return and hear what we have to say. Will you do that, Yosef? Will you at least hear us?"

Yosef wanted to say no. Wanted to tell her he had seen enough of war, had learned all he needed to know of men and their causes. But then her arms came about him and his mouth found hers and he was lost in the scent and taste of her.

"Yes, Sarah," he found himself murmuring. "I will go, and I will listen." Yosef buried his face in her neck, trying to ignore the sound of Fei Hong's voice in his mind: *When we believe ourselves invincible, we become vulnerable.*

Beyond the window, the shore of Spania rose in a jagged line, and Yosef, looking at it, felt dread and anticipation war in his soul.

59

LÆLIA
FEBRUARY, AD 693

Illiberis, Spania
Granada, Spain

Jadis's low growl alerted Lælia a moment before Tosius's silent figure appeared before her. "We have visitors," he said.

"How many?" Jadis was on her feet now, tail swinging low behind her.

"Many." There was an odd note in Tosius's voice. He was smiling, which in itself was incongruous. There had been no word from Toletum. Despite the fact that Ipocobulcola, the small town to the north of Illiberis, was well fortified and held by allies, small parties had been testing their defences for days now. Every day they fought them off. It was not open battle. Not yet.

I will not run. It was a mental refrain Lælia repeated a hundred times a day, every time she heard the clash of steel or saw another man bleed and remembered that the decisions she made now would cost men their lives. It was not, she had long realised, the fear of losing her own that haunted her nights. It was the fear of watching those she had sworn to protect lose theirs.

"Many?" As she spoke, Lælia heard a faint rumble. Jadis was very still, quivering with tension, yellow eyes on her mistress. The rumble became more distinct. Hoofs clattered in the courtyard and Lælia sprang up, the arrow she had been sharpening falling to the floor as Jadis flew from her side in a swift, silent streak of gold. Lælia called out to her as she hurried along the colonnade and out to the portico. Mounted men milled about, covered in dirt, their faces drawn with exhaustion in the late afternoon light. It was only as one swung down from his horse to find himself almost knocked over by Jadis's flying form that Lælia tasted acid relief, sharp and sudden and untrustworthy.

"Alaric!" Jadis gambolled delightedly around his tall form. Lælia would have embraced him, but there was that in his face which gave her pause. Jadis, sensing his mood, dropped low and eyed him, tail swinging. He moved forward and gripped Lælia's arms, his mouth working.

"Rekiberga," he said urgently, eyes searching her face. "Shukra sent men to bring her here, but we found two of them dead on the road and no trace of her. Did she arrive?" Lælia felt a hollow ache in her stomach. She shook her head silently.

"Has there been word from Hispalis?" Alaric's question was directed at Gratimo. The older man grimaced and looked down, shaking his head. "We have not had word from Hispalis in more than a week," he said quietly.

"A week!" The last vestiges of colour drained from Alaric's face. "Shukra sent men a month ago. They should have long arrived here, or at least sent word."

Lælia felt her heart catch. "Hispalis is lost," she said. "That is all I know, and that only because a lone tribesman brought word to Tosius. The city is in flames, hundreds dead."

Alaric stared at her for a moment, then he strode to his horse and swung himself into the saddle. Behind him his men muttered uneasily. Teudolfo shook his head. "We cannot ride back that way," he said hoarsely. "Your men will die, and so will you. You're exhausted, Alaric. We all are."

"And Rekiberga is in danger," Alaric said tightly, shaking off the older man's hand. "I do not ask any to go with me. But I must go."

His eyes were hollow and desperate. "I must, Lælia – do you understand?"

"I do," Lælia said quietly, aching with sympathy. "Better than you might think. But you will change horses here and take food. You can be gone by midday tomorrow, and I will send men with you." Her hand on the reins stilled his horse. She held his eyes until he slid reluctantly off his horse, his legs trembling. Jadis butted his leg and Alaric put an unconscious hand on her head. Teudolfo shot Lælia a grateful glance and turned to give orders to the others. "How long has it been since you slept?" Lælia asked, leading Alaric inside.

"Days. I don't know." He rubbed a hand over the stubble on his face, eyes red rimmed and exhausted. She poured him wine and he drank it in a long swallow.

"Toletum?" she asked, though she already knew the answer.

"Gone." Lælia felt a long-forgotten hollowness within, the horrible awareness of loss. She reached out instinctively and Jadis was at her side, the sleek body warm and solid under her hand. She realised Acantha was standing nearby. She had not heard her grandmother enter.

"Paulus?" Acantha asked, her voice uncharacteristically rough.

"When I left, he and my father were leading the final defence." Alaric shook his head and dropped his eyes.

"But they lived still," said Lælia. "That is something."

"You are not a child, Lælia." There was a hard, desolate light in Acantha's eyes. "Even if they survived the battle," she said quietly, "they are still dead men."

Alaric did not answer, for there was no question in her words. He looked around the villa, as if seeing it for the first time. "You must go to Septem," he said. "Now, Lælia. While there is still time. We saw a significant force on our way here, had to ride across the mountains to avoid them. Clearly Egica has more allies in the south than we knew. There will be those amongst them who know this land well. They will know how to attack it." He met her eyes. "There are encampments in every direction," he said quietly. "And they are preparing to attack. You do not have the men for this fight, Lælia."

Lælia felt cold rage grip her. "I will not run from Egica," she said tightly, then, seeing Alaric's face darken, forced herself to smile. "We will hold Illiberis," she said. "The army you passed does not belong to Egica. It is bought with Oppa's coin and headed by Giscila – the man who killed our parents, Alaric." Seeing the blank shock on his face, she went on hurriedly, stumbling over her words in her attempt to explain. "I have been preparing for weeks. I have the men to hold Illiberis. If you did not see them, our ruse is working." Lælia had not yet shown the skirmishers her Riders. Everything, she knew, rested on the attackers believing she had barely enough men to hold the fortress. The Riders remained in the mountains, learning the secrets of this new land from the tribesmen. Briefly she explained their presence to Alaric. Unlike Gratimo and Zdan, however, who had come to grudging acceptance of her plans over recent weeks, Alaric's face did not relax into a smile but grew colder and harder as she went on.

"I told Theo I would keep you safe." Alaric rubbed a hand over his face, shaking his head. "No amount of men from the desert can protect you, or Illiberis, now, Lælia. You must go. Illiberis will fall. Whether now or when Egica sends the full force of his army, it will fall. You have not seen what I have. You cannot hold Illiberis against him, Lælia. And I will not stand by and watch you try." Jadis stood between them, tail swinging low. A tense standoff was broken by a movement at the door as Gratimo bent his head to a messenger. When he raised it, his eyes gleamed and he addressed Lælia.

"Oppa left his dromon yesterday," he said. "He is halfway to Illiberis now. And the messenger says the fortress at Ipocobulcola is under attack."

"He took the bait," breathed Lælia, staring at him. Gratimo nodded, his lips twisting in a rare smile.

"Yes," he said. "He did."

Alaric glared at Gratimo. "What bait?" he growled. "You were left to protect her, old man. Now is your last chance to do that. Ride south with her, over the mountain tracks where Oppa cannot follow. Get her to Septem before everything is lost. I must ride for Hispalis, try to find Rekiberga, and then I will follow."

"It is too late for you to ride to Hispalis, Alaric." Lælia heard the note of command in her voice and saw the moment Alaric, too, recognised it. He took a step back from her, eyeing her warily. "And it is too late for arguments," she continued. "If Ipocobulcola is under attack, we will face Giscila's army in a matter of hours. I am riding for the fortress now. You may come with me, if you wish, or stay here." She held his eyes. "Either way, Alaric," she said quietly, "I will stand, and so will Illiberis. If you ride with me, I will explain as we go. But I do not have time to stand here and debate it with you." Walking past him, she mounted her horse.

Alaric looked for a moment as if he might argue. Jadis growled. Acantha looked between her granddaughter and the cat. "We have no time for this, Alaric," she said brusquely. "My granddaughter has given her orders."

Swallowing his protests, Alaric mounted his horse and gave Lælia a wry smile. "Then I suppose you had better tell me of these plans of yours," he said.

She and Alaric rode out together, Acantha ahead and Jadis running at Lælia's side. Alaric's men followed at a tired pace, some struggling to stay mounted in their fatigue.

"Tell me what happened in Toletum," she said. As they crossed the serried fields of olive trees, Alaric described what he had seen of the battle. Acantha, ahead of them, was listening, Lælia knew, but her grandmother's stiff-backed silence precluded comfort or conversation. Lælia heard Alaric's words as if from a distance. That Paulus could be dead seemed impossible to her. Her grandfather rode beside her always, his acerbic voice a constant companion in her thoughts. She listened but did not hear until finally Alaric ceased his account. After a short silence he turned to her.

"You have left only a handful of men to hold the villa, all of them old."

Lælia nodded. "Oppa knows that if we are forced to retreat to the villa, all is lost. It cannot be defended, and it makes no sense to waste men trying to do so. He must believe we throw all our resources at the army to the north."

"But you do not," Alaric guessed.

"No." Lælia did not smile. "Part of our force is hidden in the valleys around Garnata and inside the settlement. Giscila has sent a detachment to attack that approach. He will try to take the walls, which appear sparsely guarded, as they would if I had only the Illiberis thiufa to work with. The men I have left there will easily defeat Giscila's forces – none will enter Illiberis from the east. From the west, men must first take the fortress, which can only be done from the northern side, and that is where Giscila has focused his forces. Giscila will try to take the fortress." She looked at Alaric. "We will let Oppa think he has succeeded."

"Do you plan on sending word to Oppa yourself of this?" Alaric asked, not attempting to hide the derision in his tone.

"Oh," said Lælia lightly, "I have already done so. Oppa has been masquerading as Giscila, who very recently offered me his help, should I need it, to defend Illiberis. Giscila assured me he wished to make reparation for the murder of my parents." She met Alaric's eyes. "I sent a message three days ago holding him to his offer and begging for his assistance. I told him our cause was most likely lost – and that if he could not bring the men to defend Illiberis, I would need his help to escape to Septem." She smiled grimly. "According to the tribesmen hidden along the road between here and Sexi, Oppa left the same day, with no more than ten men, looking to any curious eyes to be Giscila riding valiantly to my rescue as requested."

Alaric stared at her. "Oppa is no fool," he said slowly. "Surely he knows that Giscila is the last person from whom you would seek help."

Lælia felt her smile fade. "When I met Giscila," she said, "he told me that Oppa and Theo fought side by side. Were even, perhaps, allied. He suggested that Illiberis might be the price of that alliance."

Alaric made a furious noise.

"In my message to Giscila," Lælia said quietly, "I said that I had been traded once – in marriage – but that my time amongst the desert tribes had shown me there was another way. I said that I intended to go to Dahiya and take back Illiberis on my own terms if I must. I said that I did not believe Theo had betrayed me, but that I would not wait helplessly for Oppa to play another of his games, and would seek Theo, and the truth, myself." She met Alaric's eyes. "And I told him that I had kept two hundred horses in Sexi for the past year as a gift for Dahiya, to ensure her help, should this moment ever come."

"Oppa will check that claim."

"And when he does, he will discover that for the past year, two hundred Illiberis horse have been grazing on the plains near Sexi. My tribesmen have made very certain they were well observed and that all knew the horses were recently transported, on dromons of the Karabisianoi, to Septem. Dromons Oppa himself saw as he sailed south."

"You have been planning this." Alaric was looking at her with an expression of mingled respect and wariness. "How long, exactly, have you been planning this, Lælia?"

Up ahead, the bridge was coming into sight.

"Since the day I realised that even if Theo does come back, I cannot be simply the woman who stands at his side." Lælia met his gaze steadily. "I am the last heiress of Illiberis, Alaric. This land is my birthright and my responsibility. I will defend it – or I will die doing so."

ALARIC and his men were exhausted; they had barely eaten, let alone slept, during the long ride south. As the afternoon turned to dusk and nothing happened, even Alaric, eyes burning, finally collapsed into noiseless slumber. Lælia watched over him throughout the night, her mind going over every line of the Illiberis boundary. Tosius crept to her side close to dawn. The little tribesman had a face gnarled and lined as old oak, and he arrived unseen even by Lælia's own men. "My people sent word that Ipocobulcola has fallen," he said. "Now they approach." He looked at her, eyes gleaming. "Gratimo sends word that already they come for Garnata. He will not fail you."

"And Zdan?"

Tosius grinned. "The desert man is ready. He will await your signal."

Lælia nodded and settled back against the stone. She was stiff and cold, the night chill creeping through her bones. Spring was yet to break, and over the valley the moon gleamed on snow-covered peaks, the mountains a ghostly wreath floating in the night sky. Jadis prowled the hillfort, growling low in her throat. Lælia touched her as she passed, as if she were a talisman. Her tail was straight out, uneasy, golden eyes darting this way and that. She pushed herself against Lælia's side and stared up at her, unblinking.

After a moment, Tosius said, "They are many, *dauhter*."

"Many?" Lælia asked, frowning. "I thought we knew their number."

Tosius shook his head. "There are more than we knew." He held up one finger. Then he slowly unfurled another two.

Three hundred men? Lælia felt her stomach drop away. She had known it was a large force. But even still, she had hoped for less. "Are you sure?" Tosius nodded sombrely. "And those who approach Garnata?"

He held up one finger. Lælia tried not to show her concern. Another hundred. Giscila must have had men hidden in places even she did not know.

"How far away are they?"

"They will reach us before dawn breaks."

"We must hope Gratimo holds to the east," said Lælia quietly. "It is too late to send him aid."

Dawn was glimmering grey pearl on the horizon, still a way off. The morning was overcast and still, the air stale. It felt like a day of death, and suddenly Lælia was impatient to have it over. She shook Alaric and he came awake with the exhausted alertness of those who have lived on a cliff edge for too long. "Ipocobulcola has fallen," she said.

He nodded slowly, his eyes on her face. "Your Riders will meet them on the plains, then."

"No." She heard the hard edge to her voice and tried to soften it. "Not yet. I cannot risk showing them, not until Giscila has committed his entire force. Oppa will have eyes on this battle. He must believe us defeated and that I fall back to Illiberis. For now, we fight as if there were no more than the Illiberis men to defend the hillfort. Zdan will not ride until he sees my signal."

She saw Alaric search for words, the grim line of his mouth working. "Before I left Toletum," he said finally, "Father's last words to me were to tell me I should live – and you too, Lælia. To find Theo and together create a new world, not die for the old one. He believed Spania a lost dream. At the time, I agreed to obey. But now, you are making yourself bait to trap Oppa, and Rekiberga –" He broke off, unable to finish the sentence.

Jadis growled, butting Alaric. He gave a half smile and put his hand on her head. "Shukra said he saw Rekiberga safe on the road south, and I would trust that little devil with my life. He said his best men accompanied her. I do not believe her lost yet – I cannot." He shook his head, as if clearing it from the image. "I must believe she will yet come. And even if I am to be hanged as a traitor, I will not leave Spania without her, just as you would not if Theo were here."

Lælia could not argue that. She knew it to be true.

He smiled grimly at her. "I will fight with you, Lælia. But you must promise me that if this day does not go well, you will leave Spania. Promise me you will. Find Theo. And when you do, tell him that all of us – Athanagild, my father, and I – we never lost faith. We never forgot him." Lælia's chest clenched with a tight, hard pain. She nodded, unable to speak.

"Alaric!" They swung around at the urgency in Teudolfo's tone. He pulled Alaric to his feet, thrusting him toward the ramparts. Lælia followed, Acantha at her side.

"*Xristus y Marja!*" Alaric had paled more than his friend. His hands gripped the stone before him, his body quivering.

Below, on the plains, a horse streaked down from the far ridge and into the wide sweep of the valley, racing across the plain. Astride it was a girl with long, flaming auburn hair, lit by the distant red ball of the rising sun. She rode hard, glancing behind her as she leaned forward, urging her exhausted mount onward.

Rekiberga.

She was accompanied by three horsemen. They rode with bows raised, aiming behind them, shooting even as they urged their shattered mounts forward. A handful of men rode close behind them, and in the distance a smudge on the ridge rippled, then coalesced to become a thick, black line of men, which broke and began charging down the valley after their leader. There was something oddly familiar about him. Lælia squinted into the pale dawn, trying to make out his face. Behind him she heard Alaric curse and then he was gone, running for his horse, roaring at men to open the gates.

"He can't!" Lælia turned to Teudolfo. "He will die down there."

"And if he lives, and she does not," Teudolfo said grimly, "what then?"

Lælia would have answered, but Alaric was already mounted, ignoring the winding path as he raced his horse directly down the uneven ground. The men at the gates turned fear-filled faces toward Lælia. The gates, they all knew, must be held until it was time for them to be opened. *We cannot risk allowing that force to pass,* she thought, hating herself for even the consideration.

"Do it!" Lælia commanded, her voice seeming to come from a distance. Around her, men muttered uneasily, their eyes moving from the slowly opening gates to the army riding inexorably toward them. They were less than thirty facing three hundred, and though they knew Zdan waited for their signal, it mattered little in the face of such a force.

"Notch!" Teudolfo yelled at the men on the ramparts, his face white and drawn. "Draw!" The archers on the ramparts aimed down the hill. Alaric burst through the gates, riding like fury. "Release!"

The arrows flew in a rush of wind, falling aimlessly to the earth just shy of the oncoming army. Alaric reached Rekiberga and wheeled his horse to chase at her heels, firing behind them as their pursuers them closed in. An arrow took one of Rekiberga's guards in the back, and he fell in a tumble of hooves and iron beneath the attackers, one reaching down to slice his head from his shoulders as they passed. The couple raced across the ground, nearing the cliff and the shelter of the bowmen above. Lælia ran around the wall, her eyes never leaving Alaric and Rekiberga.

They are not close enough to make the gates.

For a moment she considered sending the signal to Zdan, but she knew it was too early for his attack, that Giscila could yet turn back and their surprise be lost. Even for Alaric she could not do it, and the knowledge sickened her.

Lælia could see Rekiberga's face, white and set, turned up

toward them, Alaric's lit with blazing triumph behind her, mouth open, exhorting her onward as they rounded the western hillside.

Then a spear appeared through Alaric's neck, and his eyes went wide in shock. Jadis yowled, a pained, unearthly shriek that rang across the valley.

Rekiberga's horse faltered. She pulled it around, fighting its headlong rush for the gates, her eyes on Alaric, her mouth open in a primal scream that ripped the morning as he toppled from his horse to the ground. Rekiberga's two remaining guards spun their horses and drew steel, their faces grim as they faced the onslaught, yelling in vain at her to ride for the gates.

It was then that Lælia recognised the dark features and hooded eyes of the man who rode toward Rekiberga.

Giscila.

Beside her, Acantha made a low, furious noise.

"No!" Lælia lunged to hold her, but Acantha was already swinging onto her horse. Lælia met her eyes and saw in them the ancient grief her grandmother had always kept hidden, the ghost of vengeance never taken. Lælia heard Dahiya's voice in her mind, speaking of Acantha, and the death of Lælia's parents: *It is she who sees Giscila's face in her dreams … the pain of their loss is your grandmother's revenge to take, not yours.*

Time slowed. "I must," said Acantha simply, and Lælia knew, deep in her soul, that the decision was made.

The world snapped back into focus. Acantha did not ride for the gates. She rode directly for the ramparts where Lælia stood, putting her horse at the wall at a gallop. It was not a high wall, only four feet, made of earth and stone. But the slope on the other side was deadly, a mercilessly steep slide of shale and rock. As men watched in blank astonishment, Acantha's horse cleared the wall, seeming to fly for an endless time through the air, hurtling toward an impossible landing. For a moment every breath on the hillfort was held, as it seemed certain she must tumble or the horse miss a stride. But it was an Illiberis horse, long accustomed to the mountains, and it found its feet, landing at a deadly angle, Acantha's body jolted forward. Then she found her seat.

In a rush of stone and crumbling earth, the horse took the slope in headlong strides, hurtling down the deathly fall as the onlookers on the ramparts stared in awestruck silence. Acantha and the horse flowed like a waterfall down the slope, a poetry of horse and body so closely joined it was impossible to tell where one finished and the other began. As the horse took a final leap from the slope to the plain, Acantha reached for her bow and raised it, measuring the distance between the oncoming attackers and the girl bent over Alaric's fallen body on the plains below.

"My lady," said one of her men urgently. "Give the order to close the gates."

"Not yet." Lælia clutched the wall, her voice rough with tension.

Lælia saw the moment Giscila recognised Acantha. His horse faltered momentarily, his eyes widening in shock. Acantha shrieked her rage, a bloodcurdling sound of raw fury that cut the air and seemed to silence the day around them. Then Acantha's arrows flew through the air, each of the five in her hand taking the men around the leader, toppling them to the ground, the final one taking Giscila through the shoulder. He slumped forward on his horse as Acantha wheeled her own and took the remaining guards with two arrows, swiftly notched. She swung back past Giscila and turned, forcing his horse to a halt. He faced her, his expression clearly visible to the watchers on the wall, shock changing to resignation as she drew her sword. The steel glittered in the early-morning sun as Acantha raised it. With a savage cry she brought it across his neck with the full weight of her arm, severing his head clean from his shoulders. His body slid to one side and fell to the earth and his head rolled away, the dark eyes closed forever. Behind him the cavalry bore inexorably down.

REKIBERGA HAD DISMOUNTED. She was desperately trying to pull Alaric's inert body onto the horse when it took fright and fled, reins flapping, from the oncoming force.

"My lady!" the guard beside her pleaded. Lælia made a harsh sound.

Acantha spun her own horse and reached Rekiberga when the cavalry were barely a hundred yards away. Leaping to the ground, she glanced down at Alaric's body, and even from a distance, Lælia knew it was too late to save him. Acantha pushed Rekiberga onto her horse, standing astride Alaric's prone figure. "Go!" Lælia saw Acantha shout at Rekiberga. "Go!" She slapped the horse's quarters, sending the Illiberis mount home.

"Close the gates!" Lælia's hoarse cry broke the morning and the tall gates began to close even as she clutched the wall convulsively, unable to look away from the scene below. Rekiberga bent low and urged the horse forward, her face white and stricken as she raced for the wooden gates that were already beginning to close.

Acantha turned to face the oncoming army, raising her bow. "Stand!" she screamed at Rekiberga's remaining guards as the rumble of the coming horsemen shook the ground. "You will stand!" The guards, white faced, drew their arrows beside her, three small insignificant figures standing before a tidal wave of men, firing into the onslaught and drawing again.

Rekiberga slid through the gates a moment before they slammed shut, leaving Acantha sealed beyond the walls, the army too close to run from.

Lælia stared at Acantha standing over Alaric's fallen body, her heart clenched with pain. Acantha glanced up to where Lælia stood, her face strangely calm. Her eyes found Lælia's. She smiled. The rising sun lit her face and for a moment it seemed to Lælia that her grandmother flamed like a fallen star against the grey dawn; then Acantha turned to face the solid wall of oncoming spears barely ten paces from where she stood.

Lælia remembered Dahiya's long-ago words: *There is a time for action, and when it comes, you will know there is no choice.* Lælia raised her bow, notched a flaming arrow, and took aim. Jadis howled, a long, anguished shriek of pain and loss. *In that moment, blood will spill — and you may find you wish, very much, it had not.*

The arrow seared through the air, signalling Zdan in the mountains above, and took Acantha from behind, straight through the heart. The tall, graceful figure coiled to the ground, one last arrow flying from her hand as she did. Jadis's shriek died in a gargled cry, and the cat lowered her head.

Then the cavalry were upon the hillside, and Alaric and Acantha's bodies disappeared, pounded into the earth beneath a frenzy of hooves.

Lælia stared numbly at the place where Acantha and Alaric had stood. Teudolfo, grey faced and desolate, stood beside her. "Why?" he said roughly. "Why did you do that?"

"Because she had already chosen it." Lælia's voice seemed to belong to someone else. "And because it is what I would have chosen." Jadis growled softly, butting Lælia's leg. "I am sorry," she said softly, knowing how insignificant it sounded.

"I must take Rekiberga," Teudolfo said hoarsely. "I promised Alaric I would see her safe. She cannot stay here. And nor should you."

Behind him, Rekiberga rode into view, grief turning the beautiful features into desolate, carved marble. She met Lælia's eyes.

"Do not wait," she said, her tone brittle and hard. "They are not Egica's men beyond your walls."

"I know." Lælia gripped Rekiberga's hand, a quick gesture that said what she could not. "They are Oppa's."

Rekiberga nodded. "Do not let them win."

"I won't." They stared at each other for a moment. Rekiberga nodded, a small, painful gesture that hurt Lælia's heart, and then she turned and rode away behind Teudolfo, down the winding path toward the river.

Lælia heard the thunder of hooves and turned back to the men at the walls, trying not to look at the place below where Alaric's and her grandmother's bodies had disappeared.

Then, from the steep mountain cliffs to the west, a lone mounted figure erupted, then another, and then Zdan's Riders were pouring down the hillside and onto the plain, breaking into the deadly concentric circles that had beaten armies from Carthage to Septem. Even though she had watched it many times in training, still Lælia stood awestruck at the terrible power of the Riders as they bore down on the attackers in a relentless hail of arrows, moving so fast and with such ferocity that they had almost reached the base of the hillside fort before Giscila's force realised what had come for them.

The Riders herded Giscila's army toward the hillfort, shooting down any who fled, thinning the ranks rapidly so that by the time the force found itself trapped against the gates, barely one hundred of their original number remained. Then the Riders set upon them with spear and sword, whilst from above, Lælia and her men loosed arrow after arrow. Amidst the clamour of battle she found an odd calm in the methodical task. The men below tried to escape the pincer in which they were caught, throwing their horses at the steep slope toward the fortress, none making it more than a few strides before falling from spear or arrow. Their bodies made a natural obstacle at the bottom of the slope over which coming men must climb. Lælia loosed her arrows, picking off those who attempted it. The sounds of battle seemed to come through a fog. All Lælia could see was Acantha's face and Giscila's dark eyes, one coming over the other. She felt empty, nothing but cold hatred and the arrows between her fingers.

Tosius appeared at her side, his face streaked with gore. "Open the gates," she said to him tersely. "We need to return before Oppa reaches the villa."

"Yes, my lady," he said, his eyes sombre.

My lady. Acantha was dead, and she was the Lady of Illiberis now.

The man at her side nodded at the thick wall of Zdan's Riders herding the remaining men toward the gates. "We have them now. Once they're through the gates they'll not go anywhere." He shook his head. "I've never seen the like of those Riders," he said. "Nothing could stand against such power. Nothing." He looked at her. "We'll make certain none escape from here, my lady."

"I know you will." Lælia gripped his arm briefly.

He cleared his throat. "And I'll send men for your grandmother and Alaric. We'll not let them lie there in the dirt."

"*Awiliudo pus*," she said simply. Thank you.

Lælia waited until the gates were opened and the last of the miserable captives had been brought inside the fortress walls. She took one last look at Acantha's and Alaric's crumpled bodies, one still shielding the other. Then she turned away and rode for Illiberis, Jadis running swiftly at her side.

· · ·

485

On the plains barely miles from the chaos of the hillfort, the silence was broken only by occasional birdsong. Lælia moved through the morning as if she swam underwater, Tosius silent beside her. The world felt still and dead, as if the air were torn.

They dismounted half a mile before the villa, approaching from the drill ground below the olive groves, staying low to the earth, alert to every sound. As they came close, strange horsemen entered the courtyard, hoofbeats echoing loudly from the stone. Lælia glanced at Tosius, nodding to the rear, and he was gone, slipping silently around the villa to the east. She made a low gesture and Jadis streaked across the courtyard, silent and unseen, pulling one man from his horse and breaking his neck before the cat disappeared into hiding. Lælia gripped her knife and bow, inhaling deeply, steadying herself. She crouched beyond the wall and peered through a gap in the stone. It was a good hiding place to observe the courtyard, wide enough to shoot an arrow through if she needed to.

They wore chain mail over leathers and tunics rather than the cross-laced trousers favoured by the Gothic forces. The front rider raised his helmet. His eyes were heavy lidded and dark, taking in every detail of the villa with cool calculation, and Lælia felt the sick jolt of recognition.

Oppa.

Lælia's hand tightened on her knife. She glanced at where Tosius had disappeared. Gratimo should have been back here by now, in place, ready to surround Oppa. That she couldn't see him sent cold dread into her heart. She knew that it was too late now to change course.

Oppa ignored his men's questions as he looked around, then swung lightly from the saddle and landed with the silent fluidity of a serpent, despite the heavy mail. Although still a young man, there was a sharpness to Oppa's features that gave him the appearance of being older, and men watched him warily. "Search the villa," he ordered curtly. Oppa's men spread out, creeping silently through the empty breezeways. "It is fortunate," said Oppa carelessly to the man at his side, "that I bought the service of so many swords before we landed. It seems Giscila has met more opposition than expected. He should already be here."

"I don't like it," said his companion, looking about him uneasily. "There should be more than old men guarding these walls."

"She's sent every man who can hold a sword to the fortress." Oppa looked around him. "Illiberis cannot be held. It depends upon the fortress, which cannot hold back a force the size of that I sent, and the bridge, which she does not have the men to defend."

"Do you expect her men to draw steel against us?"

"They're dead men either way. They are outnumbered a hundred to one and more." Oppa's voice was like a chill wind. He gestured behind him, at the rows of men dismounting, men who had most definitely not ridden at his side from the south. Lælia froze. Her mind raced, wondering what had become of Gratimo, and what else Oppa had done that she did not know.

There was a faint movement at her side and Lælia swung around, knife in hand. Teudolfo crouched beside her. "They came before we could leave," he mouthed in her ear. "Rekiberga is hidden in the bathhouse. But Gratimo is not here, Lælia. Something has gone wrong. There are more men than we can safely take, and God alone knows how many more. You must leave. We do not have the men here to take him."

Lælia did not move. "I will not run from Oppa, Teudolfo."

"We can return with your Riders. But you must leave now. There is no choice. You cannot take him alone."

"There is always a choice." Lælia held up a hand to still his words, watching Oppa, trying to think.

A shout of triumph came from the direction of the bathhouse, and beside her Teudolfo swore. Rekiberga, pushed from behind by a guard, stumbled into the courtyard, her hair dishevelled, face pale and set. Teudolfo reached for a sword and Lælia put her hand on his arm, shaking her head slowly. *No.* Before he could object, she nodded to the east, where the shadows of tribesmen slipped between the silver olive trees. Teudolfo met her eyes and she gestured to the far side of the villa, the only place Tosius's tribesmen were not. "That is where Gratimo should be," she mouthed. "Join him, and if he is not there, be ready." Nodding reluctantly, Teudolfo slid from sight, his eyes on Rekiberga.

In the courtyard Oppa stared at Rekiberga, a slow, unpleasant smile stretching the corners of his mouth. "The Lady of Hispalis, I presume," he murmured. "You have your father's look. Your men led us a merry dance, I believe. Giscila spent valuable days chasing you from one side of the country to the other. I am not a man who likes to waste time." He cupped her face with one mailed hand. "Your father is dead, you know," he said conversationally. "Along with most of the traitors who opposed our rule. Their little rebellion is done. You are the Lady of Hispalis no more." Rekiberga met his eyes without flinching but did not answer.

He raised his head and looked around the courtyard, his eyes keen. "I know you are here, Lælia of Illiberis." His tone was easy and conversational, as if they sat together at meat. Lælia tensed. "You sent for me, and I came. You did not think I believed your little letter, though, did you? Or that I would walk so easily into whatever trap you think you have laid?"

He smiled coldly. "Your men in Garnata are dead," he said. "I have had a force of a hundred men waiting in those godforsaken mountains of yours to the east for more than a month. They are cold and heartily tired of snow. They will be glad to avail themselves of your hospitality – and you will be glad to offer it to them."

Lælia felt a cold trickle of fear down her spine. She forced herself to breathe slowly, to think.

"You will show yourself," Oppa went on, "and surrender your villa. There is no escape, not for you, nor for any here." His hand dropped to the handle of the whip at his side. His fingers curled around it, stroking it lovingly, whilst with the other he turned Rekiberga's face toward his own. Lælia, recalling the last time she had seen him with his whip, in the woods where he had tried to ravish her, could not suppress a shiver. Rekiberga watched his hand, fear darkening her eyes.

Shouts drifted through the air, and Lælia saw a group of tribes-men, led by Tosius, flit between the trees, their darts taking several of Oppa's men where they stood. Then came the sound of clashing steel and a group of men met Oppa's on the ground before the portico, Teudolfo racing to join them from behind, taking some of those who would retreat. Lælia frowned, trying to make out the numbers. She must be disorientated; there seemed more than she had expected, and there was something unfamiliar in their figures. Seeing the ferocity with which they fought, she felt a surge of excitement.

Oppa raised his whip, and Rekiberga gave a short, sharp scream. Across the courtyard Jadis slid between the stone on the breezeway. She eyed Lælia, who shook her head. *Not yet.*

Staying close to the stone, Lælia balanced the knife in her hand, edging toward the courtyard, her eyes on Rekiberga. She approached the man guarding the corner, who had his back to her. Lælia's knife took him from behind, slipping across his throat so his blood fell over her hands like oil from a jug. She held him until his body ceased to move and he was no more than weight in her hands, and then she laid him on the ground, not looking at his face.

The world slowed, and she no longer thought or felt.

She notched one arrow after another. The first two took men in the courtyard who were shooting into her forces. Tosius, on the other side of the courtyard, took more of them. Then other arrows joined theirs, and Oppa's men were falling, one after another.

"*Baguadae!*" one cried, just before he sagged in the saddle, an arrow straight through his heart. The horses jostled as men looked around them in confusion, then one of them pointed to the edge of the olive grove, where a small group of tribesmen stood, blood covered, chests heaving.

"*Baguadae!*" he repeated the cry, calling them by the name all outsiders knew the tribes as – savages, criminals.

His cry galvanised the men into action, and they scattered in pursuit of the small figures, who turned and ran, calling to each other as they went, leading the men into the shelter of the woods they called home. Oppa's men would die there, Lælia knew. She heard in the tribesmen's chilling cries the fury and grief of loss, and she knew this was the way they would mourn – by taking blood from those who had dared take that of their own.

They honoured Acantha with their sacrifice. Lælia would not dishonour theirs by wasting it.

"It would seem," Oppa said curtly, "that time is of greater importance than I had imagined." He pulled the whip from his side and tore Rekiberga's gown down the centre. With cold detachment he raised his arm and brought the wicked tails down hard across her exposed skin. Rekiberga screamed. "Tell me where Lælia is," said Oppa coldly. "Immediately." His men looked around warily, gripping their weapons, readying for the battle coming closer to them.

The bridge cannot fall. If it does, you have no choice but to run. Lælia heard Paulus's voice in her head. But Paulus was dead, and her days of training were over. For a moment, her arrow pointed between Oppa's eyes, and she knew she could take him; then she thought of Illiberis, of Paulus, of Acantha's sacrifice. *If he dies, I lose the only piece I hold. I will not sacrifice the game for revenge, nor give Egica grounds to name me traitor.*

Lælia stood up from behind the wall and loosed an arrow that took the man closest to Oppa even as she notched another. "Let her go," she said as Oppa turned in surprise, "or the next one will take you." Oppa did not release Rekiberga. Behind him the clashing of swords continued still; it was impossible, from where she stood, to tell who had the advantage.

"Lælia of Illiberis." The dark eyes flashed. Lælia could sense the venal excitement beneath his veneer of detachment. It sickened her.

"Let her go," she said again.

Oppa smiled coldly. "The hillfort will fall before midday, and we will take the bridge by mid-afternoon. I have men placed on every road south and two dromons at the port in Sexi filled with more who will kill any who try to take you away. Illiberis is lost. You will be captured, and you will be taken to Toletum. Call off your men now, and I will let this one live."

"No!" Twisting in Oppa's grasp, Rekiberga cried out. "Go, Lælia. Run!"

Lælia loosed another arrow. It took another of Oppa's men between the eyes, and he fell soundlessly to the ground. She took another step forward. "Let her go," she said again.

The men around Oppa shifted uneasily. The sounds of battle beyond the courtyard intensified, coming nearer. Oppa threw Rekiberga to the ground and gestured to one of his men.

"Take her to Toletum," he said curtly. "Take as many men as you need – but go straight to Toletum with her and await me there. Ride hard, and ride fast." He glared at the guard. "My father will want her intact. If she arrives other than how I see her now, you will pay with your life. Go!" The man swung onto his horse, hauling Rekiberga onto the saddle before him, his face pale with fear.

Lælia had judged the distance and tautened her fingers on the string when she felt a knife at her throat. Her bow was wrenched from her hands. She had a last glimpse of Rekiberga's agonised face and then the girl was gone, and Lælia found herself dragged into the courtyard to take her place. Oppa's eyes shone obsidian black, and his body was taut with excitement as the men threw her in front of him.

"I would have liked to take more time to enjoy this." He stroked her face with the whip. "But events, it seems, may be about to overtake us. Get the horses," he ordered one of his men curtly. "We will meet my uncle at the hillfort and return here when it is done." His knife blade was cool on Lælia's throat. "And you," he said curtly, "will come with us. I have even brought a priest." He gestured to one of the men who rode with him, a bloodied, dishevelled priest who eyed Lælia with apology in his face.

"Frauja," said one of his guards hesitantly, "we do not have enough men to take the bridge from this side. We were not prepared for such opposition."

"Then find them!" snarled Oppa. "My uncle has three hundred men. The hillfort will not stand against him."

Lælia smiled up at him. "Your uncle is dead," she said, enjoying the shock he could not hide. "And I will not go anywhere with you." She gave a low whistle and Jadis's gold body streaked across the courtyard, leaping at Oppa and knocking him to the ground before his surprised guards could so much as shout a warning. Lælia drew her sword, tense and cold, turning the steel in her hand.

Oppa's eyes narrowed. "You cannot prevail."

"Ah." Lælia smiled tightly. "That is where you are wrong. I think you will find that the game no longer belongs to you."

Oppa looked as if he might answer, then his mouth closed. He got slowly to his feet, his eyes trained on something behind her. Lælia tensed.

"Lay down your swords." The voice was a cool, unhurried drawl.

A rush of heat flooded Lælia's body, and her heart began to thud in a heavy, rich rhythm.

"We are six to your four," the voice continued, as if it were an afterthought. "I've won against far worse odds. As you are well aware, Oppa Egicason." He said the last in the same calm tone, but there was no mistaking the chill in his words.

"You were gone," Oppa hissed.

"Not quite. But unless you stand down, you soon will be." Lælia felt locked in place, unable to move. "The men you left in Sexi are dead," the voice went on, "as are those on the road south. Two hundred of Al Kahinat's Riders are at the hillfort as we speak. You know well those of whom I speak, Oppa, son of a king. No bought swords will defeat them."

Very slowly, Lælia forced herself to face the speaker. He was a tall man on a dark, sweating horse, hair blazing white in the morning sun, long and braided with no helmet to cover him. He wore leather and a tunic and carried a round shield in the Gothic style. His skin was rich brown over iron muscle, and fierce scars rippled across his face. The eyes that held Oppa's with such contempt were the brilliant green that had haunted her dreams for years now.

"Besides," he said, a savage note of possession in his tone that took her breath away, "as I've told you before – Lælia is mine." His eyes met her own, and something within Lælia's soul slipped into place. A large hand came up and covered his heart. He smiled crookedly.

Promise.

Theudemir had come home.

AFTERWORD

Writing fiction set in an era so remote from our own poses many challenges. Not least of these is determining the correct modern location of ancient place names. Where the location is not known with absolute certainty, I have drawn conclusions based on my own research. Any mistakes are mine alone.

Sebastopolis is often referred to as being in modern Sulusaray, Turkey. Sulusaray, however, is located well inland. Accounts of the battle refer to the 'Port of Sebastopolis', and it is known that the Karabisianoi fought in the conflict, which would be unlikely if the battle was fought inland. Elaiussa Sebaste is the other alternative for Sebastopolis. Close to the modern port of Mersin, and central to all the locations in which the caliph's forces threatened those of the emperor's, Elaiussa Sebaste seemed far more logical to me, and so I have used it.

The story of the Arabic forces riding to battle in Sebastopolis flying copies of the peace treaty between emperor and caliph is well documented enough to be taken seriously. Of the many battles fought between the Caliphate and the remnants of the Eastern Roman Empire, Sebastopolis was arguably one of the most pivotal, and certainly one that had far reaching consequences for all involved.

Some readers have queried why I have characters in both Northern Africa and Spain refer to citizens of the Eastern Roman Empire as 'Greeks'. Primary source materials from the time use this reference up to a century and a half before the time this book is set. By the late 7th century, Greek had largely replaced Latin as the language of the Eastern Roman Empire, based in Constantinople. This is particularly true for the naval forces, for which all the names of ranks and themes are rendered in Greek rather than Latin. The last Imperial outpost in Spain, won back by King Suintila in the early 7th century, was referred to as the last 'Greek' toehold in Spain.

Coins bearing Sunifred's name and likeness were indeed struck during the period mentioned, and the rebellion itself referred to in the records from the 16th Council of Toledo.

I have done my best to adhere to dates, locations, and historical accuracy as far as it is known. All errors and liberties taken are entirely my responsibility.